Dragon Spar

The Game Maker LitRPG Series

Dragon Spar

The Game Maker LitRPG Series

Keegan Eichelman

Published by Level Up in the United Kingdom in 2024

Cover illustration by Sippakorn Upama

Images by Keegan Eichelman

ISBN: 978-1-83919-655-3

www.levelup.pub

For God –
who dropped this story on my heart like a flaming fireball
Greg –
who's always encouraged me to reach for the stars
Chris –
the story's #1 Fan

SOMERGOT PRISON

~~EAST LANDS~~

TEMPLE MEHERN

ISTRAC SETTLEMENT

THE HIGHER PLACE

ess Cover/
ion Cover
Everywhere

SOUTHERN SEA

ities/Areas

SNARGEL

L1 Undead, Small

DESCRIPTION
Feisty Zombie Fox With Green, Glowing Eyes

STRENGTHS V. WEAKNESSES
- Keen Sense of Smell
- Ability to Fling Bur-Like Metal Balls From Tail
- Bite Damage
- Close Combat

CREATURE STATS

Hit Points: 7
Armor Class: 10/20
Strength: 6/20
Agility: 15/20

Endurance: 13/20
Intelligence: 6/20
Awareness: 12/20
Presence: 10/20

KENChEE

L4 Undead, Medium

DESCRIPTION
Vulture-Like Birds w/ Sharp Talons & Immense Wingspans

STRENGTHS V. WEAKNESSES
- Superb Eyesight
- Agility in Sky & Ability To Sense & Poach CM
- Close Combat
- Without CM, No More Than Nuisance

CREATURE STATS

Hit Points: 58
Armor Class: 12/20
Strength: 1/20
Agility: 14/20

Endurance: 10/20
Intelligence: 6/20
Awareness: 11/20
Presence: 17/20

LAXTAIL ChiRA

L1 Dragon, Tiny

DESCRIPTION
Miniature Dragons w/ Infant-Like Eyes & Tail Which Flashes Light

STRENGTHS V. WEAKNESSES
- Strong in Numbers
- Intelligent & Quick
- Swarm Bites Lower AC
- Individually Not a Threat

CREATURE STATS

Hit Points: 22
Armor Class: 13/20
Strength: 8/20
Agility: 17/20

Endurance: 10/20
Intelligence: 13/20
Awareness: 12/20
Presence: 11/20

DARKEN  — L4 Undead, Medium To Large

DESCRIPTION
Fast But Rather Dull Zombie. Gamers Become Darken When MRP = 0

STRENGTHS V. WEAKNESSES
- Sharp Hearing
- Tendency to Herd
- Drain Gamers of MRP w/ Bites
- Lacking Smarts
- Low Bite Damage

CREATURE STATS
Hit Points: 40	Endurance: 15/20
Armor Class: 13/20	Intelligence: 7/20
Strength: 3/20	Awareness: 10/20
Agility: 8/20	Presence: 11/20

RINKECLAW — L4 Dragon, Medium

DESCRIPTION
Distinguishable By Extra-Large Incisors, 6-Clawed Foot & Dark Scales On Spine

STRENGTHS V. WEAKNESSES
- Increased Strike Damage From Claws
- Spits Acid
- Lacking Smarts & Agility
- Easily Distracted

CREATURE STATS
Hit Points: 75	Endurance: 17/20
Armor Class: 17/20	Intelligence: 8/20
Strength: 19/20	Awareness: 11/20
Agility: 14/20	Presence: 15/20

VODYARACKA SKYDRAKE — L14 Dragon, Huge

DESCRIPTION
Distinguishable By Spikes Down Back, Yellow Belly & Ability to Persuade Its Prey

STRENGTHS V. WEAKNESSES
- Frightful Presence & Lulling Speech
- Shapeshifter
- Easily Angered & Egotistical

CREATURE STATS
Hit Points: 219	Endurance: 21/20
Armor Class: 19/20	Intelligence: 14/20
Strength: 23/20	Awareness: 13/20
Agility: 14/20	Presence: 17/20

Goran

Rosabella had never been in a dragon's mouth. Of course, she hadn't.

I'd protected her; I'd kept her safe. Of course, she'd never been near a beast.

Not yet.

…Not since I'd kept her secluded; she didn't even know what I'd done for her.

I watched her trot across the tot lot yard, her tangled, brown hair bumping back in the still-chilly spring wind with each running step… Her fist was full of dandelions.

Outstretched.

Towards me.

Her eyes, filled with mirth and joy.

I ruffled her hair when she stopped short in front of my sneakers. And she gave me the flowers and straightened her jumper before turning to dash back to the slide, kicking up mulch behind her and barely slowing down. And I knew in that moment that I'd never seen her so happy. Not since she'd been with me.

We lived in the city since her mother legally kept my childhood home, but honking horns were only steel and rushing businessmen had no pointed teeth, so I figured I'd done more than my job as a parent.

If a stranger were to casually stroll by, observing us, he'd see an endearing moment: *a father out at the street park with his daughter on a beautiful, New York day.*

He'd probably smile—not noticing the tears that were forming around the collar of my coat from age and wear...The way I'd glued Rosabella's tiny, Mary-Jane slip-ons together with Gorilla Glue for the fourth time. ...Would he have noticed the gap growing larger near my cheekbones each day because of the hunger? I'd seen it in the dusty mirror of the little league baseball stadium bathroom the other day. I'd pulled at my eyes and seen the blood-shot whites. I'd washed my hair in the sink there.

The majority of my food went to my little girl, and she didn't even *know* we were hiding in plain sight.

...And, worse, I couldn't tell her.

I could only remind her of the way out.

In case she ever needed it, but I prayed she wouldn't.

Because, if she needed it, it meant they'd caught me—they'd broken through the portal and found us.

Here, in our happy place.

My eyes darted down to my digital wristwatch—like yet another nervous itch I couldn't seem to scratch. My breath caught in my throat as I brushed one finger across the dark screen, discreetly scanning the stats there, again, with a palm up to shade the numbers from the sunlight filtering through the surrounding trees, shining off the metal park playground:

[GDP - 51/100]

I berated myself for checking the Game Damage Points again—*what? Was it the fiftieth time that morning?* I kept telling myself if the number hit a certain ceiling, I could breathe again; I'd know they'd be too preoccupied with the decaying Game world to come looking for me—for Rosabella. But that ceiling crept up with every daily increase of the percentage. …Ratcheting skyward with my paranoia as my satisfaction, ultimately, bottomed out. Because I could never be satisfied—never be sure.

That today wasn't the day. …The day they'd find us. Or the day she remembered. I wasn't sure which would be worse. I swiped through the screen, checking her memory stats from the day we'd left:

[Current MRP / ROSABELLA, GAME MAKER 1: 3640/6205]

I let out a breath. With Memory Recall Points that low, there was no way the girl could recall, I placated myself. *I'd done what was necessary. I'd had to save Rosabella even from her own memory.*

The smell of roasting hotdogs filled my ravenous nostrils as I turned my head, scanning the surrounding area for shadows or anyone watching, but my vision only fell on a cart nearby where an Italian man served food boisterously to a mother with a kid about Rosabella's age. And, for a second, I smiled, imagining my little girl biting into that same hotdog and getting mustard all over her face.

…Licking it off, laughing.

But my fists clenched in my pockets because I didn't have the money.

And my stomach clenched…*otherwise.*

"*Rosabella!*" I called her, watching her brunette head instantly perk up behind the monkey bars.

She always came when I called.

She always did what she was told.

She was a *good* kid.

Which I couldn't express enough how *good* that was for me.

…While we were being hunted and I needed her by my side every minute.

Because, if I lost her…

If I lost her…

No.

I wouldn't go there; I wouldn't let my mind sit on it. I'd rather *die.*

My lips pressed together as I patted Rosabella's beautiful head and directed her away from the delicious, roasting hotdogs and down the street. I'd told her we were on another adventure. That new adventure was finding somewhere to sleep for the night, and we'd conquer it, but not before I gave her the key again.

I'd give it to her over and over.

Till she got it.

Right then, it was our game—something seemingly silly or trivial. My way of giving her what I already knew she might need.

"Have you ever been in a dragon's mouth, Rosabella?" I asked her, waiting for her typical giggle which always came. Her eyes were the most perfect shade of sapphire as she blinked up at me, nearly falling as she missed a rut in the pavement.

"*No!*" she squealed in delight.

"But have you ever *seen* a dragon's mouth?" I asked playfully.

She knew it was coming; it was the same phrase I asked every day.

Her mouth curled up in the little bow I liked, "Well, I saw one once that had a purple and pink tongue…polka dots," she started, her words slurry around the gaps in her teeth and her eyes changing as she began her made-up story.

And my mouth pinched because *I could see it*—that glossed-over stare.

I knew she was there.

And I prayed that, someday, the little game we played might just save her innocent life.

4

Rosabella

He didn't even know how much he stifled me.

…These were my thoughts? I huffed, laughing a little to myself as I swung around the streetlamp, which buzzed and flickered overhead in the night sky as my fingers wrapped gleefully around the freezing, smooth base. My hair billowed out, strands getting caught in the collar of my coat and sticking to my exposed neck. The cloud of my breath warmed my cheeks and the tip of my nose, but I didn't mind the cold.

Not if it let me breathe for just a minute.

Dad thought I loved the Chinese food place at the corner.

What I really loved was the freedom—the two-minute walk where I felt like no one was watching me.

Not even him.

…Shouldn't I be worrying about talking to some crush or something? Or about homework or painting my toes a certain color?… Like any other teenage girl?

"General Tso's and orange chicken? Pre-pay?" the Chinese man asked me, holding up the take-out bag he knew full well was mine like he'd cooked it himself.

I grabbed it from him with the small bow that I knew he liked.

"Thanks, Ming!" I called over my shoulder.

…As I danced out in the drizzling rain for just a few more minutes, spreading my arms and tilting my face back to catch all the little drops of life misting down on me. The moon swam, high overhead.

But my watch vibrated.

The timer.

If I was over two minutes late, Dad would go into nuclear meltdown mode, and the food would get cold before he finished his lecture about safety, self-preservation and stranger-danger.

…I'd been getting kind of worried about him. His caution had increased to paranoia lately.

"They're getting closer; I can feel it, Rosie," he'd said just that morning, pulling back the curtains he always kept firmly secured over every window to stare blankly out at the street.

The blankness in his face scared me most. It was like he was losing touch with reality. He'd been jumpier in the last few months: seeing shadows, talking to people who weren't there while making something on the stove and trying to cover it up whenever I walked into the room…

It was probably not normal to feel like this as a teen—to feel like you had to take care of your parent.

I saw my classmates all the time, circling the street with their bikes well past 9pm.

Talking raucously.

Their jokes and laughter wafted up to my bedroom window like a lie I tried every day not to believe.

And it was hard to not want what they had:

Freedom.

No fear.

No restraints or restrictions—

It was like dangling candy in front of a starving three-year-old; there was only so much one could take.

My thick-soled boots thudded up the concrete steps of the apartment. I jammed my thumb into the buzzer button till the static clicked—sometimes, it got stuck. And I swung past the blinking elevator button to take the stairs two at a time, feeling the churn of my muscles as I hauled up each step...heard the swish of the plastic bag in my hand...

And the grime on the wall passed.

And the smell of some type of burnt beans and rice dish wafted into my nose.

I reached the top of the stairwell—

Threw my weight to wrench open the door—

And saw our door.

Our apartment door.

Also, wrenched open.

Hanging by the hinge.

I dropped the bag of Chinese food. I barely heard it hit the carpet with a dull thump.

And I raced forward, my mouth twisting in utter desperation. My heart pounded in my ears—

My mind tripped over itself more than my feet were—

The world past the doorpost blurred as my fingers clutched at it, heaved me forward as quickly as possible.

"Dad???!" I screamed.

Rosabella

The apartment was dark now; enormous shadows clawed up the nearly bare walls, flickering there from a knocked over lamp.

Now, smashed on the floor. ...A lamp that had been intact only 15 minutes before.

"*Dad?*" My heart caught in my chest.

Truth be told, even after so frequently wishing for it, I hadn't often been alone, and the feeling crept down my throat like an engulfing and expanding snake.

And the fear of if I *wasn't* alone lurked there too...

Curtains swished near the open window behind the couch.

I spun around, barely daring to breathe, but it was just the breeze outside.

There was Dad's book, overturned on the floor by the sofa and the tangled mess of wires for my Xbox controller. *Like he'd dropped the tome in a rush?* I reached for it, feeling the fabric of the old spine under my fingers. *He never did anything erratic; surely, he would have left a note... And that lamp didn't knock over itself...*

My breath hitched.

Dad taught me to be observant—always on guard. I noticed a dark reflection in the floor mirror propped decoratively in the corner...a black boot. ...That I'd never seen before.

8

And there was a leg in that boot.

I didn't give away the sheer panic on my face as I rose to upright slowly, the book still clenched between my fingers. I bit the inside of my cheek, tasting blood with the intensity I was clamping down, and I looked for exits.

Dad always said to run, not fight.

He'd always cryptically lectured me that, if anything ever happened to him, I should run and never look back—

The window.

Thank God it was open.

I shot a quick glance at the shadow in the mirror; whoever was standing there was concealed just behind the kitchen wall… *What if it was Dad?*

"*Dad?*" I called once more—a last, desperate plea.

But, somewhere along the line, I'd miscalculated.

Because a gloved hand clamped over my mouth from behind.

No!

Adrenaline kicked in.

I slammed the book towards the attacker's head.

I heard a muffled grunt. …And a thud as the book hit the floor.

I threw off the tightening fingers.

And I lunged.

For the window.

Cold air smacked me in the face.

I fell through the curtains, nearly taking them with me. And the soles of my boots heavily hit metal, clanging on the fire escape floor—

As something hit me.

In the back.

A pinprick of pain exploding even through my thick jacket.

Dazed, I reached my arm around, my fingers fumbling and recognizing a metal cylinder sticking out of the back of my coat.

I pulled it out, turning it over in my hand and blinking at it, there, in the dark on the dimly lit fire escape.

A dart? My breath created white puffs around my nose and mouth which, strangely, disappeared as soon as I saw them.

A message flashed over my head, neon letters floating in mid-air:

ROSABELLA Has Joined The Game
[System Loading Class & Level...]
[Class & Level Predetermined. No Options Available.]
Welcome ROSABELLA, GAME MAKER 1 To The Game

I blinked at the run of words.

My name—?

Floating in the—

"*Argh!*"

A woman's scream. I whipped around to find a women's silhouette, dressed in head-to-toe black, reaching for me—

But she missed. I heard her bellow in fury as her boot punctured a patch of rust and went through the metal floor. Out of the corner of my eye, I saw her struggling to pull her boot back through the fire escape platform, but the jagged metal kept catching on her black pants and bootlaces…

Five seconds. That gave me five seconds to get away…

My feet banged down the steel of the stairs, clanking—

My breath heaved in my lungs—

I slipped through the bars at the very end, shaking my head at the look of the drop to the top of a parked car below.

And I held my breath.

And eased down, putting all the weight on my straining biceps—

With a grunt, I landed.

My boots crashed into the steel roof of the minivan.

I did it! I made the jump!

[System Reward: Well-Executed Escape, +5 XP, 5/100]

System reward?

What? But thanks, System. It felt like a pat on the back. ...Except, what did 'XP' mean?

My brief celebration was met with wheezing breaths which raked through my body and a desperate hope that random-assassin, creepy-break-into-our-apartment girl didn't follow. Where was Dad? Did she kidnap him? He'd always said to run... I chanced a glance upward before I crawled off the roof of the van, sliding my legs over the edge to make it to the ground.

But, when I made it to the ground, my boots crunched on broken glass.

The minivan's windows were all broken...

And the sky was dark and filled with smog...

And it wasn't night anymore, even though a haze of gray darkness shadowed the dark city buildings towering over me.

This wasn't even our street...

...Where was I?

A megaphone screeched to life in the distance:

"Stay where you are, you're surrounded." A male voice seemed to echo from all sides.

[System Query: Would You Like To Hide Or Fight?]

"Hide!" I hissed fervently, hoping whatever system had asked could hear me. Adrenaline looped through my veins, *"Most definitely hide—please!"* More neon letters popped into view:

[Initiating Check For Hiding Locations...]

Oh my God, this was taking too long! Dizzying waves crashed over my head as my eyes darted over the surroundings. A pile of large, black trash bags were stacked high to my left. *Yep, those would do.* I scampered behind them as the megaphone blared to life again—

"Stay where you are, and this man will not get hurt."

And a male picture cracked and flashed into life mid-air, a giant screen in the center of the concrete clearing, as I blinked at it, feeling a sour urgency turn my stomach upside down because....

Because it was a picture of Dad.

Rosabella

I realized how extremely small I was then, crouching there—behind the lumpy pile of black trash bags—peering down the cracking, asphalt street.

A teenage girl. I, suddenly, felt as insignificant as an ant and as cornered as a jackrabbit, clutching my winter coat sleeves over my hands as the three men approached.

Adult-size shadows, towering over my own even in their advance.

Black body armor clinging to muscles and solid, unafraid walks.

More black boots…

[System Found 4 Nearby Hiding Locations.]

Fuck the system! I swiped the alert that popped up mid-air away like dismissing a text on my phone. *What was going on?*

A clattering behind me made me spin to see the girl who'd been chasing me slither down the fire escape—

She marched towards me, her hands clenched in fists.

And it was official.

I'd not only been seen—I was trapped.

A green dumpster to my side. The wall of trash bags, in front.

The minivan and mega-assassin to the back.

And the three approaching figures in front with the shadow of a smoggy city looming overhead.

"System, figure out a way to help me?" I squeaked, but I was pretty sure in that moment that, even if this was some RPG game world, my request wasn't going to work...

Dad had always said to run—but his life was at stake here. They'd said they would hurt him—

I swallowed hard, feeling panic well up in my chest.

"System, calculate my odds of winning a race against these four people," I hissed under my breath, hoping the nearest one—the assassin girl behind me—wouldn't hear. *Please...please let this work... Maybe I could run away, darting just out of reach. Maybe I had a chance.*

[System Understands Query...Loading Response...]

Come on! Come on! I chewed on my lower lip; my eyes scanned the approaching figures.

Their long strides.

Swinging arms.

My eyes flickered to the dilapidated skyscrapers overhead. Ming's Chinese restaurant wasn't on the street corner anymore—*I'd just left there five minutes ago!* ...And the surrounding buildings looked like they'd stood in the same, crumbling location for hundreds of years. A stray newspaper blew down the cracking street; the pavement was so faded there that the lines in the middle looked white-washed. ...*Where the fuck was I? And how was it just outside of our apartment window? Why was there this system thing?*

[System Answer: The Likelihood Of A Race Win Against NOMAD 9, WARRIOR 11 Or CODER 14 Is Not Looking So Hot... TRADER 10 Matches GAME MAKER 1's Agility With A 1 Point Lead On Endurance, Making It Nearly A 50/50 Opportunity. Do You Wish to Take This Chance?]

[Yes] [No]

Were you kidding me?! All the air leaked out of me in a huff. No, absolutely 'no'. I either was completely in front of all of them or the winning aspect was null and void. I'd hide, thank you very much. I hit the button floating in the air, and the text dissipated.

…'Agility' and 'Endurance'? It was talking about abilities like a game. Maybe…

I opened my mouth to demand to see some stat tables when I felt every eye on me. They were closing in, nearly arm-in-arm. An electronic error beep sounded, only increasing my utter terror.

[System Penalty: A Terrible Hiding Spot, -2 XP, 3/100]

-2? Negative? It seemed like XP was some sort of reward component. Did XP stand for Experience Points?

The megaphone shrieked to life again; I watched the man at the front of the pack raise it to his lips. His eyes were shimmering black even in the shadows. "I repeat: stay where you are. Don't attempt to run, or the man on the screen will die."

I flinched.

I was surrounded. They were threatening to kill my dad. What was I supposed to do? I couldn't let him die.

Maybe there was some mistake? That was it, there had to be some mistake—

Fear thrummed in my chest like a cello.

"Whatever your deal is," I growled into the group of three figures stepping closer and closer and the screen behind them, plastered with Dad's picture, "give me my dad back safe. Now." My voice shook, even on the demand part. If they each took one more step, they'd be close enough to tell my hands were shaking too.

Still, they were silent.

Unnervingly so as the circle of them closed around me and the woman behind stepped up to complete it. Like their shadows made it hard to breathe, I gulped for air.

"What do you want from me?" I sputtered.

"Good question."

A girl's voice.

I nearly screamed as a hand reached out and spun me around.

It was the assassin—the one who'd chased me down the fire escape. I tensed to dodge away from her, but she lifted a black helmet off her head. Pink hair fell out as the corner of her lips and right eyebrow arched up in amusement. It was unfair someone so smug could be so beautiful. ...

Was she around my age? She was about the same height—

"Welcome to The Game, Rosabella—" she sneered with extra emphasis on my name. She used her pinky to direct a strand of bright hair away from the porcelain skin of her face. "Only took us what felt like fourteen fucking centuries to find you."

She had to be crazy. What was she talking about? Was this a dream? ...If so, it was a nightmare.

"Where's my dad? And what is this place?" I spat back, my jaw hardening. Every hair on my arms rose, bristling for the slightest indication I should flee. Too bad the entire situation was already screaming that...

A man's huge hand clapped down on my shoulder.

I jumped and tried to spin around. My frantic breath caught in my throat—

"Hold your horses, newb," a deep voice echoed.

I looked and saw that the man's other hand, limp and easy at his side, clutched the megaphone he'd used before. His hair was pepper gray with specks of the same bristling in stubble on his jawline. The

16

outline of his body armor showed bulging muscles which looked rather out-of-place for his age.

"You said to stay still, or you'd kill my dad." I struggled against his incredibly firm hold. "I did what you asked, now let him go."

"Afraid it's not that easy with murderers—" he started.

Murderers? My jaw dropped open.

I struggled harder.

"He's not a murderer!" I screamed. "You have the wrong guy!"

"You have no idea, kid," he spouted with a chuckle. His hand twisted to easily pin me against the nearby minivan.

I tried to kick at him but only ended up smashing my toe into the metal bumper of the van, which caused his eyebrows to pitch forward in annoyance. Pain ripped through my foot as a system message popped up, floating before my eyes:

[-1 HP, 7/8]

Did it have something to do with health?

"Dad's been glued to my side practically since birth," I snarled around the pain, still trying to twist away with each biting word, "If he murdered someone, I'd have seen it—"

"Listen, stop struggling, kid," the man berated. "It's pointless. If you look at your stats compared to mine, there's just no match, okay?" The man with the gray hair thumbed two fingers, still holding the megaphone, in the air, swiping a glowing screen with two boxes into view. I craned my neck to see them, having to press my cheek into the cold metal of the van:

Name	Rosabella	Name	Callen
Class & Level	Game Maker 1	Class & Level	Trader 10, Game Warden (Disc.)
XP	3/100	XP	1043/1100
MRP	3640/6205	MRP	17885/18250
HP	7/8	HP	100/100
Baddie Points	25	Swag Points	500
Armor Class	10/20	Armor Class	13/20
ABILITIES /20		ABILITIES /20	
Strength	-1 8	Strength	+0 10
Agility	+0 10	Agility	+0 10
Endurance	-1 9	Endurance	+0 10
Intelligence	+1 13	Intelligence	+3 16
Awareness	+1 12	Awareness	+1 12
Presence	+3 16	Presence	+2 15
CM	0		

I gaped at the boxes in the air. *Like a video game…this looked like a video game…*I noted that his stat sheet didn't have a CM ability…*whatever that was…*

He swiped the boxes out of view again with a tired wave, "So stop wasting your hit points, will you? You'll need all the health you can get where we're going."

My mouth was dry. It felt like all the liquid there had evaporated, and I was left with the taste of sawdust and absolutely no conviction that I could fight these people…and, yet—yet, a fire still brewed in my stomach. Call it rightful outrage.

"I'm not going *anywhere* with you," I protested, not entirely convinced my own words were true.

What was happening? Was this some sort of hallucination or something? A joke? It was making my head hurt.

"You are if you're so hellbent on saving that man you call Dad," he quipped, raising an eyebrow.

Rosabella

"What's the trade?" I snapped.

I didn't know where I was or what was going on, but I knew about bargains.

Negotiations.

It was how I survived in the world of online gaming and had been making it through high school: *I give you this, you give me that. I do this for you, you owe me one.* If this was some sort of RPG, I had to be able to dominate and get what I wanted through good, old-fashioned communication.

...But Dad was involved here. Potentially his life. It made me feel shaky and off-balance—like the ground was wobbling, and I could fall into a vat of lava with any tenuous, wrong step.

I drew in a trembling breath, attempting to hide my unease behind steel eyes.

The gray-haired man looked me over with an impressed, lifted eyebrow, "Your L1 Determination, Bounce Back skill looks good on you. Well, you're brave for a reason; you're gonna need it. Your Dad's been taken into high-security prison custody for his crime. In fact, it's highly unlikely that anyone has enough skill to bust him out at this point—except for *this squad of sexy individuals in front of you.*"

I clamped down on my teeth, outrage stinging my eyes and the back of my throat, "You just lied to me about *killing him?!* …Because you don't have him to begin with…" I finished, annoyance grating at my tone. *I should have known this was all a trick…*

"We couldn't have you run," interrupted the pink-haired girl, shaking her hair out over the collar of her body armor like she was more interested in it than this conversation.

"I technically didn't lie about the killing part," the gray-haired man noted quickly, bringing up a finger "He's been scheduled for execution in seven days."

"Execution?!" I balked, my head crashing in dizzying circles.

Seven days? A week to save Dad?

No, I wouldn't panic. I could figure this out. I could DO this.

"How is that legal?"—the words fell out of my mouth, tripping— "I'll get a lawyer."

"There's no lawyers in The Game; what do you think this is, Phoenix Wright?" pink-haired girl scoffed, studying her nails this time.

I had to think. I had to act. But what could I do?

"You can get him out—you're sure?" My voice shook; I couldn't hide it anymore. My whole body was shaking, trembling at the thought of losing Dad. He'd been there for my whole life. If he just disappeared, my entire universe—any kind of stability in my life—might too. …What would I do…*without him?* Before, I'd imagined freedom, but now that the possibility was right in my face? …It felt like a void I didn't want to step into.

"We can save his life if you choose to," the gray-haired man replied grimly.

'If I chose to.' What kind of messed up gimmick was this?

Of course, I chose to! I couldn't let him die!

"Choose *what?*" I narrowed my eyes, but my voice was desperate.

20

"To help us."

"I'm listening." It was almost habit to say the words. …Something finally familiar on my tongue in this strange situation—something giving me a semblance of control even as I was flailing. They were the words I always typed in the game chats or said to another RPG player when someone approached me with a trade. I was always open—always willing to at least *hear* them. It should be the same in this case.

"Someone destroyed our world," The man's eyes were intense and crinkled with sudden, tangible pain. "Let me show you," he continued; his hands swiped a floating system menu open in the air:

[GDP - 85/100]

Current Gamer Population:	333 Million
Current Darken Population:	152 Million
Darken To Gamer Ratio:	~45.65%
Darkness Cover:	73/100
Dilapidation Cover:	91/100

What type of stats were these? I couldn't make heads or tails of them besides the population statistics. What was a 'Darken'? And did Darkness and Dilapidation Cover have something to do with the top number?

"GDP means Game Damage Points. Our world is decaying and filled with Darken, otherwise called zombies. We want to—need to fix it, and we need your help to do that," the man said, looking directly at me, "You help us fix our world, and we'll get your—" he paused, blinking, suddenly, as though he had something in his eye, "father out of prison safe before his execution day. I swear it."

I thought it over, tapping my foot on the ground like all the nervous energy in me had filtered to my ankles.

"…I can fix your world in a week?" I asked skeptically. I knew how obnoxious and sarcastic my tone sounded, but I was just having a hard time processing the weight of this trade…

"System, show me what I'd have to do to fix their world," I dictated with more confidence this time. I mean, this system thing did work, didn't it? I watched the groups' eyes roam over the system message that popped up:

[System Understands Query...Loading Response...]
[System Answer: Level 6 Must Be Reached To Activate
CM. Additional Requirements = Collection of 3 Creator
Diamonds. Once Activation Is Complete, Level 8 Must Be
Attained To Cast Enough CM To Repair The Game.]

CM? What was CM? I blinked at the response, attempting to take it all in.

"Ugh, CM means Creator Magic in case...in case you're wondering." One of the guys side-stepped forward to interject. He was middle-aged; his brown hair, which fluttered behind him in the wind, was straight and long, and deep freckles dotted his nose and cheeks where a gnarly, red beard didn't cover. If I'd been looking at him from behind, I might have thought he was a girl because of his locks if not for his burly, warrior stance and all that armor...

I *was* wondering what CM meant so...

My eyes slid upward, trying to catch the man's gaze which darted from the ground to the members of his black-clad group and back to me in a nervous manner. The brutish Nomad took that moment to itch at his beard.

"So...errr," he started again, pointing a sausage finger at the neon answer still shimmering in the air. "You have to get to Level 6 by increasing your Experience Points—XP—by doing and collecting..." he looked at a loss for words, "stuff. And, obviously, you need the three Diamonds. Then, you can activate your Creator Magic, Level Up to L8 and repair our world."

I couldn't help it, I grimaced openly, although I probably should have hid it. *It kinda seemed like a lot of work...Then again, I'd be trading to save Dad so...*

The pink-haired, assassin girl threw both hands on her hips, "Do you want to save your dad or not?"

"Of course!" I fumbled.

"Then, *take the deal*," she griped, one of her perfectly plucked eyebrows raising in disgust. "We're good on our end. Rainer, there, can open a steel-shut door with one, pinky finger"—she gestured to the long-haired guy who'd helped me with the CM stats. His squat muscle mass alone seemed to back up her statement—"and Dorkcus over there—"

"Dormouse—" the nerdy, sickly-looking, beanpole of a kid with dark hair, who she was pointing at, corrected swiftly.

"Not my fault you chose a shitty nickname from Alice in fucking Wonderland," the girl barked back, "...but he can hack into any electric grid, key-code or computer system faster than you can sneeze. ...He's a heck of a cipher-wiz too—"

"Coder 14, so," Dormouse wheezed bashfully, swiping a hand to catch the dark hair that nearly fell into his eyes as he ducked his head to hide the redness engulfing his cheeks.

"Aw, go on any longer about him and he'll get a crush," cooed the tough guy she'd called Rainer, feigning softness. "Not that Dormouse would ever have enough Swag Points to make a move—"

The nerd shoved him in the shoulder, but he wasn't able to even budge the guy.

They seemed friendly with each other... Could I trust them? Their leader, the gray-haired one, appeared the most trustworthy. *...Did I really have any other choice here? It was them or Dad would die. They could be lying, but it was probably unlikely...*

A system message slid into view:

**[Proposed Trade: ROSABELLA, GAME MAKER 1 Repairs
The Game World, CALLEN (TRADER 10), RAINER
(NOMAD 9), JOY (WARRIOR 11) & DORMOUSE (CODER
14) Free PRISONER 10]
[Will You Accept The Trade?]
[Yes] [No]**

"You'll get my dad out of prison before they execute him…safely?" My voice wavered slightly, like my decision.

"Sure, kid. Piece of cake," the pepper-haired Trader—Callen—nodded.

"One more condition," I growled, feeling for that one second like they might listen to me. "You tell me why this isn't my street and why you're all dressed like you're straight out of Comic-Con 2014."

Pink-haired girl laughed at that—a yapping, high-pitched snort.

"Oh damn!" she shrieked, "She's *good!*"

"She needs to shake on the deal," the hulky Nomad, Rainer, spat, shoving forward again with a sense of urgency written in the lines of his tanned face. It was kind of intense.

I backed up slowly. *He wasn't going to attack me, or something, was he?*

The gray-haired Trader lifted his hand like a peace offering between the two of us. "Sure"—his voice was even and calming—"she'll shake on it, right Rosabella?"

I looked at his hand, extended there in midair and made a decision.

Rosabella

I grasped the gray-haired Trader's hand, shaking it...feeling the firm hold of his fingers. Glowing letters popped up over our entwined hands.

[System Alert: Covenant Sealed]
[System Reward: The Very First Trade, The Start Of A Friendship? +25 XP, 28/100]

I gasped and pulled my hand back.

The pink-haired girl raised her eyebrow at me, studying my face with disdain. "What, you didn't think you were gonna get away with breaking it, did you?" she spat. "It's a *deal, a covenant—*"

She was lecturing me like I was five. I knew what a deal was. I just—

I swallowed. *...Didn't expect it to be quite so concrete, that was all.*

...I just made a promise to a group of crazy people. That had to be a rookie mistake, but how else was I going to save Dad? It looked like I'd just gained an additional 25 XP, bringing me up to the 28/100 figure in the pop-up. *...But what was this place?*

I stared up at the dilapidated skyscrapers again, feeling a wave of unease light every hair on my arms despite my heavy coat. Green ivy climbed up the walls of the nearest building, entwining through shattered glass and structural steel. Dark clouds, overhead, mirrored the dirt and grime that smudged the buildings, and the huge boulders that littered the street appeared to have fallen and broken the streetlamps in half decades ago... *Why did it look like New York City if it'd been abandoned for over 200 years? And where the heck was Ming's restaurant?*

Panic set in, seizing my heart.

If I could just find the restaurant Dad and I frequented, maybe I'd be closer to not losing my mind—

"System?" I stammered. "Why can't I remember? Where is Ming's restaurant?"

[System Unable To Understand Query...Recognizable Word = 'Remember'. Linked To Memory Recall Points. Loading MRP Now...]
[Current MRP / ROSABELLA, GAME MAKER 1: 3640/6205]

"Damn, her memory recall is low, why the hell is that?" the pink-haired girl started, her nose crinkling up at my stats.

"Joy, *just give her a moment*," the gray-haired leader urged, brushing a sweeping hand towards the other girl, "This is all new to her." His eyes swiveled to lock on mine. And I blinked into his flint-gray orbs, like seeing them for the first time—like an anchor in that moment.

"I can't remember," I panted as my mind spun. *How could I not remember why Ming's restaurant was right there—and, then, things turned? It'd been right there—I'd been there and, then... A dart? It was a dart—*

"*Rosabella,*" the gray-haired Trader spoke slowly—something I was entirely grateful for—"I'm Callen, and this is Joy."

The pink-haired girl scoffed as he pointed at her, throwing off his hand.

"She already introduced you to the other two, Rainer and Dormouse. I'm glad we found you. *Welcome to The Game.*" His voice was soft and understanding—like he could, somehow, see right into my gasping heart.

The world wasn't spinning.

I wouldn't let the world spin.

"Can someone explain where the heck I am and where my dad is again?" I asked, feeling like the words were as hollow and confused as my core.

Callen nodded. He opened his mouth to start when the pale, dorky kid—the Coder Joy had called 'Dorkcus'—stepped forward abruptly from the back.

"Your Dad's held in Somergot Prison, the highest-hold security penitentiary here. You're in The Game. It's an altered version of reality," he rapid-fire dictated, "a dimension overlapping Earth's. Technically, we existed before you so…"

He trailed off with an entitled-raised eyebrow and *that useless nugget.*

The group gaped at him, especially Callen. "Thank you, Dormouse," he mumbled, sounding like he'd rather not thank the kid for anything, "for that *incredibly overwhelming bit of information.*"

I blinked at all of them.

An alternate—

An alternate—wait—

"Hold on." I raised a hand. "You're *asking me to believe,*" I stuttered, "that I just *waltzed* into an alternate reality?"

"Dimension," Dormouse corrected swiftly, nodding his head once.

My eyes grew wider at his interruption.

"…Oh, and I shot you in the back with a portal dart so, there was no waltzing, Princess," Joy added smugly, throwing her pink hair over her shoulder and adjusting the katana on her belt.

"…*Seriously?!*" I crowed.

But the faces of the group were still and solemn.

They were…*they were serious…*

"*Have you ever seen a dragon?*" Rainer—the middle-aged Nomad with the long, brown hair—mused, chuckling a little to himself with the sheer joy of the question as his fingers played with the ruby-laden hilt of a very large sword strapped at his waist. And his question stirred something in me…

A memory? A foggy flicker…of remembrance?

[System Searching MRPs To Select & Display Correct Memory…]

…Wait, it could do that?…

"*Have you ever been in a dragon's mouth, Rosie?*"
Dad's voice.

Joking with me as I laughed—a young, happy giggle—in the background.

Dad's voice in my head.

He used to say that to me all the time when I was younger…it was our thing—

"Rosabella?"

Callen's voice.

I snapped back to…alternate reality.

"Yes?" —An automatic, embarrassed reply since he'd caught me spacing out.

He squinted at me, his gaze deep as the stubble on his cheeks wrinkled, "Have you ever been in The Game before?" His words seemed to hold a weight to him that was lost on me. It was like he was trying to prod something in me…something…deep. His gaze was so intense.

I shook my head. If he meant this place, I certainly hadn't been here before.

"Welp," Rainer interrupted, shouldering past Joy and Dormouse towards a side alley and only looking back long enough to nod at us and throw a bow over his shoulder, "I don't know about you guys, but I think we should get a leg-up on getting the Game Maker upleveled rather than Kumbya-ing. This is a results-based mission, and I get results. Missy there has a promise to keep."

His worn, calf-length, leather boots crunched over the gravel and dirt underfoot as he moved towards the gap between a skyscraper which had fallen into another building, creating a V-shaped, shadowed opening. Vines grew up one side. Rocks filled the other—which only looked like a slight hindrance to the middle-aged man as he heaved himself over it all rather easily. He must have pretty good Agility stats, I mused to myself.

"He's right, we should go," Callen noted.

I struggled to catch up mentally, "Where are we going?"

"The old trainyard," Callen clarified without clarifying.

I blinked at him, not understanding.

"To see your first Snargel," Joy said. "Learning to use a weapon and kill a host of them is one of the fastest ways to Level Up. We'll get you to Level 8 if we all have to carry you, understood?" And the mirth in her eyes, the sneer on her lips and the realization that she was discussing me killing something sped the rhythm of my heart more than I would ever want to admit.

***

"System, what's a Snargel?" I whispered, under my breath—trying not to let the others hear—as I trailed behind the group.

[System Understands Query...Loading Response...]

The group was hard to keep up with. They walked rapidly with large, easy strides.

Fording across a stream with quick steps…

All but jogging back into the thick forest filled with fledgling, lime-green sprouts shooting up towards the sky and hundreds of giant Redwood trees, enormous as castle towers.

[System Answer: A Snargel Is A Feisty Zombie Fox With Green, Glowing Eyes.
STRENGTHS: Keen Sense Of Smell & Ability To Fling Bur-Like, Metal Balls From Its Tail.
WEAKNESSES: Bite Damage & Close Combat. The Creature Isn't Particularly Deft, But Those Metal Burs Hurt Like Hell So Beware.]

Name	Snargel	
Class & Level, Size	Undead 1, Small	
HP	7/7	
Armor Class	10/20	
ABILITIES /20		
Strength	-2	6
Agility	+2	5
Endurance	+1	13
Intelligence	-2	6
Awareness	+1	12
Presence	+0	10

Great…so I was going to fight rabid zombie foxes that threw metal? What a cheerful thought in this already cheerful atmosphere. This sure was a lot of shit for just trying to get my dad back…

I scampered forward—tripping as my toe hit yet another rock—and sweating profusely in this stupid, winter jacket when it was most certainly spring here.

My hair plastered to my neck.

Annoyed, I swiped my hand across my forehead again and yanked at the jacket zipper, tugging it down with something close to anger.

Why was I so slow?! What was wrong with me that I couldn't keep up? I, physically, looked like the youngest one in the group and, yet, the two, older guys were so far ahead... *Did it have something to do with my stats? If only I could understand them better...* I mimicked the Trader's finger swipe from before to open the system menu again.

Name	Rosabella	
Class & Level	Game Maker 1	
XP	28/100	
MRP	3640/6205	
HP	7/8	
Baddie Points	25	
Armor Class 10/20		
ABILITIES /20		
Strength	-1	8
Agility	+0	10
Endurance	-1	9
Intelligence	+1	13
Awareness	+1	12
Presence	+3	16
CM		0

Unfortunately for me, not much had changed except for the experience points. *Strength 8/20? Endurance 9/20? Those were low. No wonder I was falling behind.* The budding thicket around us, loomed between me and Joy's shadow—the last one in line that I'd been following.

Thorns snagged at the flesh of my arms and face, creating little, red creases there. Some type of persistent, purple wasp buzzed around my face as I thrashed at it. It stung me in the hand.

"*Shit!*" I swore, shaking out my throbbing palm and stepping into the glade to find all four members of the group staring at me as a system update fizzled into view:

[-1 HP, 6/8]

I pulled my coat off, letting it fall like a puffy marshmallow to the dirt and grass, leaving me in a long-sleeve t-shirt which was still completely unnecessary in this balmy weather. "Is it just me, *or is it hot out here?*" I huffed.

They all continued to stare. ...Except Callen whose gaze flickered between me and his staring friends like he was going to attempt to Band-Aid the entire situation.

"We have to remember her ability level," Callen lectured the others, "She's only at Endurance 9."

"If she starts actively looking for things to collect or kill instead of complaining about the heat, she might Level Up by the time we get there," Joy said wickedly.

Callen scowled at her.

"*Don't be mean,*" Dormouse piped up...and I instantly liked him more.

"Will someone explain this stat chart thing to me?" I panted. ...*Really, I was just hoping it'd buy me more time to heave in air over my knees—*

"You're Level 1, so that's the number after your class, which is 'Game Maker'; it basically means your abilities are starting from scratch without any added benefits. XP is Experience Points, obviously," the nerd blew the fringe of his dark hair back from his eyes with a shrug. "At each interval of 100 XP, you Level Up. MRP stands for 'Memory Recall Points' which is a metric for recollection of life experience and differs per person based on age etc. HP—basically your health, how much damage you can sustain before lights out. Armor Class is for combat—how resistant you are in a fight. And your

Abilities show how sharp you are in each area. The corresponding modifiers—err, the '+' and '-' aspects—" he tripped up a bit on the words, "help with comparison to other Gamers and monsters. ...Oh, and Baddie Points are an extra—almost a gauge of attraction. More of them mean you have more persuasion or intimidation over the opposite sex. It gives you a better chance of...scoring with them so...yeah..." Dormouse blurted all of that rapid-fire, getting rather red-faced about the last part.

I cleared my throat, really hoping I didn't hear him right about one part, "Hold up, if HP goes to zero, *lights out?*"

"Yep, as in dying," Joy growled menacingly, throwing the comment over her shoulder like she was enjoying this. "Here and on Earth."

"*Oh, wow,*" I gasped.

Was there less oxygen after that fact? Or was it just harder to get into my lungs?

...Wait, I was currently at 6/8, so I'd better watch those HP closely, especially if these fox things were as nasty as they sounded...

The group slowed to a stop in a clearing under the heavy brush of giant evergreens. I couldn't find the reason for the halt other than Callen digging, preoccupied, in his large knapsack.

"Here." Callen apparently found whatever he was looking for and threw it in my direction. I grabbed at the white fabric, flying towards me in the air, trying to grasp it and—*and I dropped it. Figured. Did they have an Ability that labeled me as a klutz too?* I opened the fabric to find that it was a set of lightweight, but sturdy, white body armor. White fur lined the collar over a gold-embroidered seam inset with a small ruby at the center of the neck. I sunk my fingers into the luxurious folds, feeling strangely comforted for a reason I couldn't pin down.

"Put it on," Callen prodded with a wave.

"Oh, it probably doesn't fit anyway." I shrugged, holding the material against my body.

"It damn well should," Rainer boomed from behind Callen; the Nomad's bulky form shoved forward, "It was designed especially for you by you. It's magical and, frankly, damn expensive. It'll expand to the contours of your body—"

"What?" I gaped at the Nomad, feeling the fabric almost slide out of my grasp. ...*Did he just say I'd designed it? How was that even possible?*

Callen shoved the man in the shoulder, resuming his position in front with a troubled frown. "If you could try to let her *learn as she goes*," he hissed.

But I'd already heard.

"I—wait—I *made* this?" My voice faltered.

"*Designed*—" Rainer held up a huge, intrusive hand, pushing away the Trader who was clearly trying to get him to take a backseat in this conversation, "No—get off. She *designed* it. She didn't *make* it. Game Makers don't stitch their own clothes, though her parents probably enchanted it—"

"The main point is that it's fire resistant and strong," Callen interrupted. "Many beasts can bite right through the fabric of your clothes, or, if they're fire-breathing, their blaze will likely just catch and run straight up your body, burning you alive. This armor stops that," the gray-haired man stated bluntly.

I'd never wanted to change faster.

My fingers clutched at the fur collar and the breathable fabric. I ducked behind the thickest bush I could find, beginning to pull on the body armor, but a system update popped up, interrupting the process:

**[Object Identified: DIVINE DEFLECTOR ARMOR Increases
Gamer Armor Class To 15 Unless Already Higher, +30
Baddie Points When Equipped]
[Do You Wish To Equip DIVINE DEFLECTOR ARMOR?]
[Yes] [No]**

Yes, I told the buttons floating mid-air. And the option selected with a whooshing sound.

**[System Alert: Armor Equipped & Armor Class Increased
To 15, +30 Baddie Points, 55]**

And, suddenly, I stared down at the white bodysuit which had adhered immediately to my body. It was stretchy and lightweight with armored bits over my chest, arms and legs. White knee-high boots went with it. Everything fit perfectly in a slightly creepy way. ...Even if I was secretly wondering if I looked like a lady Stormtrooper. I tugged my hair into a low ponytail... *One could hardly fight half-dead foxes with it waving about in their eyes...*

And I tried to breathe.

Deep.

And slow—as slow as I could, anyway.

Into the holly-shaped, spiked leaves near my face. ...But my heartbeat was *racing.*

I'd designed this armor? How come I had no recollection of it? How come I couldn't remember it at all??? Yet, something felt so familiar about the material and the color—warm and comforting—like I had seen it before. *In a dream? In a memory?*

"System?" I breathed cautiously, squeezing my eyes shut from the thought that I was even asking. "System, retrieve the memory of me designing this body armor?" Almost immediately, the familiar, neon letters slid into my view:

**[System Searching MRPs To Select & Display Correct
Memory...]**

Yes!!

But there was an electronic error beep, and more text slid into view.

[No Connected Memory Found.]

What? I gaped at the message. *How could...*

"System, tell me if they're lying about me designing this body armor for myself," I persisted.

[System Understands Query...Loading Response...]

The results loaded quicker this time.

[System Answer: No, RAINER, NOMAD 9 Is Not Lying.]

Great. So that told me...nothing, really.

Frustrated, I stepped out of the bushes in a huff, making them rattle, to realize the group was in the middle of an argument.

Rainer pointed a heated finger at the ground, "She shouldn't rely on it; we know what it's capable of—"

The group's conversation instantly died when they noticed my entrance. Their embarrassed stares raked over my new outfit like it was a convenient excuse. ...What had they been talking about? Something to do with me?

"She looks good," Dormouse nodded reassuringly at me, and it was enough to push my worries about whatever they'd been discussing out of my mind. I smiled.

Just a bit.

The nerd kid kind of felt like the younger brother I never had.

"So, did I not get the memo when I supposedly designed this because this armor is white and all of your armor is black," I started, my eyes trailing to their own breastplates.

"Game Makers always wear white so they can be seen in battle," Rainer mumbled under his breath.

"...Battle?" I squeaked. Surely, he didn't mean...

But the volume of the Nomad's voice increased as he cleared his throat too readily, putting a hand to his red beard. "—Anyway, ready to see those Snargels?" The Nomad parted the looming brush with one hand before I could get a word in to confirm or deny.

And, through it, I got my first glimpse of charred forest—trees burned so black that some had gaping holes in them.

And a pack of half-dead foxes ran there—their gray-and-orange, streaked tails raised high as the decaying remains of their thin bodies darted between the trees and rusty train cars tilting off the tracks in the distance. There were a good number of them. Their eyes did, indeed, glow an unnerving green, and their yellow teeth were visible through the gaping flesh along their jawbones but…

They were all scurrying, galloping through the underbrush, away from us.

"Wait," I blurted confused, "Are they…running from something?" I whipped around to glance at the faces of the group.

The pink-haired girl looked particularly displeased; her porcelain forehead wrinkled in unease. "This is not good," she stated, chomping on her gum.

And, well…that was exactly the last thing I wanted to hear right now…

Rosabella

A high-pitched shriek rattled the surrounding trees. The ground shook with footfalls. *No wonder the zombie foxes were running!* I jumped back, knocking clumsily into the rest of the group, as a savage scream bellowed through the treetops again, rustling the branches overhead like a focused hurricane—clanging them together like each one was a different silver utensil.

Completely *shredding my eardrums.*

I clapped two hands over the tender flesh of my ears protectively, my entire body wincing and writhing painfully beneath me—could sound make your ears *bleed?!*

"That is *not* a Snargel," Rainer growled.

No shit.

[System Alert: SILVER RINKECLAW, DRAGON 4
Approximately 30 Feet Away.]

"Fuck," I heard Dormouse mutter under his breath.

And the kid's words started a seizing in my chest. My breath shortened. If ever there was an opportune time for a panic attack to begin, it seemed like right now had all the prerequisites. I gulped in air, trying to focus on what I figured was safe, sturdy ground under my feet. *...So, why was that ground shaking?*

"System, what is a Silver Rinkeclaw? Bring up its stats?" My voice trembled. My heart thundered in my chest and ears.

[System Understands Query...Loading Response...]

"It's a dragon," Rainer blurted, his bushy eyebrows twitching over a grim expression, "It's a Level 4 dragon—"

[System Answer: A Silver Rinkeclaw Is A Medium-Sized Dragon With Silver Scales And Extra-Large Incisors. Distinguishable Due To Its Sixth-Clawed Foot And The Pattern Of Darker Scales Which Run Down The Ridge Of Its Back.
STRENGTHS: Enhanced Stealth, Increased Strike Damage From Claws & Ability To Spit Acid. WEAKNESSES: Below Average Intelligence & Awareness. Easily Distracted. Just Don't Distract It By Letting It Spit Acid In Your Face.]

Name	Silver Rinkeclaw	
Class & Level, Size	Dragon 4, Medium	
HP	75/75	
Armor Class	17/20	
ABILITIES /20		
Strength	+4	19
Agility	+2	14
Endurance	+3	17
Intelligence	-2	8
Awareness	+0	11
Presence	+2	15
CM		1

"Damned nasty buggers and clearly hungry by the looks of it," Rainer griped.

But I wasn't looking at the Nomad speaking. I couldn't help it. I was laser-focused on the serpent head snaking through the underbrush, rippling muscles underneath silver scales like a swan's extended neck. The dark clouds overhead only made the beast's form seem more threatening, shadowing the ferns where the tremors in the ground told me it was stomping its feet. I shuttered. Apparently a 'medium-sized' dragon was still pretty enormous when compared to…well, my human form.

This was not a cute, Pokémon dragon…

Its eyes, sharp as an eagles', scanned the forest. Its slanted nostrils expanded, in and out, with each shuttering breath, and its silver scales glinted in the sunlight, like knife blades…

And I didn't even have one.

A thundering roar detonated over my ears. My breath caught and dried up any saliva in my throat. It sounded…*well, fucking terrifying. Had it seen us? I couldn't really tell—*

[System Query: Would You Like To Hide Or Fight?]

A shield icon with a magnifying glass overtop of it hovered beside the words.

"Umm guys?!" I turned, searching desperately for some kind of aid, "A little help here?"

Please say we weren't supposed to fight this thing. This armor, no matter how magical, certainly couldn't help much against a beast like this, and I didn't even have a weapon! I knew I had to Level Up to save Dad, but there had to be a different way—

Almost immediately, I noticed that I was the only one in our group with the hovering system query. The glowing letters in front of their system pop-ups still said:

**[System Alert: SILVER RINKECLAW, DRAGON 4
Approximately 30 Feet Away.]**

…Well, except that the distance meter was ticking down…

…25 Feet Away…

The beast sniffed at the air.

Oh my God. Even this tall brush wouldn't hide us for much longer.

"*Guys!*" I screamed.

The pink-haired girl's eyes narrowed, squinting at my system query. "Wait, why does special-sticker girl have an Examine Opportunity popping up, and we don't?" she protested.

Examine Opportunity?

"Rosabella, click on the shield magnifying glass icon next to your prompt, *hurry!*" Dormouse urged.

My fingers shook as I lifted them. *There—*

[System Reward: Congratulations, You Have Added A New Skill. +5 XP, 33/100
EXAMINE: Allows A Gamer To Inspect A Situation Or Object More Closely. Examine Opportunities Are Indicated By The Shield Magnifying Glass Icon. Manually Click On The Icon Or Speak The Word 'Examine' Out Loud To Initiate.]

I rushed through the words, adrenaline seeming to help my eyes read faster.

"Examine!" I whispered.

[System Query Examined... +1 XP, 34/100]
[Upon A Closer Look, You Discovered This Is Not A Simple 'Hide' Or 'Fight' Situation. The SILVER RINKECLAW, DRAGON 4 Possesses 1 CM Diamond In Its Nest. Original 'Hide Or Fight' System Query Dismissed.]

"A Creator Magic Diamond?" I breathed. My eyes wandered to search the groups' staring faces. "Isn't that what I need to—"

"To activate your Creator Magic, yes. One of three," Callen, the gray-haired Trader, nodded solemnly. Behind his blinking eyes, I saw a stormy sea of thoughts crashing into each other.

"So, the system is trying to uplevel her? This just proves my special-sticker theory—" Joy started, her grating voice droning at the typical one-tone pitch.

But Rainer cut her off, "*If* she gets the Diamond at all. That Dragon is a Level 4, Rosabella's Level 1 if you've forgotten." His red-tinged cheeks shook with aggravation.

Why were they all talking like I wasn't standing right here?

"I'm simply saying I think we need to consider the fact that the system may be trying to help," the Warrior girl protested. Her eyes flashed fire brighter even than her hair.

"It isn't like before. The new system is *never* trying to help. There's *always* a motive," Callen interjected.

"*Guys?!*"

This time, it was Dormouse's thin plea, not mine.

My head whipped around, but it was too late. Because, out of the corner of my eye, I saw Dormouse's system alert hovering over his sheet-white face.

...10 Feet Away...

His expression morphed into wrinkled, utter terror. Just like mine. *Oh shit! The dragon was—*

Yellowed incisors, larger than half the length of my arm, hissed directly in front of us, a wad of saliva dripping from where silver scales became black lips. *Shit.* The creature roared—a braying, bellowing war cry which shattered the air like a million sharp objects being thrown at my face—

Pointed and thundering.

Rushing in my ears.

A wall of fire blazed towards us, the tendrils of the orange and red edges licking and rolling over on each other—coming directly at my face. The scorching heatwave seared at the skin of my exposed cheeks and neck—

I shrieked and leapt away, shaking out my searing palms and slapping at the skin of my face to bring feeling back there where it'd gone smarting and, then, numb. A system message popped into view: my lowered HP.

[-2 HP, 4/8]

Fuck. Thank goodness this armor was fire resistant, or I would have been hit with even more damage—

"Rosabella, run!" Rainer yelled, hefting a battle axe high in the air.

But the pink-haired Warrior waved an annoyed hand between us, "No, idiot! We have to get her to Level 2. If she dies, so does this world. Rosabella, trades, collecting objects and combat get you XP. There's a limit, but— Trade me something you have on you now— anything!" Her bubble-gum-colored hair streaked across her frantic face in straight strands.

"I—" I stammered. Anything? God, I kind of stood with the pink-haired, Joy girl on this one; I didn't want to die—

I patted down the pockets of my body armor, but there was nothing—nothing that I had on me.

In the blurred line of my vision, I saw the dragon rear. The dirt beneath me quaked like it was afraid too. But I didn't have time for the luxury of that emotion. My fingers fumbled at the neckline of my armor, ripping the small ruby out of the gold, metal piece there. I held it up.

"You can take this in exchange!" The girl waved a dagger at me. "You need a weapon anyway. The trade XP will move you towards upleveling—"

[Proposed Trade: ROSABELLA, GAME MAKER 1 Trades TINY RUBY. JOY, WARRIOR 11 Offers LEATHER-WRAPPED HANDLE DAGGER]
[Will You Accept The Trade?]
[Yes] [No]

"*Yes!*" I shouted. And I launched the jewel at the pink-haired Warrior. She caught it with much more grace than I would have expected. The girl threw her dagger at me.

...Well, not *at* me, just, in my direction. I didn't catch it. It landed awkwardly near my feet in the grass with a soft thud.

[System Alert: Trade Accepted]
[System Reward: A Very 'Sharp' Trade...Literally, +15 XP, 49/100]

But I didn't have time for the system's jokes...

"*Go!*" she screeched, nodding her head to the side, while drawing two, long katanas from her belt simultaneously, "We'll distract the Rinkeclaw! Find that Diamond!"

I didn't need to be told twice.

[System Alert: LEATHER-WRAPPED HANDLE DAGGER Acquired. Object Will Be Placed In Your Inventory Unless You'd Like to Equip. Would You Like To Equip?]
[Yes] [No]

"Yes," My voice was a low growl at this point. How many options did I have to go through just to make it out of here alive?

The system pop-up cleared with a whoosh, and I looked down to see the dagger's leather handle no longer in the grass but secured in my fist. Awesome.

[System Alert: Weapon Equipped.]

Object:	Leather-Wrapped Handle Dagger
Required Class & Level For Use:	None
Description:	Basic L1 Weapon. A Bit of Metal, Wood & Leather Put Together. Did A Caveman Create This?
Augment Capacities:	+1 Strength

Baddie Points: **+0**

Good, whatever. I dismissed the words with a quick swipe. *I needed to get out of there.* I dodged into the underbrush while hearing the rest of the group charge towards the beast with raucous battle cries. Thorns and leaves snagged at my clothes. Behind me, I heard something splat and a man's yelp. An acid stench choked my nostrils.

I broke through the bushes, already nearly out of breath. My eyes swept the clearing as I fingered the weapon Joy had given me, pressing it more firmly into my palm and trying to force oxygen into my failing lungs.

My heart rammed in my chest—in my ears—

…What good was an all-but-glorified pocketknife now anyway?

Against a beast?

A dragon?! Or any of those zombie fox things I'd seen?

…Still, I sure as hell wasn't about to go without it.

The clearing was a maze of rusted-out train cars—like they'd been parked one day hundreds of years ago and never seen the light of movement again. Moss grew over metal and wood parts, suffocating the train cars in green where any shadow covered. Others, in the rows, were burned black, scorched from, well, *the obvious,* and falling apart or badly dented like the weight of something had been thrown against them.

I could guess what. …And I had to find this thing's nest to try to get the Diamond? Fabulous.

I lunged for cover in the nearest train car, wrapping my fingers around the steel doorframe and yanking my body inside like the pure existence of a wall might, somehow, make me feel safer. *Too bad it didn't really work.*

The metal floor creaked and wobbled as the shadow of the ceiling slid over my head. *What now?* A quick glance in front of me showed that a line of train cars connected to this one. Rows of metal seats, peeling paint from abandonment and age, lined the way forward with a narrow aisle through the center of each one. *Maybe, if I stayed in their shelter, I could peek through the windows and find the dragon's nest without facing the beast? …Or would the beast just flip the cars over it if caught me inside?*

It was a risk I was going to have to take. Still, doubt and fear hounded my mind like an unyielding fist on a door: *This was crazy. This was absolutely insane. There was a dragon out there—a real dragon?! This shouldn't be happening!*

But it was. It really was. And, if I wanted Dad back safe, I was going to have to suck it up, get ahold of myself and find this dragon's nest. I swallowed, and, feeling like a tiny field mouse, I ducked hurriedly through the length of the car, racing down the metal floor, balancing between the transition to the next and whipping into the door of a second car. My body felt like it was on fire from the adrenaline. My white boots flashed underneath me as my eyes swept what I could see outside from the windows. *Where would a dragon build a nest?* That's when I felt it.

A warm breeze fluttered the ends of my brunette hair past my shoulders, but it wasn't the breeze. I turned, leaning over a row of rusted seats, to peer out the nearest train car window. Past the metal box of the window and the clearing beyond, the lush side of the forest rose, where huge trees spiraled their lime-green torrents upwards, branches spreading out above like arms extended to the heavens.

But it wasn't there either.

I heard the Silver Rinkeclaw shriek again in the distance.

I shifted my weight; the metal floor squeaked beneath me as I looked back towards the noise but—the feeling wasn't there either.

…What was it? If I could just put my finger on it…

I turned. And it caught me again. Swept me up.

Exhilarating.

46

Like a breath of fresh air whisking towards me in the wind, diving into my mouth and lungs—reviving me, tingling there…

My eyes locked on a burrow in the ground beside the tracks, just outside the window. Rocks and dirt were kicked up into a pile, and a hole left in their place carved into the grassy bank. … *Wait, was that a shield magnifying glass symbol floating just over it? The one for an Examine Opportunity?*

I scrabbled out of the car, the soles of my white boots thudding down the exit stairs, shaking the whole car, but I didn't care. I jogged forward, closing the distance between me and the burrow. Loose dirt rolled downward with each of my steps towards it—

The feeling intensified.

Tingling and sparking in my fingers—nearly setting my hair on fire with *warmth* and *joy.* It felt…It, strangely, felt…like *home.*

"System, Examine!" I blurted, nearly out of breath from both the run and my own excitement.

[System Object Examined… +1 XP, 50/100]
[After Taking A Quick Look, You Discover That This Is Not An Ordinary Hole. You Found The Entrance To The SILVER RINKECLAW, DRAGON 4's Nest. Will You Enter?]
[Yes] [No]

Yes, of course. So, why was my body shaking like a leaf?

Rosabella

I tripped down into the opening—the hole. Actually, I realized as my eyes adjusted, it was a hole that the creature had dug, connecting to an old mine shaft. I crawled out of the narrow opening and into a room. The rectangular space, made of corrugated metal and wood walls, was dark, a stark contrast to the glaring sunlight streaming in from rectangular openings on each side, and a door next to my elbow appeared to be sealed with tar. *Was this an old entrance to a mine?*

The sound of dripping water reverberated in the space. I stood up to full height. The dirt floor was lumpy and uneven through the soles of my white boots, and the air was damp, nearly heavy with the feeling of water and earth.

That's when I caught the humming—the pulsing, purring around me like a million tiny pieces of sand vibrating all at once over and under my limbs. *The sound and feel were nearly hypnotic.*

And I, suddenly, had to squint into a side corner of the room.

Because the light was blinding.

Radiating from the sharp, turquoise angles of a floating diamond.

Hovering amidst piles of golden, glinting treasure.

Coins, necklaces, wheel hubs, silver helmets…all jumbled in falling-over piles where the dragon had stashed them against the walls.

And the diamond, hovering above.

Bobbing in the air.

Buzzing and swirling aqua and sky blue underneath the form of a clear, membrane-like container.

That's where the feeling was coming from.

Looking at it, my heart expanded. …Engulfed with the feeling of hot maple syrup flowing over the organ like a welcome hug.

Warmth.

Safety.

Belonging.

Was this what they called magic? …And why did it feel so real…so…tangible? Like pure joy? Or peace?

A low, menacing growl tensed every muscle in my body. I whipped around to see a snarling zombie fox, crouched low in an advance. The creature's skeleton and organs showed where patches of bristling, gray-and-orange, matted fur was missing. The tiny pads of its feet ground into the dirt floor while its narrow snout snapped. *What were they called?*

"System, show me the Snargel stats again—" I whispered, cowering while thoughts raced through my mind. *The thing definitely saw me. There was no hiding now. I was going to have to fight it. I needed that Creator Magic Diamond! Maybe if I could figure out some advantage…*

[System Understands Query…Loading Response…]

I clutched the dagger, ready, in my hand, feeling the leather handle slide from the sweat already forming on my palm.

[System Answer: A Snargel Is A Feisty Zombie Fox With Green, Glowing Eyes.
STRENGTHS: Keen Sense of Smell & Ability To Fling Bur-Like, Metal Balls From Its Tail.
WEAKNESSES: Bite Damage & Close Combat. The Creature Isn't Particularly Deft, But Those Metal Burs Hurt Like Hell So Beware.]

Name	Snargel	
Class & Level, Size	Undead 1, Small	
HP	7/7	
Armor Class	10/20	
ABILITIES /20		
Strength	-2	6
Agility	+2	15
Endurance	+1	13
Intelligence	-2	6
Awareness	+1	12
Presence	+0	10

…Okay, weaknesses were bite damage and close combat. Noted. And I needed to watch out for metal burs—

Apparently, the warning came too late. I looked up to see a morning star hurling directly towards my face—the metal spikey ball flying with extreme precision—

Fuck!

I leapt out of the way and—

And face-planted in the hard dirt. My lip throbbed, feeling swollen. The rocks and dark soot of the ground scraped at my palms, tearing the skin there. It stung like hell.

[-1 HP, 3/8]

Were you kidding me?! If this thing didn't hurt me, I was going to hurt myself? I grunted, rolling to the side. The floor was hard and lumpy on my back as rocks dug even through the white mesh of my bodysuit. My fingers scrabbled in the loose soil for the blade I'd just dropped—

But the Snargel was faster.

It growled, its whole, skeletal body shaking from the vibration. It lifted its tail again to throw another morning star.

No.

No, I was not going to get beaten by a zombie fox. I was not going to get beaten two steps away from grabbing the CM Diamond—not this close. Not when the rest of the group was fighting a higher-level dragon.

I took a chance.

I grasped my dagger, and I rushed forward.

I hit the fox mid-air, and we tumbled to the ground. Teeth snapped in the air, paws and limbs flew—crashing. I heard the thing bite down, but its teeth couldn't penetrate my armor. I shoved it off—

[-100 MRP, 3540/6205]

Negative Memory Recall Points? My armor must have been strong enough to stop HP damage from the bite, but I still got negative memory? Negative memory meant I was even further away from understanding my past—learning about Mom… And, something happened, then, something inside—a dump truck load of justified rage crashed over my head. My lips opened in a guttural cry.

Tribal.

Like, in this moment where no one could see me, I could unleash the beast I'd been all along. Dad wasn't here to berate me. No one was here. It was just me and this fox and—

[System Reward: Rage Promotion +5 XP, 55/100, Strength Will Increase +3 For The Next 10 Seconds]

A timer counted down the time in corner of my vision:

[10]
[9]

It was as though an unseen force grabbed ahold of me as my fist tightened around my dagger.

[8]

The smell of death from zombie flesh filled my nostrils. Course fur tickled in between my fingers, scratching at the skin of my hands. I didn't look. I jabbed.

[7]

I stabbed the knife into fur—flesh. Felt the animal squirm underneath me, shriek.

[SNARGEL, UNDEAD 1: -3 HP, 4/7]
[6]

But it wasn't enough. I wanted the thing dead. I wanted anything that stood in my way—between me and getting Dad back safe—dead. Gone. Obliterated. I plunged the dagger again, harder this time, like I could embed my very rage into the beast. Warm blood splattered onto my cheeks, but I didn't wipe it away. I felt the sticky liquid dripping over my hands and the weapon. I looked down at the carnage I'd made as the stats popped up.

[SNARGEL, UNDEAD 1: -4 HP, 0/7]
[System Reward: SNARGEL, UNDEAD 1 Eliminated, +15 XP, 70/100]
[5, 4, 3, 1, 0]

I breathed heavily, watching the timer run down to zero, and then…just then, I realized what I'd done—how much blood had soaked into the white material of my body armor…how I stood there holding fur and life that was no more…something I'd *killed*.

I dropped the body. I stared at it—the lifeless holes where eyes used to shine. I'd taken the very light out of them—*I'd* done that.

A second crappy aspect was that the body wasn't the only proof; blood slathered the front of my white body armor, staining it. I reeked of copper and guts.

But my eyes quickly refocused on the prize—on what had driven me to make that kill in the first place: the turquoise CM Diamond.

And I stepped forward.

My cupped hands outstretched—

The diamond came alive, twitching, then, zipping around the mine shaft room.

Past my elbow—

Back over my shoulder—

My hair blew back from the movement, and I lunged for it—

My fingers collided with the bubbly exterior which exploded into a ray of sizzling, blue sparks as it soaked into my hands with a zinging, wet feeling which made me quickly swipe my hands on the legs of my bodysuit.

Then, the magic was gone, and a system update bobbed in its place:

[System Reward: CM DIAMOND Acquired +10 XP, 80/100, Object Will Be Placed In Your Inventory Unless You'd Like To Equip. Would You Like To Equip?]
[Yes] [No]

"No," I told it dismissively.

Wait…my inventory? Was there a way to view that now that I had a second to breathe?

"System, show me my inventory," I commanded confidently, wiping my blood-covered hands again on the legs of my body armor; the blood just wouldn't come off. A strange sort of unexpected energy buzzed through me—satisfaction? Adrenaline? Both? I'd killed a zombie fox. I'd done that. And, now, I had an inventory. This was big stuff!

[System Understands Query…Loading Response…]

I made a quick, mental note of my XP points too: 80/100. They'd said I'd Level Up every 100 XP—*I was almost there!*

[System Alert: Per Request, Inventory Opened.]
- **1 Leather-Wrapped Handle Dagger [Equipped]**
- **1 CM Diamond**

I smiled despite myself. No way, there the Diamond was. Cool! Now, for the Leveling Up, so I could try to free Dad more quickly... Maybe there was something in this dragon's nest that could help?

My eyes scanned the now-empty room. There were two levers abutting the two doorways which were parallel to each other. I wondered what those did...

I stepped towards the nearest lever, reaching for it. The rusted metal was cold under my fingers, but surprisingly firm even after all the years.

[System Query: Will You Pull The Lever?]
[Yes] [No]

YES. I wanted to roll my eyes. Why did it even need to ask me that? I literally had my hand on it.

The lever shoved downward with a groan.

Metal scraped against metal.

Then, a thunderous bang as a corrugated metal door dropped, pounding into the dirt right beside me and kicking up even more of it in billowing clouds. I cringed away from the noise, coughing. The room was drenched in partial darkness—partial because of the light still streaming in from the opening on the other side of the room and from where water had rusted away a pretty decent-sized hole in the metal door. Hmmm, interesting. So, the levers operated the doors. The other side looked identical. ...Wait, there was a shield with a magnifying glass floating up in the rafters.

I wasn't tall enough to reach it by jumping—trust me, I'd tried— so I stacked a bunch of junk: an ancient-looking chest, several wood pallets, an overturned bucket... I stepped tenuously on the rocking junkpile before remembering that I could just simply say the command out loud. …Better that then fall and lose more HP, I figured.

"Examine!" I called upward.

[System Object Examined… +1 XP, 81/100]
[A Closer Look Helped You Determine That The Parallel Doors And Corresponding Levers Are Operated By Several Brown, Pulley-Style Belts. They Are Frayed Around The Edges But, Otherwise, Look Pretty Reliable For Their Age. Ability Needed To Cut: 11 Strength]

Hmmm so? There was no follow-up reward or other indication for how that information might be valuable. Feeling a little disappointed, I turned back to the piles of treasure stowed up against the walls. *Maybe I could Level Up if I collected more items? I was almost at 100 XP. There had to be something here to collect…*

I was going to need light if I was going to search through this stuff. I turned back to the lever, grasping the metal again.

[System Query: Will You Pull The Lever?]
[Yes] [No]

Yes. The door screeched upward again. Sunlight pierced my pupils, and hit the wall of treasure—

Something sparkled there, just out of the corner of my eye. I turned, distracted by it. I squinted at a form propped up against the cave wall.

…A sword?

There was so much metal here and piles of gems and valuables…*what attracted my eye to this?* The weapon had a silver and gold handle with straight, clean lines. It looked light and streamlined, like it'd been forged with incredible mastery. The blade was so reflective that I could nearly see my face in it. For some reason, I had to touch it. I reached out, realizing that an Examination Opportunity icon bobbed near the top of the blade. *What?*

"Examine," I requested, feeling curiosity tug me further towards the weapon.

[System Object Examined... +1 XP, 82/100]
[There's A Message Etched Into The Blade In Small, Swirling Letters: 'Happy Mother's Day! Love, Your Doting Husband & Rosabella'. The Design Indicates It Is A Sword Of Great Magical Ability.]

I stared at the message, not ready to dismiss it yet. What did it mean? My name wasn't the most common. Was it possible that this sword could have been—my mother's? My Dad never said much about her except that she'd divorced him. Was it possible she'd...been here? Wherever 'here' was?

The system message faded, but my shock from it didn't. A little perturbed, I took a shaking breath—barely believing I was about to ask—

"System, was this my mother's sword?" I asked, my voice shaking. Was I sweating? Why were my palms so sticky?

[System Understands Query...Loading Response...]

I held my breath.

[System Answer: Yes. ROSABELLA'S MOTHER'S GOLD & SILVER BROADSWORD Belonged To ROSABELLA THE GREAT, NOBLE 17, Your Mother.]

I stared at the words, my mouth dropping open slightly in disbelief. *My mother...? This sword belonged...how?* Regardless, I had to know what it felt like—to touch the one thing that, maybe, my mother also touched. My fingers wrapped around the hilt—

A system alert popped up almost instantly. *Good, maybe more information or XP?*

[System Reward: ROSABELLA'S MOTHER'S GOLD &
SILVER BROADSWORD Acquired +10 XP, 92/100, Object
Will Be Placed In Your Inventory Unless You'd Like To
Equip. Would You Like To Equip?]
[Yes] [No]

"Yes!" I blurted too hastily "Yes, equip!"

An electronic error beep interrupted my joy.

[System Error: Insufficient Level & Strength To Wield
ROSABELLA'S MOTHER'S GOLD & SILVER
BROADSWORD. Request Denied.]

Really? My shoulders sank even as my eyes raked over the weapon description.

Object:	Rosabella's Mother's Gold & Silver Broadsword
Required Class & Level For Use:	Melee - L2 w/ 10 Strength Magical - L6 w/ 10 Strength & 14 Awareness
Description:	Clearly An Advanced & Magical Sword Hand-Crafted With Intertwining Gold & Metal. Especially Sharp Blade.
Augment Capacities:	+7 Strength (Melee) & CM Increase +10 For 5 Seconds When Utilizing, 2 Times Max Before A Long Rest (Magical)
Baddie Points:	+25

Damn, if I remembered right, my Strength was 8. No wonder I couldn't pick it up. Wow, it increased Strength by seven points? Incredibly helpful…not that I could use it…I looked down to find the sword tied benignly on my belt without me having had to put it there.

Okay, so Creator Magic Diamond was accounted for. I'd gotten this cool sword I couldn't use that was, also, allegedly my mother's. What else was around here that could level me up? I started to dig through some more of the treasure, hearing gold and metal clank against each other as I shifted the pile and then—

And, then, I heard something that wasn't gold and metal.

Or wood.

Or dirt.

Or anything inanimate.

I heard a breathy grunt behind me, and a grating growl. The smell of smoke filled my nostrils.

And I froze.

Please say that was Joy or Rainer or one of the others. Please say that was NOT what I thought it was...

I pushed upward to standing slowly. My eyes snapped towards the nest entrance across from me.

And locked.

With a dragon's beady gaze.

Not any dragon.

The Silver Rinkeclaw.

Rosabella

The Silver Rinkeclaw advanced towards me, aggravated claws plowing into the dirt floor of the mine shaft entrance and churning it up. A spear and the shafts of four arrows protruded from the tough armor of its back, and a red, gaping wound slashed across the scales of its right shoulder. Apparently, the rest of the group hadn't inflicted enough damage to fell the beast. ...Just enough to piss it off. *Fabulous.* Its thrashing tail swished, annoyed, back and forth, slamming repeatedly into the wood frame of the doorway its form nearly obliterated. The muscled appendage hit the wood so hard that clouds of dirt and dust puffed out from the rafters above us.

A grating sound echoed through the small room as rock and debris fell, completely blocking the hole dug in the ground where I'd entered—obliterating it. I glanced at the ceiling nervously; *this place was centuries old. Would it just crumple and fall down on both of us?*

The dragon.

My eyes flashed back to it. Obviously, the dragon was the bigger issue here. Its nostrils and eyes flared, seething with a shrill whistle coming from the gaping rows of hissing-pointed teeth—

I'd—I'd beat the zombie fox thing; I'd killed it. Didn't that mean I had a chance at besting this thing too?

My weak knees weren't so sure. My head twisted. My body tensed to jump even as my hands held the tiny, crude dagger in front of me. *Good lot that would do if the monster did attack.* My eyes wove over the small room for exits—only the one behind me and the one behind the dragon. *If I ran for it, would I make it out alive?*

"System," I hissed, "Can I outrun this dragon?"

[System Answer: Probably Not. SILVER RINKECLAW, DRAGON 4 Has An Approximately 71% Advantage Over ROSABELLA, GAME MAKER 1. Do You Wish To Take This Chance?]
[Yes] [No]

Hell no. I gritted my teeth together. Stats. I needed to look at the dragon's stats again to see how to defeat this thing. If this was like a RPG, I needed to figure out the creature's weaknesses and exploit them... My heart jackhammered in my chest. Hyperventilation was setting in—

Before I could open my mouth to request the creature's stats, something launched.

Flew.

Right at my—

I ducked.

Squelch.

Acid sizzled into the wood doorpost behind me. The steaming, yellow liquid was far too close to my face for comfort. Nausea burned the back of my throat with its own sour acid at the stench and how quickly it ate the wood black.

[System Reward: Dodged That Acid, +3 XP, 95/100]

I turned towards the dragon. *Think, just think!* I shouted at myself in my head.

"System, show me the dragon's stats!" I blurted.

[System Understands Query…Loading Response…]

The dragon didn't care if I was looking at its stats or not. The monstrous dragon screamed, a hollering bellow, reaching for me with six razor-sharp claws—

There was nowhere to go! I leapt to the side, swinging around and ducking under its careening tail while trying to read the stats now hovering in the air…

[System Answer: A Silver Rinkeclaw Is A Medium-Sized…]

Yeah, yeah, I didn't care about that part. I was well-freaking aware—

Where was the weakness part—?!

[…STRENGTHS: ….WEAKNESSES: Below Average Intelligence & Awareness. Easily Distracted. Just Don't Distract It By Letting It Spit Acid In Your Face.]

Name	Silver Rinkeclaw	
Class & Level, Size	Dragon 4, Medium	
HP	75/75	
Armor Class	17/20	
ABILITIES /20		
Strength	+4	19
Agility	+2	14
Endurance	+3	17
Intelligence	-2	8
Awareness	+0	11
Presence	+2	15
CM		0

Easily distracted? Below average intelligence? Okay…okay, so, maybe, I just had to trick it, not kill it? Maybe if I could get it underneath one of the doors and pull the lever down to crush it there? Would it work?

My eyes flashed to the lever at my elbow. I was halfway through attempting to determine how one gets a dragon underneath the opening of a door while, simultaneously, being near a lever when I heard the beast turn, hissing.

I flipped around to see huge, open fangs with yellowed teeth—

Shit.

I had to do something fast.

I reached down for something to throw. My fingers fumbled in the dirt and treasure—

Fur. My fingers met matted fur. I looked down in horror to find that my hand rested in the mangled coat of the Snargel I'd killed. That was when I got an idea.

"Hey! Hey, Halfwit!" I barked at the Rikeclaw. Trying not to fully realize what I was doing, I used both hands to heave the body of the dead zombie fox upward, waving the carcass in from of me, "You hungry? Go get the nasty fox!"

I threw it—launched the dead fox body—right under the metal door.

The dragon lurched forward—changing direction and attitude so suddenly that it knocked me over. Hard dirt greeted me, bruising my elbows and back.

No. I had to flip the switch!

I fumbled to find my feet under me—fumbled to stand—pushing myself upwards. My fingers reached for the lever, feeling ice-cold metal—

[System Query: Will You Pull The Lever?]
[Yes] [No]

"YES!" I screeched.

And metal groaned.

Slammed into dirt—

And bones crunched.

The dragon roared in pain as its stats popped into view—

[SILVER RINKECLAW, DRAGON 4: -2 HP, 25/75]

Yes!

…Wait, only -2?

My blood ran cold. It hadn't worked? It wasn't smashed under the door?

I turned. And only the horned tip of the dragon's tail was caught under the metal door—I mean, that and the completely decimated zombie fox corpse. The infuriated Rikeclaw wrenched its body towards me, charging, but its tail was stuck. Its wings scraped at the wood beams, struggling, frantically grappling for some way to pull itself out and towards me.

Oh my God.

I should run?

I watched the end of the monster's tail begin to slide free with each tug.

No, if I ran, it'd catch up with me. Could I kill it? I glanced down at my tiny, dagger blade, clenched between my shaking, white knuckles. No, the weapon was only +1 Strength, leaving me at Strength 9. That wasn't going to be near enough against the Dragon's Strength 19. I was fucked. I was royally screwed. Think, Rosabella!

Maybe there was something in the treasure that could help? A weapon not as heavy as my mother's sword but better than the dagger? My fingers fumbled in the piles of treasure—frantic this time. I could barely catch a breath.

Leather. My fingertips wrapped around something solid and leather. Armor? The hilt of a sword? I went to pull it out. The familiar icon of a shield with a magnifying glass hovered over it. I rushed to select it.

[System Object Examined... +1 XP, 96/100]
[This Looks Like Some Kind Of Ancient Tome. The Letters
On The Front Say 'Draconic Language Dictionary'.]

A dictionary? Really?! Not what I needed right now. I went to throw
it to the side when another system message popped up:

[System Reward: Congratulations, You Have Added A
New Skill. +5 XP, 101/100
DRACONIC LANGUAGE: Allows A Gamer To Understand
And Talk To Dragons.]

Great, fucking great. So, what, was I, now, supposed to do—tell
the dragon politely not to eat me?! Panic surged through my core
except—

The dragon froze.

The world froze.

What…Suddenly, a host of glowing, emerald plus marks drifted
and spun around me, painting my vision monochrome green like I
was peering through night goggles for a minute.

[System Alert: ***Congratulations, You've Advanced To
Level 2!***]

Name	Rosabella	
Class & Level	Game Maker 2	
XP	101/200	
MRP	3540/6205	
HP	12/17	
Baddie Points	55	
Armor Class	15/20	
ABILITIES /20		
Strength	-1	8
Agility	+0	10
Endurance	-1	9
Intelligence	+1	13

Awareness	+1	12
Presence	+3	16
CM		1

[+9 HP & HP Extended By 9, 12/17. You've Been Awarded +2 Ability Points. Please Select Which Ability You'd Like To Increase.]

I gaped at the stats—or, maybe, I was gaping, gasping, at the strange sensation washing over my body. A strange feeling of restored health and energy coursed through me like someone had poured something down my throat. I almost toppled over from the sensation.

Focus. I could add 2 points to any ability?

A pulsating, green glow caught the corner of my eye—*what?* I looked down to see that my mother's sword, tied on my belt, was glowing ethereal emerald.

The sword!

It clicked very quickly.

For melee use, the broadsword required Level 2 with 10 Strength. If I increased my Strength by 2 Ability Points from the Level Up, I would meet both requirements and be able to use it to kill the dragon! It'd give me a +7 Strength which would be ample to battle the beast!

The realization propelled me forward with a dangerous source of grim confidence.

"Add 2 Ability Points to Strength," I commanded the system, "Equip Gold & Silver Broadsword!" I told it.

And I heard the acknowledging, electronic beep.

[System Alert: +2 Strength, 10/20]
[System Alert: Weapon Equipped, +25 Baddie Points, 80]

My hand grasped the handle of the massive broadsword, pulling it out of its sheath with a shrill clang. It took both of my hands to hold it, wavering in front of me, but the blade was massive and smooth. Its honed edges glittered viciously in the light like a dare. But, better than that, we were better matched. The dragon and I were more evenly matched.

Now was the moment. I had to see if I could do this. I took the deepest breath I could, stepping towards the snarling head of the beast.

For Dad.

I raised the huge sword, preparing for the attack—

Squelch.

—*Fuck!*

The flesh of my neck burned—itched. Pused. My fingers flew there and ended up burning too. When I looked down, I realized they were covered in disgustingly thick, yellow mucus: acid.

[-5 HP, 7/17]

"You little shit!" I screamed at the dragon, swinging the sword in front of me. *Not the most original war cry...*

The dragon roared, thrashing backwards in agony as sword met scale and flesh.

Sinking deep.

[SILVER RINKECLAW, DRAGON 4: -3 HP, 22/75]

And, then, there was fire.

Blinding.

Hot.

Overwhelming my vision.

[-2 HP, 5/17]

Thank God for the armor... The world suddenly swam in front of my eyes. *From the shock? From the searing pain engulfing my scalp and cheeks?* That was when I first heard the dragon in my mind—all thanks to my new Draconic Language skill...

Got you, you stupid Game Maker.

A breathy older-woman's voice crowed as I cringed, slapping my hands over my ears, but it did nothing to muffle the voice that clearly echoed through my mind.

> *You will now die a painful death!*

The monster hurled herself towards me, snapping jaws an inch from my face—

But her trapped tail stopped her.

Feet. I swore I had them somewhere. If I could only get my balance—

I stumbled backwards—tripped around. I didn't care anymore about the stats. About the win. About the probability of that win. It was time to run. It was time to bolt.

Out of here.

Far away.

As far as I could get, anyway.

But the pain seared at every inch of my skin, making it hard to walk in a straight line. My vision was blurry red as I careened forward, clutching my head and side simultaneously. I fell into the wall. The lever there jammed into my rib.

…The lever. The second lever. I stared up at the second door. I sucked in my breath, trying to fight it and the dizziness crashing over my head.

…What if I didn't have to outrun or kill the beast? What if I could…trap it?

The bottom of the metal door hanging overhead showed the portion that was rusted out—the part I'd seen before. If I could close it and, then, crawl out that hole, the dragon would be trapped.

I could probably fit.

I *had* to fit.

I bit my lip—bit back the pain and reached for the lever. Sweat slipped into my eyes—

[System Query: Will You Pull The Lever?]
[Yes] [No]

Yes.

I gritted my teeth. I pushed with all my might downward—

Thwack, thwack, thwack—

Not the noise I'd wanted to hear. *Where was the metal sound and the dramatic, heavy drop?*

My eyes darted between the dragon who almost had its tail free and the industrial belts overhead.

Shit, they were jammed—stuck; I recognized the problem right away. I watched the antiquated pulley system overhead jump and sputter. One of the belts was jammed in the corner which meant the door could only lower halfway—*no! This messed up my plan! I couldn't trap the thing unless both doors were down!*

That was when I realized the weapon I still clutched—the gold and silver sword. My mother's sword. The blade dripping dragon's blood onto the dirt floor.

Cut it!

I could cut the door free from the belts if I could reach them!

My eyes fastened on the leaning tower of junk I'd made earlier in trying to reach the belt Examination Opportunity. *Yes! I could climb on top of that!*

My feet—although not working entirely properly—tripped forward.

One foot, on a crate.

One foot, shoving up to the bucket.

I reached the sword upward.

The dragon's teeth snapped inches from me. I watched it out of the corner of my eye gathering spit in its mouth for more acid.

My shoulder strained from the reach; excruciating pain lit through my shoulder as the sword blade met with the wide belt.

I swung.

Fabric ripped, frayed—

I barely dared to breathe.

I needed one more pass. I heaved the weapon backward and forward again—

At that exact moment, four things happened in quick succession:

1) *Snap!* The belt cut.

2) The door slammed downward—*yes!!*

3) I fell. Not gracefully.

And 4) The dragon yanked its tail free.

My mouth slammed into dirt. Pain shot through my face, hands, feet and...*everything.* My HP dropped almost instantaneously:

[-2 HP, 3/17]

Shit, shit, shit! I grappled for the rusted opening in the door—

You are dead!

The Rinkeclaw shrieked—her high-pitched vibrato rattling in my eardrums.

DEAD!

I felt her huge shadow over me. My arms and legs couldn't move fast enough. I hauled myself forward. The hole was right there—

Right—

Grass greeted me on the other side. My fingers clawed at it as I shuffled my legs through the opening—

And the dragon hit the metal door between us full speed.

Good.

[System Reward: You've Trapped A SILVER RINKECLAW, DRAGON 4! Now, That Was Hard Work! +50 XP, 151/200 +25 Baddie Points, 105]

Whoa! +50 XP and +25 Baddie Points?

I lay there, gasping in the dirt and grass on the other side of that door. My heart hammered in my chest. And the sun, like the lie of safety that it was, beat down on my face like a strange reminder that everything was normal…

Still.

Peaceful.

Even though I'd just narrowly escaped with my life. My head hurt like hell. I rubbed at it. The nearby treetops swam, wobbling in my vision. Was that blood dripping from my temple? I swiped it away only to find a confirmed, red stain streaking my palm. The Snargel's or mine?

I noticed for the first time that an object sat, perched on a tree trunk by my right foot. My head felt so heavy as I lifted it to squint through the sun rays at it. It was another shield with a magnifying glass. Did I dare? The better question was 'could I move?' Every bone and muscle felt like a brick on fire.

Still, I shimmied towards it.

"Examine," I whispered tiredly. My voice sounded frail and weak even to me.

[System Object Examined... +1 XP, 152/200]
[A Closer Look Tells You This Is A Grouping Of Bandages, Ointments and Creams.]

I will KILL YOU!

Shrieked the dragon, suddenly, in my mind. My heart lurched into my throat.

I'll find you and KILL YOU when I get out of here, Game Maker!!!

I scrabbled backwards, forgetting the bandages—forgetting about anything but simply living.

I had to get away from here! I ran, kicking up dirt—the wedge heels of my boots flying up behind me as I dove into the brush—into the trees. *Anywhere but here—*

"Rosabella! Rosa—" The deep, throaty man's voice stopped short when he saw me stumbling through the brush. And, the next thing I knew, Rainer was beside me, wrapping an arm around me to support me.

"We're all looking for you," he barked gruffly, but, somehow, kindly as his sun-worn face wrinkled up in concern. "How low is your HP?"

But I didn't want to answer him. I just wanted to smile. Because something had just dawned on me.

"I got the CM Diamond, Leveled Up and trapped a dragon," I sputtered, letting the pride wash over me for just that second.

And the long-haired Nomad balked at me, "The Rinkeclow? No way! Way to do it!" He went to punch me playfully in the shoulder before backtracking on the idea—probably due to what was most certainly my ghost-white, drained face.

But I'd done it. I'd done it, and it meant I was one step closer to freeing Dad.

Rosabella

"No offense, but a fire really isn't a great idea given we know this area is infested with Snargels—just sayin'," Dormouse—the beanpole, dork kid with the dark hair leaned apprehensively over the fledgling blaze sparking to life under Rainer's fingertips. The huge Nomad raised an eyebrow, but, otherwise, paid the kid no mind.

"Oh look, Mr. Rules and Regulations has a problem with fire now," the pink-haired girl sneered, leaning over the meager heat to watch Rainer create more sparks, "Would you prefer to eat the fish we caught raw?"

"Joy, cut him some slack," Callen, the pepper-haired leader one, scolded the girl. "We all should be worried. The Snargels aren't usually this far south. It means the damage is increasing."

I noticed the heavy tilt of his voice and the way his eyebrows drew together near the lines in his forehead. The shadows from the fire flickered over his square jaw in the darkening night. Something was wrong, and, if that guy was concerned, we all should be.

The grove we were sheltering in was surrounded by towering, watching evergreens. Overhead, the almost-night sky glimmered from the light of the sun that looked like a dying ember on the horizon. Wispy clouds stretched out, covering where the peaks of pine needles ended. And all was silent…and, yet, that silence covered up a million things:

Squirrels and small animal movement in the brush.

The flapping of birds' wings overhead.

The buzzing of bugs that I kept swatting away.

And I realized that the blanketing silence wasn't so different than the silence of my own lips—covering up the anxious, dizzying movement of the thoughts inside me. The noise there. *How did I feel both numb and nerve-racked at the same time? How was that possible?*

I shifted on the log beneath me, feeling the rough bark scrape through the fabric of my body armor. *God, my feet were so heavy.*

Like my eyelids.

My head felt too hard to hold up. The effects of my lowered HP were definitely too noticeable at this point to try to hide. My body pulsed—almost as though in rhythm with the very beat of my life…hanging on by the thinnest thread…

"Can't even get a damned minute to lick your wounds around here," Rainer cursed argumentatively before using one of his huge boots to stomp out the fire. The flames relinquished with a sizzle and a sad excuse for smoke.

And our corner of the world got darker in that moment.

I glanced around at everyone's faces.

"Well, unlike the lot of you, I'm determined to make the best of this pitiful situation," Rainer growled, "Anyone want some?" Even in the near darkness, I was able to make out a smooth, wine bottle clutched in the burly Nomad's fist. He raised it at the quiet group. "Find me something to celebrate!"

"No takers?" he prodded when there was no answer. "Aye, well, I will then."

He tilted the wine bottle over his eager lips, drinking deeply. I watched as a system update appeared over his head:

[RAINER, NOMAD 9: +5 Swag Points, 765, -10 MRP, 14225/17885]

I stared at the numbers, watching the man take another swig.

[RAINER, NOMAD 9: +5 Swag Points, 770, -10 MRP, 14215/17885]

It seemed like each swallow gained him whatever 'Swag Points' were and decreased...*well, what was the MRP stat again?*

"Rainer, what do those stats mean?" I asked shyly. *If my head would stop pounding, this all would be easier.*

"Oh—" the mountain man rubbed an arm across his red beard, sighing loudly. "Alcohol is kind of a trade off here. You gain Swag Points, comparable to your Baddie Points. They—well, help you with the opposite gender if you know what I mean," he winked obtrusively at me, "But you lose some memory. Memory here isn't a big deal except that you want to keep it above 0 or else you turn into a zombie. I'm not even close to that, so I guess I always choose the women. Damn you girls," he joked, swishing a huge hand at me and Joy.

The pink-haired girl scowled at him, crossing her arms over her chest. "You make it a mockery," I heard her mutter before she turned away. Her steps crunched into the darkness somewhere past the shards of our campfire.

"Forget her," Rainer grumbled. "You want some, Rosabella?" He offered me the flask, but I waved it away.

"No, no, I'm good," I told him.

Fighting the Snargel had already set my memory back by 100 points. I wasn't even sure what it was I'd forgotten. *I didn't want to diminish my memory, I wanted to increase it. If I could just remember things, all of this would be easier. Maybe I would remember more about my mother...figure out why her sword might be here...*

"Rainer," I started haltingly, "Is there a way to increase memory?" For some reason, my heart kicked into gear even just asking the question. My stomach twisted.

But the man didn't look bothered in the least. "Oh sure," the Nomad commented, nodding as he contemplated the neck of the wine bottle and his huge fingers which were still wrapped around it, "Health supplies give you the option to add to your HP or MRP, Memory Recall Points. ...Speaking of which... Callen, Rosabella needs a pack. Her stats are low."

I watched the gray-haired leader's eyes snap towards me, alarm spreading through his expression. "Of course. Joy!" he barked over his shoulder, "give Rosabella our health pack—"

"*It's the last one left.*" The girl's hiss came out of the blackness near my shoulder, nearly scaring me. I watched her step out of the shadows and into the fading light. I'd expected, from her voice, to find anger lingering in her eyes, but the orbs were dark and...worried.

Callen didn't flinch. His tone only became more business-like, "We'll find more. She needs it right now. *Give her the health pack.*"

Joy let out a frustrated breath and made an annoyed show of it as she rummaged in a knapsack, pulling out a first aid kit. I swore I heard *'thinks he knows everything...wasting hard-earned supplies on some yuppie girl...'* under her breath. The girl's eyes were snapping lava as she extended the health pack out towards me, red cross side up.

[System Alert: HEALTH PACK Acquired. Object Will Be Placed In Your Inventory Unless You'd Like To Use. Would You Like To Use?]
[Yes] [No]

I almost hated to take it from her, the way she was acting, but I reached out for it. "Yes, equip," I breathed, feeling utter relief overwhelm me just from knowing the ache in my body might stop soon. There was an electronic beep as the object disappeared in my hands.

[+12 HP Available Or +500 MRP. Please Select Which Option You Prefer.]
[+12 HP] [+500 MRP]

I stared at the choices. *Rainer had been right. It was a decision.* My body felt so weak. As much as I wanted to restore my memory, I was going to need to restore my health first. I held my finger over that button.

[System Alert: HEALTH PACK Used. +12 HP, 15/17]

Vitality sped over me like caffeine from an energy drink times 100. My body no longer felt exhausted or weak. I patted my hands down my chest and limbs—touched my lip which had been swollen seconds before. My white body armor might have still been stained with fox blood, but I was….I was *healed. My health was restored! No way.*

"…So, you trapped the Rinkeclaw and got the CM Diamond?" Joy pouted—*err, questioned*—me from her annoyed, one-hand-on-hip stance by my elbow.

I turned back to nod at her, "Yeah."

I felt like I owed her twisted expression something. "Thank you," I tried suddenly, "…for the health pack."

"*Whatever*," she soured, turning away, "it wasn't up to me. I'm going to get the fish ready."

And, just like that, she stormed off.

I looked over at Callen for some explanation as to why the girl was being so moody, but he just shook his head, his lips a grim line, and said nothing.

How come I felt incredibly awkward when I just did what they asked of me?

How come Joy was so standoffish when I was trying to work with them?

…Without that health pack, I'd barely have been able to *stand* for very long… *Why was she so adverse to giving it to me?*

The feeling of being an outsider slinked back even though we were all standing there in a group.

"What's that on your belt?" Rainer wanted to know. I was glad for the distraction. The man's fingers pulled the sword I'd found in the dragon's nest upward so he could peer at the blade in the limited light.

"May I?" he asked, trying to untie it.

I nodded.

His huge hands easily unthreaded the knot, and he tilted the blade up into the dying sunlight. His keen eyes raked over the metal as he turned it over and angled it in the light. I noticed, for the first time, that there was an 'R' carved under the blue stone at the end of the handle. The hilt was engraved with so many ornate, swirling lines that I'd missed it before. I watched the man rub his finger over the letter, noticing it too.

"I found it in the dragon's nest," I mentioned to fill the quiet, "It's strange, but a notification popped up saying that it was my mother's. You don't think that could be true…*do you?*"

The last part was a thin plea…or a test.

Uncertain.

Trying to latch onto something…

The system had said that it was, in fact, my mother's sword but…well, I'd thought I'd heard Callen mentioning earlier that the system shouldn't be trusted. My eyes darted up to study the Nomad's face which was straight with any emotion masked.

"This is a beautiful blade," he admired, turning it again so the light reflected off it. "Elven made, precise mother-fuckers they m*ost definitely are*. …Did you know your mother?"

Not the question I'd asked.

His eyes looked curious—not harmful.

A sigh ballooned out of my body. "No," I shook my head, "Well, not really. Dad said he and her divorced pretty much after I was born, and I went with him so..."

Rainer threw a look at Callen, but I couldn't read it. My eyes flickered between them. ...*Was I missing something?*

"Come on, we'll clean your weapons and your armor," Rainer interjected suddenly, "There's a river down this way." He disappeared into the underbrush, and I stumbled after him, trying to suppress the unease creeping under my skin from all the unanswered questions.

The sound of water gurgling and rushing assailed my ears as I clamored in the darkness after Rainer. He was already by the stream, cupping his hands in the gushing flow and throwing it up on his face. I winced, my first question about the water's quality, but it strangely looked exceptionally clean. The waves glinted like black opals as they flowed over smooth river rock and fed the lush moss growing all around the bank. The glade was sheltered by the shadows of towering trees and filled with cricket song and moonlight.

I sat down on the soft, greenery-blanketed bank with utter relief as Rainer grabbed the broadsword from me, filled a curved piece of tree bark with water, soaked a brown rag in the water and began to clean off the blade with it. "Here, use this on your armor," he handed me a second rag.

"Never clean your blades directly in the stream," he lectured me as he lovingly wiped crud from the metal, "You don't want to pollute the water unnecessarily. This is an ecosystem. We honor all living things here by taking care of them." The softness of his words and touch on the weapon stopped me short. There was almost a tenderness there.

"You're a weapons guy?" I asked hesitantly as I began to work on the blood-encrusted form of my body armor. The blood smudged the rag red, making a damp spot on my middle, while I snuck furtive glances at the Nomad's careful work.

He barely even looked up as a smile tugged at his lips. "Yes. I used to blacksmith, make things," he told me, but, then, his face shadowed, "…That was a long time ago."

They'd all been keeping so many secrets. I had to know this one.

"What changed?" I prodded.

"Life," he said quietly.

But that was another non-answer.

"I don't *get it*," I stated simply, looking at the lines on my hands where dirt had dug into my skin. The rag I'd been using was almost completely stained now. I wrung it out with a twist, "You obviously love it—"

"Typical ranks of Gamers *can't* create," he said tersely, though not angrily. "Not since Reordering began. The group of us used to be part of the Game Warden class, protectors of The Game. But that class was discontinued and Creator Magic was taken away from all classes with magic. Only Game Makers and dragons can possess and use it now or Gamers lucky enough to have an alliance with a dragon—they use the dragon's magic to create."

"Reordering?" I asked. "Wait…*I'm* a Game Maker."

"Yes," he didn't look up from his work, "the last of your kind."

"The last—wait," I blubbered, "I'm the only person besides dragons who can create—do magic? In this entire place?"

"I meant what I said," The man turned away, refilling the bowl of water stoically. I couldn't see his expression around that red beard.

But my body felt fluttery and strange all of a sudden.

They needed me—they made me this trade because I was the only one who could fix their world? Me? The only one, unless they roped a dragon in? It seemed improbable. It seemed…impossible. This whole thing was impossible. Being here. Fighting half-dead foxes and—

And dragons!

That nerd said this was an alternate reality—

It was…well, it was…crazy.

"*I don't want to be here,*" I murmured suddenly, my voice a shaky, annoyed admittance. "I'm only trying to save my dad. In my world," I raised my finger; my voice wavered with emotion, "none of this is possible—"

The Nomad shook his head, chuckling with a raised eyebrow, "Well, I don't know what to tell you. In my world, *it is*—"

"Clearly," I mumbled. And my hand rubbed over the skin of my neck which I'd remembered burning from acid and dragon fire. *This was all ridiculous. It really was.*

"Rainer," I wrung out my rag again, like trying to squeeze the pessimism out of my tone, but it was nearly impossible. "I got the CM Diamond. I'm trying so desperately to get my dad back. Maybe…" my voice faltered for a minute. I cleared my throat, "Maybe I can make things right for you too."

I watched him smile, but it wasn't his typical mirth-filled one; his gaze was far away. "I hope so," he whispered longingly, "I really do."

The lull in our conversation was filled by the stream—the whispering hush of it. I watched a handful of fireflies dart through the fingers of a fern. And, looking beyond into the dark forest, I—*wait, did I recognize this place?*

"Rainer," I perked up like a dog, "This stream. It's near where you found me—where I trapped the dragon, isn't it?"

The man nodded, "Err, yeah. That's not far at all, just through the trees and underbrush—"

"I, uh," I pushed up, hastily, to my feet, brushing off my knees, "I actually dropped something there that would be great to pick up."

The medical supplies. I'd examined them, but the dragon had freaked me out too badly to actually grab them. If what I'd learned was right, a medical pack would give me the choice of applying it to my HP or MRP. I wanted to increase my memory. More than anything, I wanted to remember. *What was I forgetting? Why couldn't I connect all these dots?* If I could sneak off, and grab it, I could up my memory without making a big scene.

Rainer shoved to his feet, "I'll come with you—"

"No"—*I interrupted him too quickly, didn't I?* I froze, trying desperately to smooth my face and my words over and feeling like I was failing at both. "No," I amended quickly, "I just meant that it's not far. I'll be really quick, and be right back. No need to trouble you."

I watched the Nomad's bushy eyebrows raise, but he shrugged, "Suit yourself. Come right back though. We'll have to get back to the group soon; I have first watch."

I nodded.

Quickly.

Just so glad that he didn't ask more.

And I darted into the underbrush. It was hard to see the way ahead. The moonlight slanting through the trees barely lit the dense brush underfoot, which seemed nearly black. Bushes thrust themselves in my way with each one I sidestepped. Branches crackled and snapped underfoot. Very much frazzled and slightly out of breath, I fought my way out and into the clearing. I could see the stump from here—the one that held the medical supplies. Unfortunately, I could, also, see the metal door of the mine shaft. While it was way too easy to imagine a pissed off dragon still behind it, I wasn't about to let my own imagination dissuade my determination; I raced forward, my feet kicking up behind me.

The stump was rough under my fingertips as I moved to grab up the group of bandages.

**[System Reward: BANDAGES, OINTMENTS & CREAMS
Acquired. Object Will Be Placed In Your Inventory Unless
You'd Like To Use. Would You Like To Use?
[Yes] [No]**

"Yes, definitely," I told it, trying to resist the realization that both my hands and core were shaking. It felt like what I was doing was a little selfish and clandestine, using two health packs in the matter of a few hours for my own benefit when Joy had been so annoyed to give me the groups'. *Still, this memory. I needed to remember.* Another system message appeared:

[+6 HP Available Or +250 MRP. Please Select Which Option You Prefer.]
[+6 HP] [+250 MRP]

Yes! Just like I'd thought! Although the numbers were smaller than the other pack Joy had given me, it felt good to know I could use this to repair even a small portion of my memory. I took a deep breath and selected.

[System Alert: BANDAGES, OINTMENTS & CREAMS Used, +250 MRP, 3790/6205]

My head. My head, somehow, felt clearer with the new notification. *It'd altered something. What had it altered?* But I didn't get the chance to find out because, at that moment, both Rainer and Callen crashed through the forest tree line, sprinting towards me.

"*Rosabella?! Thank God*—" Callen's voice rung through the surrounding trees, interrupting. *Was it just my imagination or did it sound filled with...fear?* His tone was sharp, matching the serious lines of his face. Not even a strand of his gray hair was out of place even though his chest heaved up and down from lack of breath. "You'd better come quick. Darken are in the forest. We have to move—*now.*"

Rosabella

Darken? Wait—why did that word sound familiar? What did Callen mean?

I balked for a minute at Callen's warning and the tension in his voice, but Rainer's face told me he wasn't going to let either of us sit in indecision for very long. The Nomad moved—like a lion in battle. He took two, enormous steps forward. One hand went to the axe on his belt. The other fanned out, pushing me behind him as his eagle eyes scanned the tree line surrounding us.

"Stay behind me," he barked, his voice a low, wobbling tremor.

And I didn't argue. If something out there wanted to eat me, I'd definitely prefer it had to get through tough-guy Rainer first—

"Take your sword," the Nomad groped blindly at his belt for a minute, as his gaze was still engrossed in the forest and undergrowth. His sausage fingers handed me my mother's broadsword back. It was heavy in my grasp, but the blade shone, gleaming in the dark from Rainer's careful cleaning. I watched a system message pop into view:

[System Alert: ROSABELLA'S MOTHER'S GOLD & SILVER BROADSWORD Acquired. Object Will Be Placed In Your Inventory Unless You'd Like To Equip. Would You Like To Equip?]
[Yes] [No]

Absolutely, yes. There was no way I was going to fight whatever had these full-grown men scared for their lives with the glorified butterknife which was that crude dagger…

[System Alert: Weapon Equipped.]

"Come on!" Callen shooed us forward, "The other two are already on high ground."

—*Darken?*

—*High ground? What were we running from?*

I didn't have time to ask as both men took off, high-tailing it into the forest at high-speed. I tramped after them through the dense underbrush. My boots caught on the ferns—snagged on the brambles–and I fought to kick them off. *Fighting myself. I was fighting myself when the whole goal of the running was to not have to fight whatever was out here?* I felt like a bull in a China shop—loud and jarring in the silent woods. Heavy…like an elephant with large footfalls, crushing the shoots of greenery underfoot as I followed. My breath came in huffs.

Their pace was breakneck. Even with the benefit of my Level Up and the health pack, I was struggling to keep up. I clamored forward, my eyes scanning the watching trees stretching overhead like vigilant guards in formation lines. …Except there was no one to save us here–not in a place that had dragons.

…No one to act as shelter from this harsh world, except Rainer and Callen…

—*Who I might lose complete sight of if I didn't move faster!* I scrambled forward, heaving through the moss and underbrush. Ferns tickled my hands. Branches snagged across my face and neck. *How much longer did we have to hike uphill? Next Level Up, I was going to have to increase my Endurance, no matter what.* Sweat prickled under the white, fur collar of my body armor, and the muscles of my legs complained.

We weren't alone.

I felt a stare. My eyes scanned the surrounding forest as my heart nearly jumped ship from its place in my chest. But the woods around me were still: all shadows, no movement.

…Almost…eerie. *Surely, there should be at least a breeze or something…?*

"Keep up, Rosabella!" Rainer called over his shoulder from somewhere sounding far ahead.

And I launched myself into the brush again, after them, feeling uneasiness bristle on my arms and legs.

Overhead. I finally found the source of the lingering stares.

Vulture-like birds swirled in dizzying circles, craning their necks to look down at us—watching, like the trees. I wrenched my neck up to stare at the beasts. The feathers of their huge wings fluttered in the wind, and their dark shadows nearly blended in with the midnight sky. But something about the birds was wrong; the longer I stared, the more I was convinced. Their feathers were thin and twisted, missing in several spots where raw bone and muscle were exposed. A strange, black-and-red, pussing growth grew—over the eye of one, over the wing of another—

"System, what are those things?" I breathed.

[System Understands Query…Loading Response…]

I was so busy craning my neck upward at the sky to watch the creatures that I nearly bumped into Rainer who'd clearly stopped his race through the forest. I quickly straightened myself, pretending I wasn't being a total doof, but how close I ended up standing to the guy was probably a dead giveaway of my fumble. The Nomad's face was pissed anyway. He turned to me with an aggravated huff, his cheeks tinged red and scrunched up in annoyance.

"Stop asking the system about every blasted thing, will you?!" he growled, "Just ask one of us."

I faltered, almost falling back. Mostly, I was just confused. *Why was the man so mad about me asking the system?*

"Oh—uh, okay," I started, but the familiar system update had already popped into view, floating, neon, there for my perusal. I really didn't get why the Nomad was all up in arms about it…

[System Answer: The Creatures Above Are Kenchee. Kenchee Are Undead, Vulture-Like Birds With Sharp Talons & Immense Wingspans.
STRENGTHS: Superb Eyesight, Ability To Sense Nearby Magic And Magical Beings And Agility In The Sky. Capacity To Poach Magic From Magical Beings And Use It For Attack, Disregarding The Fact Of Their Own Unmagical Constitution.
WEAKNESSES: Close Combat. These Birds Like To Poach And Use Magic. Without Magic, They Are Little More Than A Nuisance, But Always Be On Guard In Case Magic Is Nearby.]

Name	Kenchee	
Class & Level, Size	Undead 4, Medium	
HP	58/58	
Armor Class	12/20	
ABILITIES /20		
Strength	-5	1
Agility	+2	14
Endurance	+0	10
Intelligence	-2	6
Awareness	+0	11
Presence	+3	17

"See that bit about poaching magic?" Rainer pointed to the description of the creature.

I nodded.

"Kenchee are verminous, loathing bottom feeders. They circle around up there," his huge finger waved in a circle over our heads,

"Hiding in the clouds like the cowards they are while they search for magic to prey on. When they find it, they attack so they can wreck havoc and take memory from as many beings as possible to increase their own levels. No system update is gonna tell you that." He lifted a self-satisfied eyebrow, but his ruddy face was still dark and moody, "Some call them spies of the Game Governor—"

"And it is *way* too late in the day for conspiracy theory rubbish," Dormouse interrupted the Nomad, stepping forward and jabbing him in the chest with a bony shoulder. "Are you gonna kill the birds, or am I going to have to create some sort of vacuum, warp-in-time hole to suck them into?"

"This one," Rainer's furry eyebrow raised as he nodded at the nerd while squinting at me like we had a secret, "He's really not as fancy as he sounds—"

Whiz.

An arrow hummed as it released straight up into the night sky.

Thud.

I watched as a glowing, system alert appeared over Joy's head; I hadn't even seen the pink-haired girl standing there. Her arms were raised, poised from where she'd clearly just released her longbow.

[KENCHEE, UNDEAD 4: -58 HP, 0/58]
[JOY, WARRIOR 11: System Reward: KENCHEE, UNDEAD 4 Eliminated, +15 XP, 1180/1200]

"We all know Rosabella's CM Diamond is attracting them. Either you're part of the problem or part of the solution," the girl barked, shaking her long hair over her back as she loaded another arrow. Her lips pressed in a thin line as she drew the bowstring taunt—

Whiz.

Thud.

[KENCHEE, UNDEAD 4: -58 HP, 0/58]

Another bird tumbled from the dark sky.

[JOY, WARRIOR 11: System Reward: KENCHEE, UNDEAD 4 Eliminated, +15 XP, 1195/1200]

"Geez, she's picking these things off like cotton candy," Dormouse mumbled.

"Give Rosabella a chance," Rainer griped, shoving me forward with probably more force than he'd meant.

"I'm about to Level Up," the pink-haired girl complained through clenched teeth, her eyes still focused on the creatures in the sky.

"Joy, play nice with the other kids. Weren't you just saying that we need to get Rosabella Leveled Up?" Callen argued.

"Whatever," the girl grunted, lowering her bow, "Let the baby take her first steps."

Wow, really? I waited for anyone in the group to tell her off, but it didn't happen. The gray-haired Trader frowned in Joy's direction and shifted a shoulder sling on his back, extending a crossbow to me. *Oh no—I mean, as cool as that weapon looked, I didn't want to... ...So why was I obediently reaching for it?*

[System Alert: SMALL CROSSBOW Acquired. Object Will Be Placed In Your Inventory Unless You'd Like To Equip. Would You Like To Equip?]
[Yes] [No]

I sighed, feeling a twinge of loss set in at the thought of having to put my broadsword in my inventory.

"Yes," I told it.

The system pop-up cleared with a whir. I glanced down to find my fingers curled around the smooth barrel of the crossbow stock. *Shit. This trying to free Dad thing was really pushing me out of my comfort zone. Not that doing so was particularly difficult...*

[System Alert: Weapon Equipped, +10 Baddie Points, 90]

Object:	Small Crossbow
Required Class & Level For Use:	None
Description:	Medieval In Design, But Deadly-Looking. The Craftmanship Is Evident Even If The Stock's Been Worn Down From Use.
	Augment Capacities: +3 Strength, +3 Agility
	Baddie Points: +10

"You load it like this," Callen expertly used a tool to wrench the string back, locking it in place. He placed a chunky-looking, sharp arrow in an indent at the front of the bow. "Just line her up and press the trigger—this lever here," he clarified, pointing.

And I raised the bow. It felt unnatural in my hands, even though it was light. I squinted into the sky, attempting to align it with the last, circling bird above…

Whiz.

No thud.

The arrow zoomed past the bird, which didn't even need to pivot to escape. My hands trembled as I shook them out. *I was such a rookie—*

"Hey, just try again," Callen's patient voice encouraged me. He used the tool again, loading another arrow. And I swallowed, pushing down the doubt that suddenly crept up in my stomach. *The Snargel and the Rinkeclaw had just been luck. I was no good at this. I wasn't cut out for killing things or Leveling Up. I just needed to get my Dad and get out of this crazy place—*

Whiz.

Thud.

[KENCHEE, UNDEAD 4: -58 HP, 0/58]

Black feathers spiraled towards the ground, several feet away. I stared at the now empty sky in shock, feeling…numb. *I'd pulled that trigger? …I'd done it?*

[System Reward: KENCHEE, UNDEAD 4 Eliminated +15 XP, 167/200]

The system message verified the kill. I turned to Callen in shock to find him smiling.

"Nice, Rosabella!" Rainer applauded, slapping a hand down on my shoulder and grinning like it was his birthday, "We'll make a warrior of you yet!"

"Slow down, it was *one fucking bird*," Joy spat sourly. "Now, we just have to keep her from becoming Darken food before morning—"

"We'll hike up to the ridge to secure the high ground and camp," Callen interrupted the girl quickly. "Don't worry," he said, turning to me, "We'll keep you protected. Rainer is one hell of a swordsman, and Joy's stare can make an enemy retreat without even a weapon." The gray-haired man meant the last part as a joke; his lips turned up in amusement at his own words, but the pink-haired girl didn't seem to find it funny.

"Cute," she sneered, turning away to lead the group up the slope and further into this misery called a forest.

As we climbed, the dense woods stretched out from the sides of our feet, sloping downward sharply.

Trees.

As far as the eye could see.

It was…*breathtaking. …Or, maybe, my breath was already taken, so that was easily achieved.* I would have considered the place beautiful if I wasn't so sure numerous things were lurking in it, waiting to kill me. *Which reminded me…*

I tried to catch up with Dormouse, jogging and reaching him even as my feet on the slanting ground below complained beneath me. I grabbed the end of his sleeve to tell him to wait up. His eyes were wide and unsure, with dark hair flopping over them, as he turned.

"You okay?" he asked.

"What are Darken?" I whispered, making sure to keep my voice low enough so the others didn't hear. "What are we running from?"

He swallowed nervously, casting a quick glance at the rest of the group and wetting his lips. "The short answer?" he whispered back.

I nodded.

He ducked his head further, "Zombies. Not like undead foxes or birds—they're...people."

The air went out of my lungs. *Zombies? We were in a video game. ...If there was one thing I knew, it was my survival horror video games...*

"Resident Evil or Walking Dead type shit?" I asked rapidly.

He stared at me blankly, "What?"

"*Zombies*," I fired back, hissing under my breath as more grass swished by my ankles, "Are they the stupid, slow kind or the fast, smart ones?"

"Oh..." he pursed his lips and shook his head. "Fast and smart," he said grimly, "...unfortunately. This is all because of a delusional imposter who took over several years back, misused the power and left us vulnerable to darkness. During that time, a giant comet hit our world. Earthquakes warped and twisted everything. The sun and sky were black for a whole week...and this hole appeared in the middle of The East Lands. Right in the middle—well, I'll just show you. System, bring up The Game Map." His command was more confident than I would have assumed from his typically mousy demeanor.

[DORMOUSE, CODER 14: System Understands Query...Loading Response...]
[DORMOUSE, CODER 14: The Game Map Successfully Downloaded]

A map popped into view.

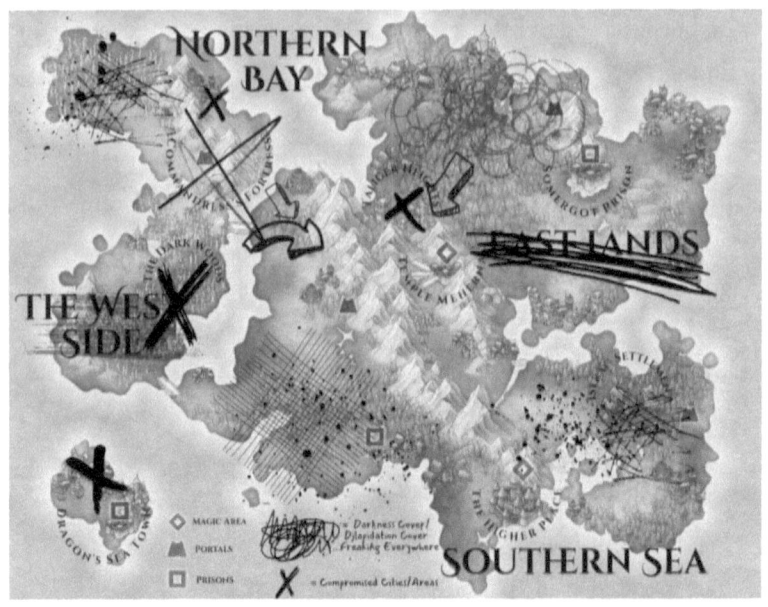

I marveled at texture and complexity of it and noted where the nerd tapped at the floating screen in front of us: *East Lands*.

"No one knows exactly what happened, but hordes of zombies appeared that week, including the undead creatures you've seen—the Snargels and Kenchee. The Game and system had always been amicable. The Gamers didn't know what the new creatures were. They hunted and ate them. Lots of people got trapped in the zombie herds and got bitten till their memory was zero. Then, they'd turn themselves. We used to call them 'the darkened' since folktales said they were touched with black magic, but it got shortened after a few years. Now, it's just 'Darken'."

"That's *terrible*," I muttered, watching my feet trail over the rocky path, dirt and grass. Rocks pinched underneath the wedges of my boots, causing me to wobble dangerously. *Some catastrophic event had unleashed darkness and death on this world?*

"After the zombies appeared," Dormouse continued, "there was a Reordering of classes. The group of us aren't Game Wardens anymore, but we still want to protect the game. Creator Magic was ripped away from classes that could wield magic—even simple kind. We knew we needed you to fix this world. We needed a Game Maker," Dormouse ran a hand through his hair, "We've been searching for you and your Dad for a while now. The Game Damage is getting worse and worse as more people lose memory and rot. I think it's at 87/100 right now. It's like something in the very fabric of the system has gone corrupt. Joy is—"

"You guys wouldn't be talking about me, now, would you?" the pink-haired girl sidled up beside us, harshly chewing on a piece of gum. Her eyes darkened, probably as she recognized the alarm on both of our faces.

"Callen, *this little shit* is spilling all our secrets to the Game Maker," she complained loudly to the silver-haired man in front.

He looked back, arched an uninterested eyebrow and waved her off.

"Here, I'll make you a copy of the map," Dormouse said, apparently trying to dodge the literal daggers that the pink-haired girl was shooting at him from her eyeballs. His long, pale fingers typed in the air.

[System Query: Please Input Code]
[*QuickObjectCopy*]
[<Action Input: Duplicate An Object Without General Restrictions>]

"Hey, um, actually, could I trade you something for it?" I asked shyly, looking between the boy and Joy, "Trades seem to help me Level Up quicker—"

"Oh, yeah, sure," the kid nodded, his eyes wide as he dropped the code, "What do you want to trade?"

I thought about the useless dagger in my inventory as the confirmation of that thought popped into view between us:

[DORMOUSE, CODER 14: Proposed Trade: DORMOUSE, CODER 14 Trades Copy Of The Game Map, ROSABELLA, GAME MAKER 2 Offers LEATHER-WRAPPED HANDLE DAGGER.]
[Will You Accept the Trade?]
[Yes] [No]

I watched the boy select 'Yes'. Suddenly, a minute version of The Game Map flashed between us.

[System Alert: Trade Accepted]
[System Reward: Trading 'Bright' For 'Brawn'. Nicely Done! +15 XP, 182/200]

The messages appeared in rapid succession.

[System Alert: THE GAME MAP Acquired. Object Will Be Placed In Your Inventory Unless You'd Like to Use. Would You Like to Use?]
[Yes] [No]

"No," I told it quickly.

"The top of the ridge is right ahead," Rainer called from the front. "I think we're high up enough to spot any incoming Darken. The guys and I will keep watch for a little while. You girls want to get some sleep?"

'You girls?'

My eyes pivoted between Joy and the Nomad. He said that like the pink-haired Warrior and I had something in common—like there was more than the common element of gender. ...Like we liked each other. *In all honesty, I wasn't very sure Joy liked...anyone... But I sure as hell wasn't going to pass up an opportunity to sleep...*

Soon enough, I was curled up in a blanket Joy reluctantly shared with me, propped against the rough bark of a wide tree. The warmth of the other girl's body, behind me, helped in the chilling night air, but she faced the opposite side and pulled herself inches away, like it'd be a sin to even be associated with me.

I wondered if she was laying there, still and blinking into the night too.

Both of us.

Experiencing the same thing, just looking separate ways. I swallowed, trying to work up the courage to say something to her, but I figured she'd just cut me off, anyway, or say something rude. ...And I didn't want to hear it right now.

I let my mind drift into the netherworld. As my eyelids sank, the shadows of my dreams flared. ...Like secrets I would rather remain hidden even if I was searching for them with all my might.

***

"Rosie?"

It was Dad's voice—the pet name he'd always called me.

"Dad?" I blinked into a long, dark hallway. The walls looked like they were made of gray stone with bars on either side. The floor was smooth concrete and freezing on my bare feet. ...Where were my shoes?

"Dad, are you there?!" I shouted.

I was surprised by the desperation in my voice and the tearing, welling—the grief twisting at and splitting open my chest. God how I longed to see him. If I could just hear his voice again—just once—"

"Rosie, over here!"

I ran towards his voice—frantic. My feet slapped on the hard floor. Why was my heart hammering so loudly in my ears?

Down the hall.

My breath snagged in my throat as the hall widened to a room where he stood, his sweatshirt pulled over his head like he usually wore it, facing a corner. ...Away from me.

"Dad?"

Why was I suddenly scared? Why wasn't he turning around?

He didn't answer. My feet pattered towards him on the concrete. I was nearly at his shoulder now. My breath rasped up my throat. I reached a hand out towards his shoulder—

He spun, grabbed my hand and—

His face was distorted.

Eaten alive from the inside out.

Red, welting flesh where his eyes should be.

Bone showing on his jaw.

He'd been infected! He was one of the Darken Dormouse had talked about!

I screamed. I tripped backwards, trying to tug my hand free—to get loose!

"Get off!" I yelled, shoving him away from me, but he wouldn't let go. His diseased face leered closer.

"Rosie!" his voice echoed in my head as the image distorted further, twisting and flashing like I was moving backwards down a long hall—

[System Searching MRPs To Select & Display Correct Memory...]

Was that a system update flashing before my eyes? MRP—a memory?

"Rosabella!"

Another voice, slightly deeper, rang over his.

Meshing.

Bleeding together. …Was it part of a memory?

"Rosie—"

"Rosabella!"

Like the voices were fighting, filling my head—too loud!

Cold fingers still wrapped around my wrist—fingers I couldn't get off—

I thrashed, jolting awake, and found myself kicking off the wool blanket. A dream? It was only a dream?

But a face snarled into mine.

And it was half-dead.

Bulging eyes.

Bulbous growth entwining up a pale face that used to be a man's and into its thin hair that only half covered a balding head.

I screamed with everything in me.

Rosabella

The zombie shrieked, its icy fingers persistent around my wrist—grabbing. Its skin was like soggy sandpaper, scratching. I tried to shake off the Darken—tried to kick at it with a scream—to no avail. *Fuck this! Oh my God, oh my God, it was going to bite me!*

Its gaping mouth, red with blood and gore snapped at me—sunk into the flesh of my shoulder. *Fuck!*

[-100 MRP, 3690/6206]

I howled in frustration more than pain. Its yellowed teeth couldn't penetrate my white body armor, but it'd lowered my MRP! I wasn't about to let it take my memories when I was trying so hard to recover them.

"Don't you *dare!*" I growled. My eyes snapped to the broadsword on my belt, but it was pinned under me from the weight of the zombie. *Could I still equip it if it was stuck? I didn't have time for the system's loading anyway–*

My fingers scrabbled in the tree roots, wrapping around a large rock. *If I could just dislodge it—*The pads of my fingertips dug in the dirt as a text update popped into the air—

[System Reward: LARGE GRAY ROCK Acquired +10 XP, 192/200, Object Will Be Placed In Your Inventory Unless You'd Like To Equip. Would You Like To Equip?] [Yes] [No]

"Yes, equip!" I muttered, clenching my teeth. What the fuck would I do with a rock sitting in my inventory? Stupid System—

"Ahhh!" I shrieked again as the Darken attacked, its jaw rattling as it tried to bite my arm this time—

[-100 MRP, 3590/6206]

"*Get off!*" I bellowed in aggravation, lifting the rock.

The creature's eyes were wild—insane. Like it wasn't a person at all anymore, not the man whose skin it wore. …Like it was only the shell of one, its soul emptied from its eyes and…hungry.

Ravenous.

Not today, zombie. I heaved the rock forward with all my strength—

Clod.

[DARKEN, UNDEAD 4: -15 HP, 25/40]

Dazed, the creature fell to the side—

SPLAT.

Bone-slicing.

Blood squirting. Nearly into my eyes. I cringed. *What? That wasn't me—*

[DARKEN, UNDEAD 4: -25 HP, 0/40]
[RAINER, NOMAD 9: System Reward: SNARGEL, UNDEAD 4 Eliminated, +15 XP, 990/1000]

The zombie fingers on my wrist dropped. I blinked past the red in my vision to see the large, hulking outline of the Nomad standing over me: Rainer's shadow. …Holding the handle of an axe buried deep in the Darken's skull.

The weight of the zombie's body fell on my chest, its blood seeping into my body armor. *Great, more blood.* Its stench of death clogged my nostrils. Having the entire scene dripping there, inches from my face, both frightened and wowed me at the same time.

"Rosabella, you good?" The Nomad leaned, peering into my face.

But I didn't—couldn't—respond. Not with words anyway.

I shoved the Darken off and into the grass beside me with a squeal. *It wasn't just a dream—that…that THING had been attacking me…* I could barely catch my breath; my hyperventilating chest wobbled up and down. The entire act of breathing seemed like a lost cause as my eyes adjusted to the early morning light, focusing on Rainer's suddenly wrinkled-up face.

"*Who was on guard?!*" he seethed, calling over his shoulder, "They did a *piss-poor job of it*—" He garbled the last few words under his breath as he shoved yet another Darken to the ground, running a dagger clean through its forehead. *Seriously, how many weapons did the guy have on his person at all times?*

"Get up," the man urged me, "We're going to have to make a break for it! Kill anything in your path!" He slashed another Darken who charged him.

…Kill anything in my…

But I was frozen in fear; I moved after his lumbering silhouette. Because shadows of Darken stumbled in the budding sunlight of our safe spot. And there were lots of us but more of them.

Kill—

Rainer had said—

My hands fumbled to untie the broadsword on my belt like my mind was fumbling for a grip on reality. *Damn, it'd just be easier if—*

"System, equip my Broadsword," I called.

[System Alert: Weapon Equipped.]

The gleaming blade appeared swiftly in my hands. Amazing. Now, if I could get my bravery to appear as quickly, I'd be on a roll…

I stumbled to my feet, feeling each thrust of my lungs as they brought in breath. Just breathe and follow the others, I instructed myself in that patient inner voice resembling a first-grade teacher. …But that was kind of a harder deal than one would think when surrounded by zombies…

Callen flagged me down from a rocky ledge just a few paces away. His face was tight and serious, and the tuft of his gray hair above his insistent eyes blew back in the wind.

Feet—work!

I leapt forward, trying to follow him, but a low growl stopped me…

…Too incredibly close to my ear.

I whirled around—

To meet dead eyes cracked with red veins, a gaping jaw and—

I didn't give myself time to think. I moved. With a grunt, I shoved my sword forward, into decaying ribs. Blood and yellow filth sloshed over the blade, dripping into to the grass and leaves below. The creature whined, the light flickering out of his eyes. I'd– I'd killed it?

[DARKEN, UNDEAD 4: -40 HP, 0/40]
[System Reward: Darken Eliminated, +15 XP, 207/300]

Whoa, cool! I was already over the L2 XP. Did that mean…? Suddenly, everything froze. The familiar gathering of glowing, green plus marks rotated around me, blurring the world in an emerald hue as they flashed in my face.

[System Alert: ***Congratulations, You've Advanced To Level 3!***]

Name	Rosabella	
Class & Level	Game Maker 3	
XP	207/300	
MRP	3590/6206	
HP	24/26	
Baddie Points	90	
Armor Class	15/20	
ABILITIES /20		
Strength	-0	10
Agility	+0	10
Endurance	-1	9
Intelligence	+1	13
Awareness	+1	12
Presence	+3	16
CM		1

[+9 HP & HP Extended By 9, 24/26. You've Been Awarded the Ability to Select One Of The Following Extras:]
[Mask Of Magnetism] [Straight-And-True Advantage]

Wow, that felt like nothing getting to Level 3, probably because of the high XP from trapping the Rinkeclaw. But did the system want me to select now? I stared at the options, noticing Examination Opportunities hovering over each one. I hurried to click on the first shield and magnifying glass option.

[System Option Examined... +1 XP, 208/300]
[A Closer Look At The Fine Print Explains The Option Further:
MASK OF MAGNETISM: A Magical Object Which Allows A Gamer To Charm, Persuade Or Convince Another Party, Regardless Of Presence Ability Points Or The Other Party's Opinion Or Will. Unfortunately, This Mask Is Disposable And Can Only Be Used Once.]

...Okay, that sounded useful, but what was the other option? "Examine," I said. Another paragraph of text bounced into view:

[System Option Examined... +1 XP, 209/300]
[A Closer Look At The Fine Print Explains The Option Further:
STRAIGHT-AND-TRUE ADVANTAGE: With This Advantage, The Wind Is Always Blowing In The Right Direction, And Your Arrow Is Always Straight. Use It In Any Combat Situation To Ensure A Solid, Kill Strike That Will Fell Any Beast Up To Level 3. Requirement: Bow Of Any Level Or Type. Restriction: Can Only Be Used Once.]

...Hmmm, I pondered my choices. This was also a helpful piece except...except, I currently had no bow; I'd just been borrowing Callen's so...

[Please Select Which Extra You'd Like.]

"Mask of Magnetism," I stated confidently, and an electronic beep followed.

[System Alert: MASK OF MAGNETISM Selected. Object Will Be Placed In Your Inventory.]

A red mask glowed in front of me briefly before minimizing and careening towards my belt. A strange sort of elation quivered through me. *Was it the increased HP? The cool, new magical object? I wasn't sure.* ...That was before time unfroze, though, and dumped me back into the realization that I'd just officially gutted a zombie at my feet. I held back the urge to projectile vomit right on the carcass.

"*Atta girl!*" Rainer remarked, coming back to life from the frozen time space, pride coloring his cheeks red as a grin spread across his face.

And I would be proud of myself—I would—except...*except I was pretty sure that was a kidney floating around in that vile mess.* My gag reflex started working overtime. And a feeling of disgust overwhelmed me. I'd killed a Snargel and a Kenchee zombie-bird-thing and, now, a Darken? *Was this how it was going to be now? Me just...killing things?*

All for the sake of freeing Dad? Was this…right? I mean, I'd like to argue that all the creatures were kind of already dead but…

But they'd still had a heartbeat.

I tried to shake the thought off. *This was a fake game, right? Some alternate reality or a dream? What I did didn't matter here as long as I got Dad back…right?* Somehow, I just felt even more like heaving.

"Come on, you two!" Callen shouted, waving even more frantically at Rainer and me, "To the river!"

Luckily, the path was clear this time. The two of us raced forward, down the hill. … *Well, per usual, Rainer was far faster than I was, but I got there all the same.* My legs burned from the angle, but, when I looked up, I found the group flagging us over to a stream. Honestly, I could barely call it that; it was a gully in the hill where water looked like it'd been draining off the mountains from rain. Still, water gushed through it, sloping downward in a series of trickling waterfalls.

"Darken don't swim," Dormouse called to me, so I understood. His voice carried even over the rushing noise in the, otherwise, silent early morning, "They're afraid of the water."

…*If I'd have known that, I would have found an island to sleep on… What were Darken's other weaknesses?* It occurred to me, suddenly, that I hadn't even seen their stat sheet.

"System, bring up the Darken stats," I whispered under my breath.

[System Understands Query…Loading Response…]

I watched the rushing water at my feet while I waited for it to load.

[System Answer: A Darken Is A Fast But Rather Dull Zombie Characterized By Rotting Flesh And A Typically Nasty Odor. Gamers Become Darken When Their MRP Reaches 0.
STRENGTHS: Sharp Hearing, Tendency To Herd With Other Darken And Their Ability To Drain Gamers Of MRP From Bites.

WEAKNESSES: Not The Brightest Bulb, Plus Their Teeth Aren't Sharp Enough To Pierce Through Armor Higher Than 14.]

Name	Darken	
Class & Level, Size	Undead 4, Medium To Large	
HP	40/40	
Armor Class	13/20	
ABILITIES /20		
Strength	-3	3
Agility	-1	8
Endurance	+2	15
Intelligence	-1	7
Awareness	+0	10
Presence	+0	11

"Rosabella, game's in here," Joy called over the sound of the water. *What? Shit. The group had been waiting for me to cross?* I swiped the Darken stats away. My boots hedged on the slippery rocks.

"Watch your feet, your Agility isn't the best," Callen warned me as I lifted a foot.

Icy liquid flooded over the tops and sides of my boots as I wobbled across. With a few, careful steps, I managed to make it to the other side as a system messaged appeared.

[System Reward: Successful Ford, +5 XP, 214/300]

Neat. And I could exhale again—I could finally breathe now that both feet were returned to solid ground. Callen offered a short smile and a hand to help me up, and I took both of them gratefully.

Rainer, however, was not in jovial spirits. "I'll ask again: *who the hell was on guard?!*" he raged, his meaty arms making frantic circles in the air—*really, with the red beard and all, he looked like some raving, Viking lunatic.*

Leaning up against the gray rock embedded in the side of the hill, everyone looked like they were suddenly in a rock against a hard place. Flashing eyes told me no one particularly wanted to answer, especially Dormouse who cowered near the thinnest part of the stream.

Finally, Joy stepped forward. Her face was rigid with frustration. Her pink hair billowed out behind her like a flag from where her expression constricted in an annoyed snarl, "I fell asleep—"

"*Oh, no, no, no,*" Rainer shook an annoyed finger at the girl. "No more excuses from you. Our lives are in your hands, do you not understand? Callen—" the Nomad turned abruptly to the gray-haired man, his arms stretched open in protest and outrage, "It's affecting her. They *smell* her—"

"Oh, cut the theatrics, Rainer," Joy barked; she seemed more worked up than typical. "They didn't smell shit. I'm still here, you know." Her face, suddenly, creased with hurt. "I'm still *a person.*"

What was going on here? My eyes darted between Joy, Callen and Rainer without uncovering anything further. I edged towards Dormouse, trying to conceal my movement. I definitely did not want to be included in their quarrel.

"What are they arguing about?" I whispered to the nerd.

"You don't want to know," he murmured back. ...But Rainer overheard us—

"Rosabella has every right to know," he stormed, "It could save her life if you lead more of the undead here—"

"I'm not leading them *anywhere!*" Joy screamed, throwing her hands down—

"*Quiet! All of you.*"

It was Callen's voice: sharp and decisive. Like his gray eyes.

"...What's going on?" I asked haltingly, wondering, even as the words came out, if it was more prudent to just keep my mouth shut;

Joy looked like she was about to draw both katanas from her belt and cut out all of our tongues.

Callen glanced at the pink-haired girl before answering. She was simmering—too hot to handle—and I was extremely glad in that moment that it was him and Rainer pushing her buttons and not me. The gray-haired Trader swallowed and began to speak slowly—calmly—directing the words at me, "Joy's a good Warrior. She's held her own in more Darken battles than probably all of us combined which means she's, also, taken on the most casualties. Her Memory Recall Points...they're—" The man's voice broke.

Joy shoved forward, past him, her hands opening a screen between us, "You guys are so dramatic; just show her. Here—"

[Current MRP / JOY, WARRIOR 11: 47/7306]

Forty-seven MRP out of that giant number? I gaped at the stats, my jaw going instantly slack. Oh my God, that was so low. How was it so low? We had to get her more health packs! I'd been so selfish to horde them for myself—

"When you reach 0 MRP, you turn Darken," Joy finished sourly, swallowing and averting her gaze from mine, "I got caught in a zombie nest. I couldn't get out. Now, Rainer, here likes to poke fun at me and tell me I'm some magnet of death or brag about how he'd rather get Swag Points than retain his MRP from not drinking because it's 'just a beer or two' and getting laid is more of a priority—" The girl's voice was sharp and bitter.

Across from us, Rainer looked particularly uncomfortable. He swiped a hand across his wide nose. "...It's not like that—"

"Really?!" Joy snapped, her eyes flashing, "'Cause that's what it feels like—"

"We'll just have to get you some health packs," I stuttered, suddenly feeling incredibly on edge and frantic for the girl's sake. "We'll all look around. I'm sure we can find something."

"The health packs don't work the same way for Joy as they do for us," Dormouse interjected sullenly, "According to The Game Code, anyone who's under 100 MRP gets an automatically applied curse. It cuts point values from health in eighths. Once you're under 100 MRP, it's hard to climb back."

Joy nodded darkly. She squatted on the ground, leaning heavily into her knees as she brushed her bright hair over her shoulder, "I just focus now on not letting the points go down any further." She picked up a small stick, tracing lines in the dirt. "And we had that emergency health pack for me, but, now, we don't so…"

Observing her bleak expression, I felt everything sink within me. …So, that was why she'd been so pissed when I'd used their last health pack. Joy was…dying—turning zombie. I looked at the girl with renewed understanding. Maybe she wasn't angry with any of us here… Maybe she was just…angry.

At her situation.

At this world…killing her.

…But part of the deal with them was activating my Creator Magic and fixing their world. Maybe, if I fixed their world, it would help…fix her.

"But if I heal your world—" I stuttered.

"You will, kid, you will," Callen assured me, holding up both hands as though to soothe the blubbering in my voice, "This is all just temporary till you can Level Up and activate your CM."

…But something in his eyes made me wonder if he actually believed that as uneasy silence blanketed us all again.

"Well, I'm up," Rainer finally quipped, thrusting his hands into his pockets, "Anyone down to find some more CM for Rosabella?"

"—As if we even have a chance of doing that without knowing where it's hidden," Joy noted sullenly, still not looking up from her drawings in the dirt. But my eyes wandered upward, trailing the mountain peaks in the distance when–shit, I actually had an idea!

"Hey!" I pointed into the egg yoke horizon where drifting silhouettes of dark bird wings circled. "Are those the Kenchee things?" I asked.

Rainer used a huge hand to shade his eyes, nodding as he realized it. "Yup. The blasted beasts are probably on to their next magic heist," he griped, "Bloodthirsty mothers—"

"Exactly," I quipped.

The group stared at me.

"Exactly what?" Joy snapped, brushing off the legs of her pants from where she still squatted.

"They poach magic, right?" I spouted, suddenly speaking fast with the excitement of my own idea. "…Which means they can lead us to where more magic is—"

"Or we could just waltz completely into a Level 15 Aswakart Allopa," Joy sniffed scornfully.

…Oh. She meant the birds could be attracted by a huge magical beast and not just CM magic… Damn it, she had a point.

"Uh…" I stammered. "I don't know what that is, but I'm hoping the Kenchee could help us locate another CM Diamond—"

"Well, I'm on board," Rainer wheezed, hefting his bow and axe onto his back with a giant swing.

"Me too," Dormouse peeped, adjusting the straps of his own backpack in white hands.

And Callen stared between me and Joy, nodding, "Let's go then—"

"You people are insufferable," the pink-haired girl complained, pushing to her feet, "If I have to walk one more mile chasing after a needle in a haystack—"

"You might not have to." Dormouse's nasally voice cut through the girl's.

She stared at him. "What?"

"Walk," the dork stated simply.

Joy shook her head in utter annoyance, "Would someone tell him to form complete sentences? For a brainiac, I sure as hell can't understand a word that comes out of his mouth—"

"I have this," Dormouse drew his hand out of his pocket, showing us all a tiny pair of sneakers with wings painted on the sides. I leaned in, squinting at them, "I got it from a wizard when I was small 'cause the other kids would pick on me. Completely forgot about it till now."

A shield and magnifying glass symbol hovered over the shoes. An Examine Opportunity?

"Go ahead," Dormouse urged me.

"Examine," I commanded.

[System Object Examined... +1 XP, 215/300]
[A Closer Look Determines These Are Not Just Baby Or Gnome Shoes. This Is An Enchanted Object Called Run-Run-As-Fast-As-You-Can.
RUN-RUN-AS-FAST-AS-YOU-CAN: A Magical Object Which Allows A Gamer Or A Party of Gamers To Advance 1 Mile With 1 Step (If Party Journeying, Please Clasp Hands). It Can Be Used For Up To 10 Steps. After That—Watch Out!—the Shoe May Slip Off And You May Go a Mile Backwards With Every Forward Step!
Restriction: Can Only Be Used Once Every 10 Long Rests.]

"If it is an L15 Aswakart Allopa, then we can simply keep running and outrun him," Dormouse blubbered excitedly, "I mean, the Kenchee are probably 5 miles from here so we'd have plenty left over. Geez, and to think the wizard just gave it to me to outrun bullies. I'd totally forgotten I had it buried in my inventory—thought all that was just old kid stuff…"

I stopped listening, noticing Joy's overt, livid posture. Her arms were crossed firmly over her chest as she stared daggers at the Coder.

"Are you *shitting me?!*" she raged. "You're shitting me. We've walked all over this Godforsaken place for *months*, and you conveniently forgot that you had super speed?"

"It's not super speed," Dormouse fumbled. "It's a mile augmenter—"

"I don't *care*," the girl spat. She turned towards the rest of us, shaking her head. "I'm going to kill him. I really am going to kill him this time—"

Callen cleared his throat as though trying to clear the air, "Dormouse, fire it up, and let's try it out." He nodded at the tiny shoes in the kid's hands, and the nerd nodded back.

"Err, we have to join hands…" the Coder glanced nervously at Joy before reaching for mine and Rainer's. The dork's hand was cold and, somehow, wet—*ew!* But I tried not to tug away.

"Great idea about following the Kenchee, by the way," he said, leaning to whisper in my ear.

And I smiled weakly at him, still looking out at the circling dots of the birds in the sky. *For Dad,* I thought to myself. *Some people had to wonder what they'd do for a loved one, but me? I was living it. And I knew I'd do anything for him but… But, honestly, I was beginning to wonder about that Level-15-whatever Joy had mentioned, myself. Was this all just a big mistake???*

Rosabella

Dormouse didn't mention the nauseousness. And, if you asked me, that was something one should have mentioned. I clutched at my wrenching stomach as the purple-and-pink sky tilted dangerously above my head. *Did we stop moving? Why didn't it feel like it?*

"I'm gonna puke," Rainer moaned. The huge Nomad held his stomach, doubling over. His typically red-tinged face looked green.

"Real delicate of you, Rainer," Joy jeered, brushing back her pink hair in a sweeping motion and looking like she was having little to no problem with the world-spinning phenomenon.

Fuck resilient Warriors.

"Where are we?" I choked out. My blurry vision sharpened on a huge building looming on the horizon.

"Right underneath the Kenchee, as promised," Dormouse told me, rocking back and forth on his feet and gleaming with probably as much chest-puffing self-satisfaction as the dork had ever seen.

"Captain Obvious over here," Joy mumbled under her breath. I watched Callen elbow her sharply in the ribs which quieted her.

The zombie birds were, in fact, overhead. The shadows of their wings crossed over my face and scattered the ground with dark, moving rectangles. I craned my neck backwards, squinting into the sun to see black, decaying wings and feathers fluttering there, watching us again. ...*But, so far, there was no giant beastie so... What was drawing them?*

My gaze fastened on the building again, and a familiar warmth stirred my heart—the feeling of safety and home and...

Magic.

There had to be magic in that building—building? Well, it wasn't just a building. It looked—

Well, it kind of looked like—

"Is that a prison?" I blurted.

The enormous, stone edifice sat on the sloping ground just off the ridge like a meditating monk, balanced and settled between two, mountainous peaks. Its square, gray towers cast a shadow that loomed over the landscape and the surrounding moat, making the place appear eerie and desolate. Steam rose from the water, billowing and distorting the gothic angles of the windows and doors. ...But all of the windows had wrought iron bars creasing their panes. If I'd had to decide if it was a castle or a prison, I'd settle on prison.

"Yep, it's a prison," Dormouse piped up. "Actually, it's the prison your dad is in—"

"*Seriously*, Dormouse? You couldn't keep that *nugget* of information to yourself for two minutes?" Joy blurted, her face utter devastation mixed with enough frustration to pound his head in.

The kid shrugged, "Just trying to help—"

"Oh my God, *I swear*—" Joy leapt at him, but Callen stepped forward, easily separating the two like squabbling siblings.

But I suddenly didn't care about whatever argument they were or weren't having. My head spun, and I gaped at the stone walls, feeling my heartbeat launch through my shirt. *Dad was in there—behind those walls? Trapped? We were right in his neighborhood only to have to walk away again before the group would fulfill their part of the trade?*

"Wait—just hold on a second," I hedged, spinning on the group. "So, you're telling me Dad's literally right there"—I pointed—"and you expect me to just continue to go through with my part of the deal when we could literally just sneak in there right now and get him?"

"It's not that easy, kid." Callen's tone was a deterrent. They all stared at me. They were all staring at me like I was, somehow, in the wrong here—like *I* was the crazy one. *No. No! I wasn't the crazy one. I couldn't just stand here and walk away from saving the one person I'd been doing all this shit to save—not when he was right there!*

"No," I stated bluntly, echoing the sentiment in my thoughts. "No, I am not just going to pretend like he's not right there—"

"You made a covenant," Joy snarled.

Something shrieked.

A high-pitched call overhead—a bird call.

Black wings dove from the sky, landing close to us. The thing was massive on the ground. Rotting flesh and diseased feathers on a body larger than a racoon's. A sharp beak pecked at the tall grass. *What was the Kenchee doing?*

Its black wings flapped. It rose, kicking a strong wind and foul odor towards us. ...And, in its gnarled talons, a turquoise diamond shone, radiating a multitude of streaming, white light. My eyes widened.

"A CM Diamond!" I exclaimed.

"That thing is going down!" Joy hollered, "Callen, I need arrows—"

"Wait!" I shouted. Because an Examine Opportunity icon hovered in the grass where the Kenchee had landed just seconds before. And I had to know what it said...

"Examine!" I shouted. Overhead, the Kenchee squawked and crowed.

[System Query Examined... +1 XP, 216/300]

[Upon A Closer Look, You Discovered The Reason For The Circling Kenchee Flock. 2 CM Diamonds Were Laying Here In The Dirt. The Bird Got One...]

I read the message at a furious pace, my mind clicking through the meaning.... *Wait, so was there a second Diamond just...laying there?*

I leapt into action—no one had to tell me twice. No one had to explain that this might just be the lucky break that secured my ability to get my Dad back. *Two CM Diamonds? I was going to take them both—*

"Joy, shoot it down!" I cried. I heard the Warrior behind me string her bow with a thrum.

And my feet were already running towards the spot on the ground where the second Diamond should be—

BrrrUGHHHHHHHHHHHHHHHHHHHHHH!!!!!!!

Shit. Oh my God, shit. A face-rattling roar lit my skin on fire. I looked up from where my fingers were inches away from their destination—buried in the grass.

To see a dragon.

Not a Silver Rinkeclaw this time.

Something bigger.

Something...*madder.*

A colossal jaw, inlaid with rows of glinting, jagged teeth and a soft tongue screamed into my face. Spittal dripped there. Fire scorched my cheeks as a ball of flames shot forward, hitting me—throwing me backwards—

"*Oof!*"

[-7 HP, 17/26]

I rushed my hands to my face, feeling the skin there. It stung like hell but was, otherwise, okay other than a little puffy. I blinked through swollen eyes at the system pop-up. *Aw, come on, not my*

HP! Not when I was so close to snagging this Diamond!! Still, self-preservation was a damn stronger emotion than I'd realized. I backed up slowly, praying with everything in me that the enormous thing would stay occupied with the CM Diamonds and forget about me...

The creature was too big; that was my first thought. The dragon was too massive. The mammoth, red beast squatted in the center of the field, swiping an enormous claw right in front of my face as it searched the high grass for the CM Diamond. The spikes on its spine jutted upwards nearly as long as half my arm, and its huge tail swished angrily through the grass like a restless python.

That Motherfucker. I am so not in the MOOD FOR THIS TODAY!

A furious man's voice bellowed in between my eardrums—in my head again like the first dragon? Thanks again, Draconic Dictionary...

"System, what the heck is that thing?" I mumbled under my breath as I tripped backwards, my toe meeting with a sharp rock that nearly sent me sprawling.

[System Understands Query...Loading Response...]

I watched the clearly agitated dragon find the CM Diamond in the grass, which it absorbed quickly into its inventory.

Where the hell is the other one? I had two! It is way too early for this—

The beast's footfalls shook the ground as it readjusted itself. It reared, spotting the Kenchee, still holding the second CM Diamond in its claws—

[System Answer: The Dragon Is A L14 Red Vodyaracka Skydrake. It Is A Large Dragon With An Uncanny Intimidation Factor Due To The Impressive Array Of Spikes On Its Back, Sheer Bulk & Ability To Persuade Its

Prey Into Surrendering. Distinctive Features Include A
Yellow Belly.
STRENGTHS: Extremely Strong, Frightful Presence &
Lulling-Like Speech Which Can Convince Prey To Do The
Dragon's Whim.
WEAKNESSES: Easily Angered & Rather Egotistical
Which Can Be A Good Or Very Bad Thing Depending—
Don't Try To Win A Persuasion Battle With This Beast.
You Have Been Warned.]

Name	Red Vodyaracka Skydrake	
Class & Level, Size	Dragon 14, Huge	
HP	219/219	
Armor Class	19/20	
ABILITIES /20		
Strength	+6	23
Agility	+2	14
Endurance	+5	21
Intelligence	+2	14
Awareness	+1	13
Presence	+3	17
CM		6

Oh damn. I did not like the sound of any of that—

Whiz.

An arrow?

I whipped around to see Joy poised in her release stance. Her arrow hit the Kenchee with a sobering thud.

[KENCHEE, UNDEAD 4: -30 HP, 28/58]

But it was a wing hit. The injured vulture floundered in the air, trying to regain its mobility.

CHOMP. Crack.

—The Red Vodyaracka's jaw shut right over the creature. I watched the system alerts appear:

[KENCHEE, UNDEAD 4: -28 HP, 0/58]
[SPARO, RED VODYARACKA SKYDRAKE, DRAGON 14:
System Reward: KENCHEE, UNDEAD 4 Eliminated, +15
XP, 1465/1500]

Black feathers wafted downwind, towards me, as the dragon swallowed, turned around and began to lumber back towards the prison. ...*It was just leaving us here? Alive? Oh, thank God!* But I celebrated too soon—

"You're welcome!" Joy shouted sarcastically after it. *What was the girl doing? Egging the dragon on?!*

"Joy, stop!" Dormouse pleaded from beside the pink-haired Warrior. ...Apparently, he and I were on the same wavelength.

But, luckily, the dragon didn't stop. The Red Vodyaracka Skydrake continued lumbering away from our group and back towards the prison even as its honey-smooth, male voice echoed in my mind:

Check out the pipes on that girl—hella ballsy. As though a dragon has to thank anyone for anything! I'll remain in my toxic apathy, thank you very much.

Oh my gosh, if Joy could hear him... But she couldn't, I realized quickly, glancing at the pink-haired Warrior's face. Apparently, the others hadn't found a Draconic Language Dictionary...

You know, I thought that watching such an enormous beast walk away would fill me with relief—like I could finally breathe again, suck in air again. But, for some reason, it did the opposite. And I realized, suddenly, why my stomach was churning and twisting. ...And it very much had to do with the fact that not only was a dragon walking away from us—so were his 2 CM Diamonds.

And I needed them. I needed those Diamonds to activate my Creator Magic and fix this world so I could free Dad. ...And Dad... The CM Diamonds weren't the only things behind the prison's stone walls as the Red Vodyaracka slid under the raised, metal gate and back inside. Dad was in there too. And I needed Dad.

Shit.

I hated the way I felt my emotions shifting—the determination and urgency suddenly filling my core. *Damn it, I was really going to do this? I really needed to do this right now? I'd JUST gotten out of harm's way.*

"I have to go after him." The words fell off my tongue even as I picked up my rubbery-and-weak-feeling feet to begin moving towards the prison. "Guys, he has two CM Diamonds. I have to go at least *try* to get them from him—"

"I think she's gone off the deep end," Rainer murmured, crossing his arms and raising a bushy, right eyebrow in a way that told me he couldn't believe the words coming off my lips. "Rosabella, you only just got to Level 3."

"There's no way I'm letting you willingly kill yourself—so, no," Joy sneered, also crossing her arms. *What, were they both trying to replace my dad with all the rule-following?*

"Then come with me!" I tried instead.

"—And, somehow, I like that idea even less," Joy griped openly.

"Oh, get over it," Dormouse ran an annoyed hand through the fringe of his tousled, black hair, "you're not going to really send a little girl into the throws of Somergot Prison and a dragon's lair alone, are you?"

Hey! I lift an offended eyebrow, eyeing the dork up, "I am pretty sure I'm older than you—"

"And she probably weighs more since you're all skin and bones," Rainer added—*kinda in my defense?*

"We'll all go together," Callen interrupted. His voice lowered into seriousness as his gray eyebrows knit over his thin nose, "Rosabella is really doing this for all of us, as much as she's doing it for herself. We defend her and our cause together—"

"God, I hate it when you go all noble on us," Joy rolled her eyes.

And Rainer laughed—a full-stomach bellow that brought a smile even to my unsure lips.

I swiped a boot across the tops of the grass, hearing the green stands hit the sides of the now-rather-muddied, white leather with a satisfying 'thwack' which somehow seemed to fill the void in my mind. "Guys, I swear he's cool," I added.

Dormouse squinted at me, "Who's cool?"

"The dragon," I told him, "I found this Draconic Dictionary, and I can hear him speak in my mind so… He just sounds kinda irritated and jaded, but not bad."

Famous last words…

Rosabella

The path towards the prison was weedy, sprouting with clumps of exuberant onion grass and sharp rocks. I wove my feet cautiously around the jagged stones and through the tall meadow. The smell of stagnant water hit me as my feet clanked over the ancient wood of a bridge across the moat. The water below grew green with cattail and lily pads. I lifted my chin to observe the thick, castle-like torrents twisting overhead. And my stomach dropped with flinty resolution.

"Which way do we go in?" I asked no one in particular as the prison walls rose over my vision, a maze of wrought iron bars and spike-armored gates. *Up close this place was kinda creepy…*

"Beats me," Dormouse shrugged. "The Red Vodyaracka Skydrake is one of the prison guards here. That's why it's maximum security. You can't get in or out without facing the beast…and, unfortunately, for far too many inmates here, that *doesn't typically end well…*"

"Dragons are a prideful breed," Rainer's deep voice echoed loudly between the stone walls, "But, if he thinks we're easy to face, he's got another thing coming to him—"

OhmyGerd!!—Gate A is for assholes who talk too loud and wake everyone up at the crack of dawn; have some respect.

There! The dragon's voice in my head! My heart rammed in my chest. My breathing shallowed. *I was the only one who could hear the dragon, right? He'd said 'Gate A'… Was it a trap or legit?* I wrangled with my own thoughts. If this was a game online, I'd make a move. I'd get a grip and make a big move. *Gate A it was then…*

I wet my lips and asked the question I was afraid would open a large can of worms, "System, where is Gate A? Is it open?" …*Or was this snarky dragon playing around?*

[System Understands Query…Loading Response…]
[System Answer: You Do Not Currently Have A Detailed
Map For This Area. However, The Game Map In Your
Inventory Labels A Gate A On Sommergot Prison. This
Gate Is Identified As 'Open'. Would You Like GPS
Directional Guidance For Locating?]
[Yes] [No]

Yes, obviously. Thanks, System. I selected the option, and a digital, yellow arrow appeared, stretching in front of me and pulsing as though waiting for me to follow where it pointed around a stone corner.

"Thought we talked about using that damn technology," Rainer mumbled under his breath.

Callen held out a hand, "It's okay. Rosabella, lead the way."

'Lead the way?'

The gray-haired man's direction made me unsteady. Back in New York, no one had ever asked me to lead anything—not in school, not in clubs, not even, really, in my online games. *I, more so, just tried to stay OUT of the way. Now, I was LEADING the way?* My breath caught and quivered in my chest. I hedged forward.

The coolness of the stone hallway before us hit my face. The directional arrow fizzled out and reappeared ahead, waiting right under the points of a metal gate…an open gate. *The dragon hadn't been kidding… Gate A was real.*

[System Alert: You Have Reached Your Destination, +5 XP 221/300]

The arrow dissipated. Really? The system's message was weirdly like my phone's navigation back on Earth... I squeezed my eyes shut, praying with everything in me. Please let traipsing back after this dragon be the right decision. Please let this end with all of us in one piece and me getting the CM Diamonds.

...But I couldn't help but wonder as I stared at the huge spikes of the gate directly overhead: had I made the wrong call here?

And the further that I walked into the prison, the more convinced I became—that my judgment had been way off. And I'd been just a little too optimistic on this one. But everyone was following me; our footsteps echoed in the stone hallway. And, since I'd only been put in charge once in my life, I kinda didn't want to turn around and admit I'd screwed up so...

Both of my hands clutched at the handle of my mother's blade— well, her supposed sword, anyway. The metal etchings there dug into my sweaty palms. Maybe it'd bring me some luck. The solid, stone walls of the narrow hallway seemed to push in on me, constricting my breathing further. My darting eyes surveyed the situation:

Long, stone hall.

Solid, metal door at the end.

No windows.

Barely any light.

Too many shadows.

No dragon...yet. ...Luckily. I swallowed all the fear stuffing itself down my throat. I could do this. I'd trapped the Silver Rinkeclaw. I'd killed a Snargel and a Kenchee. I could do this for Dad. ...I hoped.

An amused chuckle echoed in my mind. Damn that dragon.

My favorite part is how white all your faces get. Like y'all have seen a damn ghost.

123

The beast's sneering voice made me want to be even more sick. I held the sword out in front of me, watching the blade tremble in my shaking hands. *I wouldn't show fear,* I told myself, trying to pin myself together like a badly torn quilt. *I would be strong—*

But my arms were already weakening, bowing under the pressure of the situation and the weight of the weapon in my grasp even with the increased Strength from my Level Up...

"Show yourself!" I called, my demand bouncing off the walls and sounding much more confident than I currently felt.

The dragon chuckled again—a low, brewing sound.

This one's got as much of a mouth on her as her pink-haired friend. You might just be better than a cup of coffee, small one.

I heard something huge shift nearby. *Was it past the door at the end of the hall? –Closer? ...Above us?* I craned my neck upwards but only found a stone ceiling there. Despite my courageous exterior, my insides jumped and jittered like a bee in a tin can. *What was this dragon's deal? How was I going to get him to hand over the CM Diamonds?*

"Why don't you come out?" I breathed, running out of breath and nearly steps till the end of the cramped enclosure.

Why don't you come in?

The male voice in my head mused instead. I gritted my teeth as the metal door at the end of the hall creaked open. *...Like the worst invitation ever.* And the dragon was most definitely inside. If this was a trap, there was no going back now.

"He wants us to go inside," I told the group over my shoulder. I heard Rainer clear his throat behind me. Callen nodded. And that nod was enough to get me to step forward.

"Fine," I muttered to the voice in my head, deciding I only had one choice.

But it wasn't 'fine', because the doorway was dark beyond where I could see—completely shadowed like the raw, tangible uncertainty and fear coiling in my stomach had become a black monster that lurked just beyond that door frame and thick door.

I swallowed. And I surged forward. My boots made a harsh clicking noise on the concrete floor. My nostrils filled with the stink of mold and large reptile.

And I passed the doorway.

...And immediately sucked my breath in.

The room beyond was enormous. *This wasn't a prison room; this was a cathedral!* An arched, intricately carved ceiling stretched overhead, made of the same gray stone as the walls. Cathedral windows, lining the far side, opened the cave-like quality of the place with the rosy glow of early morning as the sun slipped over a pink horizon, making light glint and bounce off the excessive piles of gold coins and jewels pushed up against the walls.

Treasure.

And the mammoth Red Vodyaracka Skydrake squatted among all of it.

...Actually, the beast was rolled over comfortably on his belly, showing the yellow-tinted scales there, different from the flaming ruby ones on the remainder of him. He scratched at an armpit with one claw, barely lifting his huge horse head to acknowledge our presence, while his other claw twisted a turquoise CM Diamond like a top, spinning it on a pile of CM Diamonds. My jaw dropped. *There were so many there! How many?!* An Examination Opportunity shield and magnifying glass symbol bobbed overtop of the pile.

"Examine," I whispered covertly under my breath.

[System Object Examined... +1 XP, 222/300]
[The Closer You Get, The Clearer It Becomes That This Dragon Has A Ton of CM! Craning Your Neck Allows You

To Count 6 CM Diamonds in The Pile. The Room Is Also Crammed With Treasure That Might Contain Other Items.]

...Six CM Diamonds?! My mount went insta-dry.

"He has six of them," I croaked to the group behind me, trying to keep my statement low enough not to reach the creature's rotating ears.

Out of the corner of my eye, I watched Joy's hands go to the two katanas on her belt. "I'll distract him, you grab them—"

"No," I shook my head, "I think we should...just talk to him—"

Talk? I loooove talking. Most people find I'm an excellent conversationalist.

I froze. The dragon—the Red Vodyaracka–had heard every word.

If I have to be real with you, you really don't want to go the sword route, pretty—the one where you fight and try to steal from me, nope.

He tsked patiently, like we were deciding this together. His eyes flicked to the tip of my sword, which still shook slightly as I held it upright.

Imma flambe barbeque you and your friends crunchy Szechuan if you try that. And I already had to have a roast this morning, before you— not even dawn; it's been very busy.

He thumbed a claw at a charcoal-burned, human skeleton, dressed in a gray prison uniform, hanging by the ankles in the corner. The flesh of the corpse was burned black and the face, melted like clay. The stench coming from it was atrocious. I nearly jumped out of my skin—or passed out.

Or both.

Was the room getting smaller? The dragon's almond-shaped, dark eyes blinked at me, staring directly.

Stupid egotistical sons-of-bitches.

He scoffed in my head, shaking his own huge one.

Gotta get all caught up in their escape theories. I didn't get the best room in the house by sheer luck! …Thinkin' they can get past me—not here, motherfucker.

The Vodyaracka spat in the corpse's direction. And, suddenly, all plans were off the table. My sword felt like a toothpick in my grasp. *What the hell was I going to do?* I was very aware of the walls on either side of us—our group's tiny size in relation to the enormous dragon and just how easy it would probably be for the beast to catch us and eat us for breakfast like nuisance mice. The beast's thick tail swished on the stone floor, filling the room with its winds and curves like a huge snake come to life. My heartbeat quickened. My eyes flashed between claws and teeth and the magic I needed. *How was I going to talk the thing into giving me the CM Diamonds?*

"What's he saying?" Joy hissed, shoving a sweaty wave of pink hair off her forehead.

"I'm *working on it*," I growled back. …But, really, what I was doing was floundering and wasting time so I could figure this all out. *I'd beat the Silver Rinkeclaw through strategy. Could I do the same here?*

"System, bring up the dragon's stats again," I whispered.

[System Understands Query…Loading Response…]

So…why the visit?

The dragon's voice chimed in my head with the same inflection someone's aunt might use in finding their granddaughter on the doorstep of their home. Not like a cold-blooded killer but…well, I already had proof of that, and it undeniably matched the size of the teeth gnashing inches away from my face and the corpse in the corner.

I shuffled my feet on the hard floor, wondering what action actually caused the instant flambe. ...And, more accurately, what I could do to avoid it. "Err, I—" I stammered. *Stats, load faster!!*

Cat got your tongue?

The dragon shifted his huge form forward like propping himself up, interested, on two elbows. A thousand razor-sharp blades of his scales scratched across the floor with the movement. His eyes narrowed, blinking slits.

[System Answer: The Dragon Is A L14 Red Vodyaracka
Skydrake. It Is A Large Dragon With An Uncanny
Intimidation Factor Due To The Impressive Array Of
Spikes On Its Back, Sheer Bulk & Ability To Persuade Its
Prey Into Surrendering. Distinctive Features Include A
Yellow Belly.
STRENGTHS: Extremely Strong, Frightful Presence &
Lulling-Like Speech Which Can Convince Prey To Do The
Dragon's Whim.
WEAKNESSES: Easily Angered & Rather Egotistical
Which Can Be A Good Or Very Bad Thing Depending—
Don't Try To Win A Persuasion Battle With This Beast.
You Have Been Warned.]

Name	Red Vodyaracka Skydrake	
Class & Level, Size	Dragon 14, Huge	
HP	219/219	
Armor Class	19/20	
ABILITIES /20		
Strength	+6	23
Agility	+2	14
Endurance	+5	21
Intelligence	+2	14
Awareness	+1	13
Presence	+3	17
CM		6

Finally! But the dragon's expression morphed into…*well, he kinda looked pissed off…*

You're looking at my stats right in front of me? I am not a pig at market, small one. If we're going to examine stats like we're in a marketplace, I need to see yours. I DEMAND to see yours while you tell me what you and your friends are doing here. NOW.

The Vodyaracka roared—deafening. I nearly fell over from the force of it in my eardrums. I clutched my hands to my ears. Warmth and spittle clung to my face. It's monstrous, yellowed fangs were way too close—

"Okay—okay, I just—" I sputtered.

Shit. I was going to kill all of us. We were all going to die. We were all going to die here in a stupid fantasy world, and Dad would die too because I was too incompetent to save him—

My fingers fumbled in the air to pull up my own stats, but, between my frazzled nerves and my unsure movements, I, somehow, pulled up my inventory instead:

[System Alert: Per Request, Inventory Opened.]
- **1 Rosabella's Mother's Gold & Silver Broadsword [Equipped]**
- **1 CM Diamond**
- **1 The Game Map**
- **1 Mask Of Magnetism**

"Sorry, how do I—" I muttered. …*Wait a second…!*

Elation swept through my body as my eyes locked on the last item on the list: *the mask! The Mask of Magnetism I'd gotten from my last Level Up! I'd forgotten I had it! The dragon stats said not to try to persuade the Vodyaracka, but, with the mask, I could override any amount of Presence Ability!* Anticipation and joy bubbled up within me, making my fingers all but useless even as Callen tried to figure out what I needed, his eyes searching my face so he could help.

"System, just bring up my stats please—*now*."

[System Understands Query...Loading Response...]

It was hard to focus with the dragon this close and my closer, jumping nerves, but, strangely, I watched the beast's expression change. His mouth shut. His eyes locked on the first item in my inventory, flashing to the sword in my grasp. *Thank God, he hadn't noticed the mask...*

Wait a hot sec...Does that say 'Rosabella's Mother's Broadsword'?

The Vodyaracka squinted at the weapon in my fists quizzically, his eyes bouncing back to the text in my inventory, which I tried to swipe closed as quickly as possible.

Damn, it's been a long time since I've seen that weapon...

The dragon mused. The creature recognized my sword? This was getting too strange. I turned the handle over in my grasp.

"Wait, you've seen this sword before?" I tripped over my own tongue, "You knew...my mother?"

Your mother? Hot damn, kid. Your mother WAS NOT Rosabella the Great that—that's like saying the lifeless corpse in the corner is a thriving tap dance competitor—

But, at that second, my stats popped up like the verification I needed:

Name	Rosabella
Class & Level	Game Maker 3
XP	222/300
MRP	3590/6206
HP	17/26
Baddie Points	90
Armor Class	15/20
ABILITIES /20	

Strength	+0	10
Agility	+0	10
Endurance	-1	9
Intelligence	+1	13
Awareness	+1	12
Presence	+3	16
CM		1

The Vodyaracka's keen gaze swept over the numbers and attributes, widening especially on my Class. His huge jaw dropped open.

H-O-L-Y Hannah! Shut the front door! You're—you're Rosabella?

He looked at me with new, disbelieving eyes.

"Shut the—*what?*" I stammered; the force of the beast's words in my mind was already forming a headache. I shook my head, but it didn't help. "I'm Rosabella, yes—I mean—"

You're a Game Maker?! The last... Well shit me a brick!

His surprise was tangible, hanging in the air between us. Honestly, it confused me a bit, as did his address of my mother, setting me off balance with the way the huge reptile was staring at me.

"You—you knew my mom?" My voice was a vulnerable squeak because, in that second, I'd forgotten why I was here...maybe even that I *was* here, having a conversation with a dragon that the group behind me could only hear half of. I'd forgotten the sword in my hand and the body armor on my arms and legs...and the fact that the dragon was two-stories tall and could potentially grill me to death. I'd forgotten it because, in that second, I just wanted to know.

About Mom.

My shoulders slumped forward. My sword pitched in my grip, the tip clanging against the concrete floor. Dad had never talked about her—actually, he became nearly irate if I ever asked. And I just wanted to know...

What she'd been like…

What she'd wore…

What she'd *smelled like…*

—That last one was weird, and the dragon probably couldn't have described that to me even if he knew. I cleared my throat and tried to clear my thoughts.

Yeah, I knew her.

The dragon nodded. I hung onto every word—

I actually have a pretty vivid memory of her locked away if I could just recall…

He closed his eyes as a system update popped into view.

[SPARO, RED VODYARACKA SKYDRAKE, DRAGON 14: System Searching MRPs To Select Correct Memory…]

An icon I'd never seen before, comprised of a thought bubble outlined in a circle, bobbed in front of him like waiting for him to select it—*was that like an Examination Opportunity? Was that…the memory? Sitting there? Bobbing there right in front of me?* I had to see it. I dove forward—

Whoa, there, Nelly!

The beast extended a huge claw, stopping my advance easily with the blunt side of one talon.

It's mine. You can't just take what you want. That's called rude.

The action was similar to a cat extending a paw, with retracted claws, to nudge something back, but Rainer couldn't hear what was going on. The Nomad leapt into action, his red beard bristling and his axe raised, "You touch her again, *you die, dragon!*"

The dragon snorted, clearly bored of the whole thing.

Call off your dogs. They're getting annoying—

HE was getting annoying… He had a pile of CM Diamonds and a memory of my mom. He had everything I wanted—needed. And, more than anything, I wanted it. I had an idea for how to get them before, what was it…? My mind spun in dizzying circles. The Mask of Magnetism from my inventory! Maybe I could use that to make him hand them over!

I squared my shoulders. I swallowed. I took a deep breath. Here was the part where I got what I wanted or became a roast chicken. …At least no one could say I was acting like one in standing up to this monster.

"Everyone stand down," I stated, staring hard especially at Rainer and Joy. Then, I turned to the dragon. "I—we," I corrected swiftly, stumbling over my own words, "are in need of two more CM Diamonds, so I can activate my Creator Magic. Equip Mask of Magnetism," I murmured, clearing my throat to muffle my words, but the corresponding system alert popped into view.

[System Alert: Object Equipped.]

The eye cutouts of a satin, red mask suddenly covered my vision. Could I do this? Could I make this work? Why was there no saliva in my mouth???

I watched the dragon continue to spin a turquoise CM Diamond between pointed claws, rotating it on the cement floor as his memory of Mom flashed in front of that…

I took a hurried breath. "I want that—" My eyes locked on the CM Diamond, "I want you to give me the CM Diamond and your memory of my mother. I *order* you to give them to me now."

Briiiinnnggg! A ringing noise chimed above my right ear.

And the mask disappeared and, stranger, the Vodyaracka grinned at me—*as much as a dragon can grin, anyway.*

You know…

He quipped slowly, cocking his head and looking, suddenly, sleepy or drunk.

I like you. Not sure why, but I'm in a particularly generous mood all of a sudden. How about I do your ass a favor and give you a CM Diamond, huh? I mean, you can even have this old memory too, if you want. Will that get rid of you all? If I give you those?

[System Reward: Look At You, You Fooled A Dragon! +15 XP, 237/300]

Awesome! I'd fooled him! I quickly dismissed the system pop-up before the beast could see. *The mask had worked!* Jubilant disbelief raced in my chest—through my fingers. *I was going to get the memory of mom and the CM Diamonds!*

"That is very generous of you," I blurted, bowing low and nearly falling over from my sheer excitement. Relief flooded my heart. "We'll take them and go—"

Agreed, then.

The dragon's huge body shifted, scales rustling over the hard floor. And his claws clacked together as he flicked a turquoise Diamond and the memory in my direction. System pop-ups impeded my vision, rapidly, in succession:

[System Reward: Memory Acquired! +75 MRP, 3665/6206, Would You Like To View Memory Now Or Later?]
[Now] [Later]

"Later," I told it—I'd have to view it when I wasn't, say, trying to save our asses and Dad… A second message appeared:

[System Reward: CM DIAMOND Acquired +10 XP, 247/300, Object Will Be Placed In Your Inventory Unless You'd Like To Equip. Would You Like To Equip?]

[Yes] [No]

The important part! The CM Diamonds! No, System, I didn't want to equip yet. But my joy was cut short as my eyes read the alert again.

Wait...One? 'CM Diamond' not 'CM Diamonds'? Not plural? My heart skipped a beat—not in a good way.

Rosabella

Only one CM Diamond? I needed two to activate my CM and progress in the trade so I could free Dad. Two. Not one. Two! I smiled tightly, but I wasn't sure it was convincing; everything inside me was jumping and twisting—

"You were going to give me two CM Diamonds," I said, hoping the power of the mask somehow, still would apply. A lie, I knew it; I wasn't proud of myself. I'd fudged my delivery. I hadn't used the mask right! I hadn't been specific enough with the number of Diamonds! I'd only told the beast to give me the one he'd been playing with.

I most certainly was NOT going to give you two, small one. One Diamond and one memory is the limit of my sensible generosity. Does this look like a charity house?

Ugh! What was it with these dragons! I was tempted to throw a fit right then and there—to throw down my hands and pout like a five-year-old but...

Joy stepped forward, her eyes swishing over my wincing face and the dragon's looming one. She drew her bow and arrow, "I'm gonna just kill him. Someone let me take him out, and we'll grab the pile of Diamonds—"

"Hold up," I told her, extending an arm, "He gave me one, maybe I can—"

"You need two—" Rainer growled,

"I know," I griped. "But—"

But no dragon in their right mind would give you more than one CM Diamond and a memory for FREE. So, aren't I a gem in a pile of shit?!

I frowned at the beast. Was it just me or was the beast clearly patting himself on the back here while also completely pissing me off? I was going to have to go into begging mode and hope this worked…

I cleared my throat and fluttered my eyelashes for my best damsel-in-distress appearance—*how did one use those Baddie Point things?* It didn't feel like I was doing it right—"Listen, we really need two CM Diamonds, any way you could spare another one?"

The dragon didn't look impressed.

I rushed forward, forcing myself to plug any hole the dragon might conjure up; I was not about to let this next rejection squeeze through. "Like I said, I made a trade, and I need to activate my CM to get my dad back. This is really important," I stressed. The truth spilled out in a disorganized-feeling jumble.

Oh, honey, he's not coming back. These assholes didn't tell you that?

I scrunched my face up, feeling confused by the words ringing in my head. *What was the dragon—*

"No, you don't get it," I countered quickly. "It's not about my dad coming back. It's rescuing him. He's actually here in this prison. I made a deal with these guys that I restore your world, and they help me get Dad back—"

Oh man. Oh mannnnn.

The Vodyaracka chuckled lengthily. I stared at him, becoming annoyed and crossing my hands over my chest, "What?"

It's ironic is all. The girl who got kidnapped outta here is gonna come back and save our world? Now? After leaving us in DISASTER for over 10 years?! Now, if that isn't ironic, I don't know what is.

My mind fumbled to understand his words, feeling like an old, lagging VHS tape. What was he talking about—kidnapped? I hadn't even been in this world before. I'd been in New York. ...And I hadn't left anything in disaster! I was in no way tied to this. He was wrong. He was so wrong about me—

"You clearly have no idea what you're talking about," I started, abruptly raising my sword again between us. Maybe I was going to have to fight this brute after all.

Don't I now?

The Vodyaracka crowed, his huge nose nodding up and down, confidently now.

Dragons have this thing called prophesy. ...We know shit.

"You didn't even know who I was when I came in here!" I huffed, feeling like I had a major point...

"You tell us to attack and we're all in behind you," Joy hissed in my ear and, for once, I was glad that they were all there—right behind me. Because, right now, I needed that support. I needed to know that someone or something would catch me if—when—I fell flat on my face.

You can stand here and spout all the nonsense, small one. A sob story, whatever you want.

The beast countered, a tiny fireball spiraling out of its nostril.

But, honestly, don't you have better things to do? You're the daughter of Rosabella the Great. Your dad's death was a terrible tragedy—

That got me.

138

Like a flipped switch. Like a jolt.

"My Dad's alive!" I sputtered. "I'm trying to save him."

No, dear. Your dad is dead. He was a Game Maker too. The Class appointment runs through blood to the eldest child. How can you be the LAST Game Maker if your Dad's alive?

"He's alive," I insisted as outrage suddenly pumped through my veins, "He's imprisoned here in this prison!"

Callen placed a persisting hand on my shoulder, leaning in, "What is he saying?" But I shook him off.

Now, why would we imprison the greatest Game Maker that ever lived? The man we have locked up in here, who you call Dad, is an imposter— a murderer, a traitor and a—

"This is a trick! You're *lying!*" I screamed.

I couldn't listen to it anymore. I couldn't take his erroneous words, the sneer on his lips...his know-it-all attitude. Any of it. And, before, I'd decided to make a decision, I'd made it. I brought my sword down with a hefty war cry of a swing.

A chop.

Metal sliced through scales and flesh. Straight through the Vodyaracka Skydrake's claw.

[SPARO, RED VODYARACKA SKYDRAKE, DRAGON 14: - 2 HP, 217/219]

The huge beast bellowed in rage more than pain. His head reared—

"Attack!" I howled, "Take him fucking down!"

The group's raucous howl of battle echoed in the high-ceiling space as they clamored forward with weapons, but the dragon was faster. He let out a stream of fire in our direction.

Engulfing.

Hot and sizzling on my face. A system update fizzled into view—shit.

[-7 HP, 10/26]

My vision swam. My knees threatened to buckle.

Somewhere in front of me, I heard Joy scream—Rainer, shout.

And I dodged to the side—tripped...bolted.

I stumbled over the thing's thick, swishing tail.

Past razor-sharp talons that reached for me—

Out of the corner of my eye, I saw an arrow fly, embedding in the dragon's shoulder. He wreathed in pain and anger. His lizard-yellow eyes landing on me as he whipped around.

Oh, you've done it now, small one!

He roared.

And I had. I really had.

Because, as I scrambled down the nearest, stone hallway, I saw a locked gate at the end. I catapulted towards it. The bars were freezing on my tugging fingers: strong, resilient.

The stone walls on either side of me were solid—damp and craggy to the touch.

And I turned around.

To see the dragon's enormous head filling the opening of the hall and my friends trapped behind him and a wall of fire.

And I was trapped too—between dragonhead and bars. I was so damn trapped.

Goran – 20 **Minutes Earlier**

I awoke with a start, gasping—feeling the gag cut into the sides of my mouth and tasting blood there.

…My first thought? The realization that my hands were tied against each other in my lap and legs secured with rope to the base of a chair. A folding table plateaued in front of me. My pupils slowly adjusted to the dark, shadowed room. *Was I in a warehouse? …A castle?*

Somergot Prison. The reality dumped on me like a truckload of dirt. *Those Game Warden bastards. Didn't they know their entire Class had been discontinued?*

I pulled against the thick rope across my chest, securing me to the freezing, metal chair, hearing the legs scrape and jump across the concrete floor from the force. But I couldn't go very far with the ledge of the table jutting into my middle.

…My second thought? Rosabella.

Of course, it was Rosabella. But, by the looks of it, the world was currently against us both. *They'd found us. I'd known they were watching. I'd thought I'd had it under control—that she was safe.*

My stomach twisted at the realization that I was wrong. Because Rosie was the furthest she'd ever been from safe now, and I was in no condition to hold the bargaining power to do much about it.

"System, bring up my stats," I commanded, though my voice was completely garbled by the gag in my mouth. I spat it out, waiting to see what I was dealing with.

[System Understands Query...Loading Response...]

Name	Goran	
Class & Level	Prisoner 10	
XP	1041/1100	
MRP	1350/14612	
HP	85/108	
Swag Points	5000	
Armor Class	11/20	
ABILITIES /20		
Strength	+1	12
Agility	+1	12
Endurance	+0	11
Intelligence	+1	13
Awareness	+0	10
Presence	+3	16

Okay, so the prison guards had obviously beaten me around a little bit; my HP was lowered. I must have lost consciousness. What was in my inventory?

"System, inventory?" I inquired. My voice scraped up my throat, hoarse and brittle like it was sore—from shouting? Screaming? I couldn't remember. Had they drugged me so I'd forget? I couldn't remember how low my memory had been before...

[System Understands Query...Loading Response...]

"Display MRP too," I told it, "Compare it to MRP two weeks ago."

[System Understands Queries...Loading Response...]

It amended. I waited for the screen to pop up, swallowing heavily and feeling goose pimples tug every hair on my arms upward from the chill in the dark room. I squinted at the neon system alert when it appeared—*ugh, so bright.* It pierced my pupils.

[System Alert: Per Request, Inventory Opened.]
- **1 Hoodie Sweatshirt**
- **1 Pack Of Gum**
- **1 Broken Shoelace**

Seriously? These assholes were so predictable in taking all my weapons. ...They'd even taken my stat watch and left me with a pack of gum...generous.

"Equip hoodie," I told the system curtly, and warmth enveloped my arms with a comforting softness as the black material of it covered my arms. A host of system updates appeared:

[System Alert: Object Equipped.]
[Current MRP / GORAN, PRISONER 10: 13205/14235]
[System Answer: Current MRP Is 13205, Approximately 2.2% Less Than Two Weeks Ago (13505). Did This Answer Your Question?]
[Yes] [No]

"Yes," I grumbled. They had fucked with my memory. I wasn't going to let them forget it anytime soon.

Memory.

Rosabella's memory! Rosabella! Maybe they'd already gotten to her—altered her MRP! If she remembered, she'd be scarred for life— Fear flashed through me, setting my nerves ablaze with hasty unease. "System, bring up Rosabella's current MRP—hurry," I demanded.

[System Understands Query...Loading Response Double Time...]
[Current MRP / ROSABELLA, GAME MAKER 3: 3665/6206]

The breath went out of me—her memory was still significantly lower, though higher than it'd been at when we were in New York. *It was okay...for right now. But she'd Leveled Up to L3? Hmmm...unpredictable. I had to get her out of here.* I yanked on my restraints. *If I could just—*

"Look who's awake. I do believe we've been introduced."

I blinked into the dim room, watching a darkened figure step out of the shadows, but not exactly into the light. I recognized his voice and broad shoulders even through the body armor he wore: the clean-cut, red beard...the bald head... It all made sense now. He was always one for theatrics.

I spat the gag out of my mouth. Whoever had tightened it didn't know what they were doing—typical of this place.

"Demetrius," I scoffed, "Looks like power has been treating you well. What'd you do with my stat watch? Gonna sell it so you can afford to buy your girl some lingerie?"

I said it just to get under his skin. I knew he was a goodie-two-shoes-justice boy—a real tool most days. That's why he'd turned me in years ago. ...And when I'd offered to reward him grandly. It was a shame, really.

The man looked clean—that was the best way to describe it. In this sordid, grimy room, his pale skin was spotless: no bags under his eyes or dirt under his nails...a sword too big for him and probably just for show on his belt... He screamed 'out-of-place' and 'soft'. Probably like his big-boy hands. It shouldn't have been a surprise. It was just like he'd always been.

I watched his left eye squint, bulging slightly with annoyance at my words like I'd struck that nerve I'd been fishing for. His air of overdone moral compass still stunk like a hyena's ass. Loathing spiraled up within me like the bile I could taste at the back of my throat. *This man made our lives miserable, Rosie. He'd made Rosabella's*

*life miserable. We could have had it all, but he'd stood in the way.
...Hmmm. I supposed bygones were not bygone after all...*

"Goran," Demetrius spat back, his right, red eyebrow arching. *What did this prick have to say in defense of himself? What could he say? I'd evaded them for years. I'd kept Rosabella safe.*

"I suppose you still aren't sorry for your actions," the man goaded. His face hardened to granite, "I loved Ford like a brother—"

"But you weren't..." I hissed back, through my suddenly clenched teeth, "...You weren't his brother."

Demetrius swallowed his eyes glassy and hard, "No. ...But I wasn't the one who killed him either." His crow-black eyes sparkled with accusation. "That was all *you,* Goran," he snapped.

And something broke inside of me—like a wood pencil.

No effort—straight in half.

Rage crashed over my head.

Lies.

[System Reward: Rage Promotion—]

An electronic error message sounded.

[System Error: Rage Promotion Cannot Be Initiated When Restrained And Class = 'Prisoner'. Reward Disabled.]

Rage promotion or not, I lunged for the guy. *They didn't understand—no one understood! What I did. For Rosabella—for her mother!* They'd twisted it all—made me into a monster meant to be trapped in these restraints, but I wasn't. I knew Rosie'd see the lies for what they were if only I could find her.

The rope around my wrists and the table, now pushing into my middle, restricted my movements. The chair could only go so far. But it wasn't far enough to teach the man's smirking face the lesson he needed—

With a shove, I tried to grab for him—

The angle was too much.

I miscalculated.

I fell.

My cheek plastered against the freezing stone floor, nearly in a water puddle. … *This was what I'd been reduced to? This is what they'd reduced us to?* I hoped Rosabella was in better company.

The weight of the chair on my back and the way it pressed my chest to the floor constricted my breathing. I glowered at the man as his huge boots took two steps towards me. He lifted the sole of his boot to press down on my face. The plastic and dirt clinging there dug into my flesh—

[-3 HP, 82/108]

You filth. You absolute swine.

"What have you done with her?" I gasped as he forced his foot down again, pain flaring in my jaw—would he break it?

[-3 HP, 79/108]

But I was determined. "What have you done with Rosie?" I rasped out.

"She's about as far away from you as she can get, so that's a positive," sneered the man overhead.

"I need to see her," I snarled from under his sole, feeling my mouth distort with the desperate plea. Sweat broke out on my forehead at the thought of Rosabella locked up or as broken as I felt. "I need to know you're not lying—"

"Oh, you mean like how we needed to know you weren't lying once upon a time, and you didn't even do us the service to let us know our leader was dead—" His voice broke.

"Would you just listen to me?!" I raged.

I lost it. I admit it; I lost it at the incompetence of the asshole and the fact that I didn't know where Rosabella was or if she was still in one piece. I screamed at the man. My face shook even under the weight of his shoe. And I wrenched my chin out from under him, seething at his huge shadow above, nearly blocking out the one lightbulb hanging in the room. *I was a failure. I'd failed in protecting Rosabella—my last promise to her mother...*

"Show me proof that she's okay," I yelled, "Come on, Demetrius! You know what she means to me!"

"I can't—" he complained.

But I could see through the act. It was my guess, from the pristine state of his clothes, that he still had sentry access, if not more.

"You *can*," I growled, "I know you have the list. Show me. You owe me at least that."

Luckily, the guy had always been a little more than susceptible to following angry orders...and giving away his cards. I watched the man's expression weaken and hedge with the uncomfortable itch of making a decision.

"Let's get one thing straight, I don't owe you anything," he muttered, spitting on the floor. But he winced; his eyes darted around the room, checking to make sure the metal door behind him was sealed before his fingers swiped horizontally in the air and the chart I'd asked for appeared:

SENTRY LOCATOR MAP

GAMER TAG:	LOCATION:
Goran, Prisoner 10	Holding Room 1 - L2
Ratsby, Prisoner 7	Holding Room 2 - L2
Tony, Prisoner 13	Holding Room 3 - L2
Holten, Prison Guard 8	Door of Holding Room 1 - L2
Jack, Prison Guard 11	Door of Holding Room 1 - L2
Mike, Prison Guard	Control Room - L2
Joey, Prison Guard 9	Control Room - L2

My heart rammed even more rapidly against my chest as my eyes scanned the names and locations. I swiped quickly down the list, looking for Rosabella's name till…

I found it.

ROSABELLA, GAME MAKER 3 – Entry Room – Level 1

She was here? Only just a level below this floor?

…Two guards at the door…

Two more down the hall… I quickly made a mental note of their positions. But hope leapt in my chest. Rosabella had given me hope…and a reason to get out of here.

"You lied to me," I snapped, addressing Demetrius to allow for some time to think my plan over, "You said Rosie was far away."

"You don't have much bargaining power here," the man retorted back, righting the chair I was tied to with a sweeping motion of his arm and pushing my legs back under the table where I'd started. He scowled down at me, "I showed you she's alive, that's all I'm willing to do for scum of your likes. Drop the pathetic act. Eat your food here, mind your manners and, maybe, you'll get out in a lifetime—"

I laughed—a hollow sound.

Brimming up from my core.

It was funny. It was funny that, after growing up together and seeing The Game through similar eyes, that he still had no fucking idea of how anything worked. I was sure they already had my execution on the books. They probably had it dated the second they wrapped rope around my arms.

"You don't believe that, do you?" I scoffed.

The man's eyes constricted. Maybe he did. Maybe he really did. Luckily, for Rosabella, I knew the truth. And I was going to get her out of here no matter what it took.

A plan formed, solidifying in my mind as I rubbed the rope of my wrist restraints against the sharp, metal underside of the table. I felt the thick fabric of them start to split as confirmation of that flashed numerically in front of my nose:

[ROPE, L2 OBJECT: -3 Integrity, 9/12]

I rubbed faster, gritting my teeth and hoping Demetrius wouldn't notice if the numbers kept popping up. *System, make prompts related to the rope only visible to me,* I told it internally.

[System Understands Command. System Prompts Related To Rope Are Now Only Visible To GORAN, PRISONER 10]

Good. …Now, if I was going to pull this off, I needed a ploy…

"Come here," I told the guard. I kept my voice light and casual, but he was resistant to it; I could see it. He shook his head, "No."

"Demetrius," I cooed, really working the act; I even smiled, "We were old friends—you remember."

"I told you," he snarled back, his chin quivering. "I remember Ford."

Touche.

"I do too"—I decided to go off-script a little. Like a professional. …And, for a minute, I almost believed it myself. I let my eyes swim with memories and regrets. …Memories of my kid brother's laughter. …That look he'd get in his eyes running through the woods…The way his hair blew up in the wind…and the way he'd slap my hands away from animals, taking such care to scoop them up and cradle them, even the gross slug and frog ones, in his hands when he knew I had far more fun seeing what they'd do if I threw them—

"He was a prince of a man," I started, nodding. "He really was—"

"A king," Demetrius interjected, lifting his chin with glowing, loyal eyes.

I rubbed further at the rope, smiling a little as I watched the Object Integrity fall again:

[ROPE, L2 OBJECT: -5 Integrity, 4/12]

"Sure," I amended, shrugging.

"But he had a fatal flaw," I purposefully lowered my voice. "He had *one thing* that led his position to fail. *One thing* he couldn't master..." My jaw tightened, remembering.

Dry.

"I'll tell you," I nodded at the man who now had wide eyes, watching me. I felt the rope cuffs break off my wrists under the table...

[ROPE, L2 OBJECT: -4 Integrity, 0/12]

"I'll tell you right now," I promised, "I'll spill it all, so you don't have to make the same mistake."

The man was hooked now; I could see it in his eyes. All he'd ever wanted was to be acknowledged—to be seen as powerful...to be loved by the people who'd never given two shits about him. He leaned forward.

I gestured, "Come here—"

Like I was going to whisper it in his ear. *Just a little closer—there.* *BANG!*

I moved—lightening fast.

Bringing my hands up and his head down—smashing his skull on the corner of the table.

Practice paid off. The man crumpled beneath my hands like spaghetti; his despondent face drooped to the ground. Blood poured out of a broken nose as system updates bounced into view over both our heads.

[DEMETRIUS, PRISON GUARD 12: -120 HP, 6/126]
[System Reward: One Hell Of A Hit +30 Swag Points, 5030]

Demetrius should have already known the answer to my brother's fatal flaw; everyone else in this place did.

"*It's me,*" I crowed gleefully to the silent watching walls. *I'd, single-handedly, been the downfall of my esteemed brother.*

Demitrius's unconscious body was close enough to lean towards. I reached down, grabbed a handful of his shirt and yanked his heavy frame towards me to grasp the fancy sword at his belt. My fingers wrapped expertly around the blade's handle…

[System Alert: FANCY SHOW SWORD Acquired +10 XP, 1051/1100. Object Will Be Placed In Your Inventory Unless You'd Like to Equip. Would You Like To Equip?]
[Yes] [No]

"Yes," I told it.

[System Alert: Weapon Equipped, +25 Swag Points, 5055]

Object:	Fancy Show Sword
Required Class & Level For Use:	None
Description:	This Thing Sure Has The Gems & Carvings, But The Blade Looks Heavy & Unwieldy. Surely, A Trained Welder Didn't Make This...
Augment Capacities:	-1 Strength
Swag Points:	+25

Great, I'd been far too correct about the quality of this sword, but it'd do the trick for now... Two, swift saws and the rope fell off my ankles too.

[ROPE, L2 OBJECT: -12 Integrity, 0/12]
[System Reward: Makin' Escaping Bonds Look Easy +15 XP, 1066/1100]

I chuckled for a minute at the system message. *I still got +25 XP for this shit? I'd done it too many times to count.* I took a minute to rub at the raw, red skin of my wrists before standing and facing the one door out of here.

Hold up. I looked down at the unconscious man's body, noticing a plain dagger on his belt that I hadn't seen before.

[System Alert: LEATHER-WRAPPED HANDLE DAGGER Acquired +10 XP, 1076/1100. Object Will Be Placed In Your Inventory Unless You'd Like to Equip. Would You Like To Equip?]
[Yes] [No]

I let the flashy sword clatter to the concrete floor. On second thought, the thing was an absolute piece of junk.

[System Alert: Object Discarded.]

"Yes, equip the dagger," I commanded and the blade appeared, snug in my fist.

[System Alert: Weapon Equipped.]

Object:	Leather-Wrapped Handle Dagger
Required Class & Level For Use:	None
Description:	Basic L1 Weapon. A Bit of Metal, Wood & Leather Put Together. Did A Caveman Create This?

Augment Capacities: +1 Strength
Baddie Points: +0

I smiled looking at the stats; the weapon was simple and functional—like me. Like the two of us had a common goal with a common approach.

And I stepped towards the door out of here.

This had to work; I had to make this work.

I had to get to Rosabella before they did.

Goran

The two guards at the doorway were child's play—insulting, really. *Had this world already forgotten who they were dealing with?*

[HOLTEN, PRISON GUARD 8: -81 HP, 0/81]
[JACK, PRISON GUARD 11: -108 HP, 0/108]
[System Reward: 2 PRISON GUARDS Eliminated, 2000
More To Go... Just Kidding, +10 XP, 1086/1100]

Man, at this rate, I was going to Level Up before I even got down the hall. I wiped the blood-stained dagger blade I'd swiped from Demetrius on the thick fabric of my jeans, leaving a maroon streak behind…as well as two bodies propped up on the walls where they'd slumped as crimson rivulets ran down from slits at their throats. *I didn't want to do that. I only did it for Rosie. I only did it for her.* An Examination Opportunity bobbed over one of the guards' pockets.

"Examine," I murmured, watching as a system update popped into view.

[System Query Examined... +1 XP, 1087/1100]
[Looking Closer, You Realize There's Some Sort Of Scroll
On The Guard's Belt. Would You Like To Take It?]
[Yes] [No]

Hell yes. I selected affirmative without a second thought. Running through these system prompts felt so natural—like the one thing I was okay with remembering about my childhood.

[System Alert: PRISON MAP Acquired +10 XP, 1097/1100.
Object Will Be Placed In Your Inventory Unless You'd
Like To Use. Would You Like To Use?]
[Yes] [No]

Yes, thanks very much. A parchment rolled out before me in the air. Dark lines and angles clearly showed the walls of the prison. A room in the center of this floor, the second level, was labeled 'Control Room'. *Bull-yah. I was going to need to turn off the cameras so that no one saw my escape, but I, also, might need to unlock some doors to get to Rosabella...*

"System, show me where Rosie is," I dictated. *Demetrius's list had told me she was in the Gate A entrance room, but where the fuck was that on here?*

[System Understands Query...Loading Response...]
[System Answer: System Has Labeled ROSABELLA,
GAME MAKER 3's Location On The PRISON MAP With A
Red Dot.]

Thank you, you good-for-nothing system. Well, maybe it'd been good for that. My eyes swept to the maroon marker, tracing my path to her: downstairs...to the left. I had to get to that control room first...

I dismissed the map and slipped silently down the hall. I'd become good at silent—unnoticed. Rosabella and I did it together for years in New York City. It was an easy dance: keep your head down, keep your hood up, no eye contact, no remembrance to be tracked by.

I'd taught Rosie to blend, but neither one of us could blend here—not in The Game. It was why I was trying to keep her away—keep her safe. I pulled the edges of my dark hoodie even more securely over my face to shadow it. This was not ideal. I'd already passed two security cameras on the way down the second-floor hallway. Rosabella was on the first level. If they knew she was with me on the way out, they'd stop at no lengths to get her back. They needed her, but, more excruciatingly, they hated me. If I had any chance of keeping Rosie away and safe, I needed to make sure they didn't see us leave together. Reaching the control room to switch off the cameras was of utmost importance.

My high-top sneakers were quick over the concrete floor. The prison guards hadn't even had the decency to let me change; I was still in my Earth, street clothes. Again, hardly ideal. But what about this situation was?

I rounded the corner. The control room should be right—

I nearly passed it.

A row of windows.

I hastily ducked so the prison guards there didn't see. Even with my training, my heart rammed in my ears, echoing each ragged push of breath. God, Rosie. I wish they weren't making me do this.

I wrapped my fingers more firmly around the knife in my crouched position, running the numbers and the plan through my head like watching the scene from an action movie before it started: two more prison guards in the control room…disable the cameras, unlock any doors in the hallway, get to Rosie. Simple, solid, secure.

I didn't waste time; Rosabella might not have it. I pounced.

'Be like a panther,' my fighting instructor used to say to my brother and me when we were young, 'Never let them see the attack.' And they didn't.

Two slashes of the knife and the guards in the control room were on their knees too. …The way this entire place should have been years ago.

[MIKE, PRISON GUARD 7: -72 HP, 0/72]

[JOEY, PRISON GUARD 9: -85 HP, 0/90]
[System Reward: Hard Hitter! 2 PRISON GUARDS
Eliminated, +30 XP, 1127/1200]

The world spun in slow motion. A whirlwind of green plus marks coursed around me, tinting my eyesight army green. *I'd been right. I hadn't even gone down the hall and had already Leveled Up. This game was so predictable.*

[System Alert: ***Congratulations, You've Advanced To
Level 11!***]

Name	Goran
Class & Level	Prisoner 11
XP	1127/1200
MRP	13505/14235
HP	88/117
Swag Points	5055
Armor Class	11/20
ABILITIES /20	
Strength	+1 12
Agility	+1 12
Endurance	+0 11
Intelligence	+1 13
Awareness	+0 10
Presence	+3 16

**[+9 HP & HP Extended By 9, 88/117. You've Been Awarded
+2 Ability Points. Please Select Which Ability You'd Like
To Increase.]**

This same shit? A laugh spurted out of my throat in a sharp bark. No thank you. …But I wondered if that cheat code from all those years back still worked…

I bit the inside of my lip. "System, bring up input interface and type ZYZYSSA555." I made sure to put clear emphasis on every syllable, my tongue working off muscle memory. It'd been my favorite cheat as a kid—my one way to get back and manipulate the nanny or my brother. With the cheat code, you could forfeit your Level Up ability points and decide to decrease the memory of another Gamer. Memory was a good one to alter because people rarely ever monitored it as closely as their Abilities…plus, then the nanny would conveniently forget whatever mischief of the day I'd been up to…

[System Understands Query…Loading Response…]
[System Input: ZYZYSSA555. Enter?]
[Yes] [No]

I held my breath as I hit 'yes', watching the neon letters with fierce intensity. *Would this work?*

[System Alert: Cheat Code FOGGY REVENGE Validated.
FOGGY REVENGE: Upon Use Of The Cheat Code
ZYZYSSA555, The Gamer Agrees To Forfeit Any And All
Level Up Benefits. Instead, They Will Have The Power To
Decrease Another Gamer's MRP By 500. Please Indicate
Which Gamer You Would Like To Select.]

A thrill hummed through my bones. It'd worked! I was back! I had my control back! Now, I could have Rosie back too.

"Rosabella," I told the system. "I select Rosabella."

[System Understands Query…Loading Response…]
[System Alert: ROSABELLA, GAME MAKER 3's MRP -500,
3165/6206]

And a slow smile spread over my lips. Rosie didn't know how I was saving her each and every day—what I was doing for her constantly. Now, I just had to physically save her…

The pause from the Level Up dissipated. My eyes quickly scanned the windowed room—no more guards, only computer screens, buzzing and crackling in a wall full of squares, showing footage of every inch of the prison—a thousand, shadowy hallways. Concrete floors, bare walls and an entire panel of buttons spread before me...some red lights, some keyboard keys, some levers... Other than a few, neglected, black office swivel chairs and the bodies now dripping red onto the floor, the room was empty. My eyes darted over the controls, attempting to decide which to press.

I recognized the map of the prison at the center of one of the panels, showing green-lighted lines for open doors and red-lit lines for closed ones. I quickly did the mental gymnastics to identify which locked doors I needed to open to get to Rosie. A few key presses and I had the entire way downstairs unlocked.

I turned to leave the room, but a thought kept bugging me—niggling at my brain like a strong nudge I couldn't shake off.

...And it had to do with the row of red-lit lines throbbing on the whole left wing of the prison.

Pulsing.

Like those lines were waiting for death itself just like the prisoners trapped inside. There were rows of inmates trapped there—like I had been—in cells. And I couldn't let it go—I couldn't not do something when this world had so terribly screwed me and Rosie over. If anyone knew the evil that The Game was capable of, it was me. And, yet, the tables had turned. And I had the power to do something about it...

And, so, I turned back around.

And my fingers found the control for the prison cells, clacking over the keys.

And I set every one of those lucky bastards free. Hell yeah.

[Prison Locks Disengaged – Area 1A]
[Prison Locks Disengaged – Area 1B]
[Prison Locks Disengaged – Block 2A]
[Prison Locks Disengaged – Block 2B]
[Prison Locks Disengaged – Block 1C]

…Let them call me a freaking traitor now—not to those people. Not when I'd just saved their sorry-ass lives.

I let a sly smile spread over my face as I pivoted to the television screens on the wall, watching the bars slide up on every cell in the damn place. The prisoner's faces distorted in disbelief and, then, joy. Reaching hands became running masses… God, it felt good to play God for a second.

But I heard a roar.

My head snapped to a monitoring screen in the top, right, corner. The damn dragon; I'd forgotten about the damn dragon guard—

My heart sunk. My stomach wrenched.

Because I watched its red, rearing head and gnashing teeth. I watched it spewing fire—a hailstorm of climbing flames—

As a small silhouette darted into a tunnel with a locked door.

Oh God, it was Rosie! She was—

Cornered.

Goran

I'd never lunged for controls quicker. My eyes darted over the labels till I found the one I needed, and I switched the door open—

But it was too late. She'd already tried tugging on the door and thought it was locked.

…All as the dragon moved closer—its disgusting nose snapping only inches away from my baby girl—

Panic consumed me.

Raw.

Real.

NO! That creature couldn't kill her. I wouldn't let it happen! I'd promised—

Heart in throat, I raced down the hall, praying with everything in me that I wouldn't be too late. My feet pounded over the concrete floor, skidding as I rounded the corner. *Thank God for 11 Endurance—*

I tore down the stairs, taking three at a time.

I leapt towards the metal-bar door that Rosie was trapped against—

I heaved all my weight against it—

My breath rang in my ears. It felt like every motion was slow motion—

Rosie cowered behind the door there, her eyes closed like she'd accepted her fate against this dragon—like she'd already processed and accepted that she was going to die. *No.*

The stink of dragon and burnt flesh stung at my nostrils. *He'd hurt her.* His fire had engulfed part of her armor, although she'd stamped it out. Her cheeks were dirt-smudged and her hair, unruly like when she used to come back from the park as a child…

And the beast was still there, snarling at both of us in the doorway—its huge snout filled it. Smoke curled out of its nostrils, choking me—making Rosie cough and gag.

How the fuck was I going to kill this thing? I bit down on my lip. *I was going to have to do something.* Arrows flew at us from the other side of a wall of fire, but they bounced off on the walls around us without much damage to the beast at all. *Looked like we were on our own with this one…*

Suddenly, a war cry bellowed from behind me—*what?* I turned, but not fast enough—

A million bodies pushed through the door, jostling around Rosie and I—*the prisoners I'd set free! All escaping at once! This was exactly the distraction I needed!*

I clutched Rosie to my body, holding her there, finally safe. I felt her warm breath on my chest, felt her soft hair on my cheek. Finally *okay* as long as she was with me. A million arms and legs raced past us like the salvation we deserved after all this time, pushing against us—past us—flooding out the doorway, towards the dragon like a crowd of unafraid heathens.

But the beast wasn't about to surrender. The thing shrieked, shaking the hallway with its pure fury and loosing a volley of fire directly at us all. A million decreasing stat points popped, neon, into view, but ours were the largest, flashing so close to my face:

[ROSABELLA, GAME MAKER 3: -5 HP, 5/26]

Screams echoed in the cramped space.

Bodies burned.

The smell, sickening.

Crashing.

Hair sizzling.

Arms flailing and bumping and shoving—a million hands and shoulders. It was stifling. I couldn't breathe from the stink of fear and sweat. I gripped Rosie tighter. I shoved against the crowd harder—against these fiends that I'd unleashed. They were dying around us—screeching, moaning, running. *I had to get Rosabella out of here.*

I yanked her out of the hallway enclosure. I tripped over the dragon's tail but pulled the girl with me. Her despondent head lulled forward. Her creamy skin was ashen against the smoke in the room. *I was going to kill the beast that did this to Rosie—maybe not today but I swore it.*

The dragon thrashed, bellowing overhead in fury. Huge talons swiped towards us, shaking the earth.

More fire.

Rosie caught like a burnt offering although I tried to get her out of the way—

[ROSABELLA, GAME MAKER 3: -3 HP, 2/26]
[-3 HP, 80/108]

And I screamed.

In rage.

And I picked her up, still burning, in my arms. I leapt for the door out of there—

I knew it was open.

"*Stop!*" I heard a woman cry somewhere behind me. I turned to see a flash of pink-hair, but there was no way I was stopping for anyone.

We burst forth into the morning that wouldn't have been this pretty if it'd known the slaughter that would ensue.

…Bodies falling into the moat. *The moat around the prison!*

Rosabella was still burning. *My baby was burning;* I could smell it.

[ROSABELLA, GAME MAKER 3: -1 HP, 1/26]

Her hair blew over my face, ensnaring my vision as I struggled to read the neon popup, but the cattails and lily pads of the moat were still visible. *Her HP was still decreasing? She must still be burning; I had to save her.*

And, so, I ran, carrying her—my little girl.

Into the water.

Full speed.

The murky, filthy waves slapped against my sides and arms and soaked into my jeans, making each step heavier. And Rosie thrashed for a moment against my movements; she resisted me. But the cool water flowed over her limbs, putting out the fire. And I watched her face smooth over like the waves: white, hanging on by a thread.

But, still, okay again—no more decreasing HP. A sigh of relief rushed over my heart. *Thank God, she was okay again.*

[System Reward: Saved A Damsel In Distress, +40 XP, 1167/1200]

Breathing heavy, I swiped the update out of view. I tugged us out of the water; Rosie was heavier with her armor and hair soaked, but the peace on her face was worth it. *I'd gotten there just in time.* I sloshed onto shore, heaving us both upwards and into the grass. *Where could we run, Rosie, where they wouldn't follow us? Where could we hide so they'd never find us? …Actually, I thought I knew.*

And I shouldered the girl like I'd shouldered the burden of who she was for her entire life. And her eyes sunk shut as she clutched at my neck, too weak to talk.

Because she knew home when she saw it; she knew 'safe'. *Rosie was safe with me.*

***

I knew the perfect hiding spot. It may have led me to tramp all the way through these woods to get there, but I knew the place. Rosie's frail body, even though it was relatively light, was getting heavy in my arms after the length of the trek. Even though my stats were pretty well endowed for a man of my age, my HP kept slinking down more than I would care for as thorns snagged at my ankles, brush scrapped across my face and the never-ending forest continued as my arms strained to carry the girl.

[-1 HP, 79/108]

There it was again. I cursed the pop-up as it engulfed my vision. I wanted to save the health pack I remembered storing in the safe spot for Rosie, not myself. *That pack was for her once I got her there.*

I gritted my teeth, hoisting her body up, once more, in my arms. It wasn't much further; *I hoped she could hold on. She had to hold on. To be honest...I was scared for her.* Rosie's face was frighteningly pale, nearly see-through like I could view every green and blue vein working to keep her body alive where the burns didn't cover.

Bubbling.

Boiling burns, red and pussing.

Angry.

Her forehead was slick with sweat, caking strands of her hair to her cheeks and neck...And I swore she was shivering, her chin chattering up and down as I walked. *Look what they did to her.* Each of her shallow, shuttering breaths made me hate myself. *Why couldn't I have run faster—gotten there sooner? Why couldn't I have saved her from all this pain?*

But I knew that, in reality, I should hate *them. This world did this to Rosie—The Game. I would kill that dragon personally. I would if I had anything to say about it.*

"Water," Rosie's chapped lips parted to whisper; I had to strain to hear it.

Of course.

Water. Of course, she was thirsty after nearly burning alive. I would get her water just as soon as I laid her head down to rest somewhere safe— somewhere they couldn't track us and take her.

The willow tree was where I remembered it—its sagging branches even larger than before, after all these years, laden with the weight of its own wispy greenery. Years ago, I used to admire the look of it...like a wise grandfather sitting amidst egotistical evergreens pointing up at the sky and not much else. But, now, it just looked like a tree and a sigh of relief, because it was shelter for us.

My sneakers wove over the tree's massive root system—gnarled, shooting branches tangling the dense grass like the threads of a basket. I was careful not to trip over them as I made my way to the glitch; I didn't want to jostle Rosie.

"Just a little longer," I told the girl, whispering into her hair. "Hold on."

And I swore I saw her eyelids flutter in recognition.

Still holding her, I angled my body at the wall of the landscape behind the tree. I watched The Game flicker as I tried to walk forward; the programing ended here. I had to set Rosie on the ground for the next part. I carefully laid her in the lush grass, reaching in its matted tangles to find the handle for the trap door. My fingers wrapped around smooth wood. *Ah ha! Success!* I'd found it. A system update fizzled into view:

[System Alert: This Is A Restricted Access Area.]

It made me smile to see that Rosie's mother's privacy code still worked.

"System, input a password," I told it, softly, remembering, "Banana." I remembered her brunette head tilting back in laughter when she'd set that passcode—Rosabella's mother. It made my throat raw.

[System Alert: Password 'Banana' Accepted.]

A click sounded. I swung the wood trapdoor open, watching as the ground glitched into a square of darkness where the door opened. And the ladder was still there; Rosie's mom built it back when this was our spot. *That girl could make anything.*

I heaved Rosie back into my arms and took the ladder down with slow, calculated movements:

One foot down one rung. The raw rope scratched my palm that clutched at it.

One more step.

Then, another.

My arms were nearly aching—shaking—from the girl's weight when I reached the concrete floor below. I fumbled in the dark, straining with everything in me to reach for the light switch that I knew was on this side—

[-1 HP, 78/108]

Damn it! I shouldn't be losing HP for simply carrying a girl around and reaching for a switch!

I found the switch. Low light flickered to life, flooding the dark bunker. It was really just a concrete-walled room, a place Rosie's mother created for us to hide when we were little. But it'd more than do. Even back then, we'd stocked it with supplies in case of an emergency: a queen-sized bed made with extra blankets and leaning to one side due to a broken leg in the back...shelving stacked with food...a table that I'd stolen from one of the extra rooms when I was younger and two, wobbling, non-matching chairs. I remembered the place...exactly as I'd left it when I'd last lived there with Rosie as the entire Game world searched for us like hounds above ground.

I brushed a strand of brown hair off Rosie's forehead as I propped her up against me. She'd been too small to even write her name back then. And I'd cared for her. I'd made sure she survived. Just like I'd promised her mother.

...It was colder down here than I remembered. The stagnant air smelled stale and of dampness. But that didn't concern me now. Only Rosie did. I rushed to lay her down on the bed, taking care to place her head on the makeshift, square pillow. Her cheeks looked shallow. I needed to hurry.

The health pack was where I'd left it on top of the nearby bookcase. I easily reached to grab it from its hidden location, my fingers wrapping around the leather.

[System Alert: SMALL HEALTH PACK Acquired, +10 HP 1177/1200. Object Will Be Placed In Your Inventory Unless You'd Like to Use. Would You Like To Use?]
[Yes] [No]

"Apply to Rosabella," I told the system.

[System Understands Query...Applying SMALL HEALTH PACK To ROSABELLA, GAME MAKER 3...]

An electronic beep sounded as another system alert came up.

[+12 HP Available Or +500 MRP. Please Select Which Option You Prefer.]
[+12 HP] [+500 MRP]

The HP. I made sure I checked twice before selecting it. I didn't want to accidently hit the MRP and give her memory back...

[ROSABELLA, GAME MAKER 3: System Alert: SMALL HEALTH PACK Used. +12 HP, 13/26]

I squinted at the numbers floating near the girl's head. Much repaired from before though not even close to perfect. It'd have to do for now.

I watched color flood into Rosabella's face and most of the boils and redness on her skin dissipate. Her breathing steadied, and, almost as though the girl was an extension of myself, my breathing steadied too. Thank whatever God there was. Thank God, she was okay.

Tears welled up in my eyes just looking at her laying there with her brown hair splayed out around her. I did it. I did okay. Rosie's eyelids fluttered open like a lost princess surrounded by a world of dwarves. I watched her forehead crease as she noticed her surroundings and the dark, close ceiling. Her eyes filled with confusion till she saw me. She tried a thin smile, but I could see she was worried still.

"You're safe, Rosie," I murmured, smoothing back her hair, "You're gonna be okay."

She nodded like she knew I was right. Of course, I was right; I'd never led her wrong before. But her eyebrows creased again, and she opened pale lips in confusion. "Tell me about Mom," she whispered.

My heart clenched—stopped. A request. Her only request, and I couldn't honor it? I bit down on my lip to keep an angry retort from slipping out. I shouldn't be mad at her; they'd messed with her mind. They'd done this to her. Those discontinued Game Wardens had already pitted her against me.

"Rest, dear," I urged her. "Your body needs rest."

It was my answer to the question I wouldn't—I couldn't—answer. I couldn't talk about her mother. It would bring me too much pain. I'd drank those memories away and, then, contacted a Witch to restore my MRP, and, every day, I wished that Rosie never had to relive those spiraling thoughts—playing over and over in my head like a merry go round of horses that I knew were all dead, but that I wanted more than anything to be alive again, brightly-painted and vivid again...

Rosie's eyes fell closed, and her face smoothed once again with the peace of sleep.

The mattress creaked as I moved to reach for a jug of water and a washcloth.

The fabric was soft on my fingertips as I nudged enough water out of the clear jug and onto its fibers. I hastily retook my place on the edge of the bed, careful not to cause too much movement and wake the girl. Tenderly, I traced the burns on one of her arms, trying to get the dirt out so they'd heal. I did this not because I had to—because I wanted to. Rosie was everything to me, whether she knew it or not.

But the simple movement of washing her wounds let my mind wander to a place I'd rather it didn't. Before I could stop the movement, my mind focused on the one person I tried to keep it off: her mother.

[System Searching MRPs To Select & Display Correct Memory...]

No, no I didn't want to go there! I swiped away the words.

"Cancel," I muttered softly enough not to wake Rosie. Her mother... she'd been a beautiful human. She was called 'Rosabella the Great' for a reason; the people loved her. I couldn't talk about her, and it'd be too painful to experience the system memory, but I could think about her. My throat burned, thick even just with remembering her face. She'd loved me best—I knew it. I knew she loved me best. Her voice was a birdsong and her eyes, stars. We were friends all through childhood; I'd had the biggest crush that only rolled into adulthood. That night when I'd first kissed her and Ford didn't know…it was magical.

[System Searching MRPs To Select & Display Correct Memory...]

Well…maybe, I could go there…An electronic beep sounded.

Rosabella The Great's eyes sparkled, reflecting the moonlight under the willow tree. The tendrils of the leaves seemed to weave in with her hair.

We'd been whispering; her face was so close…her lips.

She'd reached up to brush something out of my hair, and her soft fingers lingered there.

God, I wanted her. I leaned in, and she was everything I'd expected: warm, plump lips and the smell of vanilla and lavender.

She'd whispered, our foreheads touching in the dark—

I yanked myself back from the memory, breathless—no, I wouldn't remember what she'd whispered. The words had stung me for an eternity.

…But I'd remember the day Rosie was born.

[System Searching MRPs To Select & Display Correct Memory...]

Again? I wanted to resist the system, but a strong pull coaxed me in.

Rosabella cradled Rosie, peering down lovingly at her. She waved me forward, from the back of the room, insisting that I held her.

And she handed me her, as much baby as there was blankets around her tiny form.

And Rosie was so small and soft in my hands.

And warm.

I hugged her against my chest, knowing she was the perfect daughter.

"Never let anything happen to her—vow to me," Rosabella the Great's eyes were serious, even during this joyful time, as they looked up into mine.

"I promise," I pledged as the covenant came up between us. [Covenant Sealed]

The memory spat me back out, leaving me teetering backwards and off balance. *I'd tried my best to always live up to that vow. God, that day had been so long ago…*And, suddenly, an idea dawned on me—a remembering: *tomorrow was Rosie's birthday. A special day.*

I wouldn't let her forget how special it was. I'd make her something—I'd make the day special. So, when she opened her eyes, she'd know how loved she was.

How much I loved her.

She'd open her eyes, and she'd remember that love. *I'd do this for her.*

And, instantly, my mind spun with a million ideas. *She'd need something to remind her of home. And she'd need a cake, of course. I could make her one if only…*

My eyes flickered to the trapdoor above us. *Would she be safe here while I got what I needed and swept away any traces of the glitch so our pursuers couldn't find us?* My eyes darted to her despondent form still asleep beside me on the bed.

Yes. This was a grand idea.

She would love it. She and I would be safe here together, and she would have the best birthday I could give her in this place.

I moved quickly—quietly. I grabbed my knife and backpack from the wall and crept silently towards the ladder upward.

My steps on the rope were slow and careful. I heaved the trapdoor open, excitement replacing adrenaline in my sore muscles. Rosie was going to love this and, maybe, it'd remind her of how much she loved me.

I snapped the trapdoor into place behind me and turned around, quickly threading a lock through the door's handle and into the ground where I remembered steel was bolted below. I turned the key in the lock, tugging on it to make sure it was secure.

All for Rosie.

Anything to keep her safe.

Rosabella

I awoke with a start. ...What was that smell? ...Musk? Dirt? Moss?
And a strange sound...

That, for sure was a buzzing, incandescent lightbulb. Did they
have lightbulbs in the afterlife?

I blinked my eyes open. They were heavy—my whole body was
heavy, leaden-feeling, although my head spun, light. The concrete
ceiling above me twirled and distorted. A memory tugged at my brain.

**[System Searching MRPs To Select & Display Correct
Memory...]**

"No," I batted the system prompt away. I could remember
normally without that weird, sucking-face, body-in-a-vacuum
sensation thank you very much.

*Dad's face—yes, that was it!—Dad's face had swum there, above me,
the last time I'd had my eyes open. When was that?*

My head hurt—this was too many thoughts. My hand reached up
to rub at my temple, and I noticed the patchy tears and burns in the
fabric of my white body armor; in some places, blood and wounds
showed through. ...*What?* That would explain the stinging sensation
that still sizzled there. I moved my hand down into my line of vision
to observe the reddened flesh. *Shit. Burns.*

...That dragon.

It all came flooding back: the wall of fire at my face, people screaming, arms...clutching...

Dad had been there. Dad had gotten me out.

"System, show me my HP," I said; my voice sounded warbled like I was speaking underwater—*was it just me or was everything off right now?*

[System Understands Query...Loading Response...]

A headache thudded over my temples. *Fabulous.*

[Current HP / ROSABELLA, GAME MAKER 3: 13/26]

...Well, that explained things. ...Except for the 'thing' of where I was... Did I still have the stuff I'd tricked the Vodyaracka into giving me?

"System, bring up my inventory?" I asked weakly.

[System Understands Query...Loading Response...]
[System Alert: Per Request, Inventory Opened.]
- **1 Rosabella's Mother's Gold & Silver Broadsword**
- **2 CM Diamonds**
- **1 The Game Map**
- **1 Sparo, Red Vodyaracka Skydrake's Memory of Rosabella The Great**

It was all there. My breath caught as I read the last item. *The memory? I still had it. Did I dare view it—how'd this work again?* My mouth felt so dry as I forced it into forming the words:

"System, show me the dragon's memory of my mother?"

[System Searching MRPs To Select & Display Correct Memory...]

I took a deep breath and, somehow, instinctively, closed my eyes. When I opened them, the world bubbled into a foggy haze and reappeared again.

I readjusted my enormous, red claws underneath me, but the woman didn't even flinch, she only smiled at me. Her pale face was round and gleaming—was it her smile or the kindness in her eyes? Loose pieces of her brown hair, braided down over her shoulder, flew around her face like a halo.

"Will you help me create, Sparo?" Her voice was a warm bell.

And I felt my huge, spiked head nod. And I opened my mouth wide. And she took two, unafraid steps towards me— really, the woman of her size was completely fearless.

I watched her extend her arm, her gold-embroidered bell sleeve falling down from it—felt her tiny hand on my tongue.

And I shut my eyes in pure ecstasy as the magic began to flow through us.

Gold sparks and blue twirls—intertwining, zooming, sparkling…twisting around until I heard Rosabella the Great murmur something in the magic tongue.

And there was a firework.

And I had a birds eye view of the most beautiful forest I could have ever imagined. The Fall colors were vibrant—reds, yellows and oranges cresting over the hillsides. …And the city beside it. I watched as the lights went on—as she created it from the ground up, pulling clay upwards and creating skyscrapers. The outsides, mirrors, reflecting the brilliant rays of the sun.

And her smile reflected in all of them—the pure joy in her eyes.

They sure called her Rosabella the Great for something…

Whoosh.

I plummeted back to reality, breathless, to find myself still sitting on the bed—what? Oh my gosh, had that been—

My mother.

I suddenly knew it like I knew my heartbeat, the one kicking a base drum in my ears. And, for an inexplainable reason, I wanted to puke right there and then. Was it my lowered HP or the fact that…I'd just seen…my mother? She was better than I'd thought—better than—

The image of her warm eyes and smile flashed through my mind.

This was too much. It was all too much at one time. A foreign, nervous energy raced from my core to the tips of my fingers. I had to move. I had to process this—Mom had been in The Game? Here? She'd been here?

I wasn't ready to stand, but I shoved myself upward, to my feet, so I could examine my surroundings and try to get my head on straight, but the appendage instantly revolted, and my stomach pitched again.

My mom was in The Game. I reached out to grab the nearest piece of furniture—which was, apparently, a desk. Hmmm. I looked it over: plywood variety, nearly just a simple frame of one crammed up against the bed with a lamp donning a sideways shade. The fake wood scratched my fingertips even though it couldn't answer my question: where the heck was I?

I was alone, that much was obvious. The concrete bunker-of-a room was as sparse and desolate as the cold, gray material of the walls and floors. I quickly identified the buzzing noise from before as the light flickering overhead. The place was dark except for two more bulbs, barely lighting the rows of shelving on the far walls. Other than the bed, the desk and a table and chairs, there wasn't much furniture. …And everything was old and tattered like it'd survived a war. Dad had brought me here? Where was he now?

I wandered over to the shelving unit on the far wall, tracing my fingers over the labels of brightly-colored food cans and boxes there:

beans, canned vegetables and pancake mix. It looked like someone had lived here... Survived here for quite some time...

I picked up a box to examine the best-used by date, but I paused as something caught my eye. Through the shelving, I saw a cardboard box filled with kid stuff—shoved way in the back. But it wasn't the knit, pink blanket falling out of one side or the blocks or even the pair of sneakers there that got my attention. It was the stuffed bear on top. The stuffie sat, lopsided—one corduroy arm extended over the edge of the box and one shoved somewhere inside. It had two stitched, black eyes and someone had wrapped a sliver of fraying fabric around its neck like a scarf. It tugged at something in me as I stared. Why did that bear look so...familiar?

"System, search my MRP, and tell me if I have a memory related to that teddy bear," the words slipped, breathlessly off my lips. First, watching the memory of mom and now...this? Why couldn't I remember? What was...wrong with me?

[System Searching MRPs To Select & Display Correct Memory...]

An electronic error beep sounded, and a notice appeared:

[No Connected Memory Found.]

No. No, that couldn't be right. I chewed on the inside of my lip. *I mean, I had to have seen that bear before. ...Or maybe it just reminded me of something?* I shuffled forward, pushing things off the shelf to try to see what else was in the box when I noticed that a shield and magnifying glass was printed on the cardboard front—*an Examination Opportunity? I knew it! I knew I'd seen that bear before!*

"Examine!" I demanded.

[System Query Examined... +1 XP, 248/300]

[Upon A More Thorough Examination, You Realize This Is A Significant Object From Your Past. Would You Like To Take It?]
[Yes] [No]

Yes, of course. I could barely breathe as I selected it. The teddy bear, suddenly, appeared in my hands. The fabric was worn and soft beneath my fingertips. I looked down at the stuffed animal. *I knew this bear. I knew it from somewhere, I was sure—*

I noticed a symbol drawn on the fabric scarf in marker—*wait, I recognized it.* It was the same symbol I'd seen when Sparo had extracted his memory of my Mom: a thought bubble with a circle around it. I squinted at it—

[System Reward: Congratulations, You Have Added A New Skill. +5 XP, 253/300
RECOLLECT: Allows A Gamer To Search Their Mind To Collect A Memory, An Object Or Situation To Recall A Memory Not Already In Their MRP. Recollection Opportunities Are Indicated By The Thought Bubble In A Circle Icon. Manually Click On The Icon Or Speak The Word 'Recollect' Out Loud To Initiate. MRP Will Be Increased With Every Recollection]

I stared at the words and, then, at the toy still in my hand. Was something inside me more scared of this than of a Snargel, Darken or a dragon? …Nah, the dragon had been pretty damn scary… But my fingers shook. My voice shook more.

"Recollect," I told the system.

[Object Recollection In Progress… +700 MRP, 3865/6207]
[System Searching MRPs To Select & Display Correct Memory…]

I felt the world blur and rush past my face—hopefully all this wasn't messing with my HP. I was beginning to get a little sick from all the movement…

I stood in a yellow-painted room with a strange, foggy kind of sparkle to it. I felt like I knew the place. Did I know it? A single, four-poster bed with white-sheet curtains flowing down the sides…a teddy bear tossed on the messy, pale-pink sheets— a teddy bear? My eyes snapped to it. It was the corduroy bear with the stitched eyes.

A fluffy rug comforted my pudgy toes… Was I shorter?

The white-lace hem of a nightgown trailed over my chubby knees, and I couldn't see much higher than the top of the mattress—

"Rosabella!" A warm bellow of delight rang through the room.

I spun around, finding the movement hard and bulky, nearly falling.

"Opps!" Dad's face smiled into mine as his hands reached for me, grabbing me just in time. "Don't take a tumble there. How's my big girl?"

The room twirled as he picked me up. A giggle spouted out of my lips. A feeling of utter safety rushed over me, here, secure in his hold.

"Ford?"

Another voice.

Deeper.

Dad placed me on the ground with a jolt; his brow furrowed as he turned to address someone behind him. Why were they all so tall?

It was a man with a bald head and red beard. His face creased with urgency as they spoke in hushed tones. But something confused me then…

More accurately, someone.

Because there were suddenly two Dads.

Both with the same jawline…the same, dark hair. …Identical twins? What?

I shook my head; I had to be seeing this wrong.

"Goran, would you watch her for a minute?" the first Dad— the one, Ford, who'd spun me around—asked the other who stood, lounging casually in the doorway. His voice was clipped as he nodded at me.

And the second Dad tried to hide a smile as he bustled forward.

"Of course, I'll watch Rosie…brother."

I returned from the memory with a start—with a gasping breath. The teddy bear fell out of my grasp and to the floor at my feet. I swallowed. …Because the memory I'd just witnessed burned in the back of my throat. *It was a memory, right? It was a memory of mine? From when I was little? How had I…forgotten? The teddy bear…two twins? Dad was a twin? How was that…possible?*

But my heart sunk because I was, suddenly, very aware of how possible it was, even if I wanted it to be wrong. The Red Vodyaracka had told me my dad was dead. He'd asked me why everyone would say I was the last Game Maker if he were still alive or why they'd imprison the greatest Game Maker that'd ever lived. And the dragon had a point about another part too: why would The Game be hellbent on imprisoning and killing my dad unless…

…Unless it was like the memory, and *he wasn't my dad at all. …Unless the man I'd been calling Dad WAS an imposter like they'd all been saying…my real Dad's identical twin…my…uncle…*

???

Yikes.

That was a lot. Honestly, that was nearly fucking too much right now. My head spun with unanswered questions. I backed away from the shelves—away from the bear. I backed up until my back hit cold, concrete block—till I could feel the biting firmness of a wall behind me like that could, somehow, stabilize me. But that was another lie. *A lie. Had Dad been lying to me all these years? Could he have been lying? He'd been so paranoid. My mother had clearly been in The Game. What did all of this mean?*

"System," I begged, suddenly breathless, as waves of dizziness and desperation crashed over my head, "Tell me—can you tell me about my birth parents? My actual—real—" My voice cut off. The system response slid into view, bobbing in my vision.

[System Understands Query...Loading Response...]
[System Answer: ROSABELLA, GAME MAKER 3's Birth
Parents Were ROSABELLA THE GREAT, NOBLE 17
(Deceased) And FORD, GAME MAKER 21 (Deceased).
ROSABELLA, GAME MAKER 3 Was Born In The Game.
Would You Like More Information?]
[Yes] [No]

Deceased??? I stared at the tags after the names. I was born in The Game...? Oh my God, the dragon was right? Could the dragon be right? ...Would I like more information? ...No. No, I wouldn't like more information; I could barely digest what I had already... I tried to bring air into my lungs, but it felt impossible. My vision blurred. This was... was this all possible? Could the system lie? Was it lying to me? Or was everyone telling the truth, and I was lying to myself?

I leaned against the concrete block wall, my lungs heaving. Was this what a panic attack felt like? Like dying—like drowning? Like searching for something this whole room was full of and finding too much of it. Answers. I'd wanted answers. But, now, I wasn't so sure—

Boom!

Something by my elbow fell. I spun, clutching my arms to my chest like I had any chance of protecting myself, but my heartbeat evened out as I realized it'd just been a barn door—so old and dusty that it was peeling paint and, now, laid face-down on the floor where it'd fallen. Its absence opened up a hole in the shelving; I had a view I hadn't seen before. Apparently, there weren't only shelves of food in the place. There were, also, shelves of…

Animals.

I swallowed.

They were dead, I realized quickly. The animals were dead. Eyes stared at me—vacant, glass eyes. Mounted deer heads lined the shelf that had been covered before by the door. A stuffed racoon and possum stared back at me from their positions on pieces of polished wood. There was a fox too…and a rabbit. Their fur was coarse and dry; their mouths contorted in their last dying breath.

Taxidermy? Ick. I shivered even though it wasn't cold. I rubbed my arms and was about to turn away, and, maybe, prop that damn door up again so I didn't have to look at them when I realized a symbol was burned into the wood of one of the deer heads. I leaned closer to look and saw a thought bubble with a circle around it. …What had that skill been I'd just learned? …Oh, right…It was a Recollection Opportunity.

"Recollect," I whispered, dread jumping in my stomach more than I wanted to admit.

[Object Recollection In Progress... +30 MRP, 3895/6207]
[System Searching MRPs To Select & Display Correct Memory...]

My vision fogged and melted, zooming out and, then, very far in. It nearly knocked me off my feet—*why was I doing this again? Didn't I feel sick enough? Didn't I know enough?*

The concrete floor of the bunker was up close and personal, hard underneath my bottom, as I sat, cross-legged there. Kid-sized hands extended into my vision as I played with a doll, parading it towards a familiar corduroy teddy bear seated on the floor.

"Dew, dew, dew," I sang to myself, trotting the dolly towards the bear.

"Rosie, Daddy's working."

My head snapped up to view a younger version of…Dad. Which twin was he?

The man didn't look up though. His eyes were laser-focused on an animal that he was stitching. His mouth was stretched in an annoyed frown.

My gaze dove again to the dolls, but I could hear the man muttering in the background.

"Damned Ford. You wanted me to respect animals, here's me respecting them—putting them on the shelf as a literal trophy. How's that for your bleeding heart?"

My heart thundered in my chest even if my kid heart didn't. This was the twin, not my birth father. He was making fun of his brother—my Dad?

"Daddy, I'm hungry," my child voice whined. I didn't know it wasn't my Dad?

"Of course, sweetie," the twin, Goran, responded, his voice smoothed over, omitting the bitterness from before, "We only have a few cans left, but choose whichever you want from the shelf…"

The memory faded out and the bunker faded back in. …As did my outrage. *Something was wrong here.* I was putting the puzzle pieces together faster than I liked, and the larger picture was terrible—gut-wrenching. *Goran... The guy I'd thought was my dad was...*

I suddenly needed air. Not stale, bunker air. Fresh, outdoor variety and I needed it now. My eyes searched for a window, but it was clear there were none. Instead, my eyes locked on a rope ladder hanging from the ceiling, and I craned my neck up to find a wooden hatch. *A trapdoor?*

My body ached, but I had enough strength to haul myself away from the wall and up the first few rungs. The rope scratched at the burns on my palms. My HP popped up almost instantly, decreasing.

[-1 HP, 12/26]

Damn that. I didn't have a ton to begin with. Damn this door.

I used my nails to try and pry at the place it met the grass shoots sticking through the crack, but it wouldn't budge. There was no handle on the inside.

I shoved at it, heaving my weight against the wood—

[-1 HP, 11/26]

I heard the door jangle against something—*a latch? Was it locked?* Alarm rattled through me. *Was I locked in here?* I struggled against the thing for ten more minutes before my swirling head told me to stop. With a huff, I let my arms flop helplessly down at my side. *I was stuck in here—trapped. Dad had been in here with me. Why would he lock me in?*

I was about to descend the ladder when I heard metal scraping against metal from over my head—*a key inserted into a lock or my desperate imagination?*

I leaned forward on the ladder, straining to make out the slightest sound—

Something clicked.

Not my imagination. *A key! It was a key in a lock!*

Wood and metal groaned as something shifted overhead—

I blinked up into the blinding light as a boot came down the first rung. My eyes took a minute to adjust.

It was Dad....err, I wasn't quite sure of the title yet. Emotions mixed a strange potpourri inside my stomach as I tripped down the ladder, feeling rather numb, to allow him to climb down. I watched the man close the trapdoor overhead; a smile wiped shyly over his face as he concealed something behind his back. He shook off the hood from over his head, letting his cropped, dark hair fall free in a tangled mess. I noticed there was blood on his face and hands—*from getting me away from the Vodyaracka? From something else?*

"Dad?" I started, hesitantly as his sneakers thudded to the concrete, "Are you hurt?"

"I got you something," he said instead.

His avoidance of my question made me more annoyed than typical. *Maybe it was the lock on the door or the memories or the dead animals and the spite I remembered in his voice about his brother... Maybe it was this headache that was pounding at my skull.* I gaped, incredulously, at both the situation and the now-closed-again door to the bunker above, "So...you locked me in here?"

The man did a double take. His jaw went slack as he rubbed the top of his hand over his cheek, wiping away dirt but smearing blood there, "Of course. Rosie, it was for your protection. It's dangerous out there." He nodded towards our one link to the outside world above.

He had a point; I'd just fought off a dragon. But, still, something within me fought it and his doe-eye expression. *After seeing all those memories, I just... Something was different now... Something I couldn't put my finger on. I guessed I was more tired than I'd thought.* I rubbed at my head wearily, "What'd you bring me?"

"I didn't forget"—he actually looked excited which made me feel even more exhausted—"Tomorrow, you know?"

I didn't know. I raised a half-hearted eyebrow, leaning on the safety of the bed. *How was I supposed to question him about the things I truly wanted to ask? How was I supposed to bring something like that up—just launch into an awkward conversation? ...When I was this tired?* My heart hammered in my chest.

"Your birthday," he announced with a triumphant swish of his arms.

"Oh." My voice was quiet; my breath, hitched. *I'd forgotten about my birthday. Honestly, I'd forgotten about everything human since I'd been stolen into The Game. At least that dragon hadn't completely roasted me, and I could see the beginning of another year...*

"You know," I tried to wave the man off, turning away to fidget and fold and re-fold the corner of the bedsheet over itself on the mattress, "I don't even need to really celebrate this year—"

"*Whala!*"

He wasn't listening to me. I turned to find his eyes wide as he produced a water canteen, brandishing it proudly in the air.

"A canteen?" My forehead, admittedly, crinkled up in protest.

But he winked at me, leaning in. "Ye of little faith," he tsked. His fingers unscrewed the cap of the canteen, and tiny lights zoomed out—*lightening bugs?*

The cloud of them buzzed around me, landing on my arms, and I looked down to realize that they weren't bugs at all. They were dragons: minute, kinda adorable, miniature dragons with wings like dragonflies and a tail that flashed yellow light.

He chuckled, "They like you!"

"What are they?" I asked, temporarily distracted from my swirling thoughts as my eyes darted along with the tiny dragons, watching them careen, dive and land again on my shoulders and hands—

"Oh, they aren't the gift," the man clarified, "They're called Laxtail Chira, Chira for short. They're perfectly harmless individually and rather like lightening bugs in our world. Here, you can check out their stats." He swished a system menu open in front of me.

[System Answer: These Cuties Are Called Laxtail Chira.
They Are Miniature Dragons Distinctive Due To Their
Tiny Size, Huge, Infant-Like Eyes And Tail Which Flashes
Light.
STRENGTHS: Strong In Numbers, Intelligent And Quick.
Their Bites Can Lower AC If They Swarm And Damage A
Gamer's Armor. Their Adorableness Convinces Many
Predators To Not Eat Them.
WEAKNESSES: Individually, They Are Not A Threat.]

Name	Laxtail Chira	
Class & Level, Size	Dragon 1, Tiny	
HP	22/22	
Armor Class 13/20		
ABILITIES /20		
Strength	-1	8
Agility	+2	17
Endurance	+0	10
Intelligence	+1	13
Awareness	+1	12
Presence	+0	11
CM		2

"But, honestly," he continued, "I think you'll probably be more interested in what they can do." He coaxed one onto his finger, stroking its tiny head with a fingertip and inserting his pinky into the little creature's mouth. The Chira purred, and something strange happened then. The man began to speak incoherently. Black spirals of magic shot out of his fingertips and—

And, suddenly, there was a cake, balancing on a white dish there, in his hand—out of thin air: a three-layer, white-frosted birthday cake with black swirls and lit candles.

"How—" I murmured. But, worse, *I knew how.*

Rainer had told me about magic in this world. Game Makers and dragons possessed it and could use it. Gamers who had an understanding with a dragon could, also, access the dragon's magic to create. *But that meant*—Something dropped and hardened in my stomach. *But if the man had to use a dragon to create, it meant he wasn't a Game Maker. And the dragon and my memory both told me my real Dad had been a Game Maker—that the title was passed down by blood...*

The man placed the cake on the table nearby with a soft clatter. I gritted my teeth, my blood pounding in my ears. *So, my memory was right then? This wasn't my birth father? This was his twin? I was going to have to talk to him about it—address it upfront. I was going to have to bite the bullet and just face him—*

"And, that's not all!" the man waved his fingers in the air again, black exploding from his hands this time as the Chira zoomed around like little lightening bolts.

"Dad, *stop!*" I shouted. But a container of rice appeared in his one hand...and a bowl of General Tso's rested in the other.

"Your favorite," he said simply, his smile reaching all the way to his eyes, "I thought we'd have dinner and celebrate early."

The smell of the food wafted into my nostrils like something familiar and solid in the midst of everything unfamiliar and unsolid— like these tiny, circling dragons, this room and the memories I really wanted to discredit and couldn't...

But it wasn't enough. *A birthday dinner with my favorite food wasn't going to fix this. Not even close.*

Tears stung at my eyes although I tried to hide it. My lips twisted and distorted with the beginning of a sob. *Was this all a lie? I'd been trying so hard to rescue him, and this had all been—a lie?*

The man stopped. He could see the anguish on my face. His expression dropped, dipping into utter concern. "You don't like it?"

he asked, looking crestfallen, "I know there's only so much magic I can do with these tiny dragons, but, Rosie, just say what you want, and, maybe, I can make it for you—"

"It's not that," I sniffed, crossing my arms over my chest. My throat felt clogged worse than an apartment toilet. *Oh God, could I get this out? Could I actually DO this? Ask him this???*

"I mean," I amended quickly. "It's kinda about that—"

The man leaned closer, his arms reaching out to comfort me, "Rosie—"

I tried to ignore the escalating beat of my heart and find some saliva in my mouth. "It's—" I stuttered. "It's the Creator Magic. Why do you need the dragons to create? The group I met trying to rescue you said that Game Makers can do magic on their own once activated. And the group and this dragon said that *I* was the last Game Maker which has to be totally wrong because it passes through blood, right? …Also, this place… I think I remember it. We were here together, maybe a long time ago when I was little? It's all really confusing me." *It wasn't coming out how I'd wanted it to at all. I was babbling. I was—*

But the man was frozen. His face grew white. His eyes glossed over, cold.

And I couldn't take the silence; I couldn't have him not say anything right now when I needed him to speak the most.

"You're a Game Maker, right?" I filled the empty room with my shakingly optimistic voice instead, sniffing through the words. "That's what everyone doesn't know. They're wrong about you, about us. You're my dad. Of course, you're a Game Maker. Of course, those memories are wrong."

…Why wasn't he saying anything…

I blinked at him.

"Rosie, it's different than you think—" he reached out to cocoon me in a hold, but I shrugged him off. *Because he wasn't saying what he was supposed to say. He wasn't telling me they were wrong. And there was only one way to find out for real—for concrete sure.*

"Show me your stats," I spat, suddenly, trying to hold him at arm's length. "Show me the title on your stats—"

"Rosie, every Gamer's title is obliterated and replaced with 'Prisoner' when they're impounded," he tried, "My title won't tell you anything. You have to believe me. You're jumping to conclusions."

No. No, I wasn't jumping to conclusions. He was using dragons to create. Why did he need the dragons?! …I wasn't going crazy. Why was my head throbbing?

"Show me your stats," I growled again, "It'll be your birthday present to me." My words and voice were not kind, but I couldn't help it. I needed answers. The dragon and the group of discontinued Game Wardens seemed to know more about my past than I did. The memories I'd seen were too vivid. I had to know if my dad had an identical twin and who the man standing in front of me was. …Growing up, he'd never told me his name. He'd told me he was my Dad, and that's all that mattered. *Why didn't I know something stupid like his name? I had to get some answers.*

My stare must have included daggers; he held up his hands in defeat, "Okay."

He swiped a finger horizontally, and his stats appeared:

Name	Goran
Class & Level	Prisoner 11
XP	1177/1200
MRP	13205/14235
HP	78/117
Baddie Points	5055
Armor Class 11/20	
ABILITIES /20	
Strength	+1 12

Agility	+1	12
Endurance	+0	11
Intelligence	+1	13
Awareness	+0	10
Presence	+3	16

"See?" he echoed. "The Prisoner class obscures my regular one. This doesn't really tell you anything."

But it did. My eyes swept over his name, Goran—*not Ford, my real Dad's name from the memory. Goran was the name my birth Dad had called from the doorway to watch me while he was busy. ...And there was no CM slot under Abilities like there was for mine...* My heart started to tremble.

The brother.

The man in front of me was...he was the twin.

This wasn't my dad.

I was a prisoner here.

Rosabella

I felt the color drain out of my face. *The Vodyaracka had been right. My dad WAS dead. His twin hadn't had the courtesy to even tell me.* Unease swept over my body, causing all the hairs on my arms to raise. I, suddenly, felt light-headed, but emotions were there too. I was…angry. And…frightened—*what did he want with me? How could I escape when he was so much larger and stronger?*

"I have to pee," I wheezed out, feeling like all the air was being vacuum-sealed from around me. It looked like he didn't hear me, so I repeated my statement—a little stronger now, "You have to let me outside to pee *now.*"

The man's eyes narrowed—sharpened. *Shit. I was going to have to do better than that if I wanted him to believe me.*

"Please, Dad," I hurried, hoping the title would assuage any of his fears even as fear jumped, wholly alive in me, "I'm gonna pee myself. It was stupid of me to doubt you. I've just gotta pee quick and, then, I can come back and celebrate my birthday with you. Just the two of us, like always."

And I couldn't breathe. I couldn't move as I watched the man's face, considering—

"Okay," he whispered finally. Relief crashed over my head.

"Go and come back quickly though," he warned, his face tight, "There's danger in the woods."

There was danger in here too, I thought to myself. But I didn't wait for further permission. I bolted for the rope ladder, nearly tripping in my haste. I barely felt the harsh fabric on my palms as I climbed.

—Barely heard Goran shuffling below or the Chira buzzing as I rose. All I saw was the door above me: *freedom.* Like the one hole in a ceiling of thick ice. ...And I was a seal who'd been holding my breath for far too long. *My one chance to breathe—*

I pushed upward, the wood rough on my palms. I burst out of the hole, shoving past the trapdoor. I clamored to my feet, ducked under the tendrils of the weeping willow tree above and dove into the underbrush—the woods. I waited until I'd gone a full five paces before I couldn't wait any longer. I heaved over my knees, hyperventilating as the wind blew petals and green leaves to tickle my cheeks where tears already were.

[System Reward: You Made A Risky Escape! +25 XP, 278/300]

But I didn't care about the points. Not now. I swiped the system pop-up to the side, out of the way. My cheeks were wet now. I tried to wipe the tears away, but my spasming breaths wouldn't calm. *This was all too much. This Game world had been too much, and, now, I found out Dad had been lying to me?*

Not my dad.

He wasn't my dad—he wasn't my fucking Dad!

...So, if he wasn't my dad, what did that make me? Who was I? And what else did he lie about? My head spun. *I needed to get away from here—to run!*

I whipped around to do just that when I spotted Joy crouched so fully in a bush that I probably wouldn't have seen her if her pink-hair didn't stick out through the greenery like a sore thumb. She put a careful finger to her lips, shushing me, "You alone?"

I nodded. And she stepped out of the brush. A bird call whistled through her teeth. *Summoning the others?* I heard branches crack underfoot as the rest of the group stepped out of the brambles: Callen, Dormouse and Rainer.

"Where's the traitor?" Rainer barked, his fists going to the jangling weapons at his stout waist.

I swallowed. *Goran. He meant Goran.*

"I'm always lightyears ahead," Dormouse goaded with a sigh, his fingers pattering away in the air near the trapdoor. "Passcode was 'Bananas'—amateurs. That's been like everyone's passcode since the fifth grade," he huffed.

"Dormouse, wait—" I started.

But neither him nor Rainer did. I heard a click as the trapdoor unlocked. The muscled Nomad rushed forward, axe waving. And he didn't take the ladder down, he grabbed ahold of it like the rope it was and swung down into the hole with a bellow.

Joy rolled her eyes, "The theatrics of that one—"

"What will he do to him?" I gasped, not sure why my heart was suddenly in my throat at the thought of the Nomad's unleashed fury hitting Goran, even if he wasn't my dad.

"He'll do what should have been done long ago," stated Callen seriously, running his fingers through the short strands of his gray hair.

No. No, I wasn't sure that I wanted him dead. Even if he'd lied. Even if he'd strung me along, I wasn't sure—

Panic raced through my limbs—down to my fingers. I lunged for the trapdoor hole, my hair billowing back in the wind like the climax of a terrible movie I hadn't wanted my life to become—

Goran laid, sprawled out on the concrete floor at Rainer's booted feet. A bloody gnash on his head indicated the reason for his limp limbs. A system alert fizzled into the air between us:

[GORAN, PRISONER 11: -70 HP, 8/108]
[System Alert: Covenant Ended. RAINER, NOMAD 9
Struck GORAN, PRISONER 11, Not Freed Him. Trade
With ROSABELLA, GAMER MAKER 3 Terminated.]

I blinked at the message. Our trade was off now? Goran was…here. I had no reason to fix their world. To be honest, I was really having far too much trouble processing everything…

"He's not dead," Rainer called upward, his hearty voice booming in the narrow opening.

"You hope," I retorted back, anxiously staring down at Goran's pale face.

"I know," the Nomad insisted, "No offense, but I've been doing this for a lot longer than you, tyke." The slightest grin slid over his face, nearly hidden by his red beard.

God, I hoped he was right. And, yet, I acknowledged swiftly that something inside of me, also, wanted him to be wrong—for Goran to be dead. So I could stop dealing with this—all this drama for one minute and breathe. No—I couldn't think like that. I wouldn't. I rushed down the rope ladder—to him—my hands prodding at his limp form, staring into his closed eyes. I couldn't think with my hands on the man's rigid shoulders…watching his pale face…I couldn't breathe. What had I done? My throat was raw and dry. I was shaking. I'd realized just now I was shaking. I looked down at my trembling hands, turning my palms over slowly.

Wavering.

Was I shaking to see Goran in such a state? …Or because of what I'd learned about him?

"He wasn't your father, kid," Callen shimmied down the rope ladder easily, relying mostly on a quick swing to leap agilely to the ground. He offered a hand, trying to place it reassuringly on my shoulder, "I don't know if you have enough MRP to remember but—"

"I remember." I said it sourly, staring at the man lying unconscious at our feet.

And I didn't shrug off Callen's hand, resting there, heavy on my shoulder. Even though I wanted to. Because, for a minute, it felt like I needed someone in my corner. ...And even someone I barely knew was better than no one at all... My mind felt numb. ...*Did I really remember that Goran wasn't my Dad?* A mesh of memories and voices in my head swirled together in an overwhelming clashing of cymbals—like, even if I strained to hear them, I'd only burn my eardrums or lose myself completely in the pulsing, deafening noise...

My heart ached. *God, I was so tired.* Maybe I should just jump back in that bed in the corner, pull the covers way up over my head and let my exhausted eyes close—hoping that, when they opened, I'd be in the real world.

...The normal world: New York. My...almost life. ...*But, without the man, pale-white and unconscious, near my feet, where would I live? Who would I talk to? Who would I be? An orphan? Who would make me cereal dinners or talk to me about school? Who would be there when I needed them? ...I'd only done all this to get him back. And, now, I knew he wasn't my dad... Did it make him a bad person? Why was Rainer calling him a traitor and murderer? What did he do?*

I had no answers for any of it. I swallowed several times, trying to pretend I wasn't processing all of this as Callen and Rainer stared, concerned into my face.

Rainer shuffled from one foot to the other, "Uh, Rosie—"

"Don't call me that," I snapped—so quickly that it was nearly jolting.

197

Rosie. Goran called me 'Rosie', but in the memories my birth Dad, Ford, called me 'Rosabella'. I strained, trying to remember the last time in my life I'd heard my father call me by my full name. ...But I couldn't remember.

"All I was trying to say is there's an Examination Opportunity," Rainer grumbled, pointing to a shield and magnifying glass icon bobbing just in front of me. *When had that appeared?* I suddenly kinda felt bad for snapping at the guy.

"Sorry," I amended, "Examine."

What could the system want of me now? What could I possibly have to examine in the open air with nothing around except Goran's despondent body?

[System Object Examined... +1 XP, 279/300]
[Looking Down At The Pale Body, You Realize Suddenly That Nothing Ties You To The Game Anymore. This Man Was Not Your Birth Father. You Owe Him Nothing. At This Time, You Have The Option To Leave The Game And Return to Earth. Would You Like To Exercise This Option?]
[Yes, Return To Earth] [No, Stay In The Game]

What? I gaped at the message. Had it just read my mind?

"Any food down there? I'm 100% starved." Dormouse's voice interrupted as did his head, which suddenly dangled down through the hole, his dark hair hanging down in icicles.

"Err...we're kinda in the middle of something," Rainer grunted.

"In the middle of what? Nerd—out of my way," Joy shouldered past the Coder and slid down the ladder like she'd trained in the circus.

"Let it be known no one's ever confused your demeanor with 'nice'!" Dormouse called down after her, his dark head appearing again.

Joy just rolled her eyes and folded her arms, "God, he's annoying. What is up?" She tapped her foot impatiently on the concrete floor, her eyes only darting to Goran's unconscious form on the same floor for the fraction of a millisecond. But my eyes seemed glued there—unable to move even as the group's laughter and voices slurred in the background. There he was: Goran. The man who had impersonated my father for years.

A pain stabbed at my stomach suddenly. Grief? Hate? Distress?

It felt like I couldn't breathe—weight burrowed into my chest cavity like fingers with long nails ripping at flesh. The man who had lied to my face about my entire childhood was there, passed out on the concrete at my feet and the system was giving me a chance to walk away from this all—to go back to Earth? It sounded too good to be true...

"Ask the system about the consequences," Callen insisted, chewing on the inside of his lip in thought.

Consequences? That was a good idea. "System, what are the consequences of the choice?" I asked. The expected reply came right away:

[System Understands Query...Loading Response...]
[System Answer: ROSABELLA, GAME MAKER 3 Has Two Options. A Selection Of 'Yes, Return to Earth' = -100 Baddie Points, +15 XP. A Selection Of 'No, Stay In The Game' = +30 Baddie Points, -1000 MRP, +15 XP.]

...With an unexpected answer...

My jaw grew slack. My mind spun numbers. So, the same XP either way. I didn't really care about the Baddie Points but the MRP? That was a big number! If I stayed here, I'd forget a lot.

[Please Select Which Option You Prefer.]

Okay! Enough already! The neon reminder pulsed in my face like a gnat I couldn't swat away. *A fucking important gnat. If I screwed this up—*

"Rosabella," Callen started, his tone stern but his eyes brimming with kindness and pity. "Would you like to go home? I know this has to be a lot for you. If you were to select 'yes' no one would fault you—"

"I would," Joy interrupted irately, her eyes flashing and her mouth twisting in utter disgust. "I *completely would*. Callen, are you out of your *fucking mind?!* You can't just let her go—"

"You know she's the only one who can fix our world," Rainer objected as well. The Nomad stood, wide-legged, hands on his hips. His long hair blew back from his hulky chest in the wind from the trapdoor, and he looked like a wild sight still clutching his axe to his chest.

"We'll find another way," the gray-haired leader told both of them. "Rosabella," he repeated. *"Do you want to go back home to New York?* You can't take Goran with you; he has to pay for what he's done, but you are free to choose whatever you feel is best. We are not holding you captive here—"

"What if the system *wants* her to go, have you thought of that? – Have either of you thought of that?!" Rainer roared at Callen and I. I swallowed, hating the anger on his face and the indecision in my heart. *I could go? I could really go if I wanted? What was the right choice?*

"Dorkus, come down here and tell this asshole not to let Rosabella go!" Joy shouted at the ceiling till the kid's dark hair appeared.

"What's going on?" the dork squeaked, "If there's any question, I stand with Rosabella."

The room quieted. …And they all looked at me. I was grateful for Dormouse's affirmation, but…*but I didn't know where I stood. Except that…to be honest, a part of me deep down inside knew EXACTLY where I stood.* And, suddenly, there was nothing I wanted to do more than lace my favorite pair of fuzzy, baggy sweatpants around my waist, slip on my slippers and sink into the oblivion that was the couch back home and a familiar, RPG video game.

Forever. I could do that forever.

To numb this.

To numb my pain.

To never have to deal with these fantasy weirdos or this game world ever again. And forget that I was, somehow, tied into this mess.

Yes, I wanted that—to bury my head forever in the city where everyone else was burying their head for some reason or another.

Away from these people.

Away from Goran.

Away from dragons. And Darken. And Kenchee and Chira…

…Like this was all a bad dream.

"Rosabella?" Callen asked hesitantly. "You've decided?"

And I nodded—quickly so I couldn't take it back.

"Yes, Return To Earth," I told the system. I watched their faces fall, devastated. *But I had to do what was best for me, right?* An electronic beep sounded as text flashed into view:

[System Understands Option Selection…Loading Response…]
[System Reward: One Hard Choice Made, +15 XP, 294/300]
[System Penalty: You Look Like A Wimp, Running Away From Your Problems! Your Street Cred Took A Dive! -100 Baddie Points, -10]
[System Alert: PORTAL RING Acquired. Object Will Be Placed In Your Inventory Unless You'd Like To Use. Would You Like To Use?]
[Yes] [No]

Portal ring?

"Callen?" My eyes flashed to the gray-haired man, and he nodded, his flinty eyes serious. "Yes, use it. We'll be there on the other side, okay?"

"Okay," I wheezed. And my stomach clenched as I selected 'yes'. A thick, gold ring, engraved, with a navy-blue stone suddenly appeared on my finger—*oh, okay...*

[System Alert: PORTAL RING Used.]

Object:	Portal Ring
Required Class & Level For Use:	None, 3 Use Max
Description:	Magical Portal Creator Locked In An Object. Looks Clunky & Old-Fashioned With The Huge, Navy Stone But Feels Powerful.
Augment Capacities:	+0
Baddie Points:	+0

"Close your eyes," Callen directed, "All you have to do is think of home."

"I cannot believe you're okay with this," Joy complained in the background, but I tried to block her nasally voice out.

My eyelids fluttered shut; blackness took over.

And my imagination. *I just had to think of New York? ...It seemed far too easy, right?*

Rosabella

The portal fizzed and popped in the center of the apartment living room, the ends of the circle riming with blue and red flames that were a magic I didn't even want to understand—only that it'd taken me here...home.

Back to New York.

Rainer was halfway through an awkward attempt to reattach the apartment door to the place, with his huge hands and a frown on his face, while Joy scolded him from behind the cracking screen of the portal.

"You're taking all day—" she whined.

"We can't leave the girl without a door," Rainer grumbled back, annoyed, under his breath. *It looked like he almost had the thing fixed...*

"Are you sure we should just...*leave her here?*" Dormouse hedged; his voice was laced with the nerves dancing in his eyes.

"Rosabella made her choice. She can fend for herself," Callen assured the timid kid, nodding at me. I crossed eyes with the gray-haired man. And, for a reason I couldn't nail down, I, suddenly, felt nervous myself. ...*Because I'd asked for this.*

...And I didn't know what I was going to do now that Goran was...well, not here anymore.

"*There we go!*" Rainer shouted as something metal clicked, obviously popping back into place. He tested the door with a robust swing, and it clicked closed with precision. Satisfied, the bulky guy wiped his hands together and fell into line with the rest of the group, his eyes flashing up to mine for only a brief second. "Hope it helps," he muttered, almost bashfully as his eyes darted to the floor again.

And I nodded. Because *it did—it was kind that he'd even wanted to do that and fix it for me.*

"Okay," Callen warned us all with a tight-lipped smile, "We're gonna shove off now. Be safe, kid."

"Yeah, send us a postcard—will ya?—" Joy drawled. "If you ever think of us in our *squalid, deteriorating Game—*"

"*Joy!*" Callen admonished, but the damage was already done. My tight smile waned further. Because, even if my mind was still made up, her words were like daggers twisting in my stomach. *The girl looked pissed. Was my choice a big mistake?*

Callen seemed to recognize the doubt paralyzing my face. He pointed at the blue-stone ring on my finger, "If you change your mind, you can call us using the ring. Just picture our faces and a portal will open, okay?"

I nodded at him, suddenly feeling rather emotional. The rising wind from the portal pulled at his choppy, gray hair. "Call anytime, anywhere. We'll find you."

I bit down hard on my cheek, twisting at the ring on my finger to try to distract myself because *I wasn't going to cry. I wasn't. And I wasn't going to use the ring either.* I yanked it off, slipping it into the pocket of my body armor. *This was the last time they'd see me. I was done with the crazy.*

Dormouse and Rainer waved as the portal began to fizzle into thin air like an old TV snapping off.

And text flashed over where the portal disappeared:

And, then, it was just me.

And the dark apartment in NYC.

…Honestly, I was fine until I was alone. I swallowed a sour chuckle, my eyebrow raising as I observed the mess before me—*wasn't that how it always went?* I was fine till I felt the lump in my throat I'd been pressing down so firmly that it'd only grown as thick as a tire lodged in my throat.

And, feeling like I was going to lose control if I did anything else, I looked around the place. The curtains were secured firmly over the windows. The lamp I remembered from the side table was knocked to the floor in jagged pieces.

And me.

I was, also, knocked to the floor in jagged pieces. Just ones I didn't remember. *…I felt like, for all the memories I'd collected, I couldn't remember half of it!*

Besides Goran…his fingerprints were all over this place: in the decorations and the way the books on the coffee table were stacked…in how clean everything was…It was as though he was matted into the very fabric of the apartment—like, if I closed my eyes and rounded the corner, I might open them to find him there, in the kitchen, cooking up something he'd burnt most of.

Tears prickled at my eyes. *No. I wouldn't start crying yet. This was a new day—a new chance to start over. I wouldn't begin it by feeling sorry for myself.* I'd gotten out of this mess—out of The Game. Now, I had this place all to myself. I wasn't going to waste this. I was determined to do it different—make this new.

So, I flung open those stupid curtains that Goran always kept closed. Sunlight streamed in, batting me in the face so hard that I had to close both eyes, but I persisted, throwing back the heavy, scratchy fabric. The rays lingered on my cheeks, warming them when I finally wrangled the shades open. The sash of the rear window was already open from my lunge for the fire escape, and a breeze fluttered the wispy ends of my hair back from my face.

A deafening horn sounded from below. My eyes swiveled to lock on the school bus at the street corner. The one waiting for me…

My insides scrambled. *Was I late for school? Dad would be—*

Dad would be NOTHING, I reminded myself quickly, *because Goran wasn't my dad. And I wasn't late for fucking anything because I'd just got back from emotional trauma. I was gonna do whatever I wanted today, and no one was going to stop me.*

And, so, I watched the bus, full of my classmates, whistle and grunt as it lurched down the street without me. And a strange sort of pride and giddy confidence filled me in jumping over my first decision hurdle. I half expected a system message to pop up, congratulating me on my choice—*maybe giving me a little XP or something but…*Well, the air was strangely vacant. …And nothing happened at all. *Did I care? Did I need immediate gratification? Wasn't just being here enough gratification?! Yes. Yes it was.*

I threw off my boots in the middle of the carpet. And I let my hair stream behind me and my bare feet slap all the way down the hall on the hard floor as I ran, breathless, to my bedroom—to my safe place.

The room was exactly how I'd left it: band posters taped to the wall and ceiling, my journal thrown on the balled-up covers of my bed, the fuzzy-pink lampshade contrasting the dark posters overhead and the small bed pushed up against the window-less wall. I had cases of movies and video games stacked so high beside the bed that they'd started to fall over. Seeing the place almost caused me a sigh of relief because it smelled…familiar.

Like rest.

And comfort.

And…*me.*

I tore my white body armor—the last reminder of The Game—off my body, fumbling in my dresser drawer till I found my fluffiest pajama pants. With a groan of pleasure, I slipped the soft fabric over and up my legs. *It felt like Heaven.* A white tank-top later, and I had Heaven perfected. I shoved my bare feet in slippers that had always been a little too big and busily threw my hair up in a messy bun on top of my head. Catching my reflection in the mirror, I acknowledged how flushed my face looked…how—

Free, I decided, smiling at the glass.

I pulled a few strands of hair out in front of my ears to frame my face before sticking a hand under my pillow. My fingers curled successfully around the edges of my cell phone. *The first order of business? Food.*

Dormouse wasn't the only one who was starving. We'd barely eaten, except for a bit of fish and jerky here and there, and my stomach was grumbling worse than an earthquake. Luckily, I had the place on speed dial for emergencies such as this; *they were open 24/7 for a reason.* My fingers worked quickly over the dial pad, and I waited for the ring tone.

"Hi, I'd like to place a delivery order please"—I tried to keep my voice clipped and older-sounding…like an adult who'd simply got hungry for pizza at 7:00 in the morning—"A large pepperoni…yes, extra cheese please and ranch on the side. …Extra ranch too," I amended quickly, changing my mind.

I gave the nice lady my address and phone number, and hung up, my eyes wandering around towards the ceiling, wondering what to do next. …*If Dormouse was here, he'd tell me some stupidly awesome statistic about delivery pizza…like how long it took…or a tale about a delivery driver…But Dormouse wasn't here.* I bit down my own bitterness— *shoved* it down. *Why was my brain thinking about The Game when I'd wanted so desperately to come here—to get away from it all?*

Distraction.

That was what I needed.

I changed from my slippers to fuzzy socks and slid down the hall in them, towards the couch—ice skating where the floor wasn't covered by carpet. *Goran used to tell me I was going to break my face, but he couldn't lecture me or stop the pirouettes now!* I fell in a happy tangle of arms and legs on the plush couch, reaching for the remote. The screen buzzed to life under my direction, and I loaded up one of my newer video games, reaching for the controller. The dancing silhouettes on the screen and the flashing pictures of the intro cutscene took me away from my mind—absorbed me. And it felt good to just lay there, my thumbs working magic over the joystick and the character moving forward.

Forgetting.

Forgetting that I was trying to forget.

My character rounded a corner—*shit! That was a big monster!*

The joystick clacked as I thrusted it to the side, but the avatar didn't move fast enough. The beast clipped my shoulder as I ran into a deformed claw—

The screen blanched to black—*what the?*—as red letters appeared:

GAME OVER

"What the fuck?!" I screamed at the tv. Was it serous right now? That was NOT how HP worked—I'd seen it firsthand. Even when I was battling an enormous dragon, my HP wouldn't just disappear if I bumped into it. This was bogus—totally unrealistic!

…Wait…Realistic? I chuckled aloud, hearing the noise echo in the empty apartment. Was I kidding myself? I was gauging the realism in a video game on the absolute insanity that'd been my experience with one…or a heck of a mental breakdown? Hilarious. This was insane. I was insane—

My phone vibrated on the coffee table, making me jump.

Unknown Number

Fear raced through me until I remembered the pizza.

God, why was I so jumpy? I lectured myself, *Stop being paranoid. It was just the delivery guy.*

I picked up.

"Hey…uh…" some guy with a thick accent stuttered. "Pepperoni pizza?"

"I'll be right down," I quipped, already grabbing up the money I'd laid out and swinging out the door and down the concrete steps which were freezing through even my thick socks. I saw a man's silhouette through the slit in the metal door and heaved my weight against it to open it for him.

"Pizza?" he asked.

I nodded.

"…Yep, or else I'm just keen on letting complete strangers into our building," I jested. The joke came off flat and awkward even as it left my lips, and I was left shifting my weight between my socked feet, feeling more than dorky. Joy would have had some comeback in this situation—*why was I thinking about the pink-haired girl?!*

I tried to smile and focus on the moment, but it seemed impossible. *Was it just the smell of the pizza wafting towards my nostrils or fucking everything???*

"Today's my birthday," I told the pizza delivery guy as I handed him the cash. *Wait…I just told the pizza delivery guy my…How desperate was I?*

He looked equally mortified. "Err…cool, should I keep the change?"

Dying of the shame dyeing my cheeks scarlet, I grabbed the pizza box and dashed upstairs. I was glad Rainer'd fixed the door because I slammed it shut behind me, breathing heavily against it like I'd just evaded a Vodyaracka—*would I stop thinking about this shit???!*

209

I was safe!

I was back in New York!

I had pizza! I had myself. ...That should be enough.

The pizza box was warm on my palms, and the cheese-and-meat smell overpowered me, making me salivate. I navigated back to the couch, crossing my legs and putting the box right in my lap like a warm, greasy blanket. *Who needed a plate when they didn't have a dad?* Goran would have squawked and complained if he'd seen me eat straight out of the box, but today was my birthday. *I had no cake and a fake dad in custody in a game world. ...Oh, and a dead dad. ...But that wasn't going to stop me from enjoying this.*

I opened the box.

I let the smell of it wash over my nostrils: melted cheese, plump, thick-cut pepperoni...

And I dove in. My fingers latched onto the greasy crust, pulling a piece away from the masses—dripping with cheese.

And I dangled it sloppily over my wide mouth.

And cheese tasted like nirvana.

And home.

And safety.

And everything I was lacking. *Oh God, it was so good!*

I ate; I gorged. And, as I gorged, I began to feel. I slipped into it without noticing at first...

How I needed to fill this hole inside me because...

There was pain there.

And sadness.

Dad. He wasn't Dad. He was my real Dad's brother.

He'd lied to my face.

He'd deceived me. Had he loved me?

What was I going to do without him? Here, on my own? How was I going to survive? Would I have to hide again? So they wouldn't take me into child services? I was turning 18 today. Did that mean I was an adult and could be on my own? I tried to look it up on my phone, but my fingers slid all over the screen from the grease, and, so, I gave up and just ate more—worrying.

Feeling emotion crash over my head.

Feeling…

Feeling sick.

I looked down and realized I'd eaten clean through over three fourths of the pizza. The TV show I'd put on played loudly in the background—a jarring, grating noise. And my fingers slid over the remote; *I had to turn it down… I didn't even care about the show anymore. It was just chatter, and I had enough of that in my head.*

The pizza smell was sickening now; it made me want to hurl as I leaned over it. I threw the box to the side, desperate to find some other distraction because my mind was thinking about The Game again. *Callen had said that Goran had to pay for his crimes. What did he do?*

I couldn't help it; I needed to keep my hands and mouth busy. Somehow, I found myself standing in front of the freezer and reaching for the pint of ice cream I knew was tucked in the back: mint chocolate chip. *That should soothe my bloated stomach.*

Using one hand to swing the refrigerator door closed, I reached for a spoon. And I sunk back into the comfort of the couch with my prize.

I hadn't chosen this. I was the victim here. Goran had tricked me.

And, now, I was alone, and hardened by the world, but mostly just alone.

…Just fucking alone…

A tear slid down my nose, dropping into my pint of ice cream. I watched the salty liquid absorb into the freezing treat. I looked around at the nearly empty pizza box on the couch armrest…the discarded napkins balled up around me and on the floor. The place was suddenly

211

a mess...*I was a pig. The adults were gone for one second, and I couldn't even keep it together? I was a cow—eating till I was this stuffed? I was—*

More tears came, and I couldn't stop them this time; they poured down my face. They downpoured so hard I had to set the ice cream to the side and sob into my knees, pulling myself close in a hug it seemed I couldn't give myself.

I didn't know how long I sat like that—balling. ...But, when I looked up, the shadows on the walls seemed bigger even with the light streaming in from outside. And I was done with today, even if it was my birthday. *I was so done.*

Dragging my exhausted limbs, I crept down the hallway and into bed.

Pulling the covers way over my head.

And hoping tomorrow would look better.

...Even though I knew it wouldn't.

Rosabella

When I awoke, my bedroom was pitch black. I tried to unglue my eyelashes from each other, instantly remembering the tears that had dried on my cheeks and cemented them together. And my soul sunk, and my stomach twisted. Because I knew this apartment was as silent and empty as a robbed tomb.

The digital clock on my nightstand flashed red:

9:32 PM

I'd slept my day away until it was literally time to go to bed? My feet were heavy as I threw them over the side of the bed and blinked blearily at the band poster near my headboard. Why did I used to obsess over this stuff? Everything seemed so unimportant and childish right now.

I padded into the bathroom, observing the purple half-moons under my eyes in the flickering, incandescent glow of the overhead lights and the general un-wash of my hair. A fabulous look—not.

The living room was in the same state of disaster I remembered leaving it in—trash thrown about, my boots still in the middle of the floor and me having no desire to do anything about any of it. Darkness reflected my pale face back at me in the open windows, showing the New York skyline and the grubby street below. I'd thought this place was freedom...so, why then, did I still feel like a caged mouse?

…What was I supposed to do now? Go to school tomorrow like none of this even mattered? Pretend everything was okay when it really wasn't?

A glossy picture of Goran and I glinted in the lighting overhead from its perch on a nearby end table, catching my eye. It was in the gold frame I'd given him for a birthday when I was small. He'd said then that he'd always keep it, and a picture of the two of us, in plain sight so that we'd both remember how much we loved each other. I remembered his smile as he grinned at the frame. Now, it just made my heart hurt.

I swiped at it, feeling the cheap plastic underneath my fingers as I brought it towards my face to squint at our expressions. In the picture, Goran had his arm around me, and we were grinning at the camera, having a blast. I was around the age of 10. It was the day he took me on a special trip to the zoo. "I always have time for you, Rosie," he'd proclaimed when he took off work just to give us that special day, "You remember that. You're that important to me. I'll always make time." I remembered we'd taken the picture in front of the reptile house. I'd been in love with lizards then. …Ironic because, after the dragons, I wasn't feeling the same…

…Something about the openness in Goran's face made me shudder. He'd been lying? …All this time? My heart wanted to harden, but it was like it couldn't—like there was an impenetrable foot jammed in the door there. …Like I'd rather take off my own foot than let that door close. Even after all this, why did I still…love him? Why was I getting this aching pain in my heart from leaving him in The Game?

No, I countered quickly, he deserved it.

…But did he? And what did he do?

I couldn't rid myself of the thoughts or the heartache, so I began what the receptionist at my high school called 'puttering'. I wandered, distractedly, around the living room, picking up the trash, cleaning…straightening the sofa cushions…anything to give myself time to think.

I meandered into the bathroom.

I turned the shower as hot as it'd go—which was really just lukewarm in this shithole of an apartment. …And I lathered soap into my scalp till it hurt.

But I looked the same in the fogged-over, water-dotted mirror when I stepped out of the shower, wrapped a towel around me and blinked into the glass. I still looked…

Lost.

Confused.

Unsure.

And, more than anything, I wanted to be sure.

Of what to do next. What did I do next? I felt so…empty.

I yanked on the clothes I'd been wearing before, feeling them stick to my skin from the water, and I drifted into my bedroom—

But I stopped short.

Because the white body armor I'd supposedly made for myself laid knocked-over and semi-rigid on the carpet where it'd sunk near the bed. And it was nearly verification—like a solid affirmation that I hadn't made all of this up; it hadn't just been a dream.

I remembered the ring—the portal ring the system had given me which could be used to enter The Game again or contact the group. I dug in the mesh pocket till my fingers hit it and pulled it out: solid, gold metal met a giant sapphire. I marveled at the thickness of the metal and the engravings around the side. And that's when my eyes traveled to the sword, laying awkwardly on an angle against the belt of the body armor where I hadn't even bothered to detach it.

…Mom's sword…supposedly.

I remembered the Vodyaracka's memory of her—her warm smile and hair like mine. I kind of wished I could ask the system to pull it up so I could view it again, but that was impossible... My jaw went slack—as did my fingers holding the ring. Because I realized that I was dealing with a hole much bigger than I'd thought. No wonder I'd scarfed that pizza down and cried myself to sleep! Sure, I'd learned that Goran wasn't my real dad, but I was, also, dealing with the loss of my real mother and father. ...The loss of not knowing who they were.

Goran had told me that Mom divorced him. ...But, if he wasn't my father in the first place...Who were my parents? And what was my connection with The Game? ...What was their connection with The Game? And how would I find out unless...

I pondered the ring still in my hand, rolling it around in my palm. ...Unless I went back into The Game. No. That was a bad idea. I'd just gotten here. I couldn't just—

...But Callen would answer my questions if he knew! Maybe I could summon him and ask...real quick. ...Maybe it would give me some sort of closure so I could move on.

The thought grabbed me—excited me.

Pulsing energy through my veins to the ends of my fingers. To learn about my actual parents?! That would be worth all this. That would allow me to start over. And, before I could question the heck out of it and reevaluate my evaluation, I jammed that ring on my finger, and a portal flared to life, rimming orange and aqua fire. ...In my bedroom. Which was more than semi-alarming. I leapt back, peering into the darkness in the center of the magic circle. Wait, he'd said to close my eyes and imagine his face if I needed him...I did just that.

"Callen?" I shouted into the blackness behind my eyelids. Honestly, I didn't really expect a response—

"You called?"

I jumped. My eyes flew open.

Shit.

Callen's head ducked out of the portal, and he stepped…into my bedroom. His eyes quickly swept the premises and stopped slightly on my choice of posters, which made my cheeks instantly redden in embarrassment. Kid shit. I should have ripped them all down—

"That guy's got cool hair," he noted, pointing at the picture.

And, somehow, all the cringe leaked out of me, and I knew I'd made the right decision by calling him here. This was the right thing to do.

"What do you need, kid?" His eyes were serious and wide, but there was enough kindness there to give me the boost I needed to spill.

I took the deepest breath, running a hand through my wet hair; I must have looked crazy. "I—I was just wondering if you could tell me about…my parents." My voice pitched and wobbled steeply, as did my confidence in asking the question.

I watched Callen lick his lips, taking a breath in and out too. "Okay," he said softly, "What do you want to know?"

"Everything," I blurted, excruciatingly relieved by his response. "—And I want to know about Goran too. What did he do that's so terrible?" The last question was a hurried addition. The words seemed to bleed over my lips without my permission.

Callen's eyes narrowed. His jaw tensed, "Alright," he stated, "but I need you to know that these are things that, once you know, you can't take the knowing back."

I nodded, only partially understanding. "I want to know, Callen," I pleaded, "Please."

He gestured towards my bed, "Mind if I sit?"

…And it was then that I knew it was going to be a long story…

I nodded and watched him perch on the edge of the mattress. I moved to sit next to him. …And his eyes glossed over.

"As you probably know," he started, "your father, Ford, was one of two twins—the second twin, of course, being Goran, the man we're holding hostage."

I nodded, eager to get to the part I didn't know.

The man licked his lips, "Well, Goran and Ford were always very close as brothers. As kids, they liked everything each other liked: fencing, the outdoors…animals… Well, Ford liked animals. Goran liked to torture animals," the man's face scrunched up as he recalled, "…And, when it came time to date, both brothers liked the same girl too."

I swallowed, "Meaning my mother."

"Exactly," Callen said, pausing. "Your mother's name was Rosabella, and you were, obviously, named after her."

"…How do you know all this?" I asked shyly, not wanting to interrupt, but, also, rather intrigued.

"I was friends with them," Callen surprised me by answering, "My father was a Noble in the same circle as your grandfather, except your grandfather was a Game Maker, of course. The title is royalty in The Game. Game Makers are the only ones, besides dragons, able to create The Game world, patch holes and build civilizations. It's a title that has been passed down for generations through blood. It always falls to the firstborn in any generation."

"So, my father, Ford was born first?" I guessed.

"Yes, and his brother, Goran is not a Game Maker," Callen emphasized, "He can't create. And underneath all their pleasantries, jealousy began to brew, especially when Ford wooed your mother, and they got married. Goran was close friends with your mother, Rosabella, but you could always tell in his eyes that he wanted her for his own, and…when you came along…some say it was too much…"

I could barely breathe… "Too much? What do you think it was?" I whispered.

"That made him go mad?" Callen mused, "Oh, I don't know… He's been talking since you left. He told me why. I don't know if I should believe him."

"What did he say?" my voice rasped up my throat.

Callen's lips constricted; he licked them again, taking his time with his words, "He says he did it to protect you—to give you the life and all the attention you deserve."

"Did what?" I breathed, feeling tears gathering in my thick throat—burning at the edges of my eyes—"What did he do?"

"He murdered your parents," Callen blurted boldly.

And, suddenly, I couldn't feel my limbs.

Or my face.

Or—

Oh my God. Oh my—

"Rosabella," Callen reached out, pinning my shoulder in place like he was afraid I was going to fall off the bed—maybe his fear was justified, the world was spinning—"I told you this would be hard to hear."

"He—" I sputtered. "Goran killed my parents?" I was freaking out. I was full-out freaking out. The monster! The traitor! He took EVERYTHING from me!

"Yes," Callen's face was very close; his eyes swept across my expression as though constantly gauging it, "They say he poisoned the wine in your father's bedroom. Since your father was a Game Maker, your parents lived in The Higher Place, a sort of palace with traditional and formalized, separate bedrooms. …But your father didn't drink the wine Goran left for him. Your mother did. …And when Goran came to check on him—to see if the poison worked—he found your mother dead in your father's arms…and he became so enraged that he..." He winced, pausing. "I can see this is hard for you."

Hard? It was the understatement of the century. I was breathless.

Probably red in the face.

Wholly angry and livid and terror-stricken...

I swallowed hard, "He killed him, didn't he?" I sputtered, "Goran killed his own twin?" What the literal fuck—

"It gets harder," Callen warned, nodding 'yes', "He not only killed his twin, your Dad. He shoved his body under the bed and grieved your mother's death so loudly that a servant came busting into the room. And the servant didn't know it was the brother. He thought it was Ford. ...And the absolute brute let it stay that way, preaching that 'Goran' had done it and ran. And he impersonated his brother, Ford, for months. Until we found out because he needed a dragon to create. He conned a dragon into working with him, but his crutch became too obvious. And, under his pitiful watch, the Reordering decimated our world: zombies and darkness and devastation. And, as he continued to delusionally pretend, people died in masses...The Game crumbled...and the dragons gained control. ...We eventually found your father's body, and Goran kidnapped you and ran into hiding somewhere, eventually smuggling you out of The Game to New York—"

"Stop," I held up a hand I wasn't expecting, "Please, stop."

I needed to silence him.

To stop the flow of words so that, maybe, my body could stop shaking.

But it was a stupid hope. Because there was no more pretending that this was okay—that I was okay. Because all of this was so entirely wrong.

And backwards.

And twisted.

Their world was in ruins because of Goran?! No wonder they hated him. No wonder they needed to take him prisoner right away the second we were in The Game. No wonder they'd been searching for us…

…Were they right? Were my memories right?

Was I just sitting in this dark apartment, hanging onto everything wrong?

The mattress of the bed squeaked as I stood. My hand flailed in the air, gesturing to Callen. "Can you just…can you just stay here for a minute…while I…"

But I couldn't finish.

I stumbled into the bathroom.

I closed and locked the door behind me.

And I heaved myself over the sink, both palms flat on the cheap laminate there… With my hair dangling into the sink… I stared at my haggard face as tears slipped silently down it. What the fuck? This was all so warped and messed up.

"Take your time, whatever time you need," Callen called from the other side of the door.

But that was a lie, and we both knew it.

Because I'd have to decide sooner or later.

Now that I knew how the story had gone up to this point, I had to decide where it was going next.

Rosabella

I'll admit, it took me a long while to come out of the bathroom and, when I did, my heart lurched as I reluctantly turned the lock on the doorknob. *This was my decision? Fuck this. …But I'd already made up my mind.*

My hand swiveled the cold doorknob, and the door creaked open, displaying Callen's brow wrinkled in concern as he hunched over his knees on the side of the bed, pausing in rubbing his hands together. He looked…as troubled as I felt.

"Hey there, kid," he started with a half-hearted smile. "You okay?"

I secretly wished he'd asked me anything else. My mind was spinning—my head hurt from the pressure of it.

"*No,*" I croaked. I knew why my throat was so dry, but there was nothing I could do about it: *Goran killed my birth dad and mom. Goran was responsible for their death and the decay of The Game—for the deaths of tons of people and the expanding darkness of the Darken…for Joy's disease that would probably end in her becoming a zombie…* I gritted my teeth.

Callen patted the spot next to him on the bed, but I didn't sit down. Instead, I crossed my arms over my chest and leaned against the wall, trying to command my eyes to stop smarting and whittle down the anger coiling in my chest…but it only grew bigger by the second.

"Callen, tell me this:" I began tersely, each word wrenching off my tongue, *"you let me go? Why?* I'm the only one who can fix your world, right? The last Game Maker."

I watched the man's eyes twist, but he quickly smoothed his expression over, so it was firm and steady again underneath the cropped cut of his gray hair. "That's two questions in one," he inclined his head at me in acknowledgement, "First, yes, you are the last Game Maker and the only one who can save our world. And, second…I—" He looked down at his feet for the briefest minute as his voice cracked, but I caught it. "Well, the system offered you a way out, and I thought—damn, if I was her, I'd take it. I'd take it and run. I wanted you to have a chance at a normal life again—*if you wanted one.*"

The sincerity in his face and eyes told me he wasn't lying, which made this, somehow, even harder. Thoughts raced through my mind. *The discontinued Game Wardens were good people… And their world was rotting…*

I chewed on my bottom lip. *Once I said this, I couldn't take it back. Maybe Callen was right; maybe I could have a normal life. Maybe I could go back to sleep and wake up and, somehow, convince myself that everything I'd experienced was a lie.*

That I was just a normal, teenage girl in a very real New York City.

And there was no Game.

No legacy.

No need to avenge and fix my parents' death or The Game world.

No anger knotting in my heart at the man who killed them—

Murdered them—

No.

It was impossible; it'd be downright impossible to lie to myself like that. I was NOT normal. I was Rosabella, Game Maker 3, and I carried the last of my generation's genes. I was The Game's last chance for survival. My parents' people were my responsibility now. Everything was in shambles, and only I could fix it—

Callen interrupted my inner monologue, his face scrunching into a strange sort of wince as he appeared to listen to something only he could hear. After a minute, his face straightened and his lips curled into a laughing smile, "Joy would like to inform you that portals aren't supposed to be used for intercom calls." He stifled a laugh.

"Well..." I pondered, letting the word sit on my tongue like the decision I wasn't sure I was ready to commit to yet. But, then, I decided. ...And I was right—*there was no taking this back.* My eyes hardened as I opened my mouth again, "You can tell Joy to *fuck off.* Because this *isn't* an intercom call. I'm coming back with you. I want you to take me back into The Game."

Callen's jaw dropped—that was the only way to describe it. He looked completely stunned and ran a quick hand through his hair, his eyes tracing circles on the floor like he couldn't believe it.

"*What?!*" he finally sputtered, "You—*want to go back?*"

But I was already gathering my body armor from the floor, into my arms. I turned my head over the pile of it and my shoulder to call back to him as I moved towards the bathroom to change, "Yep. Somebody's gotta face this shit and fix your world. *Might as well be me...*"

"Rosabella—" he started, shoving a hand in the bathroom door before I could close it, "*You know you don't have to do this, right?*"

His eyes were beseeching.

But he was wrong.

Because *I did* have to do this.

For my parents.

For me.

For…*some kind of peace.* Because there was none in this empty apartment, that was for sure.

Now, I felt like I had some sort of direction—some sort of *place.* A goal.

It felt…secure—like something to finally, fully lock into.

"You weren't lying I hope?" I challenged him instead of answering, "When you said I'm brave. How do you know that?" I bit my lip, putting more weight on his words than I'd ever admit.

The man chuckled, his face opened up again—lining with impressed humor as he lifted both eyebrows, "No offense, but it's kind of built into your class plus…do you know any other newb who can best two dragons?"

One dragon, I thought to myself. The second one had bested me but…well, his comment made me want to smile. *I did trap that Rinkeclaw. I fucking did it when it seemed impossible.*

I let the door shut behind me. And I stared at my reflection in the mirror, dwarfed by the huge ball of body armor in my arms and my mother's sword sticking out. And my cheeks looked ruddy, not as pale as before; and my eyes, more hopeful.

"I'm going to make you proud," I whispered to the glistening blade of the broadsword like I was talking to my mother. I slipped the portal ring—cold and thick—on my finger.

And something occurred to me suddenly—like a lightening bolt zapping through me with electricity. *I was going to do this and save their world, but I was going to do it my way.*

***

The portal thrust Callen and I back into The Game with a jolt. Immediately, a system update obscured my vision and the dark night and forest around us:

ROSABELLA, GAME MAKER 3 Has Joined The Game
[System Reward: A Heck Of A Selfless Decision Made, +45
XP, 339/300 +30 Baddie Points, 20]

The world froze. Green plus signs exploded overhead, swirling in slow motion—*Level Up? Awesome! A good way to start my journey here.*

[System Alert: ***Congratulations, You've Advanced To
Level 4!***]

Name	Rosabella	
Class & Level	Game Maker 4	
XP	339/400	
MRP	3895/6208	
HP	25/35	
Baddie Points	20	
Armor Class 15/20		
Abilities /20		
Strength	+0	10
Agility	+0	10
Endurance	-1	9
Intelligence	+1	13
Awareness	+1	12
Presence	+3	16
CM		2

[+9 HP & HP Extended By 9, 20/35. You've Been Awarded
+2 Ability Points And +5 HP, 25/35. Please Select Which
Ability You'd Like To Increase.]

Oh, thank goodness about the HP increase but what abilities to increase? I stared at the stats once more. My Endurance was low. Maybe I should increase that by 1 and save the other till I had a better feel for what I might need?

"System, increase Endurance by one and save the other Ability Point to use later," I blurted before I'd fully made up my mind. Several neon messages popped into view:

[System Understands Query...Loading Response...]
[System Alert: +1 Endurance, 10/20]
[System Alert: System Will Cache Additional +1 Ability Point In Your Inventory For Future Application. Inventory Updated.]

The world unfroze—

"*Hoeeeee*! She's back!" Rainer belted in excitement, lifting a fist over his head.

I barely had time to dismiss the system alerts and wrap my mind around the increased stats before something ran and hit me, full in the chest. I immediately recognized the dark hair and skinny, pale arms wrapped tight around my frame, "You didn't leave us!"

"Dormouse?" I asked.

The boy loosened his grip just enough to grin up at me, "See, she always remembers my name, Joy—without fail. *Unlike some people...*" He flashed an annoyed stare at the pink-haired girl who only scowled in return as she laced up a crossbow, pointing it at the surrounding trees.

"If you're not secure enough in your identity to embrace my nicknames, *that's on you*," she fired back, "As it is, you assholes are messing up my shot and, if I miss, there's no dinner—"

"Take your shot already, you've been lining it up for the past two years over there!" Rainer barked.

"*Argh!*" Joy let the arrow fly, throwing her hands down as it spun into the treetops and nothing else. A host of huge, brown birds, as big as deer, cawed and squawked, flurrying into the sky. Aggravated, Joy threw her bow into the underbrush with another scream and a thudding stomp of her boot.

"You made me miss it!" she yelled.

A shy smile lit up Dormouse's face as he nudged me in the ribs with an elbow. "She should say she missed *you* if we could squeeze a droplet of emotion out of her," he whispered laughingly. Louder, he called, "Joy, you didn't even welcome Rosabella back—"

"Welcome," the pink-haired girl snorted bleakly at me, slapping her hands sarcastically against the leather on her thighs, "Please come and eat up all the meager rations we *do* have—"

"Hey," Callen warned.

But not even the girl could rain on my parade. Because something expanded in my heart, just in seeing them all again—in being here. In this dark forest. In The Game world again.

Warmth washing over my core?

It was a surprising and strange sensation after so much cold and darkness. And, with it, came the equally foreign realization that this haphazard group of discontinued Game Wardens were becoming a little bit like family to me...

[System Reward: Looks Like You're Building Real Connections With Other Gamers! Nice Job! +10 XP, 349/400]

So strange and, yet, so rewarding to see it quantified. Without the gratifying popups, the real world had seemed empty.

"You're not hurt, are you?" Rainer immediately began checking me over like inspecting a crate or package, "Those New York thugs are the real deal—"

I tried to shove off his intense eyes and sausage fingers which pried at my wrists. "I was just in the apartment, safe and snug; I wasn't dealing with any drug dealers," I told him.

His already reddened face grew even more maroon and embarrassed by that. "Oh," he said gruffly, trying to latch onto his tough-guy exterior again and turn away, "Right."

"So, you're okay?" Dormouse asked, his eyes wide with concern and his hair falling into his eyes like usual. The skin of his face was such a stark contrast to the night sky behind him.

"Yeah," I trailed off, dusting off the body armor on my arms for something to do, "Yeah, I think I'm alright."

My fingers played with the hilt of my mother's sword at my belt as I stared up at the coal-colored sky. The woods surrounding us were dark; the silhouettes of enormous pines stretched along the horizon as the stars twinkled above. I stared at the patterns of blue and purple twisting and meshing with the glowing orbs, taking in a deep breath of the chill night hair. This place was magical. ...But my decision to come here? To do this... Was it right? Had I made the right choice?

Some of the stars were moving. I realized suddenly that the wooded glade was filled with spiraling, bright orbs. I peered closer, noticing as one ran into my arm, then, latched onto my bicep through my body armor with its claws: the Laxtail Chira—the miniature dragons Goran had showed me. Hundreds of them hovered and swirled around us, the lights on their tails flashing honey-yellow between their hungry faces like fireflies.

...Wait...hungry faces...

"Have you guys tried using the Chira to make food—like with their magic?" I asked. The words kind of just jumped off my tongue, although, admittedly, I felt awkward afterwards as they all stared at me.

"Look who's becoming a regular Gamer!" Rainer guffawed, grinning broadly and shoving me in the shoulder—an action that almost made me fall over.

"If it's so easy, let her do it," Joy snarled. And my forehead creased as I looked at her. What did she mean?

"Kid, you have to establish a bond and covenant with the dragons," Callen clarified, nodding at Joy. His eyes narrowed, "Dragons are a little finicky. Not many people have enough finesse to initiate a trade with them."

"Let me try," I blurted suddenly. "I mean, I have the Draconic Language Dictionary. I can speak to them." Oh shit. My heart spasmed in my chest at the thought. I was really volunteering? Me? My rate of failure was sure to double...

"Be our fucking guest," Joy spread her arms wide, gesturing to the thousands of dots lighting up corners of leaves and the tops of grass and bushes. Callen raised a worried eyebrow.

"Rosabella, you sure?" Rainer interjected; his bearded face looked uneasy for some reason.

"Of course, I'll try." I told him. "It's better than you guys starving." God, I sounded so confident. Why didn't I feel all of it? I swallowed. ...Right. How did one use this skill?

"System, how do I use the Draconic Language skill?" I turned away and murmured, hopefully not loud enough for all of them to overhear, but they probably did.

[System Understands Query...Loading Response...]
[System Answer: To Utilize Draconic Language Dictionary Skill, Simply Address A Dragon, And Your Words Will Be Translated As You Speak.]

Thanks, System. Seemed easy enough... But would it be? To be honest, I kinda wanted a little privacy for this endeavor. Trying to minimize the obviousness of my steps, I stole away to a tree stump a stone's throw away from the group. The Chira tittered around me playfully, squeaking and hissing. *Now to figure out what kind of dragon I was dealing with...or was it better that I didn't look at the stats? The Red Vodyaracka had been personally offended when I'd done that last time. Maybe it was better to wing it than risk their fury...*

One landed in my lap, looking confused as the curl of its back hit my stomach. It's tiny, black form rolled over, shaking itself before opening wings—

"Wait!" I breathed.

The Chira stopped. Its googly, yellow eyes—far too large for its head which made it seem infant-like—blinked up at me in astonishment and expectation.

The rock speaks!

It giggled, chattering and gnashing its teeth. The creature's tiny tail flickered to either side.

Progress! This was progress. It could hear me! "I'm not a rock," I told it, smiling a little bit despite myself.

Does the rock like to play games?

Well, this was going pleasantly so far. I didn't know why everyone had made such a stink about it. "Of course, I like to play games," I said. "If I win the game, will you help me make magic?"

Debatable.

The creature answered. Its face continued to blink blankly up at me.

"Debatable? I'm sorry, I don't understand," I tried.

Debatable that you will win. If I win, I take your sword. It's magic, I want it.

The Chira stated bluntly. ...*My sword? Well, he was turning out to be a direct little thing.* My eyes darted down to the broadsword tied to my belt where the tiny beast's eyes were already attached. *My mother's sword? Should I chance it? But, then again, I wasn't going to lose against this miniature plaything.*

"Okay," I nodded shortly, "What's the game? How do I win?"

The little dragon stared up at me; in the dim light, it looked particularly cute.

Five minutes.

Had I just gotten distracted by the cuteness? I didn't understand again… Red jumped to my cheeks. It was getting embarrassing admitting that I wasn't following the dialogue of this creature with what had to be a pea-sized brain…

I peered at the thing, "What do you mean?"

You have to survive five minutes without Game Over because otherwise you're, well, dead and I'll take your sword anyway. If you tap out, I win. You accept?

"Wait, *what?!*" I choked on my own saliva. "Survive?" *I'd thought Goran had said they were harmless!* I wracked my brain, trying to remember their stat sheet, but came up blank. The minute dragon in my lap blinked up at me. *It wasn't larger than my thumb. What could it possibly do? Plus, the group was counting on me for a meal.* I stole a glance at them, squatting around the campfire. *Afterall, I had volunteered for this. I didn't want to look like a sissy now.* The neon trade prompt hovered in front of me.

[Proposed Trade: If ROSABELLA, GAME MAKER 4
Survives 5 Minutes Without Game Over Or Tap Out,
LAXTAIL CHIRA, DRAGON 1 Will Create With Her. If
Forfeit, LAXTAIL CHIRA, DRAGON 1 Takes Rosabella's
Mother's Silver and Gold Broadsword.]
[Will You Accept the Trade?]
[Yes] [No]

"Fine, accepted," I spat, not liking any of it as the system selected 'Yes'. *This better be a cakewalk…*

[System Alert: Covenant Sealed]
[System Reward: A Risky Trade +20 XP, 369/400]

Wait, a 'Risky Trade'? Goddamn it, what did I get myself into?!

But I found out soon enough as the Chira swarmed, a million, tiny lights buzzing like a hurricane gale.

Directly at my face.

Rosabella

I won't not sugarcoat it, I ran. I ran like my pants were on fire, ducking into the underbrush, but the swarm of Chira was faster—

A thousand snapping jaws and cheeks. Lights flashed and popped like a million bulbs, blinding me, leaving my eyes stinging and bright orbs wobbling in my vision even in the dark night. Sharp pain—the excruciating prick of a thousand needles all at once—*through my fucking body armor!*

I'd thought I was facing ONE of them! Not ALL of them!

[-1 HP, 24/35]
[-1 HP, 23/35]
[-1 HP, 22/35]
[-1 HP, 21/35]
[-1 HP, 20/35]

"Get the *fuck off!*" I screamed, swatting at the masses, but it barely did anything. Their bites sizzled at my skin—

[-1 HP, 19/35]
[-1 HP, 18/35]
[-1 HP, 17/35]
[-1 HP, 16/35]

5 minutes? I had to do this for five minutes? Fuck that little shit Chira! Fuck them all! Wings filled my vision. Everything throbbed. My skin was on fire—

"Rosabella!" Callen's voice bellowed through the tornado of the assault, "They're like Kenchee, they like magic! They're drawn to it like moths. Get rid of your sword!"

Sword? My sword?! My bloody fingers slipped, trying to untie the scabbard. Fuck it.

[-1 HP, 15/35]
[-1 HP, 14/35]

"Equip my broadsword!" I hollered.

[Weapon Equipped.]

The metal swished in the air. The hum of the throng of Chira grew louder.

"There!" I yelled as I heaved the weapon upward. The swarm followed it. "Go fetch!"

And I launched it as far away from me as my complaining shoulders would let me.

[System Alert: Object Discarded.]

And the Chira dove for it like the hand of a beast. And the last few, lost ones bumped into my arms and legs, trying to join the rest but—

But it was over.

I looked down at my chewed up armor. *How the heck had they managed to mess it up when it was relatively resistant to dragon fire?* Blood and tiny wounds showed through where the rips and holes in the fabric didn't cover. I ran a hand up my neck. The tenderness there made me wince. *...I'd have to, somehow, get my broadsword from them later...*

"You alright?" Dormouse came trotting up, his black hair jostling back and forth on his head over the distress in his eyes.

I rubbed at my arm. *Alright was not how I'd phrase it.*

"I did not expect *that*," was all I could say instead, but I noticed hearty laughter coming from a few feet away, and I looked up to see Rainer, doubled over in a fit.

"She—" he huffed, breathlessly and red faced between chortles, "She ran like her hair was on fire! I've never seen you move that fast! Endurance suddenly increased! Agility 21!" he hooted.

And, something about the way he was enjoying the moment made me realize how completely ridiculous it all was. *I'd basically been battling a box of push pins...and they'd almost won!* And laughter bubbled up in me too, unexpectedly. And, suddenly, I was clutching at my side too, giggles convulsing through my sore body as neon words erupted overhead:

[System Alert: 5 Minutes Are Up. Covenant Completed. ROSABELLA, GAME MAKER 4 Won. LAXTAIL CHIRA, DRAGON 1 Must Create.]
[System Reward: You Showed Those Nasty Buggers...Kind Of... +20 XP, 389/400]

"Kind of!" Rainer hooted. "The system said 'kind of!'"

Joy raised a thin eyebrow. "It's not every day you get dinner and a show," she commented dryly, folding her arms over her chest.

"Ooh! Rosabella, what are you going to make? I'm starving!" Dormouse added.

And my face broke into a smile, "What do you want?"

"*Marshmallows!*" the kid's eyes widened, "We can toast them over the fire!"

"How about something with actual nutritional value," Joy barked.

"I'll make it all," I told them. *...Though it kind of felt like a lie because I had no idea at all how to do any of that.*

But Callen stepped up at my left shoulder like the rock-solid help he always was. "Rosabella," he told me, "just call one of the Chira. It'll open its mouth. Place a finger inside and let the magic flow through you. Imagine what you want to create—kind of like how you imagined my face with the portal ring."

I nodded. "Err…okay." And I swallowed the nervous butterflies dancing in my stomach and reached my hand out.

"Chira, come!" I whispered.

And one did, floating towards my palm in the silent night like a rose petal on the wind—absolutely nothing like the murderous flock I'd just battled. The adorable creature blinked up at me, opening its tiny mouth obediently—*was it the same one from before or a different one?* Either way, I inserted my pinky before it could decide otherwise. The pad of its tongue was wet and bumpy, but I closed my eyes. …And I started imagining food.

And words flew off my lips—ones I didn't know: *irtha hab constanca.*

And something else—a strange feeling of home—flowed through me.

[LAXTAIL CHIRA, DRAGON 1: -100 CMP 100/200]

What did that pop-up mean? I guessed it had to do with magic because, when I opened my eyes again, a plethora of dishes and plates lay at my feet in the grass, loaded with exactly what I had imagined: roast chicken, a bowl of mashed potatoes, two bags of marshmallows, five cans of soda, a bowl of apples, one of chocolate bars and a box of graham crackers.

The dragon fluttered off my palm, but everyone else dove for me.

And we gorged happily—ravenously. Or, rather, I watched them gorge while I picked. *I mean, after all that pizza, I wasn't quite as hungry as before.* And there was more light in the darkness than before, even as the Chira swarm moved elsewhere and the sky grew blacker.

I noticed Dormouse move away from the group. The boy stared, unabashed, into the vastness of the sky above us as he popped yet another marshmallow in his mouth. His eyes were transfixed on every detail of it like he saw the magic there too. And, staring up at the sky, standing there together, it was like we both understood what tiny specs of this universe we were.

And how we could be destroyed at any moment.

And, yet, how beautiful each moment could be…if we let it.

"It's still my birthday, you know," I whispered up into the Heavens like a wish I'd never gotten to request.

And Dormouse's head swiveled sharply, "Your birthday? We have the cake we found with you from the bunker—" he rushed.

"*Not the cake,*" I cut him off, "Please. Goran made that for me—"

"Right, no cake," he quickly corrected. "Did you have a smore yet? Joy, where did you put the graham crackers?" He called it over his shoulder.

"Up your mother's ass."

The girl's response echoed in the valley, catching us both off guard.

"No, up *your* mother's ass" Rainer countered boisterously, shoving the pink-haired girl who went flying to the side with an aggravated grunt. He took a long swig of the strong stuff in his canteen.

And a smile split my face.

And another laugh bubbled up from my chest.

And Dormouse laughed too.

And I knew, in that moment, I'd already gotten what I'd wished for:

A decision.

A place that felt more like home.

Some clarity.

And it was all I needed for right now.

238

Goran

The discontinued Game Wardens had been laughing and joking for over two hours around their pitiful excuse of a fire while I sat here shivering under this rock outcrop.

The utter assholes.

And they had Rosie. But they didn't have me—that was for damn sure.

I'd waited for the correct moment—waited until I heard the big one's voice slur from the liquid he'd been kicking back over his lips. I'd seen that glass bottle before; it'd been collecting dust on the shelf in the secret bunker for many a golden year. Because it was the very same whiskey that I put there the day Rosie was born. *They'd stolen it from us, my dear Rosabella the Great. They'd stolen from our bunker, and they stolen our daughter too.*

Don't worry, I wouldn't let them have Rosabella. I wouldn't let her slip between my fingers—not this time. Not ever. I'd do whatever I had to, and that was a promise. These monsters wouldn't get away with their crimes; I would kill every last one.

My wrists easily slipped out of the rope bonds, only scratching slightly on the rough fabric. The weak, beanpole one had tied me up, shaking while he did it as I made sure to glower at him the entire time. *Had no one learned to restrain people properly? Was I just a dinosaur—the last of a generation that could do this efficiently in my sleep?*

I spat on the ground and silently worked to untie the knots holding my legs together.

They wanted to play toy soldier? They had no idea that they'd just unleashed a nuclear threat that was gonna blow their little, plastic tents to the sky. …Or melt them into fucking oblivion. No one angered Goran and got away with it. These fuckers personally dug their own graves.

[System Reward: You Slipped Out Of Those Restraints! +10 XP, 1187/1200]

I sprung to my feet, crouching behind the darkened, holly bush—peering through the leaves at the campfire my captors gathered around, drinking, eating and joking loudly.

I saw Rosie there.

She was in her body armor again and looked somewhat, frazzled and bloodied. *I'd thought they'd finally taken her home and safe, but there she was again.*

"System, what is Rosie's MRP?" I asked tersely, my jaw hardening.

[System Understands Query...Loading Response...]

Work faster, damn thing. The neon letters I needed popped into view.

[Current MRP / ROSABELLA, GAME MAKER 4: 3895/6208]

My stomach dropped; my resolve steeled. It was too high; Rosie's MRP was too high. She probably knew by now—she'd probably seen it. And they had her. Those baboons of discontinued Game Wardens had her in their grips. I wouldn't have it. I always had to do things the hard way. Rosie always made me do them the hard way. ...At any rate, my hand was forced.

I quickly grabbed for the weapons the group had stolen from me: the dagger and bow and arrows. I dug in the arrow quiver, using a finger to pull out a lower value health pack I'd stashed there for emergencies like this—that Nomad guy had beat the crap out of me and had forced my hand in needing it.

[System Reward: BANDAGES, OINTMENTS & CREAMS Acquired. Object Will Be Placed In Your Inventory Unless You'd Like to Use. Would You Like to Use?]
[Yes] [No]

"Yes, use," I growled, hating the words on my tongue.

[+6 HP Available Or +250 MRP. Please Select Which Option You Prefer.]
[+6 HP] [+250 MRP]

"HP," I told it.

[System Alert: BANDAGES, OINTMENTS & CREAMS Used, +6 HP, 14/117]

I threw the bow over my shoulder, and, unsheathing my dagger, I sprinted up the hill and into the woods I knew better than the back of my hand. *Let them try to catch me now.*

***

Early morning sun filtered through the pointed, dark shafts of trees jabbing up into the sky. Most Gamers hated this part of the forest—the West Side. The dragons and Darken had burned it nearly to the ground several years back. No animals roamed here because there was nothing to eat—making for fruitless hunting—and there was no cover either; the place was stripped bare—*nearly in its underwear.* I chuckled to myself, relishing the thought of embarrassing this world that never did anything but despise me.

No new, green saplings shot up from the dirt or dead leaves that crunched under the soles of my sneakers. There weren't even any bugs to swat at or squirrels to watch darting around tree trunks and roots. This place was silent.

Lifeless.

Exactly how I liked it.

I wasn't afraid of 'silent' or 'lifeless'. Or the echoing sound of my own movement as every fall of my sneakers went:

Crunch.

Crunch.

Crunch.

In the dry leaves underfoot.

…Or the dark cloud that hung over the place in an ashen mist. A little fog didn't bother me, nor the still, musky smell that lingered: dragon's breath.

I knew what I was here for, and I wasn't afraid. *This was all for Rosie.*

I crested the hill, looking down at the utter destruction of the forest for miles: black shards of the life that used to exist here, cracks snaking through the earth like we'd ruptured the very fabric of the universe…and the stone wall no one wanted to be found near. In these parts, they called the stone wall The Blood Barrier because, if you found yourself on the other side of it without an invitation, you were as good as dead. I cocked my head, looking at it with the slightest grin. *All of that just…waiting for me.*

…Like I knew *they* were.

This place was always swarming with guards, though they would never let you see them to tip you off. They were trained in the old way… *Like me.*

"System, how many Nomads are within 90 feet of me?" I hissed under my breath.

[System Understands Query…Loading Response…]

My sharp gaze swept through the ash and darkness, trying to count them myself—*10, 11—*

[System Answer: 142 Nomads Are Within 90 Feet Of Your Position.]

Holy fuck. They were really taking paranoia to a whole new level these days… I kind of respected them for it. I sheathed my dagger and pulled my bow over my arm. My fingers made quick work of the task as I attached a tiny scroll I'd worked on earlier to an arrow shaft with a short string. I pulled it tight, knotting the white string quickly even with large fingers—tugging on the message to make sure it was secure.

I laced the arrow, yanked back the string, taking care to keep my form correct and my breathing even—

I released—

Hiss.

The sound vibrated in my ears, and the arrow flew, straight and strong.

Into the valley.

I watched as the tip of it buried in the old stone fence, the fletching on the end quivering. *Now, time for the fun part…*

I watched them swarm—Nomads' bodies so camouflaged with their surroundings that it nearly looked as though the landscape was rippling…

Running…crouching…tensioning.

All armed. All fierce with fighting skills to match.

Roughly a hundred bodies came out of the woodwork like the most genius termites. *And I respected genius termites—especially ones with mega weapons backed by the greatest dragon in the land…or the cruelest; both of those things were synonymous to me.* In fact, that was exactly who I'd come to see: that nasty dragon.

Before the Nomads rushed to start up their flaming catapults or volley a million arrows precisely into my chest, I stepped out of the woods. I knew how to play this act. I'd done it before.

I dropped the bow and dagger into the dead leaves.

I raised both palms in submission over my head.

And I watched as a huddle of them read the scroll I'd written and attached to the arrow.

"*I come in peace!*" I yelled across the vacant valley, "I come with a proposition that Ye Old One is gonna want to hear."

And it was to be expected that the Nomads turned towards me, metal clanging as their swords drew at once, rushing towards me with bloodlust in their eyes and tensing their fists wrapped around bludgeons and blades.

And it was to be expected that I let them come to me.

Unarmed. Like a lamb to slaughter.

Except that I knew they wouldn't harm me. … *Ye Old One always loved a good business deal.*

I was doing all this for Rosie, I told myself. *I hoped she'd see that eventually.*

I was only making a deal with the devil to free her from this place— these evil people and this terrible Game. I was ready to make the whole thing cannibalize itself; it was what they all deserved anyway.

"Did you read the note?" I shouted as the first ones came barreling towards me. Their muscular frames appeared even larger underneath the layers of fabric of their warfare camouflage. Some of the guys literally looked like boulders—their shoulders covered in moss, leaves and earth…their faces streaked with clay and black paint. They'd be terrifying to Rosie. But, to me, they just looked like another lie.

Another game. Another way out of this mess.

…Another way to get to Rosie—to save her. And I wouldn't let them shake me. I was good at deception. I always had 20 aces in my pocket. And I would play one here. I wouldn't let Rosie or her mother down.

The first guard grabbed me by the hair, pushing me to my knees. Pain ripped through my skull, but I bit my lip to keep back a scream as my HP flashed into view.

[-1 HP, 13/117]
[System Penalty: Count Yourself Officially Captured -50
XP, 1137/1200]

These assholes didn't know they were dealing with an experienced warrior. The Nomad's face leaned mockingly into mine, so coated in grime that I could only really make out the red and whites of his leering eyes. *... The guy needed a shower. When they said 'death smells', they didn't describe how it really was a certain flavor.* Fearing I'd vomit, I tried to hold my breath, but that wasn't a good long-term strategy—*you know what I mean?*

I gritted my teeth and kept my face stone; it was the only way I'd get through this alive.

"The Commandress will decide what to do with you," the Nomad garbled, gnashing his teeth too close; his stinking breath invaded my nostrils.

And the rest surrounded me in a swarm of loud, boisterous cries. *No one said they were 'advanced' termites—only 'genius'.*

"*Take me to your Commandress, then,*" I demanded.

Like I was in control.

Because I was. Even if they didn't know it yet. I was going to bring down darkness and destruction on all this land, and their dragon was going to help me.

245

Rosabella

"I don't think you understand," Callen's terse voice woke me, although he was clearly talking to someone a few steps away, "He's gone! *Who tied him up?!*"

His voice was raised and frantic; he did *not sound happy.*

I wiped the sleep out of my eyes and rolled over on the hard ground, though I couldn't wipe the crick out of my back from sleeping in this blanket; I felt every rock and bump under my spine through it... *Wouldn't a magical place like this figure out a way to make magical beds for all this camping they did?*

"It was me," I heard Dormouse's shaking shout. "I tied up Goran—"

"Well, *he's gone now*," Callen huffed, throwing down his hands in clear disgust.

And I felt the color drain out of my face as I realized what they were talking about. The forest blurred around everyone's tense faces— Callen, Joy and Dormouse, arguing in a circle and Rainer just propping himself up from sleep on the ground. *They'd had Goran tied up, and he'd escaped? Goran was...free?*

I swallowed. *How long would it be till he tried to find me—tried to take me back again? Put me in some kind of bunker I couldn't get out of this time?* I squeezed my eyes shut, trying to shut out the terror suddenly running through my veins. *I shouldn't be scared. I was safe with the group. I was going to help them fix their world.* If I repeated it to myself, it slowed my heartbeat and shaking breaths a little.

"At least we have the girl," Joy let out a sarcastic chuckle, gesturing to me.

Dormouse narrowed his eyes at the pink-haired girl, "You mean, thank you Rosabella for helping us repair The Game."

Joy frowned, shrugging, "Whatever."

"But how much damage will Goran continue to do to The Game even if we work with Rosabella to repair it?" Rainer grumbled, shifting to his feet. His face was grumpy and beet red—maybe from all the alcohol he'd drunk last night. He swiped a massive hand across his forehead, spitting into the grass.

"What do we do?" I asked all of them, getting to my feet myself. My head shifted and my vision of the woods swam after an unrestful night. The bright light of the sunrise felt like a million swords stabbing at my pupils. I stepped to the side to avoid it, shading my face and trying to read the grim expressions of the group against the backdrop of the trees.

"Well, you have to get the last CM Diamond you need to activate your Creator Magic, and we need to get you Leveled Up a bit further," Callen replied, tight-lipped, "You ready, kid? We're going to have to do some searching around." I noticed today that it was less of a question as the gray-haired man turned and began swiftly into the woods. He was clearly not in the mood to hear otherwise.

I grabbed up camp supplies, helping Rainer shove them in his pack. And we all trotted after him.

"…So, Callen's pissed," I started after what seemed like over half an hour of walking in awkward silence.

From my shoulder, Dormouse's face collapsed in a mortified wince, "*At me.* It was *my fault.*" His chin quivered on the last, whispered part. "I'd offer to use my Run-Run-As-Fast-As-You-Can extra, but, honestly, I just kind of want to keep my mouth shut right now. I think I have like half of the miles left. System, how many more miles do I have on the enchanted object?"

I watched Dormouse's system answers pop up over his face.

[DORMOUSE, CODER 14: System Understands Query...Loading Response...]
[DORMOUSE, CODER 14: System Answer: 5/10 Steps Or 5 Miles Are Currently Left In Your RUN-RUN-AS-FAST-AS-YOU-CAN Object.]

Rainer shot the boy a narrow-eyed stare, "I taught you to tie people up, what went wrong?" He barked the question, but his voice wasn't accusatory...it was more 'trying-to-understand'.

"He was—*staring at me*," Dormouse shivered, shaking his arms out even in the balmy weather, "It was unnerving—"

"Oh, *boo hoo*," Joy pushed between all of us, advancing to the marching front behind Callen. "Go cry to someone else," she snapped, "Not like this blunder is going to kill any of you or anything."

I swallowed, seeing the black tendrils of flesh that now crawled up her neck and into her hairline where she'd swept her pink-fire hair up into a high ponytail. ...*She was talking about how she was turning Darken. I really couldn't blame the girl for being bitter.*

"By the way, what the *fuck* happened to your armor, Rosabella?" the girl lifted a condescending eyebrow, "You know it stops acting like a defensive barrier if it's ripped to shreds, don't you?"

"It lessens the armor protection when the fibers are compromised," Dormouse filled in when I probably looked excruciatingly lost. "Check your armor stats quick to see."

"Oh, I—" I stumbled over my own embarrassment as I tried to request the information. My fingers ran over the fraying holes and rips on my arms, still rimmed red from my own blood, "System, bring up my armor stats."

[System Understands Query...Loading Response...]
[Current Armor Class / ROSABELLA, GAME MAKER 1:
11/20]

It'd been 15 before, hadn't it?

Rainer whistled, "Damn! You took a beating from those Chira. Don't worry, we'll patch you up somehow—"

"Hold up, everyone hold up!' Callen shouted from the front.

My boots ground to a halt under me as all of our eyes searched the horizon, alarm speeding pulses and making our ears crane for any sign of danger. And there was one but—

But, honestly, it didn't make much sense…

"Is that—is that rap music?" I breathed, utterly confused. My eyes hopped from face to face, trying to understand the faint beat in the distance—a flurry of rapid rapping, coexisting and in rhythm, strangely, with a faint thudding underfoot…shaking the ground.

Tha-thump.

Tha-thumb.

THUMP!

I jumped as the ground vibrated under foot, "What is it?"

But no one was particularly paying attention to me. The group's gazes were intertwined like a huge spiderweb over my head, flickering and narrowing.

"We can use my mile increaser to get closer," Dormouse said, "I have up to five miles—"

Joy rolled her eyes at Callen who appeared to be considering it, "Oh my God, seriously? You want to go towards it? We could be crushed."

"Or we might find that CM Diamond Rosabella needs," Rainer interrupted, a burly hand burrowed in his thick beard.

What were they talking about?! "…Anyone want to clue the lost girl in?" I blurted, chewing on my lip.

And that was when I heard the roar—hair-lighting.

Ear-splitting, raking through the trees.

Furious.

And a second roar—louder. Like a counterattack.

Dragons.

"Ever heard of a Dragon Spar, kid?" Callen asked.

***

No. No, I did not know what a Dragon Spar was and, as Dormouse whizzed us through space even closer with his mile augmenter, I suddenly realized that I didn't want to know.

The shriek of an enormous beast ballooned through the evergreen treetops overhead—sharp like an eagle's cry. But I could barely make it out behind the thunderous music pulsating through the woods. It WAS rap music. What the heck?

The forest was dense here, the trees snug together in their tall ambush like they'd commiserated and were forming a fence, not a forest. The bushes grew thick too—wild, tall and thorny. I could barely see the way forward, though I didn't need to see to know it was a shit show. The ground trembled—leapt—underneath me. Brush snapped and popped from the movement of something huge just beyond. A thud shattered the air. A roar detonated.

You good-for-nothing spot stealer! Tell them you don't want it then!!!

Heat bristled, blowing upwards over my face as the bush in front of me caught fire—

[-3 HP, 11/35]

Stars swirled in front of my face with the heat—*magic or my imagination?*

I do want it!

Hissed an older woman's breathy voice in my mind—*a different dragon?*

"Rosabella, *get down!*" Callen hollered.

My ears rung. Someone grabbed me by the fur collar of my armor and tugged me backwards. I fell, my ass hitting the ground hard—*oof.*

A giant, red-scaled foot landed in the dirt where I'd just stood, squashing the brushfire, unbothered by it as the flames grew up like thorns around its talons. The red dragon reared. The treetops bent. And magic flowed and spiraled out of its mouth like a tornado, mowing down the branches, launching—

Creating a deafening gale all around us.

Towards another dragon, just visible, stomping through the woods. It's snaking, purple tail rammed into a tree—

Wood splintered, cracking—

Music blared.

"*Duck!*" Joy screamed, leaping for me.

And, suddenly, my face was in the dirt again—Joy, nearly on top of me. I scrambled to my feet as the world rocked again.

"Brilliant idea, guys!" Joy shouted sarcastically as she picked herself up from the ground, brushing dirt off her bodysuit. Her eyes were as fiery hot as the flames around us. But mine were fastened on the red dragon bellowing overhead. Its yellow stomach and the spikes along its spine…

"System, is that the same dragon from before?" I whispered, nearly in awe.

[System Understands Query…Loading Response…]

251

Low to the ground like this with the beast's shadow looming over us, the creature looked larger than ever. Its ears were flat against its head, pissed, and its huge, leathery wings flapped angrily in the wind.

I EARNED my rank! You can't just take it.

...It definitely sounded like the Red Vodyaracka Skydrake from before. ...*What was his name? The system would know...*

Watch me take it.

Hissed the second dragon's voice as classical music flared to life with a cymbal crash, decimating the rap music. Fireworks of red and purple magic exploded overhead. An update popped into view, distracting me for a minute:

[System Answer: Yes. The Dragon Is Sparo, The Same Red Vodyaracka Skydrake From Somergot Prison. Recently Demoted And No Longer A Prison Guard.]

Ouch. ...So that explained the dialogue running through my head... And it, also, meant the beast had CM Diamonds that I needed, the sooner the better.

"Hey!" I screamed at the dragon—at the treetops—"Hey! Can I talk to you?" I waved my hands over my head before realizing that probably at least one of them should be holding a weapon...if I had any sense of self-preservation. I mean, the last time we'd met, he'd nearly set me on fire...

"Are you trying to get yourself killed?!" Joy hissed, looking like she was about to punch me.

But the dragon had heard. Lumbering footfalls shook the ground...towards me. A huge, red head snaked downward—close enough to lick. The beast's yellow eyes scanned my form up and down while its nostrils flared with annoyance.

Girl who tried to kill me, no offense but I'm kind of having a rough day here, and I don't need you to make it rougher, you catch my drift? Bug the fuck off.

The male voice rattled in my mind. The head snaked upward again. A claw came down way too close to my feet, throwing me backwards and out of the way as the dragon turned—

[-1 HP, 10/35]

"Ah!" I screamed—squeaked—as the claw grazed my body armor.

Unless you're here to help me get vengeance, I'm so not interested.

The Vodyaracka droned in between my ears. Of course. Of course, I was going to have to do something to get a CM Diamond. Of course, I was going to have to put myself in a stupid, harm-filled situation…again. …If I really wanted to do this. If I was committed to repairing the world of my parents. Shit. The mind guilt trip alone was stifling.

What kind of vengeance? I asked, my thoughts vibrating with a strange confidence inside my skull and upward at the beast. Whoa, that felt different—

[System Reward: Congratulations, You Have Added A New Skill. +5 XP, 394/400
DRACONIC TELEPATHY: Allows A Gamer To Communicate Telepathically With Dragons. To Use, Speak In Your Mind, Intending The Creature To Hear, And It Will. +1 XP Will Be Rewarded At The Beginning Of Every Conversation. Warning: Communication Is A Two Way Street. This Skill Is Not Responsible For Any Information Or Thought Leak That May Accidently Occur Between Gamer And Dragon.]

My eyes scanned over the text. Oh, wow. Okay…so now I was a total freak and could telepathically communicate with dragons? At least the rest of the group couldn't hear if I fell flat on my face with it…

What kind of vengeance? I insisted.

[Draconic Telepathy Used… +1 XP, 395/400]

Above me, the creature shook its massive head like a dog shaking out its coat. Its lips rippled backwards in a low growl, showing teeth.

No offense, but I don't really want to be responsible for the death of a small human—not today.

It turned to waddle away.

"No, *wait!*" I couldn't help it; the words hurled off my tongue, far more desperate than I wanted them to be. *Everything was riding on this. I needed the last CM Diamond, so I could activate my Creator Magic and fix this world—do something that my birth parents would have been proud of. I needed that final CM Diamond…so, maybe, I could make myself feel proud about something I'd done…anything.*

Just tell me what to do, and it's done if you'll give me a CM Diamond. I attempted to speak clearly in my mind, and it worked. I watched the beast hesitate, swaying like the treetops above me.

Listen, I'll give you your damned CM Diamond, but you're not going to like the quest. This purple asshat stole my Guard position at the prison. While I fight her, you and your group hit her where it hurts—her lair. It's three miles from here to the north. She hordes Darken. Wipe them out, and, maybe, we'll mutually respect each other.

His eyes narrowed at me.

I squinted back at him, my heartbeat racing. *Darken? He wanted me to wipe out zombies for him.* The corresponding message fizzled into view:

[Proposed Trade: ROSABELLA, GAME MAKER 4 Slays Helladore's Darken Horde, SPARO, RED VODYARACKA

SKYDRAKE, DRAGON 14 Gives ROSABELLA, GAME
MAKER 4 1 CM Diamond.]
[Will You Accept The Trade?]
[Yes] [No]

"Done," I spat, selecting 'Yes'—God, why did I always speak
before I thought about it?!

[System Alert: Covenant Sealed]
[System Reward: A Trade With A Dragon +20 XP,
415/400]

My vision tinted green as all movement around me slowed to a
stop. The music halted. Branches and leaves overhead paused mid-
bend. Even the dragon above me froze. The Vodyaracka's massive face
looked surprised or smug, I couldn't tell which exactly; *interpreting
giant lizard facial expressions felt a little difficult given I had nothing to
base them on.* Emerald plus symbols rotated all around me, floating
upward. *A Level Up? Awesome, I needed it if I was ever going to get to
L6 to use my Creator Magic…*

[System Alert: ***Congratulations, You've Advanced To
Level 5!*]**

Name	Rosabella
Class & Level	Game Maker 5
XP	415/500
MRP	3895/6209
HP	19/44
Baddie Points	20
Armor Class 11/20	
Abilities /20	
Strength	+0	10
Agility	+0	10
Endurance	+0	10
Intelligence	+1	13
Awareness	+1	12

Presence	+3	16
CM		2

[+9 HP & HP Extended By 9, 19/44. You've Been Awarded The Ability To Select One Of The Following Weapons:]
[Machine Gun W/ 2 Belts] [5 Cans Of Mass Pandemonia Gas]

Whoa. The first one seemed self-explanatory, but the second? I noticed Examination Opportunities hovering over each one and clicked on the shield and magnifying glass option over the second choice.

[System Option Examined... +1 XP, 416/500]

[A Closer Look At The Fine Print Explains The Option Further:]

Object:	5 Cans Of Mass Pandemonia Gas
Required Class & Level For Use:	None
Description:	Spray A Can of This On An Enemy And Watch Pandemonia Ensue. Confuses Enemies For 5 Minutes, Giving You An Attack Advantage. The Cans Seem Rather Sturdy For Travel, But Is This Glorified Pepper Spray?
Augment Capacities:	+0 Strength
Baddie Points:	+0

Hmmm. To be honest, I wasn't super impressed by it. Confusion would be a good thing when trying to defeat a zombie herd but...well, would it be enough? I wasn't convinced. I clicked on the Examination Opportunity over the first option to check that out instead.

[System Option Examined... +1 XP, 417/500]

[A Closer Look At The Fine Print Explains The Option Further:]

Object:	Machine Gun w/ Two Belts
Required Class & Level For Use:	L3 w/ 11 Strength
Description:	Machine Gun Made Of Heavy Metal. Looks Like This Thing Can Do Some Serious Damage. Two Belts Of Ammo Come With It.
Augment Capacities:	+10 Strength
Baddie Points:	+40

Wow, +10 Strength?! That was even better than my broadsword! ...But I'd need 11 Strength to use it. Currently, I was only at 10. That's when I remembered I still had an Ability point cached from last Level Up. Perfect.

[Please Select Which Extra You'd Like.]

The message popped, neon, in my vision.

"Machine Gun with two belts," I told it. The system beeped.

[System Alert: MACHINE GUN W/ TWO BELTS Selected. Object Will Be Placed In Your Inventory Unless You'd Like To Equip. Would You Like To Equip?]
[Yes] [No]

"No," I stated. I had to upgrade my strength first. "System, please add my cached Ability Point from the last Level Up to Strength."

[System Understands Query...Loading Response...]
[System Alert: +1 Strength, 11/20]

"Equip the Machine Gun," I commanded—*was it just me or was that resolve embedded in my voice?* I gritted my teeth together as the bulky weapon appeared in my hands.

[System Alert: Weapon Equipped. +40 Baddie Points, 60]

Cool. Time unfroze in a whirlwind. And, suddenly, the deafening music returned and the dragon overhead…and the coiling dread in my stomach as I realized what I'd just agreed to. *Fuck my life.*

"Where the hell did you get that beauty?" Rainer shouted, nodding at the gun in my grip.

But I didn't have time for a Q&A. "Dormouse!" I yelled at the storky kid, "Do you have enough steps on your mile increaser to get us 3 miles north?"

The Coder nodded, "Uh, sure—"

"Everyone clasp hands!" I commanded as the wind threw my hair into disarray around my face…as the music and screaming of the dragons as they clashed again pounded at my eardrums. "Dormouse, take us there!"

And I shut my eyes.

A strange sensation of urgency and electricity coursed through my body because, suddenly, I was the one giving orders. I was the one taking charge—leading. And it should have felt unnatural. It should have felt foreign or strange. But, it didn't. It felt like, somewhere along the line, I'd been built for this.

Rosabella

"You made a deal with *the dragon?!*" Rainer bellowed as soon as we rocked back on solid ground. The magic of Dormouse's mile increaser blurred and sizzled behind us—as did the music, now a far-away thud instead of piercing. I shook my head, trying to reduce the ringing there. Emotionally, I was torn between fear and relief. *At least I was away from whatever that dragon fight was...*

"I got us the CM Diamond," I corrected the Nomad. "Now, we just have to work for it."

"I keep telling you all, I'm not a mercenary," Rainer grumbled, running his fingers up and down his arms as though to soothe his own annoyance, "I fight the battles I *choose*—"

"Well, I guess we're fighting this one," Joy interrupted curtly. "All of us. If Rosabella can get the last CM Diamond, activate her CM and, somehow, fix this world so I don't end up losing my memory and turning Darken, I, at least, am all for it."

I gaped at the girl and her strange affirmation. Her eyes were burning flames, nearly challenging the rest of the group, ringed in thick eyeliner as her straight ponytail fluttered in the wind behind her head. She nodded at me, her hooded eyes narrowing. ...Like we had an understanding or unexpected respect. And, somehow, that look in her eyes fueled me—gave me the edge to grind forward.

Even though my throat was bad-cornbread dry, I shaded my eyes with a hand and looked out into the horizon. "What was all that—between the dragons back there?" I asked, trying to make my voice casual although the jumping of my heart underneath my torn body armor was anything but.

"Err, it was a Dragon Spar," Dormouse quibbled, stepping forward. "It's basically the clash of two magic-wielding creatures, obviously usually dragons—a formalized fight. Since both are magic, they use spells and brute force to one-up each other. They even have music, trying to overpower and intimidate the other—like fighters in a ring. …Um, so, not to be rude, but why are we here again?" The boy blinked at me, and his face was as lost as the rest of the group's stares.

"There," I pointed through the trees where the landscape turned open and brown. Something had caught my eye: something dark below us in a rounded crater of earth.

Callen held a warning arm over our group though none of us had moved. "There's something down there."

I bet I knew what.

In the silence of our uncertainty, I heard a hum hushing the valley.

Soft.

Grating gasps and cries.

It sounded like suffering.

And it matched what my eyes saw as we all stepped forward to where the earth sloped downward under our feet. The crater was darkened—not with rocks or brush. It was infested with Darken—a swarm of zombies, blotting out the dirt and landscape, stumbling against each other in a massive herd, stuck in the confines of the hole. Their heads lolled to the side and their arms were limp—their mouths gasping. The darkness had taken over their flesh, ripping it into melting boils and wounds. Their hair was as wilted as their lifeless limbs and the torn clothing still hanging on their thin bodies. And they walked—jumbling into each other. *There must have been hundreds of them. This was the purple dragon's lair.*

"What fresh hell is this?" Joy wanted to know, her face constricting in an even deeper frown than normal.

"I've seen herds, but why are there so many of them?" Dormouse wondered, "It's statistically improbable—"

"It's the purple dragon's horde," I explained, my lips tightening into a grim line. "The Vodyaracka wants us to destroy it. That's what I have to do to get the CM Diamond."

And it, suddenly, sounded far worse saying it than I'd thought. It sounded…*morbid.*

I peered down over the crater in the valley, clawed into the earth probably with the purple beast's own talons. The Darken there stumbled and twitched, moaning and braying even in the harsh sunlight.

"This is *fucked up*," Joy spat, her arms crossing over her chest, "I've done a lot of shitty things in my life, but this? This is wrong. Those are *people* down there—Gamers who have lost their memory—"

Dormouse raised a finger, "Not all Darken are Gamers who lost their memory. Some came out of the initial darkness appearance during the Reordering—"

"Why are you so nerdily unhelpful?!" Joy threw her arms down at her sides; her face darkened with an unscrubbable shadow. "I'm having a moral dilemma over here, and I don't have many of those." *I secretly wondered if the pink-haired girl would feel differently about it if she wasn't turning zombie herself…*

"You said it yourself, Joy," Callen interrupted, stepping forward, "We have to do what is necessary to fix our world. If the Vodyaracka will give Rosabella the CM Diamond she needs for doing this, we might just have to bite the bullet." The man's face was serious and steeled. ...*He...agreed with me?*

"Our world is dying," the gray-haired man continued. "We either kill this group of a few hundred zombies or we all become them in a the not-so-distant future. It gets worse every day now, accelerating. System, bring up the Game Damage Points," he barked.

[System Understands Query...Loading Response...]
[GDP – 87/100]

Current Gamer Population:	336 Million
Current Darken Population:	172 Million
Darken To Gamer Ratio:	~51.19%
Darkness Cover:	80/100
Dilapidation Cover:	94/100

Silence blanketed the group as uncomfortable gazes burned between us and the numbers. And the reality of my trade hit me square in the face, looking down at the horde—and the weight of it. *I'd said we would kill them? ALL of them? And their entire world hung in the balance? Gulp.*

But Callen looked at me, his eyes intense and determined. ...And I realized that there was no way around this one.

"How bad do you want that CM Diamond?" Rainer huffed, yanking his battle axe off his back and raising a bushy eyebrow. "If you're in, I'm in," he vowed.

And I shifted the weight of the machine gun in my grasp to shake out my trembling hands. The nerves under my skin jumped with fiery fear as I took an immense breath and said the words I didn't even want to hear, "Let's do this."

Because, as much as I didn't want to, I had to face this. I had to man up and face it, or my decision to come back to The Game was all but null and void. ...I'd fail the legacy of my parents—fail them in protecting the world they'd loved. *And I sure as hell wasn't about to do that.*

I raised my chin higher, "You guys with me?"

My answer was the clatter of weapons drawing. I bit down on my lip and leveled my own. And I nodded. I let my boots take me...

One step.

Two steps.

Three...

Through the tall grass. Towards the zombie crater.

My heart hammered inside my chest, decimating my eardrums with the force. My throat was so dry that I had to swallow three times before any wetness found it. I stared at the mass of zombies.

"For my parents," I whispered under my breath, as the wind carried my feeble words away. And, so, I reached inside then, to find the courage. I reached inside to steady my faltering steps—

I was Game Maker Rosabella.

I would honor my parents.

I would get that CM Diamond. I would put these Darken out of their misery and win the magic that could save my parents' world. My fingers tightened around the metal of the gun.

"For the record, I still think this is messed up!" Joy shouted from behind me as I began down the steep slope. The soles of my boots slid in the deep mud and thick grass.

"I agree!" I spat back, biting my lip. *I'd never agreed more.*

I tripped down the remaining slope, nearly falling at the end. The thin, fabric part of my body armor on my calf sliced open on the jagged rocks I moved by, making a ripping sound. *Ugh, not more damage to it! I didn't want the armor class to drop further.* The tearing noise was all I could hear besides the swaying of the grass...each of my own breaths...and the moaning.

...Of the undead.

Like the saddest sound I'd ever heard layered from a million lips.

They hadn't seen me yet, but I knew that'd only last for another minute or so. I'd seen how quick they were; I remembered from that day…

[System Searching MRPs To Select & Display Correct Memory…]

The Darken latched onto me with slimy, unyielding fingers, its teeth snapping in my face—

Ew, no! I pushed the memory down, shivering. I clutched the gun tighter.

Think tactical, I told myself. *Pretend you're back in New York playing a video game. Where was the best vantage point for a fight like this?*

"Rosabella?! What are you doing?!" Joy hissed from above.

I looked around and instantly realized my mistake.

High ground.

What was I thinking coming down the slope?! High ground was ALWAYS the best when dealing with a horde like this. I was already letting fear cloud my judgment. *I needed to turn around—*

"Get up here!" Rainer shouted.

But I'd been seen—spotted.

A raspy growl rattled right in front of me. And my eyes latched onto the empty eyes of a Darken only a foot away. Its mouth leaked saliva and blood.

Its bony fingers reached for me—

With a shriek, I jumped backwards—towards the slope behind me—

But the shriek was a bad move too.

Because, as my ankles and boots became ensnared in the underbrush, the entire Darken horde heard.

And turned.

And the rest of my group might have been, literally, backing me from above, but, down here, I only had me.

And the gun.

Fear thudded rapid-fire in my chest.

Rosabella

SHIT. I kicked my feet free of the entrapping grass and roots holding my boots captive. I heard the brush snap.

And the growls of the Darken. *They were too close to me!*

My heartbeat rammed in my ears—

An undead hand grabbed for my sleeve even as I heard arrows whizz through the air from Joy and Callen above—*hopefully they wouldn't hit me.*

"*Uhh!*" I hauled myself upward, the grass sticky against the palm of my hand as I leaned on the slope, trying to edge up the ridge, but it was too steep to keep an even footing. I tripped, falling hard on my hip on the firm ground. I watched my HP appear over my head, like a bad reminder of the stamina I didn't have against this horde.

[-1 HP, 18/44]

The Darken were closing in, forming an impenetrable semi-circle around me filled with snapping jaws and rotting flesh, reaching—

"Rosabella, aim and pull the trigger, easy-peesy!" Rainer instructed, yelling from the ridge above. *Sure, easy-peesy.* I gritted my teeth, tightening my trigger finger on the heavy gun in my grasp. *It was kill or be killed time. ...Otherwise, known as machine gun time.*

I swallowed.

I squeezed my eyes together for the briefest second, praying that I was making the right choice here in killing these things. ...*Honestly, it wasn't much of a choice at all*, I reminded myself. *It was the only option. I'd been shoved in the corner of 'kill these things' or 'let them eat me', and I certainly wasn't THAT courteous.*

I pulled a shallow breath into my lungs. I squinted into the scope of the gun, wondering if lining this up was anything like a video game...

And I made the decision. I pulled the trigger—

The solid, metal end of the gun rammed repeatedly into my shoulder as bullets exploded from the tip. The pain of it tore at the soft flesh there.

[-1 HP, 17/44]

Rat-tat-tat.
Rat-tat-tat.

[HELLADORE'S DARKEN HORDE, UNDEAD 8: -300 HP, 7700/8000]

The inflamed sound of the gun was deafening, making my ears smart, ring and pop as the weapon jumped in my determined grip. I wrapped my fingers more fiercely around the cold metal.

I bit my lip.
I bit down any of my doubt.
And I aimed.
I mowed their asses down.
Rat-tat-tat.
Rat-tat-tat.

[HELLADORE'S DARKEN HORDE, UNDEAD 8: -1000 HP, 6700/8000]

I'd only ever done this before in video games, but I watched the impact of the bullets, thudding into thick, Darken flesh—through their torn clothing, sinking into skin and bone.

Rat-tat-tat.

Rat-tat-tat.

[HELLADORE'S DARKEN HORDE, UNDEAD 8: -500 HP, 6200/8000]

Damn, I'd gotten less of them that time. Still—I watched the surprise on the zombie's faces.

As blood splattered.

As they fell into a scrambling pile of reaching arms and dying moans, still trying to claw at me even as their bodies grew cold.

Filth and flesh sprayed across my face and hands: warm, sticky, disgusting. I wanted to vomit, but I couldn't stop.

There were more of them.

More Darken.

Climbing over the bodies of the fallen to get at their meal: me. And the arrows from overhead were helping some, but not as much as I'd hoped. I watched the HP from them fly up, the damage increasing slowly... Not fast enough.

[HELLADORE'S DARKEN HORDE, UNDEAD 8: -50 HP, 6150/8000]
[HELLADORE'S DARKEN HORDE, UNDEAD 8: -50 HP, 6100/8000]

Not like what I could do with this hulking piece of metal in my grasp.

I turned the gun—so leaden in my weak fingers that it nearly felt like I already had a bruise on my arm from supporting it. And I ripped the trigger back again with as much strength as I could muster—

[-1 HP, 16/44]

Rat-tat-tat.

Rat-tat-tat.

I could barely hear the incendiary sound of it, now, from being so close. Only the ringing: sharp, high-pitched screaming in my ears.

[HELLADORE'S DARKEN HORDE, UNDEAD 8: -500 HP, 5600/8000]

Only the thudding movement of the thing: spearing my shoulder, over and over again, with the kickback.

Only the way I was struggling—gritting my teeth and using all my vigor—*just to hold on.*

"*Rrraaaaghhhh!*" I screamed, digging deeper into my own strength than I'd thought was possible.

[-1 HP, 15/44]

Gone was Rainer crowing at the zombies over my head and the wind, kicking up dust around me. Gone was Dormouse on the crest of the hill, shading his eyes to watch as his fingers worked Code in the air. *All I saw were the Darken*—the ones keeping me from getting the Creator Magic I needed.

An enemy—*any* enemy.

Just an oppressor to latch onto in this moment—something to pour my pain and fury at the injustice of my life into, so I didn't have to bear it for another second.

And I did.

I unleashed my rage—channeled it into the fight.

—My anger at Goran; the utter betrayal there.

—My outrage at my parent's death.

—The way I secretly despised the discontinued Game Wardens.

—And my disbelief of how I, also, *might love them.*

…My desperation to find love…acceptance…

All coming out in a volley of bullets, spraying into the diseased flesh of the stumbling dead as system updates popped into view.

[HELLADORE'S DARKEN HORDE, UNDEAD 8: -1000 HP, 4600/8000]
[System Reward: Rage Promotion +5 XP, 422/500, Strength Will Increase +3 for The Next 10 Seconds]
[10]

But the tears came unexpectedly.

And I could no longer see as I heaved the gun to move my fire up and down the rows.

[9]
[HELLADORE'S DARKEN HORDE, UNDEAD 8: -400 HP, 4200/8000]

Only *feel.*

Only struggle to see the jumbling silhouettes of the Darkens' rotting flesh—

[8]
[HELLADORE'S DARKEN HORDE, UNDEAD 8: -200 HP, 4000/8000]

The gun clicked.

Short.

It stopped—*what?*

[System Alert: Equipped Weapon Out of Ammo]
[7]
[6]

I jammed my finger against the trigger in shock, but it wouldn't budge. *No—I was out of bullets? This couldn't be happening—*

[5]
[4]

[3]

"*I need more bullets!*" I screamed hoarsely at the ridge, feeling sweat drip down my face. I hastily wiped it and the tears away from my eyes.

[2]

I watched Callen's face crease with concern. His hands pumped frantically in the air, "We don't have any ammo for weapons like that. You're just going to have to use your sword—" *Damn it, the Rage Promotion would have been more helpful for the sword but, now, it was almost out...*

[1]
[0]

"*ArghhhH!*" I swung at a Darken who was far too close. Its freezing hands wrapped around my arm. Its bulging eyes leaned in towards my face—

"*Get off!*" I shrieked, brandishing the machine gun as a bludgeon and hitting the thing bluntly in the skull.

It melted to my feet, blood spurting from the head wound.

[HELLADORE'S DARKEN HORDE, UNDEAD 8: -20 HP, 3980/8000]

...But an advanced club wasn't going to save me from the rest of this swarm. There were too many, and the gun was too heavy to lift repeatedly. My arms were already shaking from the effort; I was too exhausted.

Callen was right; there was only one choice here. ...*Again.*

I dropped the heavy gun in the grass. The system immediately responded:

[System Alert: Object Discarded.]

And I pulled out my mother's sword with a swish of metal.

[System Alert: Weapon Equipped.]

The blade glinted savagely in the overhead sunlight. *Now, for the hard part. ...I hadn't really chopped anyone's body to bits before...* I swallowed. I took a tenuous step forward with my arm outstretched in this barren crater of the earth—towards the zombies.

I held my breath—

Resisted the urge to close my eyes and—

Slash.

The metal hit flesh with a sickening jolt.

[HELLADORE'S DARKEN HORDE, UNDEAD 8: -20 HP, 3960/8000]

And body parts fell.

Blood squirted.

The monsters screamed.

I stared, in horror, at my own bloody hands, wrapped around the hilt.

"*Keep going!*" Rainer screeched behind me.

I twirled around. I faced the closest undead monster, tightening my fingers over the sword's handle and trying to steady my breathing: ready to slash.

...But, somewhere along the line, I'd miscalculated which Darken was the closest. Because pain ripped through my shoulder as teeth met with the base of my neck. I watched my HP and MRP drop, blinking furiously in my view.

[-3 HP, 12/44]
[-100 MRP, 3795/6209]

My armor had obviously been compromised by the rips, and the Darken was now able to bite through—shit. The bastard was taking my memory and my HP was getting low...much lower than I'd like. Everything felt muted. Slow... Slow motion? I felt liquid run down the skin of my neck. Zombie spit?

I reached up and looked down—to find my fingertips slick with red. My blood...

I screamed with fury and brought the sword sideways, slicing the Darken who'd bit me in half.

[HELLADORE'S DARKEN HORDE, UNDEAD 8: -20 HP, 3940/8000]

His body sloshed to the dirt and grass as more moans filled my ears. *The rest of them.*

I put a hand to the tender flesh of the bite at my neck, bringing my palm back to my face to gauge the blood loss. *The answer? Too much.*

[-1 HP, 11/44]

I steadied my boots in the dirt underfoot for the next round of Darken, bracing myself—

A shadow crossed my face, blotting out the sun above. Enormous wings flapped overhead, kicking up a wind and the smell of large reptile which soured my nostrils—*a dragon?* Fire spewed from the Heavens.

[HELLADORE'S DARKEN HORDE, UNDEAD 8: -1000 HP, 2940/8000]

I figured I'd help even the fight a bit. Like I said, I'd prefer no small humans getting killed today—I felt bad, okay?!

I recognized the red scales and yellow belly of the beast. Not just any dragon: the Red Vodyaracka Skydrake. He'd come to help?

Here, small one.

Something dropped from the sky, thudding in the grass.

I whipped around, my eyes locking on it and—

*...And it kinda looked like a grenade launcher from one of my video games... Was it? I'd never seen one in real life...*I grabbed it off the grass.

[System Alert: Weapon Equipped, +30 Baddie Points, 90]

Object:	Grenade Launcher
Required Class & Level For Use:	L4
Description:	It's Heavy, Black, Slick, Deadly & Looks Like It's Straight Out Of A Military Movie. Point This Thing In The Direction Of Your Enemy & They're Toast.
Augment Capacities:	+10 Strength
Baddie Points:	+30

I picked the heavy weapon up, marveling at the intricate details of it.

You're welcome. I swear, I'm not even sure why I have a soft spot for you human girls...

The dragon spoke in my mind as its enormous body wavered over the bright sun; I could barely look up at the thing.

Thank you, I told the creature telepathically.

[Draconic Telepathy Used... +1 XP, 423/500]

Three rounds—you have three shots!

The Vodyaracka shouted in my head.

I'm not a fairy godmother. I only have two CM Diamonds on me. It's the best I can do—that and help you roast a few more of these motherfuckers.

The creature dove towards the rear of the herd, spewing more fire. Flesh caught and sizzled, smoked, choking off my nose and throat. Zombies screamed and ran from the flames—unfortunately, at me...

[HELLADORE'S DARKEN HORDE, UNDEAD 8: -500 HP, 2440/8000]

The dragon didn't need to tell me twice. I lined the weapon up with the largest Darken group.

I prayed and squeezed—

Metal rocketed into my shoulder. Shattering pain exploded in the bone there.

[-1 HP, 10/44]

Whiz!

The shot flew through the air...and, then—

Then, a thunderous explosion.

BOOM!

[HELLADORE'S DARKEN HORDE, UNDEAD 8: -1000 HP, 1440/8000]

Parts of Darken flew.

The earth shook.

I stumbled backwards.

I tried to put my hands over my ears, but I was holding too much gun. Smoke and dirt stung at my eyes. ...But there were still silhouettes lumbering towards me through the fumes—

I scrambled to my feet. *Do or die,* I told myself. *This was do or die.*

I lined the weapon up and got ready to fire again, wincing this time before the release—

Trigger.

Pain in my shoulder.

[-1 HP, 9/44]

Whizz!

…

Explosion.

The world rocked. My ears rung. Everything hurt: my body, my head. The Vodyaracka roared in the sky. Arrows shot overhead. Part of the crater caved in, probably from Dormouse's efforts—

[HELLADORE'S DARKEN HORDE, UNDEAD 8: -200 HP, 1240/8000]
[HELLADORE'S DARKEN HORDE, UNDEAD 8: -50 HP, 1190/8000]
[HELLADORE'S DARKEN HORDE, UNDEAD 8: -100 HP, 1090/8000]

If this would all just stop! The screams of the zombies filled my ears. Shards of their bodies littered the ground—

One more. The dragon had said there was one more shot… I dragged myself upward.

I looked for any survivors. I could barely make out the valley anymore. Thick smoke rose in tendrils from the explosion sites and dragon fire that still burned. But there was one more group—I could just make out their staggering forms. I felt numb as I lined up the shot.

Just this last one, and I was free. Just one more pull, and I'd have the CM Diamond and I could work to activate my Creator Magic. Pain ripped through my shoulder when I took the shot. I screamed out, unable to keep the ripping pain in anymore.

[-1 HP, 8/44]

Whiz…BOOM!

The Darken howled.

[HELLADORE'S DARKEN HORDE, UNDEAD 8: -1000 HP, 90/8000]
[System Alert: Equipped Weapon Out Of Ammo]

I dropped the empty gun. I pressed my hands firmly to both ears, bringing my knees to my chest.

[System Alert: Object Discarded.]

"*Shut up!*" I cried into the destruction that I had caused.

The death.

All around me that *I* brought…

Something *I'd* made.

Because I had to.

The crater was a hole of slaughter now—dirt and smoke mixed with still bodies twisted, desiccated and decimated, in this unholy place. Grime smeared over the gaping faces of the dead Darken. Limbs laid strewn about, blood seeping into the dry dirt like the earth was hungry for a vengeance that it couldn't take for itself.

And me, just its actor.

Its angel of death.

Doing the will of a dragon just to get a CM Diamond. *All this was for a CM Diamond? All an empty attempt to save the world? But what if I couldn't? What if all this was for nothing—all this death…and pain…?* Tears smarted in my eyes. My throat was raw. More arrows shot overhead, barely visible in the smoke.

[HELLADORE'S DARKEN HORDE, UNDEAD 8: -20 HP, 70/8000]
[HELLADORE'S DARKEN HORDE, UNDEAD 8: -20 HP, 50/8000]
[HELLADORE'S DARKEN HORDE, UNDEAD 8: -50 HP, 0/8000]

And I couldn't move. I couldn't move away from the carnage I'd caused all around me. I sat there in the grass, the coppery stench of blood pulling at my nostrils. And I watched the horizon clear. …Heard the beat of the dragon's wings over me as it landed on the ridge above with the rest of the group. And, when the smoke did clear, I realized that I was the only thing left standing in this lifeless crater.

[System Reward: HELLADORE'S DARKEN HORDE, UNDEAD 8 Eliminated—That Was An Impressive Effort! +70 XP, 493/500]

Just me, surrounded by death.

The one survivor—the one survivor that I'd needed to be.

And it was enough of a realization for me to shove myself to my feet; I had to use the handle of the grenade launcher as a crutch to help me upwards because my HP was so low. My vision blurred red as I traced the slapping tail of the dragon with my eyes; its scales were just visible amidst the smoke trailing up the ridge.

"I did it," I called feebly, "I did what you asked."

[System Alert: Covenant Completed. ROSABELLA, GAME MAKER 6 Eliminated Darken Horde. SPARO, RED VODYARACKA SKYDRAKE, DRAGON 14 Must Surrender 1 CM Diamond.]

I stumbled forward—towards the Vodyaracka and the group. If I stood much longer, I'd pass out. I knew it. I'd slump to the ground like all the stiff zombies around me and be counted among the dead.

You can have your CM Diamond, small one. You've earned it. You're quite the warrior for such a tiny thing.

The dragon's chuckle sputtered to life between my ears.

I could have it? Relief coursed through my otherwise unfeeling body as a turquoise Diamond fell from the sky like a descending star. Warmness emanated over me, washing away the grime and soot of the scene around me—lifting me to a care-free feeling.

That everything was *right*.

That everything was *as it should be*.

I felt…

Happy…

The glowing Diamond came to rest right in front of my eyes, bobbing. I cupped my dirty hands to reach for it, and the shape soaked into my skin with the whisper of two ocean waves meeting each other.

[System Reward: CM DIAMOND Acquired +10 XP, 503/500, Object Will Be Placed In Your Inventory Unless You'd Like To Equip. Would You Like To Equip?] [Yes] [No]

"No," I murmured. I could barely get the word out. The last bit of strength leaked out of me even as the thoughts surfaced and the world froze. *I'd done it! I'd gotten the Diamond and it looked like a Level Up too!*

I fell to my knees as my stats box and the plus marks popped up in front of my eyes.

[System Alert: ***Congratulations, You've Advanced To Level 6!***]

Name	Rosabella	
Class & Level	Game Maker 6	
XP	503/600	
MRP	3795/6209	
HP	8/44	
Baddie Points	90	
Armor Class 11/20		
ABILITIES /20		
Strength	+1	11
Agility	+0	10
Endurance	+0	10
Intelligence	+1	13
Awareness	+1	12
Presence	+3	16
CM		3

[System Error: HP Extension Has Failed To Load.
Retrying...]

The message was the last thing I remembered as I crumbled to the ground, and everything went black.

Rosabella

"I don't understand, her avatar is locked and almost offline—just give me a second to figure it out—"

Dormouse's voice—over my head? Why was everything so muffled? It was dark behind my eyelids, which felt too heavy to open. I couldn't feel my limbs—*were they numb? Tingling? Could I move them?* I had no desire to try.

"Hold on. The issue was with her HP, maybe the loading is, somehow, stuck due to her Armor Class which I can fix—"

The Red Vodyaracka's voice. …But not in my head… What was going on?

"Anything would help at this point." Dormouse again. The kid sounded panicked.

…What happened to me? Was I…

…Dead?

…Fucking again?

**[System Alert: SPARO, RED VODYARACKA SKYDRAKE,
DRAGON 14 Has Gifted You An Armor Repair Which
Will Reinstate Your Armor At AC 15 (Currently at AC 11).
Will you Accept?]
[Yes] [No]**

The bobbing neon letters behind my eyelids barely registered—
what? Yes, I accept, I acknowledged mentally, but, honestly, it was
weakly. *Man, it felt like I'd been hit by a bus—*
Beep.

[System Alert: Armor Repaired, Armor Class +4, 15/20]
[System Error Overridden: Reloading Level 6 Level Up
Message...]

"*Yes!*" Dormouse cheered. *They could see the prompts too?* My head
throbbed as another system update appeared.

[+9 HP & HP Extended By 9, 17/53. You've Been Awarded
+2 Ability Points. Please Select Which Ability You'd Like
To Increase.]

My body hurt like hell, and little dots of gray and black peppered
my vision in a dancing jumble that confused me for a minute. I
blinked my eyes open slowly—*they were so heavy!*—and trees came
into blurred view overhead.

Then, Dormouse's face—*whoa.*
Too close.

His nose jutted into my vision, looking far too large, and his dark
hair nearly brushed my forehead. His eyes widened in excitement,
"Guys! She's awake!" I watched him dismiss the system update and
another one pop-up.

[System Alert: System Will Cache Additional +2 Ability
Points In Your Inventory For Future Application.
Inventory Updated.]

Footsteps on packed earth—louder than they should be. My
ears *hurt.*

Crunching grass. More faces crowded into my vision, blotting out
the view of the treetops.

The whole crew was here except…*except who the heck was that?* A dark-skinned man leaned over me…a warrior with chiseled muscles showing through a cut off t-shirt. He rubbed a large hand over his buzzed hair, showing more armpit and muscle mass. Light glinted off a gold chain inset with tiny, red rubies around his neck.

"Damn, girl—whew, you gave us a scare!" The Vodyaracka's voice—*coming from the unknown man's lips? Had I hit my head on the way down?*

"W—*who are you?*" the words tumbled out over unsure lips, "Where's the dragon?"

"Aww, now that's cute; she asks for me right when she wakes up." The dark-skinned stranger elbowed Dormouse in the chest, his lips sliding into a white-teeth, grinning chuckle that instantly had me off balance.

I gaped at him, holding my head as I tried to sit up. The surrounding tree line spun right-side up as I did. "Wait—*what?*" *I hadn't asked for him, I'd asked about the Vody—*

Wait a second…

I peered at him, then gaped.

"Now, she's understanding—" the man started. *The Vodyaracka's voice was still coming out of the man's body…*

"Wait, he's—he's not a dragon?" the words fell, shocked out of my mouth as I turned toward Rainer. Suddenly, I felt like crying—like caving in on myself. I'd trapped the Silver Rinkeclaw. I'd just killed a purple dragon's Darken horde. *Were those dragons also…human?*

The dark-skinned man studied me, one eyebrow raised, "For having a mega hard-on for CM, she really doesn't know anything about it or dragons, does she?" His eyebrows creased with a know-it-all flare deep in his lined forehead as he turned towards Callen. The Trader opened his mouth to respond, but Dormouse beat him to it.

"She's working on it," the nerd said defensively. *God bless the kid but…*

…But that was when I felt the flush—the blush of strawberry, magenta monstrosity creeping up my neck and cheeks. *Was it that obvious I had no clue what I was doing?*

The stranger laughed, a bizarre, barking noise that spurted up his throat and through his lips like he wasn't used to it. "You're kinda cute when you're not trying so hard," he told me, "Listen—"

He extended a hand. "Hi, I'm Sparo, and, yes, I'm the dragon who gave you the CM Diamond—two of them now," he clarified. I didn't shake his hand.

"…So, you *are* a dragon?" I stuttered, even more confused than ever.

"Ohmygerd, *he's a dragon shapeshifter!*" Joy huffed. "We'll be here *all day* at this rate," she murmured under her breath, "Vodyarackas are shifters, plain and simple. Now, we have to get your CM activated and quickly if we have any chance of getting you to Meherna so you can attempt to fix The Game."

"Wow, *someone's in a rush*," Sparo commented out of the side of his mouth.

"Actually, we really are," Callen cut in, his gray eyes bothered as he slung his pack over his shoulder, "We're trying to save The Game world which, as you probably well know, is deteriorating by the day. And Joy has every reason to be concerned, she's close to turning Darken. Rosabella is the last Game Maker. We need someone to help her activate her CM magic so she can repair the darkness." His eyes were laser-focused on the dragon-non-dragon who pointed a dubious finger to his own chest.

"Oh no…don't look at me like that. Why is he looking at me like that?" The dark-skinned man traded glances with Rainer.

"We can't do magic and can't guide her," Callen opened two empty palms in a display of helplessness, "Rosabella will need the help of a dragon. Surely there's something that you'd be willing to trade—"

"Your sorry asses don't even know," Sparo massaged his neck with a large hand. The shadow in his eyes looked…sad…*dejected?* "The ridiculous part is that what I want I can't trade for. I've suffered a fate worse than death—"

"Worse than death, eh?" Rainer griped, "Well, that's where we're all headed—a good lot of Darken wandering around, empty inside— if Rosabella can't fix this. Check the Game Damage Points, you *poor wee little dragon*—"

He used a swipe of his sausage fingers to display the stats like proof between all of us:

[GDP – 88/100]

Current Gamer Population:	336 Million
Current Darken Population:	173 Million
Darken To Gamer Ratio:	~51.48%
Darkness Cover:	82/100
Dilapidation Cover:	94/100

But Sparo's eyes widened irately, "Wee little—? Oh, you *humans get under my skin!* You want to know a fate worse than death? One prisoner—*one bloody traitor!*—stole EVERYTHING from me. My status! My street cred. I'm basically on a performance plan here now. *ONE ASSHOLE lets all the prisoners go, and I could only fry about half of them till they made it to the moat…* Now, you all come waltzing in here like you're the ones on top after one simple Darken fight, asking me to help some girl when her baby fingers can barely even hold a weapon—"

One asshole. My brain cranked at a million miles a minute, remembering…

Fire.

Smoke.

Goran carrying me.

One asshole? I bet I knew which one.

Sparo was still ranting and raving, his hands flying in the air, "The only thing I want—truly—is to sink my teeth into my replacement's neck and watch her squeal like she's lost something as painful as I have… which is what I was *trying* to do when you interrupted me in the middle of a Dragon Spar—"

"What if I could help you get revenge on the man who set the prisoners free—at the prison? Was it a man named Goran?" Before I knew it, the words had leaked out of my mouth—before I fully knew what I was offering or had a concrete plan.

But the dragon-non-dragon was hooked already. His face snapped towards me. His eyes locked on mine. "Prisoner 11, Yes, Goran—that pathetic wretch who's still haunting this place." *Geez, did no one like the guy?* "*Tell me how,*" he stated. No snarkiness this time. No joke. Just greed in his voice.

Vengeance.

It made my blood run cold.

I drew in a deep breath, trying to quickly concoct an answer, but it turned out I already had one. It sped off my tongue with a quickness that I was nearly frightened of. "Goran killed my parents. He decimated your career here. *I'm going to find him,*" I started, my voice holding more conviction than I would have thought possible (especially when I realized it was probably *Goran* who was going to find *me*, not the other way around), "*When* I find him, I'll bring him to you and you can help me decide what happens to him, but I need you to help me activate my Creator Magic first."

The words felt powerful coming off my tongue. I was a little in shock of my own speech, as it seemed were the discontinued Game

Wardens who looked on with respect. The system description of the trade slid into view in the middle of all of us.

[Proposed Trade: SPARO, RED VODYARACKA SKYDRAKE, DRAGON 14 Helps ROSABELLA, GAME MAKER 6 Activate CM. ROSABELLA, GAME MAKER 6 Locates and Delivers GORAN, PRISONER 11 To SPARO, RED VODYARACKA SKYDRAKE, DRAGON 14.]
[Will You Accept The Trade?]
[Yes] [No]

I watched Sparo's eyes. He observed me carefully—barely breathing he was so still. His index finger twitched under a crossed arm at his belt. He seemed to chew on my words for a moment, but he snorted, crossing his muscled arms again.

"Yeah, *counteroffer*," he said shortly. "I help activate your CM and you let me kill him after you deliver him to me."

An electronic beep sounded as the system amended the trade:

[Revised Proposed Trade: SPARO, RED VODYARACKA SKYDRAKE, DRAGON 14 Helps ROSABELLA, GAME MAKER 6 Activate CM. ROSABELLA, GAME MAKER 6 Locates And Delivers GORAN, PRISONER 11 To SPARO, RED VODYARACKA SKYDRAKE, DRAGON 14 Who Has License To Kill Him.]
[Will You Accept the Trade?]
[Yes] [No]

Kill Goran? I stared at the 'yes' and 'no' buttons bobbing in front of my face. My heart twisted. My stomach jarred. *KILL him? I hadn't wanted to take it that far; I wasn't comfortable with taking it that far.*

"Take it or leave it, peach," Sparo looked me up and down.

"Rosabella—" Callen warned.

Except Sparo's keen eyes caught my wince. His face contorted, "Oh, you have some attachment to this monster, Goran? …Why are you protecting him?" His words might as well have been a spear to my gut. I clenched my fists, my nails digging impressions into my palms, but the pain didn't steady me. *Why was I protecting Goran? …Because he'd always protected me? Because I'd thought he was my dad for all those years? Thought he knew better… Because any dad was better than no Dad?*

My face hardened. *No. He had to pay for his crimes. He'd killed my parents! I couldn't turn a blind eye to this. I was angry at him—enraged! …So, why wouldn't I make the decision that had to be made?*

"Don't fuck this up, it's a good offer," Joy spat. And I knew that should have made me want to take it more, but it didn't.

I swallowed. "Okay," I said tartly. But the truth was that I barely had the breath to get the word out.

[System Alert: Covenant Sealed]
[System Reward: One Heck of a Trade +25 XP, 528/600]

My heartbeat stirred in my chest, jumping like the nerves in my fingertips. *Had I just agreed to that?*

ThE OLd TRAiNYARd

Watch Out 4 Dragons...

ICONS TO LOOK OUT FOR...

Examination Opportunity [Opportunity to Explore Object or Place Further]

Spell Retrieval [Opportunity to Pick Up New Spell]

Recollection Opportunity [Opportunity to Recall Past or Forgotten Memories]

How To Activate CM:

ACTIVATE CREATOR MAGIC

- Reach Level 6
- Collect 3 CM Diamonds

NOTE: Once Activation is Complete,
Level 8 Must Be Attained To Cast
Enough CM To Repair The Game

Burning Bridges at
TEMPLE MEHERNA

[GDP - 85/100]	
Current Gamer Population	333 Million
Current Darken Population	152 Million
Darken To Gamer Ratio	-45.65%
Darkness Cover	73/100
Dilapidation Cover	91/100

Burned Black, Desolate Forest

THE WEST SIDE

ROSABELLA

Class & Level		Game Maker 1
XP		3/100
HP		7/8
MRP		3640/6205
Baddie Points		25
Armor Class		10/20

ABILITIES /20

Strength	-1	8
Agility	+0	10
Endurance	-1	9
Intelligence	+1	13
Awareness	+1	12
Presence	+3	16
CM		0

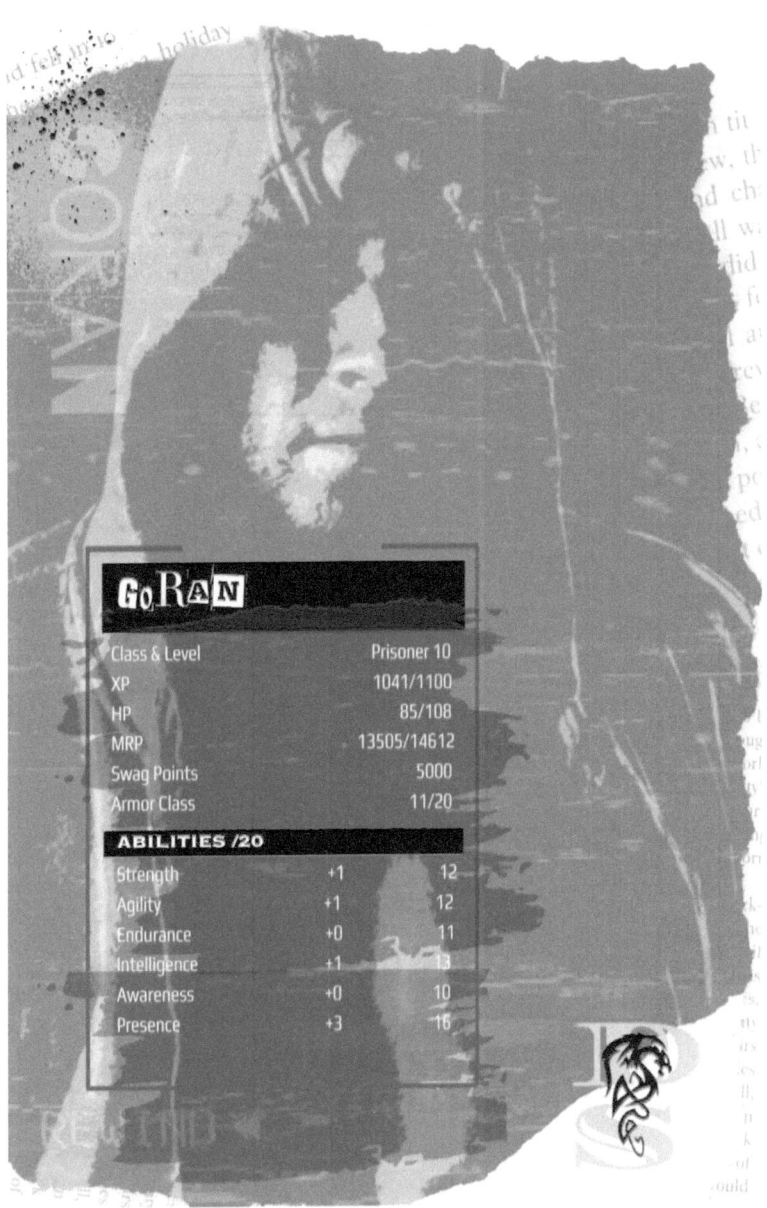

GoRAN

Class & Level	Prisoner 10
XP	1041/1100
HP	85/108
MRP	13505/14612
Swag Points	5000
Armor Class	11/20

ABILITIES /20

Strength	+1	12
Agility	+1	12
Endurance	+0	11
Intelligence	+1	13
Awareness	+0	10
Presence	+3	16

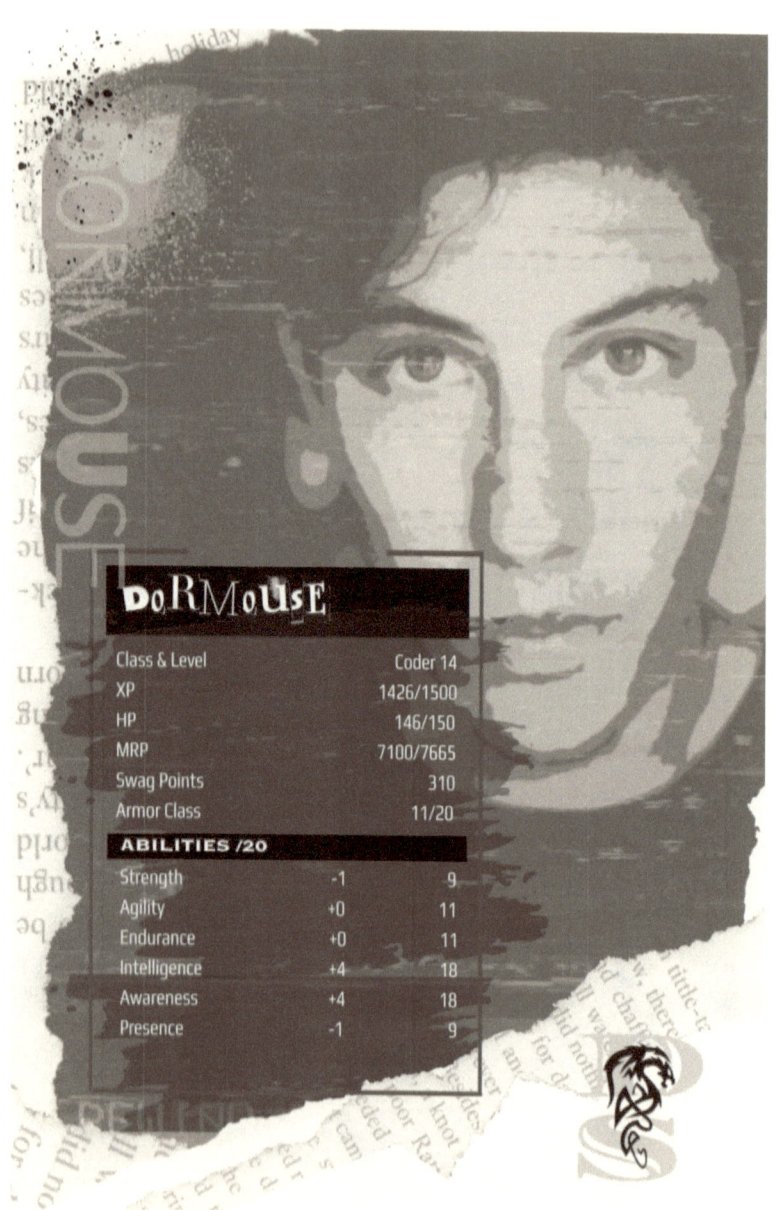

DORMOUSE

Class & Level		Coder 14
XP		1426/1500
HP		146/150
MRP		7100/7665
Swag Points		310
Armor Class		11/20

ABILITIES /20

Strength	-1	9
Agility	+0	11
Endurance	+0	11
Intelligence	+4	18
Awareness	+4	18
Presence	-1	9

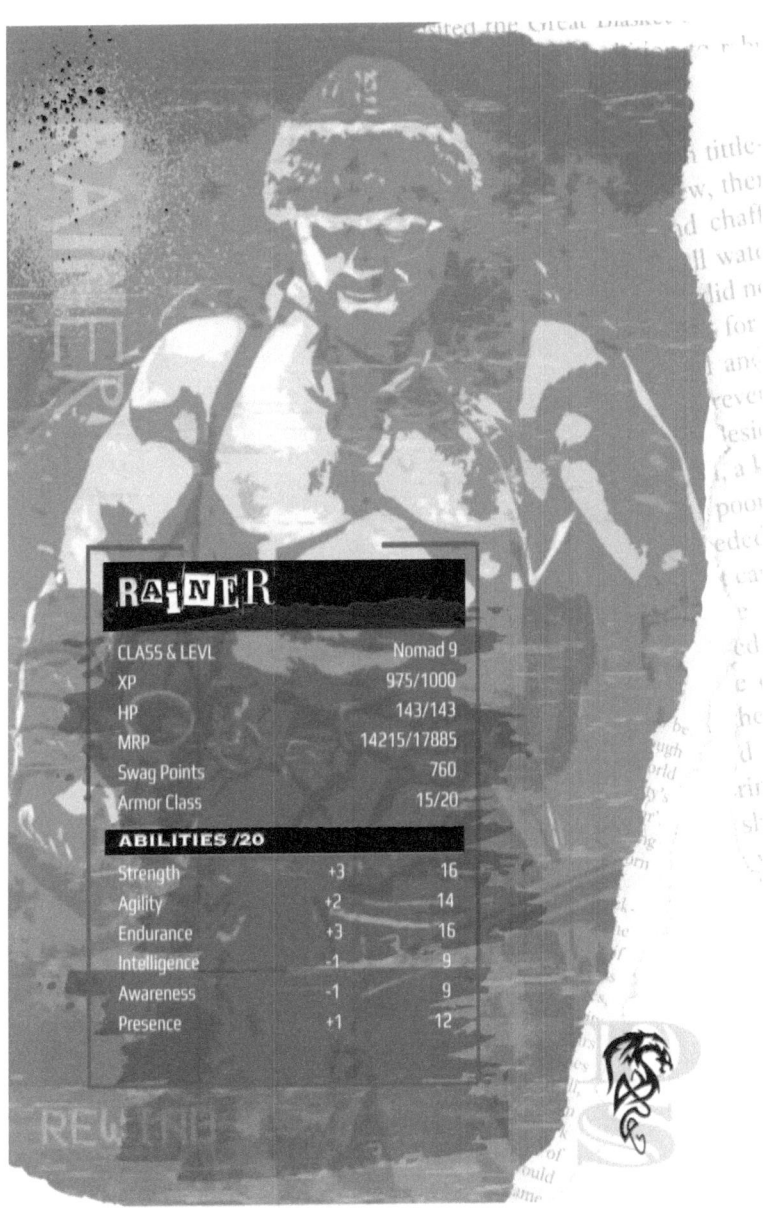

RAINER

CLASS & LEVL		Nomad 9
XP		975/1000
HP		143/143
MRP		14215/17885
Swag Points		760
Armor Class		15/20

ABILITIES /20

Strength	+3	16
Agility	+2	14
Endurance	+3	16
Intelligence	-1	9
Awareness	-1	9
Presence	+1	12

SpaRo

Class & Level		Dragon Shifter 14
XP		1465/1500
HP		219/219
MRP		11480/11680
Swag Points		4500
Armor Class		19/20

ABILITIES /20

Strength	-1	23
Agility	+0	14
Endurance	-1	21
Intelligence	+1	14
Awareness	+1	13
Presence	+3	17
CM		12

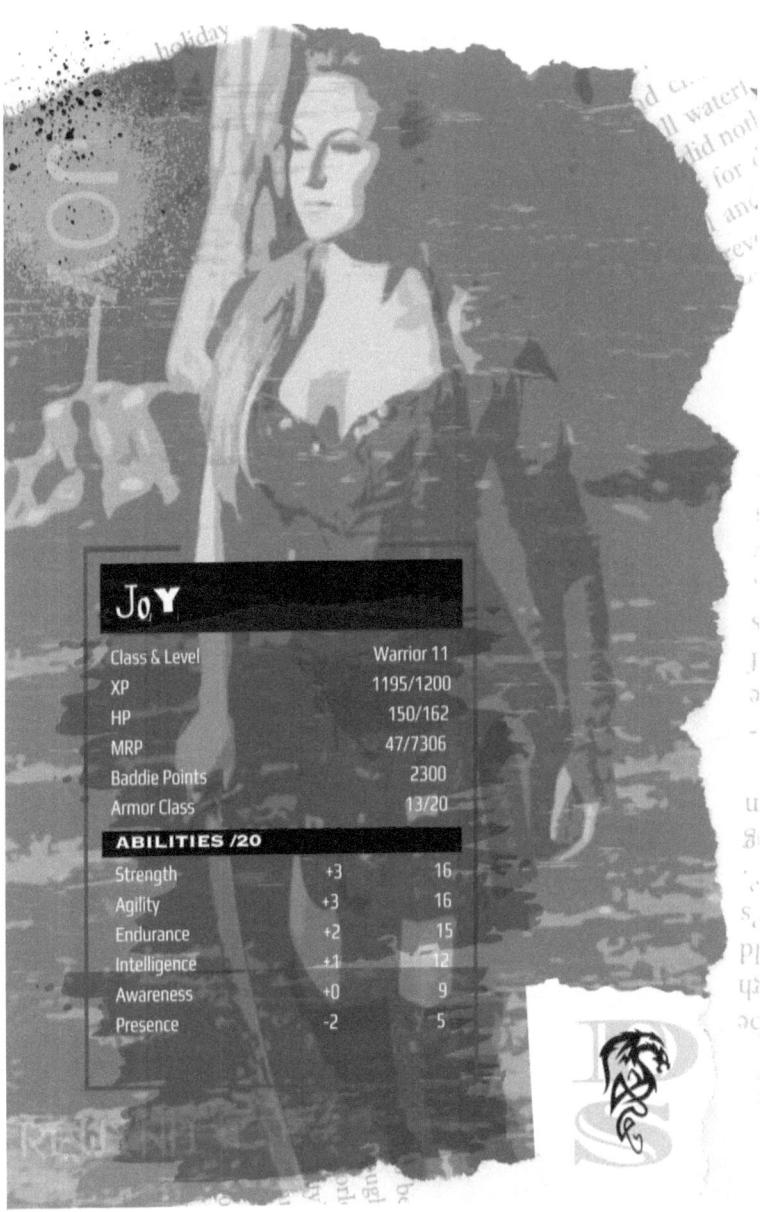

JoY

Class & Level		Warrior 11
XP		1195/1200
HP		150/162
MRP		47/7306
Baddie Points		2300
Armor Class		13/20

ABILITIES /20

Strength	+3	16
Agility	+3	16
Endurance	+2	15
Intelligence	+1	12
Awareness	+0	9
Presence	-2	5

CALLEN

Class & Level		Trader 10
XP		1043/1100
HP		100/100
MRP		17885/18250
Swag Points		500
Armor Class		13/20

ABILITIES /20

Strength	+0	10
Agility	+0	10
Endurance	+0	10
Intelligence	+3	16
Awareness	+1	12
Presence	+2	15

Rosabella

I'd just agreed to that. I'd just agreed to Sparo killing Goran, and it shook me to my core more than I wanted to admit. Why did I have this terrible headache? My head felt split open at the seam. I tried to move the blankets over my legs to the side, but my hands blurred from the movement, and my head jogged painfully. I grabbed at it, "Ouch."

"Hey—" Rainer reached down for me. His brown eyes were deep and kind, even foggy from my vision this close, "Take it slow there, soldier. With your HP this low, your next fight might just be standing up."

I winced, trying to turn over onto hands and feet. My HP? Where was it again? My head felt foggy, trying to remember.

[System Understands Query...Loading Response Double Time...]

...Oh, or the System could remember for me...helpful.

[Current HP / ROSABELLA, GAME MAKER 6: 17/53]

Great, so that was basically floor level. Rocks and dirt speared my palms. The grass smelled like dew and morning. *How long had I been out?* Shakily—and leaning heavily on Rainer's stout form—I heaved myself upwards, to my feet. Sparo rushed forward to help support me too. To be honest, I was still trying to figure out how I felt about the guy.

"There she is," Rainer said cheerfully, smiling like I'd done something grand instead of something pretty much everyone over the age of one had mastered. He kept a supporting hand on my arm as I tried a few steps.

"I don't know what happened with the Code," Dormouse scratched at his dark headful of hair, "It was like the system locked you up—"

"Well, she's better now," Joy cut in, "She can do what she came here to do—activate her CM magic. Dragon, you got this from here? I was on watch all night and need one hell of a nap—"

"Got you," Sparo nodded at the girl, "Go fire up some zzs."

My eyes wandered between the group and Sparo. They were friendly with him—like they had some sort of trust between them. I should be grateful to him, not resentful because of the trade. I mean, he'd all but saved my life in the Darken crater by creating that grenade launcher…then again, I wouldn't have been in the crater in the first place if it weren't for him…I wasn't really sure which side the scales balanced on. I felt a little shaken up after the Darken fight—frazzled—and, as I looked around the group, I wondered if they saw me different after it. Because I saw myself differently. I even…*felt* different.

A quick look down showed a summary of the battle without words. The front of my body armor, though repaired from Sparo's magic, was smeared with dirt and grime. Blood blotched over patches of the exposed skin of my hands, and pieces of my hair hung limp and dirty near my chin. A waterfall of dried red extended down the side of my left shoulder. That was when I felt the pain again. *My neck! The wound in my neck from the Darken biting me!*

I reached up but found in surprise that it was padded with fabric. …A makeshift bandage.

"One bit me"—I couldn't help it as terror rode into my voice, and my eyes flashed to Callen's face—"One of those things bit me. Does that mean I'll turn Darken—"

Before the man could answer, Joy leaned over me, a devilish, bemused look raising her right eyebrow. "You think this is The Walking Dead or something?" she sneered. "Cool your jets, Michonne." And she clapped a hand down on the wound.

So hard that I winced.

"That's enough," Callen warned the pink-haired girl, slapping her away, "Go get that sleep you've been carrying on about. Sparo!" he called over his shoulder, "Can you help Rosabella activate her CM now?" And the dragon-non-dragon stepped forward, his dark head and wavering smile contrasting with the morning light behind him. I watched him nod.

"Let's give them some air," Rainer's gruff voice suggested. And the group dissipated.

And, then, it was just me.

And Mr. Grenade-Launcher Magic.

And the treeless glade.

And for a reason I couldn't pin down, I didn't feel like I needed to put a show on anymore; all my defenses dropped.

"So, I'm confused because you sent me to my death in that crater, but, then, also saved me from it with that gun so…I'm not really sure where that leaves us," I hedged, wiggling a finger between his chest and mine.

The guy chuckled a little at that. He raised an eyebrow, "You know, not every Prince Charming rides a white horse," he quipped. "Mine's a red-as-fuck dragon, and you were sooo hellbent on that CM Diamond—" He shook his head, rolling his eyes.

301

"I was," I agreed.

"And, so, you got the giant pit of death," he shrugged. "Saved me a shit ton of revenge-getting though. ...Plus, I *kinda think you liked it*—"

My jaw dropped at that. I opened both of my arms wide, displaying the blood and guts sloshed down the front of my armor, "Look at me, I did *not* like it!" I protested.

"Oh, come on, now," he batted me away with a dismissive hand, "That's what all you girls are always sayin'—you don't like something when you really do. It's like y'all are just tryin' to create mental gymnastics for anyone with a Y chromosome—"

Was he kidding me right now?! He was really trying to convince himself that I'd LIKED being in a bloodbath of zombies, so he felt better about things?

"To clarify," I huffed, "I did not like having to chop up zombies like salad."

"To clarify," the dragon-non-dragon huffed back, mimicking me, "I kinda *did* like saving your ass though—" He flashed his white teeth at me and—

[System Query: Would You Like To Flirt With SPARO, RED VODYARACKA SKYDRAKE, DRAGON 14? Use 30 Baddie Points To Flirt?]
[Yes, Flirt] [No, Thank You]

Wait...what?! My cheeks flushed brilliant red. My flustered fingers flew in the air, trying to swipe away the system menu prompt. *No! No, of course I didn't want to! What was the system up on?*

Luckily, the man wasn't paying attention. His eyes were lowered into the grass as he ducked his head, brushing a hand over it. "Listen, I..." he stuttered. "I felt bad about the trade, that's why I came to help you. And that's a pretty big thing for a dragon to feel bad about something because...well, we're a selfish breed, you know? A lonely, selfish breed—that's why we horde magic. It makes us feel something—some type of warmth. And I haven't done much for anyone but myself in a long time so…" His eyes ducked up to me as he pulled down his cutoff shirt. "So…that's something at any rate…"

[System Query: Would You Like To Flirt With SPARO, RED VODYARACKA SKYDRAKE, DRAGON 14? Use 30 Baddie Points To Flirt?]
[Yes, Flirt] [No, Thank You]

The prompt popped up again with an electronic beep.

"No!" I protested, dismissing it quickly.

Sparo squinted at me. "No—what—?" He looked lost.

"No, really, *thank you*," I stumbled. But there was an insistent meaning in the last two words. "Thank you for saving my life." The crazy thing was that I really meant it. I really meant to thank him for saving my life. Selfish creature or not, he'd done that.

And I looked up.

And Sparo looked down.

And we were so close in that moment—our faces. His wide chest, heaving up and down under his burlap shirt. And the look in his eyes swept any breath I had straight out of my lungs—gone.

Because, even in this world that sometimes felt like bullshit and barriers, there were none between us. Just…

Skin.

Nose.

Eyes.

…Lips.

My eyes lingered there as I licked my lips in anticipation—

[System Query: Would You Like To Try For A Kiss With SPARO, RED VODYARACKA SKYDRAKE, DRAGON 14? Use 100 Baddie Points To Try For A Kiss?]
[Yes, Kiss] [No, Thank You]

Whoa—no! What was this?

I pushed it down.

I watched him shove it down too. He cleared his throat.

Awkwardly.

Or maybe that was just a reflection I had because I, suddenly, felt awkward—suddenly, noticed every place that my body that was willowing towards him like a breeze blew us together in this windless valley. And, suddenly, I needed some space. I tried to take a few steps away, but my feet had other plans. I pitched backwards, wobbling dangerously. My foot rammed into a hole—damn this low HP!

[-1 HP, 16/53]

...And, now, it was even lower...

"Hey there," Sparo called, reaching out to help, "Damn women always trying to be so independent when they can barely stand—"

...And there was his joking facade again, smoothing right over everything—replacing it like it had never even happened. Good thing I hadn't chosen a flirt option—

I gritted my teeth. Why did the pulling away feel so familiar?

"I need to do this on my own," I told him, resisting his fingers even though I felt the weakness taking me under its waves. And I wondered for a minute what it would be like not to have to do it on my own...to have help. To have...someone.

Him.

To have him.

I swallowed. "Listen, I know you want to help," I started, "and I appreciate everything you've done for me, really, but I have to be able to at least stand and walk. I need to be able to activate the CM and fix the world here."

I said it so confidently, but I could see that the man saw through it. His forehead creased in worry, "What you need is a health pack, and, even with my Creator Magic, that's the one thing I can't make you—"

"Then, screw it. I'll have to go without," I told him firmly. But I couldn't even stand firmly. My feet teetered on the hard earth below me—weak. I tried to disguise the movement as I reached to steady myself on a nearby sapling, but Sparo's eyes flickered to catch my hand on the peeling bark. ...It was almost like he could see the nausea crashing over my head—see the way the world was blurring and churning around me. How much blood had I lost from the Darken bite?

"You can't do magic like this," he complained, "I know I'm supposed to show you how to activate your CM and that everyone's on a freaking productivity train around here, but, in your state, I'm not so sure it's a good idea—"

"I—" I sputtered, suddenly feeling a little more than off balance, "I'll be fine."

He raised two, solidly unconvinced eyebrows at me, his forehead wrinkling. And I looked at him. I tried to keep my face still and solid: think tree, think impenetrable, fucking unmoving tree. ...But I was positive my expression was sliding into pale white. Whatever poker face I never had was long out the window.

"I—" I tried again, but faltered. "I...so don't got this," I admitted.

That's when my knees collapsed. I braced myself for the jarring dirt and rock below—

But I didn't hit the ground. Because Sparo's hands were there. And he lifted my whole body up, swinging my legs into his grasp like I was the weight of a child.

"What—"

"You so do got this," he told me quietly. I could nearly hear the beat of his heart through his shirt, but I tried harder not to notice lest those system prompts come back again.

"You negotiated with a dragon, me," he shifted my weight in his arms, grunting softly—I took back the weight of a child thing—"fought an entire horde of Darken…trapped a dragon—"

He watched me closely as shock crossed my face. "How—" I faltered, feeling my cheeks turning scarlet with mortification. He knew about the Rinkeclaw?

He squinted sarcastically at me, "Oh, word gets around in the dragon world, you know?"

I didn't. I could barely feel my limbs.

"Here," he carefully helped sit me down on the log of a fallen tree just inside the shelter of the forest. The shadows of the leaves overhead slid over my face with a coolness that I didn't know I was longing for. The smell of lush greenery filled my nostrils…and a hefty slice of silence filled my ears—more wonderful than anything I could describe.

Sparo's huge hands propped me up. "Sit up," he prodded. His voice was gentle, but, for some reason, I still wanted to fight him—fight the concept that I needed someone else in this minute.

"Why?" I held onto the stubbornness as I blinked at him, my lids heavy. I felt like I was going to keel over again…like my vision was going to fade…

But Sparo was there, leaning into my weary face, prodding me on. "We're gonna start the CM activation now, okay—if you still want to"—his voice was like honey…or gold…I couldn't think clearly to determine which.

I nodded but, per usual, doubt stood like a brick wall in my way.

And fatigue was there too.

How could someone win against those two, burly soldiers?

Rosabella

I should listen—no, I *had* to listen. Sparo was going to tell me how to activate my Creator Magic to save The Game world but…*well, it was hard to listen when your bones ached.*

…When your mind was numb… And your body, number. When you felt like you might just fall over, sitting down. My arms trembled even from their resting position in my lap—a shiver that seemed to run through my very blood like a nudge I couldn't control or help. *What was wrong with me? What was happening to my body? Had I ever felt this…drained? Depleted? …Empty? Even while my mind whirled with thoughts?*

My HP was pathetic right now, that much was for sure. I could barely sit up straight—barely open my eyes long enough to watch Sparo's face, still leaning close to me…nearly so close to me that his forehead touched mine. He seemed to sense my fight—how hard I was struggling to focus on only his eyes. He put a steadying hand on my shoulder, and I pressed into it. It was nice not to have to hold all the weight for just a minute.

"I'm not doing so good," I conceded shakily to him.

He nodded. "We'll make this quick."

I could see in his face that he understood; his forehead creased with concern. "It's okay," he told me, "Everything's going to be okay. I'm just going to tell you a story, alright? Dragon's love lore, and it's important to understand the story behind your CM."

I blinked sleepily at him—*was it really necessary though?* The world slid in and out of the darkness behind my lids, as I tried to stay awake. "Okay," I breathed.

And it was suddenly like I was reduced to the shell of a little kid again, listening to a bedtime story as I sat there, propped up by his hand.

...As the dragon-non-dragon began to speak...

"In the beginning, there was only emptiness, only darkness," he told me, his voice soft and husky, "but a great dragon reared its head out of this darkness. No one knows where this dragon came from—a different dimension, created from nothing? —There are only speculations. But this first, grand beast was the original Game Maker for he made The Game, you understand?"

He spoke softly to me—the question hung in mid-air like the quietest prod as he leaned into my face, making sure I was catching his words.

I nodded. "The first Game Maker was a dragon," I rasped out, too aware that my voice was hollow and rough.

He nodded, "Yes, but this was an extraordinary dragon with an exceptional amount of Creator Magic. This dragon created humans to populate the beautiful Game world—we call them The Gamers. And these Gamers, at first, revered and loved the dragon for his care of them...but they soon became restless. Some were jealous that the Grand Dragon could create, while they could not. They wanted the Creator Magic for themselves. Legend has it that they rose up against the Grand Dragon—"

"Did they kill it?" I wanted to know, trying to steady my quaking fingertips by squeezing my hands firmly together. The cool quiet of the forest seemed to press in on me on all sides, even as I was just perched there.

Sparo shook his head, his lips creating a firm line, "No, but they pissed him off. *And you know how dragons are when they're pissed off…*" One of his eyebrows snaked up in jest. He tried to shove me playfully which made me smile, but everything about me was weak at the moment. I had to use all my energy just to focus on what he was saying.

"What happened?" I asked, now more intrigued.

Sparo snorted, readjusting himself on the log. "The Grand Dragon gave up trying to please everyone. And he learned that day that no matter what you create, it is best to create for yourself because you'll never make everyone happy. They say that's why dragons are a selfish breed—why we use our CM only for ourselves and those we make treaties with. …Because of the lesson from the grand elder who started this whole world."

"That's a *terrible lesson*," I muttered, tracing the patterns of the green undergrowth near my feet with my tired eyes, "It sounds like it's every man for himself—"

"Every dragon," Sparo interrupted, winking. "But, because, we dragons are pretty smart, the Grand Dragon knew there'd be all-out chaos if he just handed out CM and let every human Gamer create whatever they wanted. He didn't want the responsibility of creating something the humans wanted, but he didn't want the world to break in two…so, first, he created the system to help govern the world under his command. He, also, gifted the Creator Magic to one human man: the first Game Maker. Turns out he was a lovebird, and his wife became pregnant. It was decreed that the first child of every Game Maker would continue the Game Maker tradition. They'd have the ability to create and patch The Game world…almost a government of sorts—"

"And, now, I'm the last one left." I didn't mean to, but I said it sourly. The words tasted bitter on my tongue, and Sparo noticed.

Before I'd realized what had happened, he'd grabbed my chin.

Gently.

His fingers barely brushing the skin there.

As he lifted my chin upward.

So that we were seeing eye to eye.

So that I could see the fire and respect brimming in his gaze.

"Yes, you, Rosabella, *are the last Game Maker*"—he almost whispered it in reverent awe—"you have been given this gift. You have the magic within you."

I batted his hand away.

Partially because I suddenly felt like I wanted to cry.

Partially because I was too weak for this shit.

Partially because, if I fell off this log and into a deep sleep, I would *not* complain at all—

"I didn't *ask for this*," I said quickly and with more emphasis than I'd intended, "I get that it's important, but I just want to fix The Game in some wild hope that it will make up for what happened to my parents and be done with things here."

The words gushed out of me—rapid and blunt. And I watched Sparo's face turn granite—*I hadn't expected that. ... What did he expect from me? That I was going to try to walk in my parents' enormous footprints? That I was here for something other than revenge?*

Oh, God, was I here for revenge?

Or to set things straight?

... Why was all of this such a muddled mess in my mind when the motives were clearly polar opposites?

I swallowed. I tried to take in a desperate breath of air, but barely found any. "Are you going to show me how to activate the Creator Magic or not?" I whispered quickly, my eyes darting up to meet

Sparo's. And I watched his shoulders sink in a way that made me want to take the words back.

"Sure," he said, turning away, "I just thought…"

He didn't finish the thought. Only a woodpecker in the distance did. And we sat on that log, that I'd just realized was wet and was seeping into the seat of my pants, longer than I wanted to admit.

In silence.

"I'm trying to *help*," I said finally.

He smiled faintly at me—not even a trace of the brilliance I knew he was capable of—as he slid to face me, his hands churning in his lap, "I just thought…that, if you're the last Game Maker…you might…Never mind, I'll show you about the magic."

Unexpectedly, he got up from the log.

And it felt empty, there, without him. And I wasn't sure if it was because I'd been leaning so heavily on him or if there was another reason. And I, suddenly, wanted the system to ask me if I wanted to flirt with him or kiss him again—just so I could dismiss it. Just so I could feel like, maybe, there was some connection between us. *Had I already screwed this up?*

"*Wait—*" I called out, my hand reaching after him.

He turned to look over his shoulder; his eyes were an unnerving, dull brown. "Well, I can't show you how to activate your CM in this form," he told me, "To create with a human, I have to be in Vodyaracka form."

And it made sense. *He was turning back into a dragon.*

The breath whooshed out of me, as a wind began to kick up through the trees. I watched him close his eyes and cup his hands up towards the sky.

And there was red smoke.

Suddenly.

Filling the woods around me, stinging my eyes. Biting into my pupils and nose—

"*Sparo?*" I called into it, coughing.

**[SPARO, RED VODYARACKA SKYDRAKE, DRAGON 14
Has Changed Form]**

And, then, there was a giant snout there. Red scales and…
Teeth?

Rows of pointed fangs opened only inches from my face. The Vodyaracka's nostrils flared above them, sending out puffs of black smoke which choked up my eyes and throat.

"Sparo, *you're scaring me*," I admitted, my voice wobbling dangerously as I tried to back away from the creature's jaw.

Open your inventory, and tell the system you want to use all three CM Diamonds. You're at L6, right?

The dragon's question echoed in between my ears.

Level 6? I nodded. *Yes, I'm at Level 6,* I told him in my mind as a system update popped up.

[Draconic Telepathy Used… +1 XP, 529/600]

Good, then put your hand in my mouth.

Put my hand in—?! I recoiled from both him and his words echoing in my head.

"Look," I argued, sudden anger coiling in me, "I might be young and, sometimes, stupid, but I'm not dumb enough to—"

You humans are infuriating!

He huffed.

I saved your life! I made you a freaking grenade launcher! Would I have done all that only to kill you now? Don't you….trust me?

The hurt desperation in his voice shocked me—made me feel even more off balance than before...*like I might just teeter right off this log—*

It's an old tradition.

The dragon continued, more stoically.

One that the Grand Dragon put into place. If a human can truly trust a dragon, he can place his fingers securely in its mouth. Only then, will they be able to combine their magic and create together—only if there is mutual trust and respect.

"O—okay," I stammered. "I'll do it. System, open up my inventory."

[System Understands Query...Loading Response...]
[System Alert: Per Request, Inventory Opened.]
- **1 Rosabella's Mother's Gold & Silver Broadsword**
- **3 CM Diamonds**
- **1 The Game Map**
- **Cached +2 Ability Points**

I'd forgotten about those cached Ability points. I was going to have to use them soon.

"System, I'd like to use all three of my CM Diamonds," I announced. The corresponding responses fizzled into view.

[System Understands Query...Loading Response...]
[System Alert: Objects Equipped.]

'Atta, girl. Now, your hand...

Sparo droned. His words were warm, and a pleasant breeze blew past my exposed neck, ruffling my hair as he spoke in my mind. I swallowed, lifting my fingers closer to his glistening jaws. *Could I do this? I could do this.* But every hair on the back of my neck stood up. *I just had to put my hand in the dragon's mouth...*

[System Searching MRPs To Select & Display Correct Memory...]

I jumped. I didn't think I was ever going to get used to these popups.

"Have you ever been in a dragon's mouth, Rosie?"
Goran's voice echoed in the recesses of my mind, "But have you ever seen a dragon's mouth?"
My giggling laugh. My kid laugh—filled my ears.
Mocking me, tormenting me, suddenly.

Goran had told me about this? Ever since I was a child he—he'd prepped me to combine my magic with a dragon's? ...Why had he prepped me? My brow creased in confusion.

<u>*You okay?*</u>

Sparo asked. I could see him peering around his huge mouth at me in worry. And I was, suddenly, more confused than ever. I nodded—*maybe a lie.*

"I'm okay," I said aloud like it might help it be less of one. And I took a deep breath, rejecting all the cringe and uncertainty running through me.

And I placed my tiny, white hand into the jaws of the red beast.

His tongue was sticky—his breath hot. But a different warmth flowed over me too like warm, welcoming honey. That feeling of...home: magic. A system message bobbed into view.

[System Query: 3 CM Diamonds Will Be Used To Activate Your Creator Magic & No Longer Available In Your Inventory. Would You Like To Activate Your CM?]
[Yes] [No]

This one felt obvious. "Yes," I told it. An electronic beep followed.

[System Understands Query...Loading Response...]

A wind kicked up around the dragon and I—stronger than I'd expected. It rushed and hummed in my ears. Three, turquoise Diamonds appeared and rose between us. Blue sparks erupted from them, showering down in a hail of transparent, diamond shapes. My vision pitched blue, and the world froze like this was a Level Up. ... *Was it?*

[System Alert: ***Congratulations, Game Maker! You've Successfully Activated Your CM! +3 CM, 3/20***]

Name	Rosabella	
Class & Level	Game Maker 6	
XP	529/600	
MRP	3795/6209	
HP	16/53	
Baddie Points	90	
Armor Class 15/20		
ABILITIES /20		
Strength	+1	11
Agility	+0	10
Endurance	+0	10
Intelligence	+1	13
Awareness	+1	12
Presence	+3	16
CM		3

[System Reward: Congratulations, You Have Activated An Ability. +5 XP, 534/600]

Activated? That was it? It was that easy? ...Not that getting the CM Diamonds had been 'easy' but...well, I was just surprised was all. Thank goodness because I wasn't really in the mental or physical state for it to be otherwise. I noticed the three under the CM spot. 3? Really? All this work for 3/20? An Examination Opportunity magnifying glass over a shield icon spun next to the CM Ability.

Examine! I told it.

[System Object Examined... +1 XP, 535/600]
[Congratulations! If You Are Reading This, You Now Have
The Ability To Collect & Use CM Or Creator Magic. The
Ability Points Listed Show How Many CM Diamonds You
Have Collected. Each CM Diamond Is A Point /20. The
Higher Your CM, The Greater The Influence And
Endurance Of Your Magic. Be Aware That There Are A
Limited Number Of CM Diamonds In The Game & Most
Don't Want To Share. Collecting Them Will Not Be As
Easy As You Think.
CM DIAMOND: Collect And Use A CM Diamond To
Increase Your CM.
CREATOR MAGIC (CM): Allows A Game Maker Or
Dragon (Class & L6 Required) To Perform Magic And Use
Spells. Spells Can Be Found & Collected Throughout The
Game. Magic Comes With A Learning Curve. Each Spell
Requires 1 Use Before It Is Perfected. Some Spells Take
Longer To Master. Please Reference The Spell Stats.]

Well, that was a textbook. I dismissed the verbiage with my mind,
and it flickered out of sight only to be replaced with another popup—
something else now?

[System Reward: Congratulations, You've Been Gifted
Your First Spell. +10 XP, 545/600]
[NO MORE NOISY NEIGHBORS ABSORPTION HEX]

What the—?

What in the name of the Grand Dragon is that?!

Sparo raged in my ears.

Fucking beginner spells are the absolute worst!

I gaped at it and the Examination Opportunity bobbing over the neon letters. Did I want to know? This spell, from the name, didn't seem particularly helpful.

"Examine," I whispered anyway.

[System Object Examined... +1 XP, 546/600]
[Leaning In Closer, A Spell Stat Sheet Appears. Hmmm, Maybe It Tells You About What The Spell Does...?]

Spell:	No More Noisy Neighbors Absorption Hex
Required Class, Level & Ability For Use:	Game Maker Or Dragon L6, CM 2
Description:	You May Not Be Able To Control If Your Neighbors Are Nosy, But, With This Hex, You Will Be Able To Stop Them From Being Noisy. Simply Cast In The Direction Of The Sound, & It Will Instantly Be Muffled. Goodbye Being Woken Up At 3am From The Woman Upstairs Rearranging Her Furniture!
How To Cast:	Speak 'Shirtaloon Mufalato'
Augment Capacities:	None
Learning Curve Required:	1 Use
HP Needed To Cast:	-1
Baddie Points:	+0

Okay, so that's useless.

Sparo's voice in my mind said it before I could even think it.

Still, try it out, small one. The first time it always goes awry, so better get it out of the way, you know?

317

I wasn't sure I did, but I nodded.

Close your eyes, and let your mind do the work. You have to dive into yourself.

Dive into myself? Well, that sounded like a load of crock—

I can hear you!

Sparo objected.

Shit. "Sorry!" I exclaimed out loud, "I just—" But it seemed I'd run out of excuses. *There was only one thing to do here...* I closed my eyes. I felt the sharpness of Sparo's teeth under my fingertips as, somehow, I instinctively knew—instinctively begin to sink deeper...

Down...

Like I'd practiced this before. Like I'd known the way all along.

My mind stilled, and, in that stillness, something stirred: swirls of color.

Vibrating. Combining.

Vibrant blues and pinks and greens and purples... As I squinted, I recognized a keyhole in the center of the swirling magic...and I looked down and realized with amazement that my fingers curled around a solid gold key—*what?*

You've got it now.

Sparo's voice hummed in approval.

And, then, a different voice spoke—deeper...throaty:

You are a creator. You were born all this time TO BE a creator. You can make this Game. You can patch it. You can make anything you wish—any world you want. It is all at your fingertips.

The thrum and rush of the voice whisked me away for a minute— filled me with momentum. And power—so full I could burst. *I could create anything! I could DO everything that Callen and Rainer and all of them had said I could!*

318

The world blurred.

"Shirtaloon Mufalato!" I bellowed into the swirling, choking haze but—

[System Alert: NO MORE NOISY NEIGHBORS ABSORPTION HEX Used]
[-1 HP, 15/53]

But something was clearly wrong. Yellow spiraled out of my fingers, forming a spongy wall hanging in the air in front of me. The foam material looked diseased and warped. It slid downward, making a pile of gushing grossness at the toes of my boots. And whatever sound-muting effects it was supposed to have were equally slush piled. *So, the first cast never worked?* But that wasn't the only thing that was off. My vision pulsated. My HP flashed into view again…

[-2 HP, 13/53]
[-2 HP, 11/53]
[-2 HP, 9/53]
[-2 HP, 7/53]
[-2 HP, 5/53]

The world glitched.

"Sparo?!" I called in desperation. *The spell was only -1 HP. Why was it subtracting more? Something was wrong.* I heard my heartbeat pound in my ears. *Something was really—*

Rosabella?!

Sparo answered back—his voice just as alarmed as mine.

Rosabella! Hold on! I'll—

But his voice crackled into silence just like the world around me. My vision hitched, then, split—going dark. I blinked into the blackness—*what?*

"Rosabella!" It was Callen's voice this time, coming from somewhere overhead.

"Sparo! Help me wake her!" Callen sounded frantic.

"I'm here!" I shouted frantically into the abyss around me, "I'm okay! I'm right here!"

"She's dying," Callen yelled, "Sparo, wake her! If she dies here, she dies altogether—We're losing her, *goddamn it Sparo!*"

[SPARO, RED VODYARACKA SKYDRAKE, DRAGON 14
Has Changed Form]

It was obvious they couldn't hear me. *Was Callen right? Was I…dying?* My heart leapt in my chest.

"I didn't mean to—I don't know what happened. One moment she was fine and then—" Sparo's desperate voice mixed over my head.

"Where's the nearest health pack?" Callen demanded, "You're a dragon. You know these parts, where is one?"

I heard the Vodyaracka pause, "It's crazy—"

"Right now, I'm you kinda into crazy," Callen growled, "Let's get her there, now! Dormouse! Joy!"

And I felt myself slipping as someone picked me up. And I finally slid into the quiet behind my eyelids.

…At last.

Sparo

I didn't mean to do this. Had I done it—was I responsible? The system almost seemed to go rogue. Humans were so frail—Grand Dragon, even Rosabella, the daughter of a legend. I could literally see the strength in her, but her vessel was so weak, crumpling at almost nothing. No wonder we dragons had scales and teeth—*better to keep all this bullshit out.* …And the fear that came with it. Fear was such an asinine emotion when you were the size of a house. And, yet, I was scared for Rosabella

My massive heart thrummed, pounding against the flesh of my chest. The air currents billowed and pushed against my giant wings. I felt the scales there bristle from both the urgency lighting every nerve in my body and from the lift—pressure scooping under my wings and hoisting me up. The landscape hurled and rushed by below my outstretched talons, foggy tendrils of green and yellow colliding and mixing.

I'd carried prey before.

And prisoners.

But, never, an unconscious, human girl who I cared about.

Were my talons too sharp? My grip, too hard? I was hoping I didn't accidently crush her. Her face was so pale against the lush landscape racing under us.

"Not to be a pain in the ass," a different girl's voice filtered into my swiveling ears, "But could you slow the fuck down? I'm gonna hurl chunks—"

She must be the one with the pink hair clutching at my scales painfully; it felt like one heck of an earache.

A wicked grin slid onto my face without my consent because, I couldn't help it, her complaint just made me want to go faster out of spite. I'd been noticing that girl's general dislike of Rosabella, and it got under my—

"Don't listen to her," Callen called—the gray-haired, leader one— his voice clear even with the rushing of the wind this high up and his placement at my shoulder, "We have to get Rosabella that health pack as soon as possible."

I said I'm on it; I'm on it, I growled back before remembering I had to open up the Draconic Language channel so they could all hear me—_apparently none of them had the language skill Rosabella did…_

[Draconic Telepathy Channel Opened. The Humans Can Hear You Now. +10 XP, 1475/1500]

I wasn't entirely convinced that opening up the communication channel was a good thing yet. The gray-haired one's direction frankly annoyed me. If we were being completely honest, dragons had a far better track record of keeping their word than humans; I'd told him I'd fix this, and I would fix it. I'd even managed to get all the humans on my back, and this load was heavier than I'd typically carry…

Hold on, Rosabella, I whispered gently into her mind, knowing she couldn't hear me but, somehow, still hoping she could. _What was wrong with me? …Getting sentimental over a human, another species…again?_ I'd thought I'd learned my lesson on that one already…And, yet, here I was scouring the earth below for the one place that I should have burned to the ground decades ago.

—Before it burned me.

And, yet, I hadn't.

Maybe, now, it was a good thing because Rosabella needed a health pack. …*Maybe.* …*Did I need a health pack too? Perhaps I could bargain for both of us.* Under my wing was still sore from where that purple beast Helladore had taken a bite out of me.

System, open my stats, I growled. I would have used a claw to swipe them open, but I didn't want to chance dropping the unconscious girl in my grasp. The typical system alert bounced into view, obscuring my view of the mountain tops with neon letters:

[System Understands Query…Loading Response…]

Name	Sparo
Class & Level	Red Vodyaracka Skydrake, Dragon 14
XP	1475/1500
MRP	11480/11680
HP	100/219
Baddie Points	4500
Armor Class 19/20	
Abilities /20	

Strength	+6	23
Agility	+2	14
Endurance	+5	21
Intelligence	+2	14
Awareness	+1	13
Presence	+3	13
CM		4

HP 100/219? Well, if I could barter with the woman for one, I'd try but…

Even just the thought of the woman we were going to visit had my heart frantically trying to get out of my chest. I had to get it together; I'd need a level head to deal with what came next—

There.

I saw the place.

The familiar slate, gable peaks and flat portions of the roof—white but weathered with age—like a memory surfacing even though I'd long tried to suppress it. The shrubbery around the place had grown up so far that I could barely make out the stone fence that ran along the perimeter of the parcel and the garden which used to sit out front. A thought bubble icon, rimmed in a circle, bobbed over that damn garden. I knew it was a Recollection Opportunity, but, frankly, I didn't want to remember anything about the place. *Perhaps she was as bitter about what had happened in that garden as I was and had decided to let it decay like the rest of the place...* My heart hardened at the thought. Maybe this was a mistake coming here. And, yet, Rosabella needed that pack. I clenched my teeth, fighting inwardly with myself.

Hold on, I told the group on my back as I dove downward.

I took the pitch a little harder than I should...just for that pink-haired one with the mouth on her. The wind swept past my face, bringing me back to life with the thrill of it as my jowls flapped against my teeth. But I had to be careful, I reminded myself, as I watched Rosabella's brown hair fly back from her despondent face. I had to make sure not to harm anyone in the landing.

I hit the grass in the front courtyard like a discarded school bus that my cousin, Darklin the Dumpyard dragon, was done with. The force of it slammed into me with a jolt. My talons scrabbled in the dirt, tearing up the lawn—a fact which I was most certainly not sorry for. But the hand holding Rosabella stayed steady—still. And her head only lolled a little to the side as I rushed her forward as the rest of the humans slid off my back and to the ground.

"I've heard of this place," the nerdy looking one stared over his head at the grand mansion with a sense of awe. "An enchantress lives here—a Witch—"

You wouldn't be so enamored if you knew what she's like. Hell in a hand-basket that one— I started, but I was rudely interrupted by none other than that stupid, pink-haired fiend. *There should be a law against people like her.*

"I heard there was a dragon who was in love with the Witch who lives here, but things ended badly," she placed a hand on her hip, throwing an accusatory eyebrow up in my direction, "You wouldn't happen to know that dragon…would you?"

I wished it didn't bother me as much as it did, but I couldn't let that show now…

You first, annoying one, I spat, gesturing for the pink-haired girl to lead the way in. *If there were any traps, at least she'd blow up first.*

The place really had gone to shit, which, sadly, was probably a decent omen regarding what to expect of the mental state of the woman waiting inside. Ivy had nearly decimated the remaining shell of the building; it laced up what used to be stately, Roman columns—now peeling paint and plaster—and covered a full side of the manor where the overgrown shadows of trees didn't. The front porch steps were broken in several places and the black lantern there hung askew from a broken chain. Brick, like a bone skeleton, showed through around the gothic windows where the plaster had cracked away. It looked…nearly haunted.

But, now, it was Rosabella's only hope. This Grand Dragon-awful house and the mad woman inside were the small one's only hope.

I shoved the pink-haired guard forward first as the chunky Nomad drew an axe and stepped after her, his eyes swishing back and forth between dark corners. I knew from experience that the doors were too small for my entry, but, way back when, she'd blown a dragon entrance in the back, using dynamite, and covered it with a purple cloth door. If the hole was still there, I'd find it.

Down the side alley, around to the rear, I told the group. We couldn't waste any time. Rosabella's face was growing whiter by the second. I cradled her in both gnarled talons, now, as my awkward and heavy footfalls took me towards the rear of the place.

Around a sagging marigold plant.

And a hedge grown up against a white-washed wall that should have been trimmed years ago. *The place was nearly unrecognizable. I wouldn't have even known I'd been here except—*

I heard the Warrior girl sniggering from the front, and I pulled up short to find the hole I'd been looking for—papered with posters, faded from the sun and crinkled from the rain...

With crude, hand-written messages scrawled on them and elementary doodles.

Of a red dragon.

Of me.

With big 'x's over my chest.

'IF YOU'RE SPARO, YOU CAN KISS MY ASS' 'IF YOU'RE AN EMOTIONAL DRAGON, TELL IT TO SOMEONE WHO CARES.' 'SPARO CAN SUCK MY—'

There was even a picture. ...*Real mature of her.*

[System Penalty: Reputation Smeared -200 Swag Points, 4300]

A low growl slipped up through my teeth as I swiped down both the system message and the propaganda with one annoyed thwap of the spikes on my tail.

The pink-haired girl whipped around, that smug smile all but stitched on her impish face. "Anything you want to tell us about, Sparo? Background we should know walking in?" she goaded.

Oh, she was loving this too much.

Anyone who wants to mention a word about this is walking back, I hissed, *I'm going in.*

And I brushed past the purple velvet that had seen better days like we all had. And I was careful to keep it from slapping Rosabella in the face as I entered with her limp body in my hands. If you'd told me I'd be here today, I would have laughed in your face. I would have told you 'not in a million years'.

So, this small human must have had something over me if I was standing here—in the back of what used to be a parlor. And, to be honest, it scared me a little bit. Even more than this shithole. For some reason, this dragon who'd seen more death than he could count couldn't let Rosabella die—*what was it about this girl?!*

"This place is like a relic—a time capsule," the nerdy kid inspected the room without fear, running his finger over the table and peering into the large, gold mirror balancing on the fireplace mantle while the rest of the group clutched their swords. It was ironic.

It was a museum back in the day—a place where people would tour to learn about the architecture and old way of living and such, I told him, wincing as more glass crunched under my enormous feet. I couldn't move in this place without breaking things; I never could. Typical of human dwellings, the room was filled to the brim with fragile objects.

Fine china dotted an ornate dining room table, surrounded by dusty cushions of the chairs. The curtains, somehow, had made it through hell and back—still hanging regally with faded gold and white threads from the gothic-style windows framing the room. A lonely fireplace sat at the head of the table with smashed glass glinting on the floor near it and ivy trailing up the wall to a crooked picture of a serene-looking woman.

NOT the woman inside.

"It's a puzzle!" the nerd kid exclaimed excitedly, his hands tracing over the detailed carvings on the mantle, "This entrance is a puzzle—

brilliant. I bet we have to find a lighter and burn something in this fireplace to get through to a secret room—"

Step aside, exuberant one, I dictated bluntly. *You don't need a lighter. You have a dragon.*

And, before he could step to the side, I let a volley of fire out—towards the fireplace. I knew I had good aim.

[System Alert: Blazing Past Illusion...Literally +10 XP, 1485/1500, +20 Swag Points, 4320]
[Secret Entrance Revealed]

...Well, at least the system thought I was cool...

The dork ruffled an embarrassed and sheepish hand through his dark, almost-singed hair, "Oh, err—right, sorry." But the light flickered right back into his eyes as the fireplace grew, and the white back wall of the fireplace melted into an enormous wood door with a wrought iron, lion knocker. "Oh cool!" he exclaimed.

But he shouldn't get so excited yet. All I could do was pray that the crazy woman behind the door could help us. An electronic beep sounded as a message popped up.

[System Alert: Passcode Needed.]

The nerd rolled his eyes at the alert. "Okay," he nodded, "I could run a quick program and see if I can hash out the password—" *Humans. They always got so bothered over the little stuff.*

Entara, I spoke, the magic rolling off my tongue A fizzing spray of yellow sparks exploded around the door.

[System Alert: OPEN SESAME COMMAND SPELL Used]
[-3 HP, 97/219]

Ouch; I was feeling that. This had better be worth it...

...

Nothing.

Nothing? I blinked at the door, dumbfounded.

"Was something…supposed to…happen?" the pink-haired loser twirled her hair around a slender finger as a know-it-all, expectant expression slid onto her face.

That's when it dawned on me: that bitch changed the passcode and blocked my magic. Assholes be assholes.

The nerdy human's fingers fumbled in the air again, bringing up the system interface, "I really can hack into it—"

[DORMOUSE, CODER 14: System Query: Please Input Code]

But I didn't have time for bullshit. Rosabella didn't have time for bullshit. I stomped my huge foot, shaking the floor—the longer we messed around with this, the closer to death's door she was…

Prickgada! I roared; I knew she could hear my mind telepathy. *Open the damn door! It's an emergency.*

There was silence.

Then, the slightest creak as the lock popped open. *Thank the Grand Dragon—*

I shoved the door in to find the woman I'd been avoiding for the last three decades standing there, a hand on one very annoyed hip.

"Hello, Sparo," she sneered.

Sparo

Grand Dragon, Prickgada looked like a trainwreck. That wild abandon raging in the enchantress's green eyes used to be what I liked about her, but it looked like it'd grown untamed like the ivy outside, shooting up and suffocating the youth in her. She'd always been a beautiful woman, but that beauty looked tired now—like every inch of life and zeal in her had been squeezed out and replaced with savage unkemptness. Her dark hair, once lush and long, protruded from her face in a frizzy and curling, dark mass. Her eyes were a fierce, stabbing green with none of the sun I remembered. Only ice. *This was the woman who'd broken my heart all those years ago?* It looked like something'd broken inside her too. *Her spirit? Replaced with bitterness and anger.* I could see it raging like one of those untethered thunderstorms she used to like to chase in the mountains.

[System Searching MRPs To Select & Display Correct Memory…]

…Oh, Grand Dragon, I wasn't sure I wanted to recall this…

"Whoooeeeee! Faster, Sparo!" Prickgada screamed gleefully into the rushing wind.

Her nails dug into the scales on my back, and, somehow, it only exhilarated me more. The wind ripped through my teeth, electric like the crackling and sizzling sky around and over us.

My talons dug heavily into the tallest plateau as I landed, grinding to a halt.

And I felt the Witch's slight form slide off me, her hand trailing along my neck with a warm tenderness.

And she watched the dark clouds.

The storm stretching out from underneath this cave and our toes, her excitement palpable as she barely dared to breathe.

But I watched her.

As the entire show flickered and raged in her avid, emerald eyes...

I shook my head, coming out of the memory. ...Grand Dragon, I had to stop it; I didn't want to relive my time with her. It'd been so long ago.

Her lair, however, I could have visited yesterday; it looked nearly identical to how it was before. It was a stately room—or would have been if not for the clutter. Gold wallpaper, an ornate tray ceiling and heavy drapes gave the place a Victorian feel, but the chaos of it matched the chaos in the woman's eyes: a chair pushed up against a huge painting, sitting on the floor, strewn with jackets and scrolls of parchment...a rug so stacked with books and random vase ware that you could hardly make out the pattern underneath... Honestly, the entire place had a general feel of claustrophobia—all lit with the golden glow of a single-shade lamp.

I watched the group of discontinued Game Wardens duck inside the door, peering at their surroundings. But Prickgada peered at them even more suspiciously. I knew that, as far as she was concerned, I'd brought the police to her criminal lair.

"I suppose you didn't see the posters," her eyes and lips narrowed in obvious distaste even at just seeing me.

How could I miss them? I mumbled to myself—words that didn't escape her keen mind as her eyes snapped to mine like a rebuke. *This was a mistake coming here. I'd told Callen it was crazy.*

"*Who's this?*" Her words were as sharp as her eyes. She flicked an impatient finger at Rosabella—her limp form in my outstretched talons. And I suddenly felt very vulnerable, standing there—an enormous dragon crowded in my ex-lover's lair, holding a human who I was still scrabbling with the thought that I might have caught the feelings for. *… Wasn't this one giant shit-show.*

I used one claw to clear the surface of a jumbled desk, hearing jars smash as they hit the ground and papers flutter.

"*Watch it!*" the enchantress warned, but I wasn't here to ask for permission.

She needs a large health pack…maybe two, I rushed, staring into Rosabella's pale face which was growing grayer with every passing minute. *I know you have a stash of them. With your unlimited HP cheat code, they're all but useless to you. Give her the health pack, and I'll trade you whatever you need for it—*

"*Whatever* I need?" Her eyes lit with sordid interest that made my heart tick into uncertainty for a second. "I trade those health packs with the locals for my food," she elaborated squarely, as though driving a hard bargain that I, honestly, cared nothing for.

…Did I not speak clearly? I growled back, the scales near my ears bristling. Without fail, the woman always put me on edge. She knew I was good on my word—

Beep.

I watched a health pack appear at the Witch's spidery fingertips. An Examination Opportunity with the shield and magnifying glass bobbed over it.

The Witch raised a plucked eyebrow, "Have a look for yourself." Her gaze could have been a stare down. Honestly, it was making me a little itchy in the armpits.

Examine, I commanded cooly in my mind, trying to hide the fidgeting going on in my huge body…everywhere—*why were my scales so itchy?*

[System Object Examined… +1 XP, 1486/1500]
[A Closer Look Tells You This Is Not Your Typical Health Pack. It's A FIRST AID DREAM CASE, Filled To The Top With Everything From Basic Supplies To A Defibrillator. This Jumbo Medical Case Will Fully Restore HP No Matter How Low Or Contribute +2000 MRP.]

Holy shit. I knew the woman dealt with cheat codes and illegal augments, but this was next level almost in an uncomfortable way.

"Thank God," Callen rushed forward to take the medical case from her, but Prickgada snatched it back, away from him.

"I'm not sure I entirely trust the word of this dragon," the enchantress hissed, her narrowed eyes bouncing to my face.

"Well, that makes two of us," the pink-haired girl agreed, stepping out of the shadow of the corner and into the light of the lamp so we all could observe her crossed arms and skeptical expression. Seriously? Humans were utterly terrible creatures… If they wanted me to play the dragon card, I would happily play it—

Give Rosabella the health pack, or I'll eat you, I threatened the Witch, growling low.

She chuckled, raising an unafraid eyebrow, "Now, there's the Sparo I remember. Here—"

She extended the pack, which both I and Callen reached for at the same time. *Naturally, I was faster.* I thrust it towards Rosabella.

[System Alert: FIRST AID DREAM CASE Acquired. Object Will Be Placed In Your Inventory Unless You'd Like To Use. Would You Like to Use?]
[Yes] [No]

Apply it to Rosabella, I told the system.

[Restore Full HP Available Or +2000 MRP. Please Select Which Option You Prefer.]
[Restore HP] [+2000 MRP]

I selected the HP option with a careful claw. *Grand Dragon, I hoped this helped her.*

[System Understands Query...Applying FIRST AID DREAM CASE To ROSABELLA, GAME MAKER 3...]
[ROSABELLA, GAME MAKER 3: System Alert: FIRST AID DREAM CASE Used.]

I watched it integrate into her HP:

[ROSABELLA, GAME MAKER 3: +48 HP, 53/53]

A collective sigh of relief ran through the room as the human girl came to life with a gasp on the table, coughing and sputtering. And, I couldn't help it, like a magnet, I was drawn immediately to her side, peering into her face just to make sure—

And she blinked at me, and I knew she was okay.

But, then again, Prickgada knew something too. Her eyes raked over both of us and came to the same realization, restarting my jumping heart. *Was it just me or did jealousy flash through her eyes?*

"In terms of payment—" the Witch started.

Wait, I still need your help. The words fell out of my consciousness and into the woman's before I could help it. I took a deep breath as Prickgada studied my face more deeply than I would have liked. She twirled a dark curl around her fingertip coyly. "...You know I like it when you *need* me," she toyed.

I ignored her line.

You know magic better than any other human I've seen, I said slowly, wording everything with as much care—and flattery—as I could muster. *I know it's not Creator Magic, just cheat codes that you use, but can you tell me about magic and its effect on humans?*

I forced the words out; it was hard admitting that I needed her help. Staring at Rosabella's recovering face, I realized I needed Prickgada more than ever. But the Witch turned away, her nervous eyes dancing to the group behind me. They might have been discontinued Game Wardens, but the small caveat in front of their title probably wasn't enough sway for her. The effects of Reordering hadn't quite soaked in for some Gamers in these parts…

"I don't use cheat codes—I would never," she tittered, "Cheat codes are against Game Law—"

WERE against Game Law. Reordering has changed a lot. Plus, you're not fooling anyone, I hissed. *You can trust this group. They're with me.*

The Witch let out a clucking huff, but I caught her uncertain eyes flickering over us all again. "…As far as the magic, I certainly *hope* I can do magic…" she huffed. "Unless I've just been perfecting these potions to grow my hair, which I certainly have; can you tell?" She leaned towards Dormouse with the question. His eyes only widened like a scared rabbit as she looked his scrawny form up and down, full hungry panther mode. "This one's my type in a spindly way…"

"Come on, Sparo, grab Rosabella, and let's go," Rainer's tone hedged on a dangerously thin line, like his face which looked more than uncomfortable as his eyes wandered around the room, and he nodded towards the exit. "Give her payment, and let's get out of here—"

But I couldn't leave. Not till I understood what had happened with Rosabella's HP back there—

I was teaching this girl how to activate and use her CM, I started, my voice heavy and level as I gestured towards Rosabella. *It's why she's in a critical level. It's like the magic was draining her or the system was. I don't know. She was using a spell, and it just kept taking her HP. This doesn't happen for dragons. Why would it happen with humans? A Game Maker?*

"I can take a look, but it will cost you," the woman said, her tone clipped as she turned, business-like, towards her potions. I looked from her back to the color returning to Rosabella face. *With Prickgada there was always a cost… She was a shrewd businesswoman. …But the group had to know in case it happened again…*

Take a look, I ordered her.

She nodded. And, sending another edgy glance at the discontinued Game Wardens, she opened a hidden drawer in the side of the desk Rosabella laid on. She reached out and turned a delicate, black nob with swift quickness. And she carefully drew out a crystal ball, perched between her two bony hands like a relic.

"Sparo, I'll need your assistance," she whispered hoarsely. The proposed trade beeped into view in front of my face.

[Proposed Trade: PRICKGADA, WITCH 15 Performs Divination, SPARO, RED VODYARACKA SKYDRAKE, DRAGON 14 Will Be Responsible For Payment.]
[Will You Accept the Trade?]
[Yes] [No]

Very vague, per usual with the woman but… I selected 'yes'.

[System Alert: Covenant Sealed]
[System Reward: Dodgy Business With An Enchantress +20 XP, 1506/1500]

The world froze for a minute. I recognized the backdrop as the Level Up screen. *Right now in the middle of things?*

Name	Sparo	
Class & Level	Red Vodyaracka Skydrake 15	
XP	1506/1600	
MRP	11480/11680	
HP	111/233	
Swag Points	4320	
Armor Class 19/20		
ABILITIES /20		
Strength	+6	23
Agility	+2	14
Endurance	+5	21
Intelligence	+2	14
Awareness	+1	13
Presence	+3	13
CM		4

[+14 HP & HP Extended By 14, 111/233. You've Been
Awarded +2 Ability Points. Please Select Which Ability
You'd Like To Increase.]

Congratulations, I don't care, I told the system in my mind,
dismissing the update.

[System Alert: System Will Cache Additional +2 Ability
Points In Your Inventory For Future Application.
Inventory Updated.]

The Witch nodded at me, but I didn't need her direction. *We'd
been there and done this before.* I opened my mouth wide, and she
placed the glass orb inside, balancing it there on the rim of my teeth.
The smooth surface froze my tongue, but I knew the sensations were
only about to get stranger. The Witch sent a scalding glance at all of
us before putting her hand in my mouth as well and looking back into

the glass. Blue and white magic flashed around my nostrils, tickling…
Her eyes glossed over as the magic took her in.

"Demosia Futura," she whispered.

[PRICKGADA, WITCH 15: System Alert: THE EYEBALLS OF THE FUTURE DIVINATION Used]
[PRICKGADA, WITCH 15: -5 HP, 138/143]
[PRICKGADA, WITCH 15: System Alert: HP Cheat Code Utilized, +5 HP, 143 /143]

Looked like she still used the cheat codes on herself too…

Then, just as quickly as she swiped away the system updates, she shook her head, and the gloss on her eyes was gone. And the crystal ball in my mouth lay cold and inactive on my tongue instead of warm and moving.

The Witched turned to me, her pupils sharper, dark knives pointed at each one of us in accusation. "There is a darkness on her—fingers grabbing for her constantly. She needs the Presence Ability cheat code to create a barrier between herself and this grabbing darkness, or she will drain and die every time she practices magic—"

Do it, I told her, my voice firm. 1,000% no hesitation. That's dragons for you, bitches—

"Hold on," Callen stepped forward with a raised hand, interrupting; he spoke directly at me, "How do we know this is safe? You trust this woman?"

I wouldn't go that far, but…

Yes, I lied—a little. I just didn't trust her…*generally.*

Prickgada is the best at what she does, I assured the man. *If she says something with magic is so, it is most certainly the case—*

"We're still kind of Game Wardens," Dormouse interrupted, cutting us both off, "I mean, sure, that tile was discontinued under Reordering, but we were supposed to keep The Game environment safe by hunting down glitches and eradicating them. I can't let her input a cheat code in front of us—"

"*Then leave,*" the Witch hissed. "This girl needs the Presence Ability cheat, or she won't be able to do what you've asked of her. You do want to fix The Game world, don't you? Doesn't that duty to The Game trump all others?" Her eyes were beadier than a raven's as she stared the dork down.

And, after an awkward minute, he nodded shortly. "Right...right, I get that. I'll just...I'll just...shut my mouth now." And he stepped back, his face draining of protest and color.

"Proceed," Callen told the Witch.

I swallowed as Prickgada swiped into Rosabella's account in the air over her head. Her spindly fingers darted with a proficiency that had always amazed me. A blank code box appeared:

[System Query: Please Input Code]

Her fingers continued to type without hesitation.

[*Whizzkid19786332*]

An electronic beep ensued.

[System Alert: Cheat Code Utilized]
[ROSABELLA, GAME MAKER 6: System Reward: A Witch's Hack Explored +15 XP 561/600]

A system reward for cheat code utilization? This new system since Reordering was bizarre. But my gaze darted to Rosabella as her eyes blinked closed. And she was still again...

Too still.

Rainer rushed forward, "*Did you hurt her?!*"

But the enchantress extended a hand over the Nomad's thick chest to stop him from moving any closer. "She'll need a second to integrate," she told us, turning with a sweep of her bell sleeves to address the group.

"And I'll take this minute to give you all *fair warning.*" Her eyes constricted, "You've put so much pressure on this girl—plucked her from her world, placed her in The Game and given her all the responsibility of fixing a universe she *hardly knows.*" She stared them down, "You ask why she's not strong enough. Her skills have *barely been built!* Her body can't handle this yet! You want her to build, but you see her as a singular member—a savior. And, yet, she is part of *your group.* You cannot heal the whole without working on the whole. You cannot fix it all without exploring it all. You are blind to what needs to be done. The darkness, destruction and zombies that cover our world aren't random. Dark attracts dark. You all harbor bits of the same, and it needs to be eradicated if you wish for this girl to repair this world. *You have been warned.*"

She turned to brush to the back of the room.

"…Well *that* was a load of mumbo-jumbo *bullshit…*" the pink-haired girl commented dryly, shaking her head in disbelief.

"Take Rosabella, and let's get out of here," Callen directed, "Sparo, can you fly us back to where we were?"

But my eyes were still trained on Prickgada. …Because I had a bad feeling I wouldn't be flying them *anywhere.*

[System Alert: Covenant Completed. PRICKGADA, WITCH 15 Performed Divination. SPARO, RED VODYARACKA SKYDRAKE, DRAGON 15 Is Responsible For Payment.]

I swallowed, but my dry mouth made it difficult. I shifted my huge body in the cramped space, ramming into a wooden chair and upsetting its contents.

System, narrow my telepathy to only Prickgada, I told it.

[Draconic Telepathy Channel Narrowed. The Human Group Can No Longer Hear You. PRICKGADA, WITCH 15 Can Hear You Now.]

Great. Honestly, I really didn't want to talk to her but...

What is the payment? I asked the woman in her head.

The green orbs of her eyes were serious as she turned back over her shoulder to face me.

"*You,*" she murmured low enough so the preoccupied others didn't hear. In my mind, she added.

You and your magic will help me form some of my newest products. You can't say no. You made a covenant.

And I nodded solemnly back. That I had. And Rosabella was worth it. Rosabella's life was worth it to me.

"Well, come on then," the hulky, warrior one waved me forward, "Rosabella's lighter for you to carry than for the rest of us—"

System, open the telepathy again, I told it through thought.

[Draconic Telepathy Channel Opened. The Humans Can Hear You Now. +10 XP, 1516/1600]

I won't be going back with you, I said. They gaped at me.

"*Why?*" Dormouse squeaked.

Payment, I replied back grimly. *The enchantress is taking me as her prisoner.*

Joy

The minute I was outta that hoarder Witch-bitch's lair, I was scheming. I mean, I was scheming before—*in* the Witch-bitch's lair—but this was a new type and, honestly, more frantic. Because I needed to get away from the rest of the group long enough to integrate the code.

...For the 20-point Presence Ability cheat, of course.

Whizzkid19786332

"System, save this memory," I murmured under my breath. *Obviously, memory saving was automatic for all Gamers, but I wanted to be extra sure with this particular nugget, especially given my MRP was spastic lately...*

[System Understands Query...Loading Response...]
[System Alert: Per Request, Memory Saved.]

With what little MRP I had, I'd still be able to open it if I wanted...hopefully.

"System, show me my MRP again," I mumbled.

[System Understands Query...Loading Response...]

God, what, was I checking it 20 times a day regularly? I chewed on the inside of my lip.

[Current MRP / JOY, WARRIOR 11: 47/7306]

A two-digit number had never scared me as much as that one did. Zero meant I was kaput—zombie Darken version. If it got to that point, I just hoped someone would kill me…didn't I? If I could just stop holding onto life with these clenching, white knuckles! …*But, to be real, that wasn't really my personality…*

I swiped the pop-up away quickly, clearing my throat, brushing a strand of pink hair behind my ear and following the group like everything was normal but… well, inside I was fuming. *I wasn't letting that lame-ass Rosabella bypass me on Ability levels when she could barely hold the swords on her belt. If the rest of this group was letting her tote the cheat for Presence, you could be sure as hell I was going to do the same. Rule-breaking 101. Someone had better keep an eye on that girl. I didn't trust her as far as I could throw her though—come to think of it—I bet I could throw her pretty far.*

"We'll stop for water here," Callen announced grandly, swiping an arm upwards so our tired feet ground to a halt near the rocky portion of a stream. The water rushed over the toes of my boots, soaking the soles and weaving around the mossy rocks there. The fresh scent of it made me wish I could find rest in…anything.

The all-knowing Callen; it was a wonder we hadn't gotten lost in these woods yet.

Rosabella was finally feeling well enough to walk so that was…*something* at least. She kept looking at me with wide, frightened eyes and, to be honest, it was creeping me the fuck out. *Couldn't the last Game Maker have been someone more…well, normal?*

"I gotta take a leak," I announced quickly, my heart ramming in my chest from the nerves I didn't typically get about anything anymore; this Presence cheat code shit seemed to really be getting under my skin.

"Don't come looking for me if I fall off the face of The Game or anything." My sarcastic jest ended flat and false in the awkward silence between the group. I heard the others shifting their feet in the grass, but their mouths stayed stretched in unimpressed lines.

Rainer raised a thick, furry eyebrow, speaking under his breath to Dormouse at his elbow, *"Don't worry, we won't,"* he chuckled.

I'd rather he threw his ax at my head than say those stupid words. I quickly drew my knife and gripped it in too hard of a grasp—something for my fingers to do, so I didn't punch the brute straight in the jaw. Of all of them, I probably like the hulking warrior the best...even if he did occasionally make smartass remarks. I lifted my thick-soled boots over the line of the underbrush and turned my back on the group. I made sure to bring my feet down in exaggerated stomping noises through the wood because...

Well, Rainer'd pissed me off with his comment.

...Snickering with Dormouse like they were all buddy-buddy in some guy posse, and it wouldn't even matter if I disappeared... Well, lucky for them, it was highly likely I would.

...Assholes... I tried to shake it off. *I had the Presence cheat code. They could all kiss my feet when my mere aura demanded attention.* I just needed somewhere to slip away, unnoticed, for a minute so I could add it to my stats—

I tromped over some more brush as the trees leaned over my heads like friends. I welcomed their cool shade on my hot skin and the playful tickling of the ferns against where my knee-high boots and black miniskirt didn't cover. Callen had dared me to fight in a miniskirt so...*let's just say I was in the middle of proving a point.* I'd caught Dormouse staring earlier when I'd bent over and had to slap him upside the head.

Absentmindedly, I reached back and scratched the base of my neck. My fingernails scraped over the gritty bumps there and came back plastered with dried blood and blackened pieces of peeling flesh. *This was what happened as your MRP lessened. You became forgetful and the darkness literally adhered to your skin, readying to turn you zombie.* The Darken rash itched so bad, especially in this heat. ...It was getting worse—even though I didn't admit it to the others—and so was the pain. The darkness was creeping up on me. Worse...*there was this voice...*

No, I wasn't going crazy; there had to be a reason for the voice. ...*Except that something inside me knew it had to do with the black spreading on my skin...*

This morning, I'd found a small, dime-size patch on my cheek. I'd pulled my hair around my face to hide it, but I'd thought Callen had noticed. I hadn't lost any MRP for a little while, but the applied curse was real. I'd had trouble finding health packs, my memory was foggy and...well, they said that when you reached 20 MRP, a countdown timer started...on your life. If you couldn't find a health pack by then, you were as good as...undead. But this Presence Ability cheat code...maybe it was the lucky break I needed. With it, maybe I could increase my personal power or influence ability on others. ...Maybe I'd...find my will to live again because it was getting weaker each day.

I made sure I was far enough away from the group, secure among a grove of sycamores and high bushes, before drawing up my stats in the air.

Name	Joy	
Class & Level	Warrior 11	
XP	1195/1200	
MRP	47/7306	
HP	150/162	
Baddie Points	2300	
Armor Class 13/20		
ABILITIES /20		
Strength	+3	16
Agility	+3	16
Endurance	+2	15
Intelligence	+1	12

| Awareness | +0 | 9 |
| Presence | -2 | 5 |

...The Witch had worked so quickly. There had to be a bar on the side or something with an option to input the code manually into my account. I tried a few different options, but it wasn't what I wanted— A jarring, beeping noise jolted me: Urrr.

[System Alert: Access Denied]

Urrr.

I closed my eyes, trying to smooth over the frustrated lines gathering on my forehead, "System, show me the memory I saved earlier from the Witch's lair," I dictated.

[System Understands Query...Loading Response...]
[System Searching MRPs To Select & Display Correct Memory...]

...Was it going to work?

The cluttered, Victorian room fizzled into view. The Witch leaned over Rosabella, her black curls falling onto the girl's chest—

"Hold on," Callen stepped forward with a raised hand, talking to the red dragon. "How do we know this is safe? You trust this woman?"

No, it was further than that part. "Fast forward," I whispered, aggravated.

[System Understands Query...Loading Response...]
[System Searching MRPs To Select & Display Correct Memory...]

"Right...right, I get that. I'll just...I'll just...shut my mouth now." Dormouse stepped back.

"Proceed," Callen told the Witch.

Prickgada swiped Rosabella's stats open in the air over her head. Her spindly fingers darted through the air—

Bzzz—

Hit—

LskAksdfs ksfwslkslkf slkfslflskdflsjdlfjsdff—

The memory froze, chalking up with rectangles of color like a damaged VHS as gibberish squeaked and hawed, nonsense—*no! Not again.*

[System Error: Insufficient MRPs To Display Current Memory...]
[System Error. Attempting To Reload...]

I tried frantically to swipe out of the messages. If I could get them to disappear, maybe I wouldn't have to deal with what I knew was coming next—

[System Error. Attempting To Reload...]
[System Error. Attempting To Reload...]

No!

[System Alert: Message For You]

"System, dismiss the message," my voice shook, "System, delete the message, you get it?!" My voice rose as I threw my hands down at my sides, "I don't want to hear the—"

[System Error. Attempting To Reload...]
[SYSTEM MESSAGE]

An electronic woman's voice started—my voice. My own voice which had been doing this creepy thing since a few months back—

"System, *stop it!,*" I begged. But I knew it wouldn't.

[System Error. Attempting To Reload...]

[SYSTEM MESSAGE:]
[You're stupid, Joy. Your mind is numb. It's no longer
functioning. No longer for your use. THIS IS JUST THE
BEGINNING OF THE END.]

"Argh!" In a fit of utter vexation, I chucked my dagger into the nearest tree—

Something rustled in the underbrush. I grabbed the weapon out of the bark with a quick tug, raised it, twirling around to find—

Dormouse. Blinking stupidly at me.

"...Whatcha doing?" the nerd quipped shakily.

I could have killed him with my knife. My hand wobbled, holding the weapon. *I could have seriously injured the spindly guy when he was just accidently creeping up on me—*

"Please say you did *not* follow me to watch me go pee," I sneered, re-sheathing the dagger at my waist and using sarcasm as a cover up to swipe the creepy system message out of view behind me.

His face twisted as his dark hair fell from a wide, pale forehead into his eyes. "I'm a little insulted you didn't *just ask*," he pouted.

"Ask what?" I played dumb. I played innocent, wide eyes and pink-hair stupid with an annoyed hand on my hip for extra flare.

But the kid was smarter than he looked—I knew that and, unfortunately for me, he looked Harvard smart. His eyes crinkled up at the corners, "If you're trying to utilize a cheat code, all you have to do is bypass the initial security protocol and bring up the secondary screen—"

I stared at him. "Do you speak *English?*" I asked—while thoroughly acknowledging the irony of his knight-in-shining-armor timing. *Thank God! I'd been hitting a brick wall with it...*

"Why don't you just do it for me?" I suggested, pulling up my stat page with a quick swipe.

The geek's white fingers typed rapidly in the air, pointing and clicking till he came to the familiar pop-up box:

[System Query: Please Input Code]

It sat there, blinking at us while Dormouse waited.

"Whizzkid19786332," I recited rapidly; *at least I could remember that part.* "You can integrate it into your account too if you want to—" I watched him type it:

[*Whizzkid19786332*]

He shook his head, tight-lipped, "No way. Sometimes it's better not to try to play Superman, you know?"

I didn't. I raised an eyebrow at him. *I wanted my Ability stats as high as I could make them. I wanted to know and be everything: how to defeat this darkness, how much time I had and how I could make sure that little shit Rosabella fixed our world so I could live in it.*

Whole.

Again.

An electronic beep ensued.

[System Alert: Cheat Code Utilized]
[System Reward: You Took Advantage Of A Nerd's Hack,
Plus You Did It On The DL, Making You A Badass +15 XP
1205/1200, +30 Baddie Points, 2330]

I chuckled a little at that. Obviously, the system didn't know me at all. I WAS a badass.

The world froze as green plus marks swirled around me. Case in point; I was at another Level Up already…

[System Alert: ***Congratulations, You've Advanced To
Level 12!*]**

Name	Joy	
Class & Level	Warrior 12	
XP	1195/1200	
MRP	47/7306	
HP	160/172	
Baddie Points	2300	
Armor Class 13/20		
ABILITIES /20		
Strength	+3	16
Agility	+3	16
Endurance	+2	15
Intelligence	+1	12
Awareness	+0	9
Presence	+5	20

[+10 HP & HP Extended By 10, 160/172. You've Been Awarded The Ability To Select One Of The Following Weapons:]
[Morning Star] [Set of 5 Throwing Knives]

Whoa, the Presence cheat code showed already, plus I got the option to chose another deadly item for my belt? That was what you called winning.

"I want the blade set," I told the system, not even caring to evaluate the Examination Opportunities bobbing over each option. I'd lost my last set in the hides of four angry Dratameercrew, and I needed a replacement.

[System Alert: SET OF THROWING KNIVES Selected. Object Will Be Placed In Your Inventory Unless You'd Like To Equip. Would You Like To Equip?]
[Yes] [No]

No, I said. The world unfroze which, unfortunately, consisted mostly of Dormouse's face leaning into mine.

"You might feel a little whoozy as the Presence cheat code integrates," the nerd warned.

Tiredness washed over me. *Wait…tiredness was for losers, not me.*

"I thought I had enough Endurance and Strength to bypass this," I complained, reaching out to steady myself on a tree as my head pirouetted. The rough, peeling bark steadied my fingertips only for a second till my mind spun again. I shivered remembering the disturbing system message. *What was wrong with me? Was it already too late to fix this?*

"Help me back to the group," I commanded the nerd. He was younger than me and highly helpful in an annoying way—*why not put it to good use?* But I pulled up short when I heard the others through the brush.

"I'll go first," I hissed in a whisper, moving past my nausea just enough to use logic and step through the bushes alone, "I don't want them to suspect anything—"

"A thank you goes a long way!" he called after me. I ignored him. *…No wonder people said I was a bitch.*

I held my head high as I strode back to join the others, feeling a strange, new energy gathering in my veins as I flipped my pink hair back over my shoulder to hide the black spot on my cheek. The Witch said something about all of us working together to fix this. I was going to find out what that meant. …At least I had time to figure this shit out.

Goran

They had no time, and they didn't even know it; this was checkmate.

Not boxing a knight in.

Not penning a queen.

The king—fallen.

Dead.

And it made me want to smile although I kept my face straight, grim and powerful under the scrutiny of the watchful eyes of the wasteland Nomads. This was the best plan I'd had yet, and it had to lead me back to Rosie. *It had to.*

"You'll wait for the Commandress's decision," one of the guards barked, his voice echoing in the vast chamber they'd been holding me in.

"Look," I held my hands up in open protest, "I'm not even asking for an update, bud. I'm just sitting here."

'Squatting here' was more correct. I tried to ensure my voice was casual and light. They couldn't mistake me for someone powerful. I'd have to appear like a friend—helpful, but not pushy. I was in their domain after all.

This had all worked out perfectly—down to the nitty-gritty details. *Was I a genius, or was I a genius?* The Gamers were wrong to have put all their trust in my brother. He hadn't been the brains of the family—I was. …And, now, they'd all just have to squirm and suffer in the squalor that was the result of their giant miscalculation.

Justice.

Finally.

And Rosabella back.

To me.

Two of the most important things—the most important goals—perhaps finally accomplished. Fifteen more minutes and, maybe, we'd see.

I squatted in a puddle in the rutted, cave floor. Water soaked into the toe of my sneakers, creating a wet, rounded line as it seeped into the fabric there. It had probably dripped from a stalactite in the shadows way over my head; even if I craned my neck upwards, into the blackness of the ceiling, it was hard to see.

…Everything about this dragon made me respect her; the Commandress had built her fortress in a cave concealed from the rest of the burned, West Side forest. Even the entrance of the place held walls carved in bronze, copper and wood—vast columns and intricate etchings displaying the sheer size and nobility of the place. I'd been chained immediately upon arrival—these guards were good…actually effective. Two solid, metal handcuffs, connected by chains, restricted my arms and feet and a third, metal collar was secured around my neck. They didn't mess around; I respected it. This place and its warriors were already proving my hypothesis to me; I'd been right. The dark dragon was the key. Her magic combined with my skill and strategy would be unstoppable. *Now, I just needed her to take the deal…*

I chewed on the side of my lip, watching the two, dimwit Nomads at the door exchange a hushed word. Their faces, plastered in black warpaint, constricted, and they shuffled towards me; the animal skins and leaves plastered to their robes dragged heavily on the ground, "She's ready to see you—"

A deafening roar shattered the air.

Then, claws scratching against wood—splintering it.

The enormous doors the Nomads had been standing near suddenly engulfed in hissing and spitting flames. And, as the wood blackened and crumbled, jagged talons broke through the solid form like easily pulling back blackened paper.

And a huge dragon's eye, yellow and bulging, peered through.

And, then, the bronze scales of a massive snout.

Smoke clogged my nostrils and heat scoured the cheeks of my face.

[-1 HP, 12/117]

I'll speak for myself.

The Commandress hissed in my mind.

Come here, fake Game Maker. Together we will remake the world.

Everything in me suddenly leapt with jittering exclamation. *I'd done it?!*

I barely dared to breathe. I bowed my head low, even secured in these metal chains and so close to the still-simmering fire, "Commandress, I am so honored—"

Shut your mouth, and let's get to work. Humans talk too much.

I inclined my head even further in a show of humble respect. The floor shook as the dragon turned around, waddling back towards the golden, glistening weaving of a red-velvet-stitched throne behind her. The guards hurried to detach my chains from the floor. They popped free with a metal, grating sound, and they let them drag heavily on the floor behind me as I took my first tenuous steps as a completely free man...towards the dragon.

Now, free of worry.

Or shame.

Or guilt.

Only filled with utter elation at the realization of the miracle I'd created for myself. *Oh, how the tables turn, Rosie, when you rig the system…*

I want those doors replaced by nightfall, vermin.

The dragon tiraded at the closest guards. Her talons clicked on the hard, rock floor and, then, softened to pale thuds as they lingered on the red carpet near the golden throne.

I told you, no more wood. This last door set has barely lasted a week. Poor craftsmanship.

Honestly, the blackened bits of the door looked like the durability had nothing to do with its design. I bit the inside of my lip to stop any sarcastic comment from slipping out. I had to make sure to play this just right—

Join me, fake Game Maker.

The beast's address of me tightened a fist in my heart. And I, suddenly, wanted to lash out—to throw away everything I'd accomplished using this respectful, smooth face by losing it and yelling at the thing. *I didn't care if she was a Bronze Sydatladon and her ego was the size of—*

Fake Game Maker?!

—I'd show her fake Game Maker!

…But I couldn't 'lose it'. Because I'd only lose Rosie. I'd throw away every chance I had of fixing this mess. I had to stay calm. I bit back every retort that'd risen to my lips.

"If you'd please, your excellency," I gritted my teeth, even in asking, to keep the hardness out of my voice. My hands clenched at my sides, "Could you please not call me that."

Fine.

She huffed, swishing her giant tail to the side in annoyance.

Join me, man who killed his brother for his child.

I opened my mouth to protest but found the Commandress staring at me with such fire that I didn't dare say anything at all. She gestured, with her enormous head, to the throne.

Wait, she wanted me…

She'd elevated me to the level to sit on her…throne?! The breath nearly died in my lungs. My head felt giddily light.

Forgetting about my brief quarrel with her, I tripped towards the throne. *I knew this would happen! I knew I'd win her trust!* I took a deep breath, closing my eyes slightly as I grasped both arms, ready to finally take my place on the seat—

Dratamore, secure him!

The Bronze Sydatladon cried.

And a Nomad nearly popped out of the wall, rushing towards me. And he grabbed the ends of my chains in his solid grip. And nailed them to the leg of the throne.

…The dragon hadn't wanted me to sit. She'd wanted to restrain me? I whipped around to see the dragon's leering head, snaking high above and over me.

"If we're going to do this, we need to trust each other," I snarled, taking a quick half step forward and feeling the pressure immediately—regretfully—in the metal collar at my neck. The chains rattled as I yanked against them.

Oh, I do trust you.

The Commandress cooed, lowering her bronze head so her eyes were level with mine. She blinked slowly.

Never mind, I take that back. I don't but…well, I trust you are doing this for your own interests, and it just so happens that our interests align. Tell me again.

She began.

How do we burn the rest of the world and wipe out any chance of power returning to the humans? How do we do all this and end with one sole ruler of The Game…me? I don't care what you get out of it. I care what I do. And I want to hear it again.

I could see the lust for it in her eyes—her need for power. That was something I understood too clearly. Because I needed something too. I needed Rosabella back or my whole world would crumble.

"I have access to and control over the last Game Maker," I told the dragon squarely, repeating what I'd told her earlier, "She's here, right now, in The Game. If she seizes power, the Gamers will back her—we both know this. I can stop her. I can make her disappear…never to return. She trusts me. I'll convince her to leave this world and return to New York with me. You won't see her again. You can rule Game Makerless—as powerful as the Grand Dragon. If you work with me and help me do magic…if we work together, we can multiply the current army you have, enhancing their skills, and advance on your nearest rivals while moving towards the Game Maker. We'll corrupt food sources, and your Creator Magic will ensure that you can make enough to eat for your army and yourself. We'll give the surrounding dragons the choice to join us or die. We'll combine forces as we move over the land, growing more and more powerful, and the Game Maker won't stop you. You will ensure the Game Maker and me our lives and safe passage back to reality, and that little problem will be out of your hair…forever."

I said the words confidently, glossing over the panic rising in my chest. The corresponding system trade appeared between us, hovering:

[Proposed Trade: GORAN, PRISONER 11 Gets
ROSABELLA, GAME MAKER 6 Out Of The Game And
Aids THE COMMANDRESS, BRONZE In Taking Control
Of The Game World, THE COMMANDRESS, BRONZE
SYDATLADON, DRAGON 18 Will Help GORAN, Make
Magic And Ensures No Harm Will Come To Him Or
ROSABELLA, GAME MAKER 6 And That They Will Have
Safe Passage Back To NYC.]
[Will You Accept the Trade?]
[Yes] [No]

My eyes scanned hurriedly over the lines, verifying it wasn't
missing anything. *The Commandress had to agree to this. If she didn't—*

Okay, man who killed his brother for his child. We fight together.

The dragon's oath. The words that cemented draconic
covenants—*yes!* I resisted the urge to yank my fist down at my side.
Neon words popped into view between us:

[System Alert: Covenant Sealed]
[System Reward: Power Move Made & Successful +30 XP,
1167/1200]

And I smiled this time; I didn't hold back the grin. Because the
Commandress was eating out of my hand now; I had her.
And, because I had her, I had Rosie back. Finally. I would find her
and take her back to NYC to restore everything that we'd had
together, and I'd break this pathetic world in two as I did. *So many
dragons with one stone.*

When shall we start?

Echoed the dragon in my mind, her blazing eyes filling with the
wrath and yearning that'd been itching under my skin for some time
now.

I turned to her, my face glistening with glee. "Right now," I whispered. "We start right now."

Joy

If I wasn't so damn sick, I'd joke about who's baby I was having. My stolen, covert Presence upgrade had, apparently, screwed me over physically; I was so nauseous that I could barely stand. I clutched at my stomach as the trees whirled overhead. I bit my lip, but even the pain didn't steady me. *What was my HP? Why was I feeling like this?*

"System, why is the world spinning?" I growled, bent low, "Show me my HP and Presence Ability Points."

[System Understands Query...Loading Response...]

I didn't have to try too hard to shield the impending pop-ups from the group. I was already so far behind. I blocked the sun from streaming into my eyes with a hand as the answers populated:

[System Answer: Calm down, You're Not Having A Baby. Your Account Is Integrating The Presence Ability Point Cheat Code. Recalibration Is Expected To Take Approximately....1 Hour, 15 Minutes and 22 Seconds Longer. Would You Like to Cancel Recalibration?]
[Yes] [No]

Fuck! No. "No, don't cancel," I told it, pouting. Apparently, I was just going to be in living hell for the next hour and some change…

[Current HP / JOY, WARRIOR 12: 160/172]
[Current Presence Ability Points / JOY, WARRIOR 12:
20/20]

I swiped the other pop-ups out of view. The group took another break, boots thudding to a slow halt in front of me and crunching in the dry dirt and grass. I saw they were trying not to make it look like I was the reason for the slow down…again. But they were getting impatient. Rainer raised a confused eyebrow at me, but I turned away before he could say anything.

Damn. Normally, I was leading this herd of spineless fools. Today, I could barely trail them. Maybe I shouldn't have integrated the Presence cheat code after all…

Rosabella was being oohed and ahhed over by a fascinated Dormouse. Apparently, she'd found some sort of spell. I watched as the system updates seemed to crown her head with neon—*like a fucking halo. How glorious that our golden girl had, once again, done something to gain the enthrall of the group.* I snorted, rolling my eyes.

[ROSABELLA, GAME MAKER 6: System Reward: You've
Found A Spell. +10 XP, 571/600]
[ROSABELLA, GAME MAKER 6: FIND THINGS
HOPELESSLY LOST HOCUS POCUS]

Goddamnit, she was such a goodie two shoes. I didn't particularly want to press the play button on the rest of this show. …Plus, maybe now was my moment—while the rest of them were all wrapped up in Girl Wonder.

"I'll be right back," I yelled over my shoulder, pretending I was going for a piss by tramping off into the thick underbrush, but, when I reached the shelter of two, larger trees, I just squatted there, heaving in air and trying to steady myself by staring at the brown dirt and entwining roots by the toes of my boots.

The side effects of this integration were terrible. …How was I going to hide it when we had a full day's trek to Meherna Temple—the place where Rosabella could augment her magic to save our world? I could barely walk a few feet without getting winded. Fucking Rosabella was in front of me with her low Endurance levels—it was embarrassing.

I scratched at my head and pitched my gloved hands down in front of my angled knees in frustration. Squatting there, I noticed that, through the rips and tears in the fabric of the gloves, my skin was coal-black. My breathing grew even more ragged with fear. What the—?!

I threw the gloves off like they might burn me—watched them fall, limp, to the ground. And, then, I stared.

At my hands.

Scaly black.

…Even the palms, covered like I'd dipped my hands in dark ash.

—Itching like wildfire with a trail of dots leaving the wrist and traveling up my arms. …Just like the rash on my neck…

This shit was scaring me. It felt like every breath was getting me closer to Darken. I did what I always did when shit scared me; I immediately covered it up. My heart thundered in my ears as my fingers fumbled in the dirt and grass for the gloves, plucked them up and yanked them back over my hands—

"Joy."

I whipped around, but it was too late, I could tell. Rosabella leaned on the tree over me. Her eyes snapped to my hands—my arms… She'd seen.

"Leave me alone," I huffed, standing too quickly for my spinning head and trying to brush past her, "What does a girl have to do to get some privacy to take a piss—"

"You're hurting." In one, swift movement, Rosabella reached out and caught my arm. …Could you believe that? The little shit finally gained some reflexes in this exact moment? Her eyes raked over the diseased skin there.

I recoiled from her, trying to pull away as her fingers dug into the tender cells there, "Get off me!"

But, somehow, she hung on. And, for some other reason, I wanted to cower back from the girl...because it'd just struck me that she was a Game Maker. ...Or, maybe, it was the fire of knowing burning in her eyes. This Presence Ability cheat code was weird. Was it making me suddenly...respect her?

...No...

"I'm dying, okay, Rosabella—is that what you want me to say? Of course, I'm fucking hurting." The words were brittle and hoarse coming off my tongue as I attempted to shove the girl off. All I wanted was to be left alone. Honestly, all I wanted was time and my memories back—it was ironic, wasn't it? After all I'd been through that I, finally, just wanted more time to live—to remember? When, my whole life, I'd been wishing both of those things away? And, yet, my draining MRP was going to kill me. Maybe it was just my excellent karma nailing me in the ass again...

"I can help you," Rosabella insisted, her fingers still on my arm.

She thought she could help me—the newb? I had to laugh. I had to chuckle at that thought. Because, although it was my one, main wish right now—that anyone could help get me out of the dark hole of my impending doom—the thought of the girl doing anything helpful was far beyond me at this point.

"You couldn't even kill a dragon," I hissed, "Why should I believe you?"

The girl's wide eyes flickered to mine, and, somehow, stopped me in my tracks—stopped the disdain in my voice just for a second. She didn't know it, but I desperately needed her to counter my sarcasm. I desperately needed her to tell me that I was wrong—that she was going to prove me wrong. I'd never needed to be wrong so ardently in my life.

"I don't know exactly how I know that I can help you," the girl started again, her gaze steady, "but I think I can."

And I watched her close her eyes.

Felt her clutch at my arm—clasped tight there in her fingers as her mouth worked in some strange chant.

And I closed my eyes too—

[ROSABELLA, GAME MAKER 6: System Alert: FIND THINGS HOPELESSLY LOST HOCUS POCUS Used]
[ROSABELLA, GAME MAKER 6: -1 HP, 52/53]

Air whooshed by my face. My breath drew in sharply as my eyelids fluttered open because we were no longer in the forest. Wetness misted over my cheeks and hair. My boots stood firmly on the dark asphalt of a soaked street...and the looming silhouettes of city buildings stretched up overhead. *An alley? We were in an alley? ...Wait, I knew that sign...*

The neon one flickering in the distance:

The Wicked Cross

Oh my God. Were we...

Welcome ROSABELLA, GAME MAKER 6 & JOY, WARRIOR 12 To The Side Mission
[Side Mission Objective: Find The Key.]

Side mission?

"What the fuck did you do?!" I raged, spinning towards Rosabella who was inspecting her hands, turning them over repeatedly under her gaze like it might tell her something.

"I—" she stammered, her cheeks flooding red, "I forgot the first time you do a spell it messes up. Sparo called it a trial run—"

Neon words interrupted her lame-ass excuses.

[System Alert: Joy, This Side Mission Is Yours As Is The Reward If You Complete It. Upon Side Mission Objective Completion Earn +2000 MRP, Fully Restored HP Or A Powerful Mystery Object. The Choice Will Be Yours. Now, Make The First Choice To Begin. Begin The Side Mission?]
[Yes] [No]

My throat went dry reading the text. Wait, the system was saying that I could restore my MRP–that I could save myself from turning Darken? Without a mention of the curse or any downsides or—

"System, is this…a joke?" I blurted, throwing my pink hair back over my shoulder.

[System Unable To Understand Query…Recognizable Word = 'Joke'.]
[System Answer: You Are Looking To Laugh. Do You Want Me To Tell You A Joke?]
[Yes] [No]

I clenched my fists together, all of my hope almost fizzling out of me—*why couldn't this system understand real, human language?!* "No, I don't want to be told *a fucking joke.* I want you to tell me if the side mission rewards are legit," I pouted. An electronic beep sounded.

…Hopefully, the system would recognize the word 'legit'—not great wording on my part…

[System Understands Query…Loading Response…]

I let out a sigh of relief.

[System Alert: Yes, The Completion Rewards Are Valid & Can Be Collected Upon Completion Of The Side Mission Objective. Good luck! Begin The Side Mission?]
[Yes] [No]

"Yes!" The word just jumped out of my mouth. Oh my God, this was my chance! This was my way out of becoming a zombie!

[Side Mission Confirmed]

I turned towards Rosabella, breathless, to find her inspecting our surroundings. "Is this New York City?" she asked, her face scrunching up, "I don't understand. This isn't my street…"

"No, it's not," I remarked quietly, swallowing hard as the realization crashed over me. "*It's mine.*"

The girl whirled around, a piece of her brown hair getting caught on her mouth which she pulled downward, hesitation written in her face, "…What?"

"Is it *so inconceivable* that a monster like me could also be from your hometown?" I asked, leaning into the sarcasm in my voice. *Yes. I was from New York City too…with one huge difference that I would never vocalize: Rosabella had escaped FROM The Game to NYC. I'd escaped NYC TO The Game.* Just seeing this place made my stomach clench with dread.

"But there's been game pop-ups," Rosabella said, "When I was in NYC before, it said I *left* The Game—"

I nodded, "That was reality. This is still The Game. You've created an alternate dimension within The Game. The program is smart. I guess your messed-up spell launched us into a side mission which is pulling from my memories. Side missions are supposed to fast-track our progress and growth as Gamers; they have wicked prizes. I could barely believe the ones that came up. I could win back a huge chunk of my MRP. This is insane. …Maybe you were right that you *can* help…"

The admittance tasted bitter on my tongue, but I had to consider it. I chewed on the inside of my lip, looking down at the skin of my arms. *If I could win this… What was the objective again? Conquer the objective, win the MRP. My mind, suddenly, had a singular focus.*

"System, show me the objective again," I commanded, my voice ringing in the empty, wet alley.

[Side Mission Objective: Find The Key.]

The neon words floated into view. I frowned at them. "Could they be more vague?" I complained. ...*Or was it vague?* The NYC in this side mission alternate reality was a match to NYC in reality. I couldn't remember using a physical key for anything back then...even my past apartment had had an electronic card to unlock the door, since it was a former hotel which had been converted into efficiency units...

That's when it hit me: a memory of a key in my hands. *I'd had a key to lock up the Wicked Cross at night—the nightclub down the street where I'd worked. ...But the manager had made me hand it back in when they'd fired me...*

I took off down the street, sprinting—my pink hair flying past my shoulders in the wind as rain pelted me in the face.

Just determination.

And speed.

All nausea gone.

I heard Rosabella squeak in surprise and, then, trot after me. "Hey! *Where are you going?!*"

"Maybe in your parallel dimension, I can get my fucking job back," I yelled over my shoulder.

And I knew my words made no sense to her, but—*well, this side mission was all about me, wasn't it?*

I stopped short under the Wicked Cross's neon sign. I'd always, not-so-secretly, loathed the place, even though it was pretty much solely responsible for all the food I'd put on the table in those days and Mom's medication. The pink glow of the neon strips overhead lit my face as I paced by the overflowing smoke stand, piled with cigarette butts, and yanked open the steel back door. Rosabella was annoyingly right behind me—*did the girl know about personal space?* I nearly elbowed her in the stomach, trying to open the heavy door.

…And the familiar, dim lights greeted us as I stepped onto that nasty linoleum that no one had cleaned in probably two years because the mop boy was usually just making out with one of the server girls in the closet while on payroll…

I reached into the nearest locker without even thinking about it. An electronic beep sounded.

[System Reward: Stealing Isn't Always Bad…Is It? Item Stolen. +10 XP, 1215/1300]
[System Reward: BUNDLE OF LAUNDRY Acquired +10 XP, 1225/1300, Object Will Be Placed In Your Inventory Unless You'd Like To Equip. Would You Like To Equip?]
[Yes] [No]

"No," I grumbled, but I saw a shield and magnifying glass hovering over the bundle—an Examination Opportunity.

"Examine," I whispered.

[System Option Examined… +1 XP, 1226/1300]
[A Closer Look At The Laundry Pile Shows You've Acquired Two WICKED CROSS WAITRESS UNIFORMS.]

For once, the gods of chance were smiling on me. My fingers dug into the fabric as I shoved a handful of the black fabric at Rosabella, "There's a bathroom over there, put this on." I nodded towards a grimy back door. But the girl *had* to look. *Of course, she fucking had to look.* She unraveled the black material, squinting at me when it was all too clear it was a corset and black shorts.

"This isn't a *strip club*, "I spat. "It's the uniform for the nightclub waitresses. If you're going to judge, you can stay in this back room while I—"

That got her moving—*finally.*

Sending a quick glance at the doorway to make sure no one was coming, I slipped my weapons belt to the floor and my body armor off. I quickly laid the fabric of the corset over my bare middle too, pulling it tight at the back—

[Object Identified: WICKED CROSS WAITRESS UNIFORM Decreases Gamer Armor Class To 8 'Cause It's Hard To Do Anything In Heels & Shorts This Short, +500 Baddie Points When Equipped. Do You Wish To Equip WICKED CROSS WAITRESS UNIFORM?]
[Yes] [No]

OMG, I'd forgotten about the Baddie Point increase. I could literally MOW OVER most dudes with that type of influence in this getup—forget battling dragons though; the AC was poor.

Yes, I told the buttons floating mid-air. And the option selected with a whooshing sound.

[System Alert: WICKED CROSS WAITRESS UNIFORM Equipped. Armor Class Decreased To 8. +500 Baddie Points, 2830]

And—*zroom!*—the black shorts immediately adhered to my body: spandex. *At least my repeated squats weren't going to waste; my thighs looked tight.* I wobbled a little as the system added the black heels. *Now, I was keeping these;* they fit my feet like the sexiest of gloves. Whichever girl I'd just robbed was going to have to deal like I'd had to all those years.

Rosabella ducked out of the bathroom, holding an armload of her clothes to her chest to cover up the corset she now wore. The sight of her almost made me want to tell her to change back...or laugh. I wasn't sure which. Her enormous, innocent eyes shone like scared, full moons, taking up a majority of her face, and her stringy, brown hair laid flat against her cheeks from the rain. Feeling strangely sisterly for all of two seconds, I moved closer to fluff the strands over her shoulders for her. But we didn't have the luxury of time. *We'd better move before someone saw us.*

I shoved a round tray at her. "Don't talk to anyone, act busy and…" I faltered, looking her timid form up and down, "*Look older.*"

If I'd had some eyeliner, I could have had her doctored up in two minutes, but I didn't have my bag. This was going to have to do.

"*Blend,*" I hissed again as we ducked through the doorway and out into the bustling pub.

Joy

The place was hopping tonight. The neon lights pulsed over a crowded bar as servers, dressed like the both of us, wove in and around customers, their black trays held high over their heads as colorful drinks wobbled in fancy glasses there. The music was so loud that I could barely hear myself think—

"Well if it isn't my favorite, pink-haired lady!" a man's throaty—and clearly intoxicated—voice bellowed from the bar. I located the owner of it quickly, honing in on a red-faced, middle-aged man with a ginger beard which looked like it hadn't been combed in over a year. *Not this—not fucking Pirate Pete when I really didn't need his shit.*

The inebriated man's sausage fingers pointed directly at me as he continued, loudly, "*There she is!* You used to mix the drinks strong. I knew it was because you had a special liking for me."

[PIRATE PETE, BAR PATRON: System Query: Would You Like To Flirt With JOY, WARRIOR 12? Use 30 Swag Points to Flirt?]
[Yes, Flirt] [No, Thank You]
[PIRATE PETE, BAR PATRON: -30 Swag Points, 2600]

Oh, God, he was trying to flirt with me again like when I'd worked here?

Pirate Pete tried to wink.

And failed.

Just like he did at nearly everything else. He hiccupped, almost falling off the stool.

[PIRATE PETE, BAR PATRON: System Alert: Flirtation Rejected, -10 Swag Points, 2590]

"Don't *flatter yourself*," I growled, "I only mixed the drinks strong so you'd pass the hell out on the bar and not punch a hole in the drywall of the men's bathroom again."

A hoot of laughter bubbled up from around the bar—those within earshot of my comeback. One guy raised a beer in a toast. "You tell him, sweetheart!" he whistled.

[PIRATE PETE, BAR PATRON: System Penalty: A Girl's Calling You A Drunk And Vandal In Front Of Your Friends! -50 Swag Points, 2540]

Pirate Pete's eyes went dark as he threw a hand sideways to dismiss the system pop-up—his lips rippled into a frown. "Last I heard"—he said, blurrily raising a furry eyebrow—"you was thrown outta here. Quite the spectacle. Got thrown outta here and drowned yourself in the bottle if you know what I mean…" I couldn't escape his dark stare.

I knew.

His words hurt; they *burned my soul.* …Because he was right. I'd lost it that night. I'd lost *everything.* That night that Mom died, I couldn't hold anything back anymore. It was like a dam had opened up inside of me when I'd seen her ashen face in the bed and known I'd missed it. I cared for her all that time, and I'd missed her death—hadn't been there to save her. She'd slipped away in the middle of the night, tucked underneath covers as gray as her face. The cancer had eaten her from the inside out and, no matter how many extra shifts I'd worked, I couldn't buy enough treatment to fix it.

No. I bit my lip. It was too hard to remember things like that—not because my MRP was broken but because...because I was afraid I'd break if I did remember. I swiped the system message away, remembering how I'd felt. Everything had seemed meaningless after Mom's death—without her. Meaningless and dark.

And I'd taken it out on this place—on this stupid nightclub that hadn't ever been enough. Just like I hadn't been—not enough to save her—my one job.

I'd split open—in half that one night. I'd drawn a pocketknife on a rude customer.

Worse, I'd thrown him across the bar.

Broken a full bottle of top-shelf brandy and—I think they'd said—seven cocktail glasses.

They'd thought I was drunk. But that wasn't till later.

As I sat on the cold, tile bathroom floor of our apartment with only a bottle for company, staring at the caulking connecting the stained bathtub to the wall and floor...

Only a bottle.

A gun.

And a decision.

And I'd almost fully made it too—I'd almost fully decided to make it. I gritted my teeth, remembering. Till—

...Well, till the Game Wardens saved me.

All the memories welled up in my eyes, stinging there. And, suddenly, I wanted nothing more than to wrap my hands around what had reminded me of them and kill it—squeeze the life out of it.

"I'm gonna kill him," I mumbled under my breath to Rosabella, "If I kill him here, will he die in real life?"

I didn't know if Rosabella opened her mouth to answer—the place was too loud and Pirate Pete was in my face, swaying so close that I got way too good a view of the gnarly scar running down his left cheek; I was pretty sure he'd swapped the word 'bear' for 'bar' when he'd been describing which fight he'd gotten it in. ...And I knew one other thing: the burly Nomad was blocking my way.

"We're looking for a key," Rosabella reminded me, yanking on my arm as though she could see that I only had one foot in this reality and the other buried and lost somewhere in my past, "We have to focus. He's just a loser. Let's get the key."

Her words seemed to steady me even though the brute was so close. I latched onto them: find the key, replenish my MRP, stay alive. Good plan—better than dealing with this asshole. I needed to get the key to this place back from my boss; I needed to find the man. He was probably in the back at his office...

"Move," I told Pirate Pete, trying to step past him—today was not the day to fuck with me.

...But the man's solid, hairy calves, showing through capri shorts, stood squatly in front of me, refusing to move above thick, black, leather boots. Don't force my hand, I begged him in my mind, Don't make me repeat what I'd done years ago in this same bar. I was about ready to snap in two like a brittle branch. My hand flew to where my katana typically hung on my belt but found only the seam of this stupid outfit.

"Get out. Of my. Way," I growled savagely. One more threat and this guy was going down. But Pirate Pete's face split into an unexpected smile under all that beard. He leaned drunkenly towards me, raising a beer in the air, "Awe, if the lady drinks a pint, I think we'd have no problems here, right boys?" The men around him nodded and murmured their agreement as he thrust a beer mug, bigger than his fist and filled to the brim, at me. And an electronic beep sounded as the corresponding trade fizzled into view. …And I, suddenly, didn't like where this side mission was going—not one bit.

**[Proposed Trade: JOY, WARRIOR 12 Drinks Beer Pint,
PIRATE PETE, BAR PATRON Lets JOY WARRIOR 12
Past.]
[Will You Accept The Trade?]
[Yes] [No]**

The system pop-up made me feel unsteady—like the world was swaying around me…or I was swaying. I chewed on my bottom lip. This was fucked up. I had to drink and loose MRP so that I had a shot at getting a huge amount of my MRP back? Revise that, I WAS fucked.

Rosabella's huge, worried eyes swam into my vision between me and the brute, "Joy, you don't have to do this."

But I kind of did. And I didn't need her pity. I gritted my teeth and raised my chin, my gaze locking on the Nomad's. "I accept," I proclaimed to the hushed bar.

**[System Alert: Trade Accepted]
[System Reward: A Dangerous Volley Of Power +15 XP,
1241/1300]**

Shit. This was stupid; I was too stubborn—

The music boomed in my ears, making me dizzy. A cheer erupted from the dimwits all around me. Glasses clinked together as they used my unfortunate situation to continue their drunken stupor. Fists pounded on the wood bar, suddenly deafening and matching the beat of the music.

"Drink! Drink! Drink!" they chanted in a clashing baritone of death.

"Honey, pour her a tall one, would you, sweet?" Pirate Pete called over the raucous noise to the woman who might as well have been me behind the bar—she looked kind of like my waitress friend Alison, not important—

And the cold glass landed in my fingers, the piss-yellow liquid and froth sloshing over the edges making my skin and the mug sticky, like this was some sort of nightmare except...except I was most definitely awake. *Fuck my life.*

"Your move, girly," Pete winked at me, all egotistical mirth.

"Call me *'girly'* one more time and you won't be able *to move*," I snarled back.

"Oooooooooh!" A trail of hoots and amazement rippled through the surrounding group.

"Drink the damn beer or me and my friends will happily escort you out," the Nomad spat.

He was right. It was ironic as fuck, but I had to drink the beer. I had to chance this to win the MRP back. I stared down at the fizzing liquid, and I made my decision. The thick glass rim was cold on my lips as I tipped it back. The bite of the beer in the back of my throat tasted like familiar defeat as I swallowed.

[System Alert: Beer Goes Down Easy +5 Swag Points, 2835, -10 MRP, 37/7310]

I swiped the back of my hand across my mouth, dismissing the froth, and took a shaking breath as I read the pop-up. The rowdy group was too busy laughing and nudging each other to notice—to notice that I was completely balancing on the very edge of brutal death.

"There, I drank it!" I announced—*why wasn't the 'trade completed' alert coming up? Why wasn't the damn system alert coming up?!*

"We agreed you had to drink *the pint*," Pirate Pete corrected, his bushy eyebrows furrowing, "Bottoms up, eh?!"

No. No, this wasn't happening. It was -10 MRP for each swig? It could take me at least two handfuls of sips to finish this. That'd be over -100

MRP, and I only had 39 left! I'd turn Darken standing here in this spot. And, if I got down past 20, the countdown from the curse would begin— My heart kicked into frantic overdrive. My eyes swept the jumbling throng. *Should I break the covenant and just make a run for it? …But, then, I'd probably lose the side mission and my chance to restore my memory…*

"I'll drink it for her!" Rosabella shoved to the front of the crowd, breathless—*so much for a low profile.* I stared at the determined fire burning in her eyes and…*Damn, she'd do that for me?* Unexpected gratefulness and respect blossomed in my chest for her.

The Nomad looked her up and down, his eyes wrinkling up in approval, "Doesn't work that way dear, but, by the looks of you though, I might just spend me own money to buy you one too."

A guy from the back whistled.

Rosabella frowned.

"*Back off, weirdo,*" I jabbed an elbow in the man's chest, but my joint met with solid armor, and it didn't seem to affect the sheer bulk of him. He bent over me, his red beard bristling; his mass was huge above my form—

…But, then, he winked at me. "Two li'le ladies, how about that? And the first one's going to drink! Bartender, a second mug for her friend!" he shouted towards the bar, waving his half-finished beer in the air—*half-finished? He'd already downed it in nearly two swigs?!*

…*Wait…* My brain clicked. *…If each swig was -10 MRP, maybe I could get away with fewer sips! I'd have to chug it like I was at a frat party or something but…but it might work!* Elation raced through me as I eyed the rest of the beer in my mug. I brought the glass to my lips, and I opened my throat—

The acidic liquid flowed over my tongue and down the back of my throat like a gushing fire hydrant. I choked, nearly giving up as beer dribbled out of the corners of my mouth and down my chin, but I kept swallowing. *The glass was empty.* I blinked at the blurry, glass bottom of the mug over me in shock—*the glass was empty! Had it worked?!* I held my breath as I lowered the mug and wiped my face. The crowd around me was raging with shouts of surprise.

"Damn! That girl can drink!" someone called from the bar.

An electronic beep sounded.

[System Alert: You Made It A Party! +5 Swag Points, 2840, -10 MRP, 27/7310]

Relief flooded through my body. It'd worked! The system had only docked 10 MRP! I was...okay!

[System Alert: Covenant Completed. JOY, WARRIOR 12 Drank The Beer Pint. PIRATE PETE, BAR PATRON Must Let Her Past.]

A huge hand clapped down on my shoulder. I braced myself, looking up, but it was only Pirate Pete, grinning down at me, "A deal's a deal. You can pass."

And I didn't wait for any further permission. I twisted behind and around rows of men smelling of alcohol and girls vacuum-sucked into their dresses... I left Rosabella to fend for her fragile self and tried to leave the past behind me too, but it was all around me—in every nook of this place. *How could I hide from something I was living?*

Joy

After walking through enough perfume to kill a horse and getting jabbed in the stomach only five million times by unsuspecting oafs too drunk to stand, I finally shouldered through the darkness and crowd to make it to the rear office where my old boss, Henry, was in his typical place—his enormous, walrus form seat-belted behind a plywood desk so thin that it bowed in the middle from the amount of stacked papers and shit he had piled there.

Let's be real about it: it was a janitor's closet converted into an office.

…And his ass was too large to be squatting in a janitor's closet.

They called him Hungry Henry for obvious reasons. The half-devoured burger laid lovingly out on its fast-food wrapper and the extra-large, fountain drink beside it, displaying dark cola through a see-through cup, were only further evidence. …And he had two, crisscrossed fries dangled just before his lips in two pudgy fingers. He only delayed his munching for one second as his eyes barely flickered up from the paper he was holding—probably a bill for this place—as he nodded at both my entrance and my torso.

"Who'd you steal that from?" he mumbled, meaning the uniform.

[System Query: It Appears You Are Trying To Sway HENRY, NIGHTCLUB BOSS's Opinion Or Obtain

Something. Would You Like To Flirt with HENRY, NIGHTCLUB BOSS? Use 30 Baddie Points To Flirt?] [Yes, Flirt] [No, Thank You]

Ew, gross, no. I wasn't that desperate yet. I scowled at his massive form, my hip leaning against the doorframe as I noticed the wad of mustard clinging unbecomingly under his lip.

"I want my job back," I hissed.

He shoved the fries into his yapper, chewing furiously with a huff and, then, talking around the food, "I want a lot of things, ladybug: the roof fixed, my rent paid, to hire some servers who aren't completely incompetent—"

Ladybug. I freaking hated how condescending his ass was. I chewed on my lip, attempting to bite back the rude retort that wanted to fly out as the Baddie Point prompt appeared again.

[System Query: It Appears You Are Trying To Sway HENRY, NIGHTCLUB BOSS's Opinion Or Obtain Something. Would You Like To Flirt With HENRY, NIGHTCLUB BOSS? Use 30 Baddie Points To Flirt?] [Yes, Flirt] [No, Thank You]

I swatted it out of sight. Let me use some logic for this one…

"I used to train the younger girls," I told him confidently, "I'm good at what I do. Let me have another chance. I was just going through a rough patch—"

He threw his hands down, disgusted, on the desk. His fists landed amidst the wrappers and papers there, nearly upsetting his soda. He looked at me directly, now, clearly irate and belittling at the same time—the combination that usually set me off the edge—

"I hate to break it to you, pumpkin," he started, "but trying to stab a customer is not a normal reaction for 'going through a rough patch'. I had a hell of a time pulling this place out of the review dungeon as a literal nightclub stab-and-grab. If you want my opinion, you need psychological help."

That was it.

The last straw.

The one that broke the camel's back...or, in this case, the waitress's.

But I wasn't a waitress anymore; I was a Warrior. And I didn't take advice from misogynist deadbeats.

Even in heels, my steps were huge as I rushed towards his desk, grabbing him by the front of his collared shirt and yanking his face close to mine.

"Psychological help?!" I sneered, "You're the one sitting here in a closet, stuffing yourself sick with greasy nonsense and giving demands to half-dressed girls half your age—what does that say about you?"

But his eyes were only annoyed, dark marble. And his jowls didn't quiver.

"Joy, get out of my office. Now." he growled.

...Wait... Had I met someone I couldn't intimidate? The shock of the realization made me loosen my grip on his shirt, falling backwards and nearly twisting my ankle in these high shoes... What were his Presence Ability points? Mine were supposedly 20/20 now. Was there some kind of lesson here from the system that I was missing?

"I—I need the key," I insisted. I couldn't lose this side mission because of this god-awful baboon! He needed to give me the damn key!

"System," I murmured desperately under my breath. "System, bring up the flirting option again," I pleaded.

[System Understands Query...Loading Response...]

Neon letters popped up with an error beep.

**[System Error: Baddie Points Are Not Able To Be Utilized
At This Moment.]**

I tried to manually override the alert; my fingers typed rapidly in the air where they were shielded from the oaf's line of sight by a mound of paper, but it wasn't appearing to work…

[System Error. Attempting To Reload…]
[System Error. Attempt Denied]

"Fuck you!" I growled at the floating words.

But it seemed like the man thought I was talking to him. His face grew red, "Really, coming in here and *swearing* at me? I'll have you forcibly removed if need be. Thanks to your antics, we now have bouncers 24/7 at the doors…" His pudgy finger paused over the red intercom button on his desk phone. He wouldn't even need to move to press it. *Of course, the man fought his battles sitting down—having others do his bidding. So typical.* A system alert popped into view:

**[System Penalty: Not The First Time Being Thrown Out
Of A Bar -5 XP, 1236/1300]**

Were you kidding me?!

"Joy, we should get moving…"

I whipped around to find Rosabella standing in the shadows outside the doorway. Her eyes were wide and worried. …Wait, leave and my loss of MRP would be for nothing?

Hungry Henry's round face cocked to one side at the turn of events, studying Rosabella and, obviously, liking what he saw. "Is this your friend?" he cooed, "She's much smarter than you. Move along and put those clothes back where you found them. …Unless, the girl here wants to fill out an employment application…" He nodded at Rosabella.

"You can go fuck yourself," I snapped, "She's coming with me."

The man shrugged, "Suit yourself. Go get a job somewhere else where it's acceptable to stab patrons—"

"You cockroach!" I screamed, lunging at the man.

But Rosabella grabbed my arm. "Let's go," she insisted.

And I tugged my arm out of her grip.

And we left that stupid man behind us, slipping back into the crowd which still did nothing to mask my seething face. I should have played the conversation different. I should have convinced him to give me my job back, so I could get the key! …But he'd been so hostile—so unbudging—and I hadn't wanted to stoop to flirt with the guy. How was I supposed to conquer this side mission when assholes like that were in the way?

I gripped my fists at my sides more tightly. "This is pointless," I hissed at Rosabella.

She shook her head. "We'll find another key—another way." God, I hated her optimism right now. I was about to tell her to bug off and stop being so sunshine-and-rainbows when a flash of light caught the corner of my eye. I turned, my hair billowing out—

…To see a young woman leaving the club.

It was obvious she was dressed for a late night out, but it looked like the night had gone sour. Tears ran, mixing with black mascara, down her cheeks as she clutched a fur wrap over pale arms. When she shifted to tear out the revolving door entrance, I caught sight of what had grabbed my attention.

Her necklace.

It was a golden key pendant.

Shimmering even in the dim light.

"Find the key," I repeated disbelievingly under my breath—so quietly that Rosabella, who was standing quite close, didn't even hear.

She squinted at me, "What?"

"That girl…" I pointed at the willowy form just disappearing out of sight, "She's wearing a key necklace."

I didn't wait for Rosabella to figure it out; I slipped off the heels, currently keeping me captive, and bolted out of the building with the pumps in hand, swinging beside me as I ran. The sidewalk and street were drenched with rain, and the wetness of it tingled on the pads of my feet as I ducked behind the nearest corner and into the shadows as Rosabella trailed after me.

"System, show me the side mission objective again!" I huffed excitedly as I sped further down the street.

[Side Mission Objective: Find The Key.]

Yes. It literally said 'find the key'. Maybe the key was a sign. Was I supposed to follow this girl? Hope spiraled inside me.

I didn't know if it was my Warrior side or what, but I didn't want to let her see me.

[System Reward: Stealth Promotion +5 XP, 1241/1300,
Agility Will Increase +3 For The Next 10 Seconds]
[10]

I pressed my back up against the brick wall there and spied.

The girl from the club was younger than me…maybe even younger than Rosabella. *How had she gotten past the bouncers?* She was still sobbing and swaying back and forth, there, in the middle of the street from both the height of her shoes and, probably, how many drinks she'd had. I watched her slip off her high heels, throw them in the nearest puddle and slink down the sidewalk. Her shoulders were slumped. …*She was rather pretty.* A flash of jealousy ran through me as I imagined trying to pull off the same silver-sequined dress without any luck. *She was a little skinny thing. Why the hell was she so tormented? She could have any boy she wanted.*

[9]

[8]

…But I realized something as I crept closer and heard the girl dial a number. A male voice picked up.

She couldn't have the boy that *she wanted.*

They were arguing. I heard snippets of the conversation.

[7]
[6]
[5]

The man calling her a bitch.

The girl screaming in fury and accusing him of sleeping with her best friend.

[4]
[3]
[2]

And she threw the phone. In a different puddle.

[1]

And ran under the shelter of the corner convenience store's neon lights, ducking inside.

[0]

"Watch her," I told Rosabella, pointing at the store, "Tell me when she comes out."

My mind was distracted as I looked around the dark night. …Because I recognized the concrete block building rising up over my head. It was *home*—my old home. It was the apartment where Mom and I lived before…

[System Searching MRPs To Select & Display Correct Memory…]

I swallowed.

Mom had died in one of those upper rooms—

Shit, I wasn't sure that I wanted to go there yet. I brushed the system box away as quickly as it'd appeared, feeling the back of my throat grow tight with fresh grief. *Yes, she'd died in one of those upper rooms.* I'd used to be able to pinpoint exactly which window was ours. Now, they all looked like a jumble—a puzzle which my scattered brain could hardly fathom to solve. I craned my neck backwards, trying to remember: *Was it the one on the corner? Or the one two windows down?*

"System, tell me which room," I croaked out, "Which room was it?"

[System Searching MRPs To Select & Display Correct Memory...]

An electronic error beeped, and more text slid into view.

[No Connected Memory Found.]

I felt all the blood run out of my face. I—I'd forgotten? My low MRP had wiped it out, or was it that I'd blocked it out for so long that it was nearly impossible to try to resurrect—like something dead for years? Was I as dead inside as my MRP told me? Tears surfaced in my eyes.

I'd been okay with pushing down the memories of Mom. In fact, I'd been more than okay with it until...today.

Right now.

Because I kind of wanted to see where I'd lived again.

I kind of wanted to remember because—remembering felt like life again...like maybe there was life inside me worth fighting for. And, maybe, it would do more than let me remember Mom... Maybe, it'd let me remember...myself.

I held up a finger to Rosabella. "I'll just be a minute," I promised, never taking my eyes off the building above, "Come get me if the girl comes out."

And I let my feet slip up the concrete steps to the entrance of the familiar, imposing building. I pushed on the glass door, palms flat. …And red carpet greeted my aching feet inside. And an outdated chandelier overhead. …And couches arranged like building blocks, in square seating sections. An icon with a circle around a thought bubble bobbed overtop the nearest couch—a Recollection Opportunity?

"Recollect," I whispered, my voice hushed like this was some kind of library…or a tomb. If I'd had to pick between the two, I'd have said it was the latter. The system beeped.

[Object Recollection In Progress… +2 MRP, 29/7310]

…Man, the system was so fucking stingy with this freaking curse…

[System Searching MRPs To Select & Display Correct Memory…]

The world rushed past my face, dumping me into the past…

The carpet was threadbare under my toes. The furniture looked worn and the front desk's wood veneer had rubbed off in some places.

"This apartment looks like a hotel lobby."

My voice.

Coming out of my lips as I strolled through the apartment lobby in a different time, looking around, with a woman at my elbow. My heart skipped a beat. Was it—

"They probably didn't do much to it when they remodeled."

The older woman's voice. Just like I remembered it.

Mom?

Akskdjf—

Nononononononononononononononon—

387

I turned, the tip of my pink hair trailing along my arm, but, when I looked, I saw that the woman's face was a gaping circle. White. Blanked out.

And fear jumped in my chest like a live lobster—what had she looked like? What had Mom looked like? I couldn't remember?

I gasped for air, resurfacing from the memory as system alerts flashed into view:

[System Error. Attempting To Reload...]

Not this again.

"System, stop—" I started.

"Can I help you?" the girl behind the receptionist desk appeared too chipper and helpful.

I jumped. She probably couldn't see the tears in my eyes. I turned away from her quickly, just to make sure. Of course, I couldn't just waltz in here after all these years. Of course, I wouldn't be able to see the apartment where Mom and I had lived. I didn't have a key card...if I could just get my MRP to act normal—

I swiped at my eyes. "I'm fine," I called over my shoulder, "I'm just—"

That's when a girl with a fur wrap and a plastic, shopping bag catapulted through the glass door, nearly running me over in her hurry—

And Rosabella hurled in after her.

I whirled around. It'd been the girl with the key necklace.

"I'm just—with them." I pointed at the girl from the club and Rosabella, both of whom were almost disappearing into the elevator lobby. When I caught up, I threw a warning arm across Rosabella's chest as she tried to follow key necklace girl into the elevator. My

Warrior stealth promotion wasn't going to do jack squat if we didn't even try for regular stealth.

"We'll take the next one," I yelled at the key necklace girl, trying to keep my face hidden as the elevator doors closed.

Rosabella was all but squawking at me. Her eyes were frantic as she hastily pushed off my hand. "How are we supposed to know where she gets off?" she huffed.

But even if my MRP was having a lousy time working on the level of a five-year-old, I could still remember a few things from my past. And I didn't need to talk to answer her question. I pointed a finger up.

Towards the digital pad over the elevator doors which had just closed. And, together, we watched that red number tick up.

...2
...3
...4
...5
...6

It stopped there, hovering.

"Our girl lives on the sixth floor," I said, allowing a smug grin to cover whatever expression was tracing my face. *It was time to take the stairs.*

Joy

I always did things the hard way—call it 'stubbornness' or 'sense of adventure'…my Warrior side. …But I could see Rosabella calling it 'stupidity'—there, behind her annoyed eyes—as we raced up five flights of stairs. I'd forgotten about her Endurance. Mine, of course, was flawless; I was barely breathing hard when I reached the top level emblazoned with a huge '6' next to the door. Rosabella, on the other hand, threw herself over her knees.

"*Really?*" she spouted, heaving in air through raking breaths, "*We couldn't have taken the elevator?!*"

But I couldn't listen to her crassness. *I had a side mission to win unless I wanted to become Zombie #24395777.*

I peered through the vertical glass pane in the door, my gaze sweeping the maroon-carpeted, apartment hallway for the girl with the key necklace. It still looked like a hotel up here, and the view tugged at the back of my brain like a word I couldn't quite find—something I'd forgot I'd forgotten.

[System Searching MRPs To Select & Display Correct Memory...]

I quickly swiped the alert out of my airspace; it wasn't like it'd find the memory anyway…"System turn off auto recollect," I growled. *The damn thing was getting annoying. It was one thing to have forgotten most of my life, but it was another to be reminded of it every five steps.*

Steps. I needed to move.

Glowing sconces lined the hallway's wainscoted walls. The place stunk of burned grilled cheese and boredom. I yanked the heavy, metal stairway door open, transitioning from freezing cement to worn carpet under my bare feet. *I'd run up those stairs. I'd hauled ass. There was no way I'd lost her.*

Sweeping the walls for threats, I advanced down the hall—

Past a drying rack where someone'd hung out their clothes.

Past a fake, potted plant.

Holding my breath, I turned the corner, my hand going to my belt where the hilt of my sword no longer rested—

The hall was vacant.

Shit— ...*And I'd left all my weapons at the club...*

But my eyes centered on a shield icon with a magnifying glass over it, bobbing over an ajar apartment door. ...The only ajar apartment door with a plastic, store bag left just outside.

Bingo.

"Examine," I whispered, nearly breathless.

[System Query Examined... +1 XP, 1242/1300]
[Upon A Closer Look, You See That The Grocery Bag Is Emblazoned With The Emblem Of The Convenience Store You'd Seen The Girl With The Key Necklace Run Into Earlier. You Also Notice A Light On Inside The Apartment. It Appears Someone Is Home. If You Can Find Something To Trigger Your Stealth Promotion, Maybe You Could Get Inside...]

Thanks for the pro tip, System. I rolled my eyes—what, was this a L1 side mission with that huge hint? But my lips curled into a smile because...I'd found her. This was game, set, match now, and I was going to win this fucker. I whirled around—

Rosabella smacked right into my chest with an 'oof'. I scowled at her. For a second there, we were a tangle of scuttling hands and feet, trying to weave around each other in the cramped hall. …Worst partner in crime ever…

"Double back," I whispered to her, "I found her door, but we need an excuse—"

The girl's eyes crinkled up at the corners, confused, as she took a hesitant step backwards, "An excuse?"

I didn't particularly feel like babysitting in the moment, so I just brushed by her shoulder—to my destination. My fingers easily plucked a baseball cap and sweatshirt off the drying rack in the hall. They wouldn't miss just a few things. They had, after all, left their laundry out in an open, public area unattended…

[System Alert: BASEBALL CAP And SWEATSHIRT Acquired. +10 XP, 1252/1300. Objects Will Be Placed In Your Inventory Unless You'd Like To Equip. Would You Like To Equip?
[Yes] [No]

Absolutely. The clothes vacuum adhered to my skin, over the waitress uniform as I selected 'yes'.

I threw a t-shirt at Rosabella. We'd run out of the club so quickly that we still had the corsets on. I couldn't have the key necklace girl recognizing we'd followed her.

"Put it on," I hissed. I watched her select 'equip' from her system pop-up too, and our excuse was, now, in full mode. I wiggled the brim of my hat far down on my head.

[System Reward: Stealth Promotion +5 XP, 1257/1300, Agility Will Increase +3 For The Next 10 Seconds]
[10]

God, I loved the perks of these stealth promotions with my Warrior Class and, apparently, I'd found what the system wanted me to do…

[9]

"Follow along," I urged Rosabella as I crept back down the hall. She looked like she wanted to complain, but we didn't have time for it. *I needed the key around that girl's neck if I was going to win this side mission and stay human, not Darken.* My heartbeat thundered in my ears as I slid up the wall, towards the cracked door. My fingers reached for the plastic, convenience store bag, looping quickly through the handle. Immediately, I raised the other hand to knock on the wood door.

[8]

"Hello? Grocery delivery!" I called into the dark crack between door and doorpost. But there was no answer.

…And it almost sounded like…

[7]
[6]

"Do you hear that?" Rosabella wanted to know, leaning towards my face.

And, for once, she was helpful. …Because she was right. Music was playing. The girl who lived there probably couldn't hear my knock because of the music…

[5]

Carefully, I took a step forward and shoved the door inward. The hinge squeaked faintly… *I wouldn't have long before my stealth promotion faded…*

[4]

"*Grocery delivery!*" I tried again, a little louder.

"*Joy*—" Rosabella warned, but I was too far in this shit to back out now. *I was going to win my life back, or I was going to die trying.*

[3]

The apartment was dark, save a sliver of light coming from around a door in the rear—where the music came from. The shadowy form of a couch and two chairs, an old-fashioned dining room table and a refrigerator clung to the sides of the room like the place had only ever been seen as something temporary. There was no art on the walls…no curtains. There *was* a good bit of trash. An empty pizza box lay open on the coffee table, and the kitchen bar was scattered with soda cans and paper plates. …*Was there a party here, or was this just the result of one person and several meals?* The place reeked of stale food and—honestly—depression. As I rounded the elevated kitchen bar, I noticed that the sink was piled high with dishes, and a tired-looking rug lay skewed over a checkered tile floor. Four alcohol bottles lined the counter: the hard stuff. *This girl wasn't joking.*

[2]

Holding a hand out to caution Rosabella I was moving forward slowly, I inched towards the lit door. I realized, as I did, that water was running—a tumbling, rushing noise.

[1]

A tub. It must be a bathroom. She was filling up the tub.

Shit, my stealth mode was out. I was going to have to freestyle this. I strained to peer through the slit where the door didn't meet the frame… And I dropped the grocery bag. Something animalistic overcame me—emotions crashing over my head in a nauseating way:

Electric panic.

Shock.

Fear.

I lunged through the door—

"Joy?" Rosabella yelled over the water and music, but I could barely hear her.

All I saw was the girl—with the key necklace still sparkling gold around her neck…

As her head drooped next to her neck in the bathtub…

And scarlet blood dripped from cuts on her wrist.

Long.

Deep.

Self-inflicted; the razor blade was still cupped in her other hand while a Goddamn Taylor Swift song blared in the background.

NO.

Maybe it was all too familiar—the scene. This cramped room—the dingy, white tile floor and pedestal sink. The fact that she was even younger than when I'd attempted something similar in the very same spot; it was suddenly personal.

Like this girl was an extension of myself.

And I was no longer detached. I was fucking invested—all the way fucking in. Panic scrambled my thoughts and shook my hands as I struggled to pull the girl out of the tub.

"Show me her HP!" I rasped, my voice shaking with fear, "System, show me!"

[System Understands Query…Loading Response…]

Why did it feel like it was taking forever?! Why was her body so heavy in my arms?

[Current HP / SAMANTHA, KEY NECKLACE GIRL: 12/72]

The breath whooshed out of me. Still alive. She was still alive except—

[SAMANTHA, KEY NECKLACE GIRL: -1 HP, 11/72]
[SAMANTHA, KEY NECKLACE GIRL: -1 HP, 10/72]

I watched the system alerts populate over her head. …Except who knew for how long if she kept losing blood like this.

"Rosabella! Fabric!" I screamed, "Bedsheets—something to cut it with! We need to stop the bleeding!" My voice pitched crazily. And, suddenly, all thoughts of The Game and this side mission were burned.

Buried.

Gone.

Only my heart, wrenching in two for a girl whose life she thought was too unimportant to keep. So, instead, she threw her heart away. Instead of facing the searing pain there, she'd decided—made the choice—to cut it out. And, in that moment, I realized I couldn't blame her or look down on her. Because, so long ago, I'd done the same thing. I'd almost literally done the same thing, but—even when the Game Wardens had found and saved me—I'd done it again. I'd taken a metaphorical knife to my heart, and I'd cut out everything that hurt.

I'd carved the memories of Mom out of my chest—I'd become a Warrior and, sometimes, even relished when the Darken would bite me so I'd forget the pain.

I'd buried my innocence, and the girl who'd emerged was hard, indifferent, untrusting and more sarcastic than ever. Because armor was a natural response to war. And I'd waged one with myself years ago… Till I couldn't even remember her face—Mom's face. I couldn't recall it—not with my lowered MRP. Tears stung at my eyes. I'd let myself die inside, but I sure as hell was not going to let that happen to this girl.

[SAMANTHA, KEY NECKLACE GIRL: -1 HP, 9/72]

I grabbed a towel from the towel bar above my head and wrapped it around the girl's thin, shivering frame. Her lips, still plumped with lip gloss, tripped over a row of twisted words that sounded too familiar:

"No—please, let me go. I *want* this. He doesn't love me. No one loves me."

[SAMANTHA, KEY NECKLACE GIRL: -1 HP, 8/72]

I seized her by the shoulders.

I shook her.

I watched her head loll, streaks of dark mascara still smudging her pale skin under half-mooned eyes.

"*You don't mean that*," I told her, "You're just in a low spot. It's going to be okay—"

[SAMANTHA, KEY NECKLACE GIRL: -1 HP, 7/72]
[SAMANTHA, KEY NECKLACE GIRL: -1 HP, 6/72]

Crimson blood poured over my palms as I tried to hold them to her wounds to stop the bleeding. *Rosabella was too slow!* Trying to only use one hand, I scrambled to rip the sweatshirt off, over my head. I tried to use my teeth to tear at the fabric—

"Here."

Finally.

Rosabella handed me a knife.

My fingers slipped on the handle, but I slit through the fabric with it, making quick use of the tool and creating a makeshift bandage. I wrapped it tight around the girl's arm, watching the red trying to seep through.

[SAMANTHA, KEY NECKLACE GIRL: -1 HP, 5/72]

But it still was. Oh God, it still was.

[SAMANTHA, KEY NECKLACE GIRL: -1 HP, 4/72]

"It's not holding," Rosabella whispered.

I whirled on her, everything clenching within me—my teeth, my hands— "You think I can't see that?!" I raged. *I had to figure out something. I had to save her. I had to help her live.*

I spun back towards the girl's paling face to find something there that wasn't before: a system query—*what?*

[System Query: Would You Like To Save The Girl Or Steal Her Necklace?]

The sweat ran cold on my forehead. Steal her—who the fuck did the system think I was?!

"Save her," I begged, "System, please save her." My throat was so raw. I looked down at the palms of my hands, smeared with blood, feeling entirely helpless. I'd trained for war—for standing up for myself, for killing. I didn't know about saving. I didn't even know how to save myself. I'd found the key. I'd found the damn key, and, now, I couldn't even save this girl—

Beep.

My eyes flashed upward.

[Initiating Check For Saving Life Options...]

Saving life options? What was this? I watched the girl's HP tick downward—almost out.

[SAMANTHA, KEY NECKLACE GIRL: -1 HP, 3/72]
[System Alert: The System Presents You One Option To Save SAMANTHA, KEY NECKLACE GIRL. She Attempted To Cut Down Her HP And Is Close To Death's Door. JOY, WARRIOR 12, You May Gift +20 MRP And +50 HP Points From Your Personal Account To Revive Her. Will You Revive?]
[Yes, Revive -20 MRP, -50 HP] [No, Do Not Revive]

My heartbeat shattered my eardrums. Wait…I could…but I only had 29/7310 MRP. That would… It would kill me. If I chose to revive her, I'd turn Darken instead.

[SAMANTHA, KEY NECKLACE GIRL: -1 HP, 2/72]

"Joy, *don't!*" Rosabella insisted. "Can't I offer the points for you—"

Normally, I would have snapped at her. I would have whirled on the newb and bit her head clean off to the tune of 'don't you get how the rules work by now?! This is my side mission. The option is only for me.'

…But all the fight had, somehow, leaked out of me. Straight into the ground. My shoulders slumped because—

Because it was finally time. To let go. Of myself. To be the hero for once because—because, if I didn't, I'd feel dead inside even if I was physically alive. I had to revive her. I had to take the chance that it was what the system wanted me to do because…maybe, for the first time in my life, it was what *I* wanted to do—to do something bigger…than just me. I knew the curse countdown would start when I was under 20 MRP. I knew this meant it was goodbye but… but, somehow, I was okay with that. *Or, at least, numb to it…*

"Rosabella," I turned to the girl, my voice uncharacteristically soft as I shrugged at her, "Save the world, okay? Tell the others it's been fun—"

"Joy, no—"

"*Yes,*" I spoke firmly. *If it was going to be my last word, I wanted it to be firm.* I looked down at the girl bleeding young life over my hands and onto the bathroom floor. "Yes, revive."

The system beeped. And I closed my eyes as neon letters flashed under my eyelids.

[System Alert: Revive Option Selected. Points Gifted From JOY, WARRIOR 12's Personal Account, -20 MRP, 9/7310, -50 HP 110/172]
[SAMANTHA, KEY NECKLACE GIRL: +20 MRP 5572/6200, +50 HP 52/72]

A blaring alarm sounded. My eyes flashed open.

[System Alert: MRP At Critical Levels. Find & Equip A Health Pack Now. After 20 Seconds, Darken Class Will Be Assigned If No Health Pack Is Equipped.]
[System Alert: Countdown Started.]
[20]
[19]
[18]

I'd thought that the choice was the hardest part, but the waiting, it turned out, was far worse.

The key necklace girl gasped to life in my arms, her eyelids fluttering rapidly—matching every last beat of my heart with a corresponding number like something I should cherish although it was going by too fast—

Thump [17]
Thump [16]
Thump [15]

I heard Rosabella tearing apart cabinets in the kitchen—her thudding run down the hall. "There has to be a health pack in here somewhere—*damnit!*" I heard her scream.

But I just stared, unmoving, at the key necklace girl's wide eyes as she righted herself, pushing upward to sit and smoothing her hair down. "You—you saved me—" Her chin trembled.

Thump [14]
Thump [13]

Yes, I'd saved her. I'd done the right thing for once and—for what? She was okay. I was going to die. Guess it turned out that life bit you in the ass in the end, after all.

Thump [12]
Thump [11]
Thump [10]

Burning pain started in my chest. I screamed out—*fuck!*
Beep.
…An electronic beep again? What, was the system going to mock me further in my last breaths? I grabbed for my chest. Air whistled up my throat—wheezing through my nose and mouth.

Thump [9]

The key pendant around the girl's neck started glowing. *It wasn't my eyes, it was—*

Thump [8]

"Take it," she urged me, sliding closer on the floor, "You deserve it."

I deserved—? I reached out, hesitantly, and poked the glowing form with a curious finger—

Thump [7]
Thump [6]

Beep. The key pendant absorbed into my palm like a med pack.

[System Alert: Key Acquired. Side Mission Objective Completed. Victory Established. +30 XP, 1287/1300]

I blinked stupidly into the neon letters floating overhead. Hope leapt in my chest—wait, victory established? Did that mean the numbers weren't counting down anymore? Did I have a chance of—

But my joy was cut short as key necklace girl's face became pixelated.

And her body disappeared—square by square.

Thump [5]
Thump [4]

And the bathroom dissipated as well—wiped clean like this was all a bad dream. Except the dream froze, mid-disassembly as a jumble of words and letters filled my vision:

[System Alert: ***Congratulations, You've Won The Side Mission!***]
[As Promised, You've Been Awarded The Ability To Select One Of The Following Rewards:]
[+2000 MRP] [Fully Restored HP] [Powerful Mystery Object]
[Please Select Which Extra You'd Like.]

I didn't have to choose. I didn't have to think! I lunged towards the +2000 MRP button. "MRP!" I shouted, breathless. Was I in time? Was I going to live?

[System Alert: +2000 MRP Selected. +2000 MRP, 2009/7310]

The world unfroze. I jolted forward. Air flew by my face and I found—

Rosabella and I stood, side by side.

In the forest.

Once more.

My hands patted over my body. There was no pain in my chest— no heaviness in my lungs. My flesh was solid, not diseased—

I stared up at the trees, stunned as more messages streamed into view:

Welcome Back ROSABELLA, GAME MAKER 6 & JOY, WARRIOR 12 To The Game

I blinked at the words and at my body beneath me. *...I wasn't...I wasn't zombie...I wasn't...*

"System, show me my MRP," I rasped out.

[Current MRP / JOY, WARRIOR 12: 2009/7310]

I blinked at the confirmation staring me in the face, feeling something strangely warm in my heart...*disbelief? Relief?* And an even more alien sensation occurred on my face. I felt something wet...

I brought up my fingertips to brush it away—*was it rain?*

But, no. It was tears. Was I...*crying...? I hadn't cried for a long time. The girl with the key necklace...she was fake? This was all just part of a messed-up side mission?*

"That was *fucking rude*," I whispered, wiping away the wetness, "Whatever your Creator Magic just did, it—*this didn't happen.*" I told Rosabella, meaning the tears and what we'd experienced together.

And she swallowed a little bit of a chuckle, using the back of her hand to shield it from my view, but her eyes expanded in shock as she stared at me. "Your—your MRP. Your hands..."

We looked down at my hands at the same time and realized—*there was no more black rash there!* Rosabella rushed to pull my hair back from my neck to check there.

"Only a small patch at the base of your hairline," she sputtered. — *Like some kind of twisted memento but nothing like the dark rash before?*

"It—*worked*—" I choked out.

"Rosabella?! Joy?!"

Callen's voice.

We both startled as the man came crashing through the underbrush.

"There you are!" his eyebrows creased in frustration, "We've been looking all over for you—thought you'd wandered off or met with some Darken. We need to pick up the pace if we're going to make it to the temple. Come on."

And, after everything we'd just been through, it was suddenly back to 'life as normal'. Except nothing about it was normal at all.

A Laxtail Chira buzzed by my hand, brushing the skin there like a further reminder that it was clear of the rash. And I watched the tiny dragon spiral upward and into the brush. And my heart felt different there, beating in my chest. It felt...*alive.*

Rosabella

I tried to shake off the side mission as I watched Joy take huge strides in front of me. The rash on her neck and hands *was* nearly gone. *She was healed—no longer on death's door and turning Darken? The generation of the side mission had been an accident—a spell gone wrong— but really…it'd gone really right… Was fate finally on our side?*

Joy and I had returned to The Game in the same clothes we'd worn before, and numerous swords jangled on the pink-haired girl's belt. Somehow, watching her got me in my head again—really one of the main downsides of walking with the group in the almost complete silence that had blanketed our hike and the surrounding forest for the last hour. *Couldn't someone just talk and distract me for a few minutes?* But the thoughts—questions—continued to circle like ravenous vultures in my mind.

…I'd only overheard part of Joy's conversation with her past boss in the nightclub. From what I'd heard, muffled by the office wall and the music, it'd sounded like she'd almost stabbed a customer. …*Seemed like the pink-haired girl, anyway…*

And, yet, I'd seen another side of her on that side mission. I'd seen a softer side—an inner part that had almost leaked out through her eyes as she'd stared at the despondent girl in the bathroom. …Something…*emotional*…and hurt. Something that made me want to stop judging her and see her in a new light. *She'd chosen to save that girl—to give her her last bit of MRP to save her life…*

"*It's right up ahead!*" Callen called from the front of the group, "Rainer, you, Joy and I will do a perimeter sweep—make sure it's safe."

I craned my neck over their heads to see the place.

Callen had mysteriously been calling it 'The Temple' for the entire walk. I saw, now, that the building was the remains of a Hindu sanctuary. Like seemingly everything else in this world, the carved pillars and walls were crumbling with age and overgrown with persistent ivy. The domes of the roof were outlined against a graying sky—*was it going to pour?* The building looked as though, at one point, it was extremely grand. Even the shell of it had gold etchings and vibrant turquoise-and-white tile still showing through the dirt on the floors visible through an open doorway.

The group, somehow, thought this place would augment my Creator Magic, but right now—to me—it just filled my heart with dread.

Because we were at that line in the sand.

The part where I either performed correctly and was able to save their dying world or…

Or I failed.

My throat went dry at the thought. *I barely knew what I was doing with this magic stuff. A backfired spell had gotten Joy and I into the side mission. How was I going to fix a whole world? What if the group had misplaced their trust in me? …What if I was just—*

Not enough.

…What if…what if I couldn't do it?

Dormouse, apparently, didn't hold any of these churning worries in his stomach. He playfully teetered on a fallen column, trying to balance on one foot as the others disappeared into the thick, surrounding greenery. His ease and the smile on his lips almost made me jealous for a minute. *He was like a kid...*

...A kid that knew everything technological about The Game...wait.

I might not know everything needed to understand how this whole universe functioned, but...well, *the others did. ...What if I just asked?*

Anyone who'd judge me for doing so had disappeared into the brush to do a security check... *I could ask Dormouse...real quick...*

"Hey Dormouse," I called, "can I talk to you for a second?"

The boy looked up, swiping a hand across his dark wave of hair and happily hopping off the pillar to trot towards me. "Sure," he quipped, "What's up?"

His eyes had an open and hoping-to-help shine to them. Somehow, it made me a little nervous. I pushed down an anxious chuckle, "Well, before whatever it is they want me to do here, I was wondering if you could tell me what you know about side missions." The words all kind of rushed out in a jumbled mess, but the boy understood.

He nodded, shoving his hands in his pockets, "Uh—okay, so side missions can occur at any time in The Game. It's just a way for Gamers to uplevel—grow their skills—and a way for the Game to offer you opportunities. The system gives you a challenge, and you have to accomplish it to win. It's done in an alternate reality within The Game. Usually, the algorithm selects an optimum time for these missions, but you have Creator Magic; you can literally *make* them happen."

He was looking at me like I was God. It felt...*weird.*

...And I kind of wanted to know how I'd accidently done it for Joy...

"So, *hypothetically*," I hedged, uneasily stepping on the insides of my boots in the thick grass, "the first cast of a spell which goes sideways could make them happen...I mean, I guess?"

Dormouse looked excited, like he was so glad I'd asked. He whisked a grin in my direction, "Absolutely. And you can learn to do it on command too. I've heard Game Makers can just shut their eyes and focus on the person they want to deep dive with. It's so cool. Supposedly, The Game literally takes you into the other Gamer's memories."

I winced a little without meaning too. *Yep. I, unfortunately, had experience with that one.*

"But, like, there wasn't a person with CM here for years," Dormouse blubbered, clearly already on a rant I couldn't keep him from. "So, I mean, a bunch of The Gamers on these hacking sites I had to monitor said there was a work around. Basically, you just bypass the Creator Magic bit by locking it in artificially with code like this—"

He swiped a hand mid-air and a sheet filled with code popped up. A prompt blinked at the bottom of the code sheet:

[System Query: Please Input Code]

His fingers jumped into action.

[*SideMissionStart101*]
[<Action Input: Start Side Mission Without General Restrictions>]
[<Begin Reboot>]
[<Initialize>]

An electronic beep ensued.

[System Alert: Work Around Utilized]

Before I could stop him, his moist fingers landed directly on my arm and—

Welcome ROSABELLA, GAME MAKER 6 & DORMOUSE, CODER 14 To The Side Mission

[1st Side Mission Objective: Report To Field Training.]

What—!!

Dormouse and I suddenly stood together in a dirt clearing where a huge, abandoned office building tilted upwards, over us—mostly smashed glass and weeds now. The white, modern lines of it were obscured by growing plants and streaked with dirt. Gone was the Hindu temple. We'd clearly just jumped into an alternate dimension. I threw down my hands—*oh no, no, NO! I'd JUST got out of the other side mission and was exhausted! To have to deal with another one?! Immediately?????*

"*Opps*," Dormouse squeaked the exclamation, like it was a joke, "I've always been a bit of a hands-on learner—"

I glowered at him. *I was going to kill the kid—*

"*Take us out of here!*" I protested, admittedly throwing a half temper tantrum like a squalling three-year-old. "You got us in, take us out!"

"Oh, *come on*," Dormouse prodded me, "what harm could an extra, little game do to pass the time? Where's your sense of adventure?"

Back with the girl who almost died in Joy's arms…

…The girl who'd been a computer simulation.

I gritted my teeth. "Dormouse, *I'm not really in the mood*—" I started, but, when I looked back up, the boy was already wandering away, gesturing me after him with a looping hand as a system pop-up generated over his head.

[DORMOUS, CODER 14: System Alert: Dormouse, This Side Mission Is Yours As Is The Reward If You Complete It. In This Side Mission There Will Be 2 Side Mission Objectives. Upon Completion Earn +700 Swag Points, Fully Restored HP or a Powerful Mystery Object. The Choice Will Be Yours. Now, Make the First Choice to Begin. Begin The Side Mission?]

[Yes] [No]

"Damn! This is awesome! It worked just like they said! Shoot, I could get some cool mystery object? That's bound to be something you can't get even with a Level Up. ...And, hey, the utilization of the memories is amazingly integrated. This is literally part of my hometown before I made Warden," he yelled back over his shoulder, "I'll show you around."

And I sighed. *Because it didn't look like I was winning this battle OR this war.*

"Fine," I told him, "But slow down, will you? I'm kinda worn out after all the hiking..." *...And Joy's side mission... This was just a royal rat's nest...* I watched him select 'yes' to begin the mission, and the corresponding system alert populated.

[DORMOUSE, CODER 14: Side Mission Confirmed]

Fuck my sorry life...

"So, the objective said to report to field training. You're gonna love it," Dormouse sputtered, clearly over-excited again as I joined him, all but dragging my boots in the dirt as we walked from my lack of enthusiasm. "I know it's super apocalyptic here, compared to your world, but...well, high school is kind of a universal thing no matter where you are. It's our version...plus, like, survival skills like how to deal with Darken and dragons...how to make fire, you know..."

My two-page essay on the most influential person in my life was suddenly looking like it'd be used for kindling here...so much for 'universal high school'.

"But, hey," Dormouse quipped, jabbing me in the stomach with a kidding elbow, "You're doing pretty great at negotiating with dragons even without the classes."

I tried to return the smile, but it, honestly, fell incredibly flat on my lips.

"So, this is the main shelter," Dormouse told me, pointing at the looming office building above with tinted windows almost shining black and navy blue in the sun, "It's just a hop and a skip away from the village, and it's where all the kids stay while we train—kind of like a boarding school I guess you'd say. After you pass here, you're grouped into Classes and shipped out into the real world. I was selected as a Game Warden…before they discontinued them so…"

He seemed kinda proud about that, hanging onto the straps of his backpack as we walked forward with his measly chest pumped out a bit. I was glad the kid felt important. From what I could tell, he was super smart.

"Training is right in here," he continued, ducking under a low, concrete beam. I followed him, having to squat lower than my knees currently agreed with, but I made it through. Darkness instantly cooled my face and, as I looked up, I recognized that we were in the lower level of a parking garage which adjoined the office section. The concrete had held steady over the years, and huge, rounded columns stood like stern war generals in lines across the vast space. The few cars there had been pushed to the side like ancient skeletons. …It looked like the place was being used as a gym; red and blue floormats dotted the hard floor.

And a line of kids, the same age as Dormouse looked now— younger even than he was in The Game—stood at attention in the center. He urged me forward, and we joined the formation.

Beep. A pop-up interrupted our vision.

[DORMOUSE, CODER 14: System Alert: Report To Field Training Executed. 1st Side Mission Objective Completed. +15 XP, 1428/1500]

…*Well, that was much easier than Joy's but…* But, as I turned, I noticed Dormouse's face had crumpled in on itself. *What?* I opened my mouth to question him when he cut me off.

411

"Oh my God, *hide me*," he whimpered, hurriedly grabbing me by the shoulders and switching spots to cower behind my outline.

"What are you—"

"She's here," he sputtered, his face bone-white, "Maude's here."

"*Who's Maude?*" I asked. I figured I'd said the words at a normal volume, but they sounded bigger, reverberating in the nearly-vacant room—off the hard walls.

Dormouse cringed, cowering in on himself like his shoulders could hide him, "*Not so loud!*"

That's when neon letters swiped into view again. ...A game pop-up:

[Side Mission Objective Updating...]
[2nd Side Mission Objective: Ask Out Maude.]

"No, *no, no, no*," Dormouse seemed to plead with the electronic box, "*Anything* but that—"

He really needed to get his shit together.

"*Who the heck is Maude?*" I hissed, taking care to lower my voice this time as I stared at a nearby concrete wall.

And he pointed.

I had to turn to see her, and, when I did, I understood his panic. Because, from across the parking garage, she sauntered towards us.

Long, blonde hair billowing out around her.

Hips swaying on a lean-muscle frame.

Her blue eyes were so bright and intense it nearly looked like there were stars in them.

...Oh my God. This WAS fucking high school. And I'd just met the head cheerleader.

"Her name's...Maude? Seriously?" I spat. *Maude was an old lady name. Maude sounded like she had saggy, baggy—*

"Don't you *dare* make fun of her," Dormouse countered rapidly, growling, "She's perfect. She's a 10, and I'm a 1.5 if we're being generous. There's *no way* I can ask her out—"

"You want to forfeit?" I offered, seeing my chance to get out of this side mission and taking it.

"Of course not," he whispered back. "Then, I don't get the cool bonus. ...I got it!" His eyes suddenly sparkled with mischievous and, maybe, misplaced hope, "I'll make her jealous! I'll pretend I'm into you, and she'll be jealous and try to get me back—"

"She never *had* you to begin with," I huffed, interrupting him. "It doesn't work like that—"

"*Oh yeah?*" he raised a convinced eyebrow, "I've watched a whole of two chick flicks, and I'm pretty sure that was the majority of the plot—"

[DORMOUSE, CODER 14: System Query: It Appears You Are Trying To Gain The Attention of MAUDE, APPRENTICE. Would You Like to Make Her Jealous By Flirting With ROSABELLA, GAME MAKER 6? Use 30 Swag Points to Flirt?]
[Yes, Flirt] [No, Thank You]

Was the system on the same loony train as this kid?! I watched his thin finger hover over the 'yes' button.

"Oh my God, Dormouse, don't waste your points!" I pleaded with him. "That's a terrible plan—"

She was coming over; Maude was headed straight for us. Dormouse's finger landed on 'Yes, Flirt'.

[DORMOUSE, CODER 14: -30 Swag Points, 330]

He grabbed for my hand.

I shook him off, "*Get off me.*"

[DORMOUSE, CODER 14: System Alert: Flirtation Rejected, -10 Swag Points, 320]

"Act cool with it," he spoke through non-moving lips; his freezing-cold hand reached for mine again as his anxious eyes raked over the approaching blonde, "Act like you're into it."

I batted his clammy fingers away, rolling my eyes.

[DORMOUSE, CODER 14: System Alert: Flirtation Rejected...Again, -10 Swag Points, 310]
[DORMOUSE, CODER 14: System Alert: Dude, She's So Not Into It -2 XP, 1426/1500]

"You're tanking my points!" the boy hissed back, but he didn't make another grab for my hand—*thank God.*

...As much as I didn't want to admit it for Dormouse's sake, *this mission was absolutely, fucking hopeless.*

Dormouse

I was sweating. I hated it when I sweat—when I got like this. It was like everything clogged up in my body like a shower drain that wasn't draining anymore…just a weak, slow spiral that didn't even do half the job.

…And, usually, this entire fiasco of a situation was just a minor inconvenience on the list of things I couldn't do that day unless—*damn it, unless it was in front of Maude.*

I lost all motor skills, all ability to use my tongue or voice and, sometimes, it was so bad that my left eye started twitching.

Uncontrollably.

Yeah, it was weird. …And I felt like even more of a freak whenever it happened, thanks for asking…

…And that whole picture probably made me look like a stretched out, pale version of a Pablo Picasso cartoon that the girl would barely glance at before *definitely wanting to turn it off*—one push of a button and a guy like me was zipped into black oblivion with no chance, whatsoever, at redemption. Usually, I just ended up standing there, sweating, in front of her like I was wearing a turtleneck in July and too busy to talk while I searched for something else to look at while turning the color of a brilliant, brick crayon. That was typically when I started praying to every God I didn't know while, simultaneously, hitting myself mentally over the head with a baseball bat so… Needless to say, *I had a good indication of how this was going to go;* the simulation had been run, as they say.

This was a simulation, in and of itself. It was a side mission; I knew that, *so why was the damn game system so great at messing with my brain???*

'Cause Maude looked real. I could nearly feel the heat coming off her pale skin—so close to my own body as she walked towards me. Strands of her blonde hair blew backwards, delicately, off her shoulders. I caught a whiff of her perfume as she breezed straight by my face and took the place in line right after me. I thought it stopped my heart.

And lungs.

How was I supposed to compete in field training when I was holding my breath? …My face felt both flushed and drained of color. *How did other guys do this so easily?*

—*Act normal in front of their crush?*

—*Confidently ask them out?*

It seemed like I was already miserably failing at both of them… *And I'd have to do it to win this side mission? Maybe I should just give up while I was ahead…*

"Okay, we'll start," the instructor called, bracing his hands on his hips over a wide-legged stance in front of all of us.

"Wait—"

It was Maude's voice.

I turned. …And *melted. Goddamn this girl!*

She had her hands over her head, slowly wiggling out of her t-shirt, pulling it slowly over her blonde head. Till she stood there, only in a pink sports bra and her black jeans. Her abs were tight and sculped—as I would have expected—and her boobs— *Damn it! This was a personal moment; I didn't have to share my thoughts!* I watched as the neon letters of a system alert fizzled into view over the girl's head:

[MAUDE, APPRENTICE: +20 Baddie Points, 7562]

And, trust me, she'd earned them.

"Everyone at attention," the instructor barked, making my dazed head spin towards him, "We are going to do fight sequences today in partners. I'll group you based on the line here. Maude and Dormouse, you'll be first. Step over here, please." …His words were the second most terrifying bit of information today.

I had to fight…*Maude???*

In front of all my classmates?

"Jeez, this side mission just won't take it easy on me," I muttered out of the corner of my mouth to Rosabella before stepping forward, onto the blue mat the instructor had gestured to.

"Choose your weapons," the teacher told Maude and I, nodding at a wall behind him filled with glinting metal and different size bows. The corresponding system prompt populated in my vision, filtering through options:

[System Alert: Duel Initiated.]
[System Alert: Please Select Your Weapon For The Duel.]
[Dagger?]
[Long Bow?]
[Club?]
[Broadsword?]
[Axe?]
[Morning Star?]
[Katana?]
[Hammer?]

...But I dismissed the menu because my weapon wasn't listed there. I wasn't like the majority of the others in this line up. My *fingers* were my weapon—*my brain.*

Maude, unfortunately, *did* find a weapon among the lot. She chose a light and deadly-looking Katana from the menu and wall, swishing it in front of her to test the weight of it. I swallowed. *It looked too sharp.*

"You forfeit choice of a weapon?" the instructor's eyes bored into me.

I nodded curtly. *Didn't he know me by now?*

[System Alert: System Registers No Weapon Selected For The Duel.]

"Begin!" the man yelled.

And Maude locked freezing, blue eyes with me. *Was it hot in here, or was it hot in—*

She lunged forward, her blade slicing through the air centimeters from my shoulder. I dodged. I saw her set up another attack. My fingers were quicker. I swiped a code box up:

[System Query: Please Input Code]

And I began typing rapidly—

[<Action Input: Place Black Hole Under MAUDE, APPRENTICE'S Left Foot>]
[<Enter>]

I hit the 'enter' key with a forceful fingertip.

Off balance, the girl pitched backwards, her leg stuck in the hole I'd created in the concrete. Her face scrunched up in shock and utter confusion that gave me an unexpected boost of serotonin. *Who was the tough guy now?!*

…But she was quicker to recover than I would have imagined. With a scream of rage, she brought her sword up over her head, swiping it down—

Metal clanged against cement as I jumped out of the way. *Thank God for Agility 11.*

[System Error: Duel Regulations Violated]

"Aim to *disable* your opponent only," the instructor warned from the side, "we don't want any accidents…"

My fingers hurried in the air again as Maude's sword slashed forward—

[<Action Input: Block MAUDE, APPRENTICE'S Attack
With Glass Wall>]
[<Enter>]

The girl's blade clinged against glass—the invisible barrier. She lifted it again. I blocked it again.

One time.

Two times.

Three—

My pale fingers blurred white in the air. Sweat beaded on my forehead. There was too much pressure. Everyone was staring, and Maude was making excellent headway. She was the best swordsman in the class. Strands of blonde hair stuck to her forehead; her lips were pulled in a grim line of determination and frustration.

My glass wall flickered, glitching slightly.

[<Action Input: Hold The Glass Wall>]
[<Enter>]

I commanded with the code, but I wouldn't be able to hold this shield for much longer. I needed a new tactic.

Swish.

[-2 HP, 148/150]

Pain.

In my ankle.

Shocked, I looked down to see my pants-leg sliced open and blood dripping from a cut there—

"*Huh!*" Maude shoved me back in the chest with a grunt. For that second, her face was so close—like I could kiss her. Her skin shone from the effort of the fight. Her lips were plump pink—

Then, I fell backwards.

In slow motion.

My back thudded into the concrete—hard.

I hit my head.

[-2 HP, 146/150]

Ouch.

Worse, I'd hit my ego because the little, blonde girl stood over me, her huge sword aimed at my neck for a kill shot she couldn't legally make in this classroom. And I was on my ass—technically, on my back—trapped. Breathing hard against a blade that'd conquered modern technology. Shit. So much for looking like a badass guy...

[System Alert: Duel Terminated/Completed.]
[System Penalty: ...Well, Chalk That One Up As A Loss, -10 XP, 1416/1500]

"Winner!" the instructor proclaimed loudly—his voice screeching in my ears like a siren—"Break! Take a break you two."

And the sword was gone—from my neck. And, instead, a tiny, white hand extended in its place: *Maude's hand.* She looked down at me through the blonde hair falling over her cheeks. *She wanted to help me up? It was...sweet of her.*

I way too gladly took that hand; it was as I expected—firm grip, soft fingers. I bounced upward, trying to appear like all the muscles in my body weren't as completely liquid as they felt.

**[System Query: Would You Like To Attempt To Start An
Interested Conversation With MAUDE, APPRENTICE?
Use 15 Swag Points To Break The Ice?]
[Yes, Break The Ice] [No, Thank You]**

I swallowed all the nerves dancing in my head and spinning in my chest. *Shit, if I was going to ask the girl out, I was going to have to talk to her...* I used a finger to peck at the 'yes' button before she'd notice...

[-15 Swag Points, 295]

System, hide your prompts from everyone but me, I told the thing internally. I didn't need my failure to be a bulletin board for my already bully-inclined classmates.

**[System Understands Command. System Prompts Are
Now Only Visible To DORMOUSE, CODER 14]**

"Good fight," I tried. But Maude was already turning away with a half-grin and a hand, tucking her hair behind one ear. I imagined myself doing the same—using my fingers to gently tuck the strands of her long locks carefully behind her ear for her. ...How she'd look, smiling shyly up at me...

...Oh my God, I was standing here grinning like a numbskull, and she had walked away...

**[System Penalty: Break The Ice Ignored, -10 Swag Points,
285]
[System Penalty: Talking To Yourself Is...Awkward -2 XP,
1414/1500]**

Oh...great.

I turned to realize Rosabella was up next to fight. She moved towards me, punching me in the arm softly and nodding at Maude who'd now ducked outside of the parking garage to probably cool down. *"Go get her, tiger,"* she encouraged, but, somehow, it only made my stomach queasier. *Easy for her to say. Her Baddie Points probably weren't almost negative...*

Time.

Wait, I probably didn't have that much time. Code junkies, like me, knew that side missions timed out if you didn't complete the objective within a certain number of minutes. *...Maybe I could hack into the code and figure out a way to see what kind of time I had to ask Maude out. It could be days! ...Or it could be minutes.*

I quickly excused myself from the group of students, ducking into a corner and clandestinely swiping open the code box again.

[System Query: Please Input Code]

My fingers danced over the air until I tweaked it *just right—*

[<Action Input: Bring Up Side Mission Timer>]
[<Action Input: Make Side Mission Timer Visible To DORMOUSE, CODER 14 Until Side Mission Is Completed>]
[<Enter>]

A watch appeared on my wrist. Cool. ...Except the neon, red letters glowing on the watch's digital face were NOT cool:

0015

Fifteen what? Days? Hours? Minutes? Seconds? My nervous eyes kept bouncing back to the unmoving number. ...Well, it couldn't be fifteen seconds, because it would have changed by now—

0014

Minutes. I drew in a sharp breath. It was fucking 15 minutes.

My heart jumped to my throat. I had to ask Maude out—I had to flipping ask her out basically right now??????!

No. No, I couldn't do that.

…I could do it? …Maybe? This was just a stupid game—a simulation. I could do this.

I bit the inside of my cheek and clenched my fists at my side, steeling myself like I was on a spaceship rigged for going to the moon, and we were mid take off. Because this was my moment. I could either do this and be a hero in my own eyes, or I could be what I was used to being my whole life: a downright chicken.

Freaking Chicken Little. …Constantly scared the sky was falling.

Not today, Chicken Little.

My boots snapped over the concrete floor as I moved towards the toppled cement beam outside—to follow Maude. I barely could find the breath to stand after ducking underneath it, but, when I did, I saw that this was my moment.

The girl stood there.

Outside.

Alone.

Her back towards me and her arms crossed over her chest, looking up at the vast, rotting skeleton of the office building I'd once called home here.

"So…that's like coding or some shit?"

I started out of my comma and realized she was talking to me—Maude. The girl peeked over her shoulder in my direction. I took the biggest breath I could manage and two steps forward, so we were side by side, staring up at the office building together.

"Yeah, it's pretty simple really," I wheezed, my nerves definitely getting to me and making this more difficult, "It's just like building blocks that you can rearrange to make what you want…"

Make what I wanted... And, suddenly, I got a brilliant idea. I had to ask this girl out, but, right now, this time and place didn't feel right. ...But my watch was still counting down:

0013

And I only had right now... What if I could change the code of 'right now' and make this better? More romantic?

"...Actually," I started, turning towards the girl as my voice wobbled crazily—was I really doing this? Was I really going to do it? A system alert popped up as though to confirm the dread in the base of my stomach.

[System Query: Would You Like To Attempt To Start An Interested Conversation With MAUDE, APPRENTICE? Use 15 Swag Points To Try Again?] [Yes, Try Again] [No, Thank You]

Yes, fucking try again, I told the system in my head, glad these prompts were, now, clandestine.

[-15 Swag Points, 270]

I turned towards Maude with what I hoped was a casual grin, "I can show you if you want."

She shrugged noncommittally, but not completely uninterested, "Okay. Your name's Dorpus or something, right?"

Dormouse. I cringed.

[System Alert: Try Again Received, +5 Swag Points, 275] [System Alert: Damn, Somehow You Got The Girl To Bite +3 XP, 1417/1500] [System Penalty: Then Again, She Totally Can't Remember Your Name... -1 XP, 1416/1500]

Fuck that... But it was something so...yay?

"It's actually Dormouse," I corrected. I'd been following her around like a puppy dog ever since we were small, and she didn't even know my name?!

"Right," she laughed a little, "I'm Maude."

[System Query: Would You Like To Flirt With MAUDE, APPRENTICE? Use 30 Swag Points To Flirt?]
[Yes, Flirt] [No, Thank You]

I hit 'yes' before I had the chance to rethink it.

[-30 Swag Points, 245]

"*I know your name*," I rushed—too quickly—"See?"

And my fingers flashed over the air, faster than I'd ever coded anything in my life—*this adrenaline thing apparently was the shit.*

[System Query: Please Input Code]
[<Action Input: Create Cluster Of The Most Beautiful Roses Known To Mankind, Tie Them With A Ribbon And Decorate Them With A Sign Saying 'MAUDE'>]
[<Enter>]

And roses appeared.

Pink.

Plush—just like I'd hoped.

A whole cluster of them tied with a ribbon.

And there was a sign right in the middle of the perfect buds, glowing red with tiny sparkles: '*Maude*'.

"Oh!" Her eyes got a strange glint in them. *Surprise? …I couldn't tell if it was a good 'oh' or a what-the-fuck? 'oh'. How did other guys tell this?*

[System Penalty: Flirtation Rejected -10 Swag Points, 235]
[System Penalty: …Well, You Royally Fucked That Up -2 XP, 1414/1500]

...Oh, this was how other guys knew...shit.

0010

0009

The timer. Counting down to my failure. My hands started trembling. My heart was pumping furiously while my mouth was bone dry. Another system prompt flashed before my eyes.

[System Query: Would You Like To Attempt To Start An Interested Conversation With MAUDE, APPRENTICE? Use 15 Swag Points To Try Again?]

[Yes, Try Again] [No, Thank You]

It was getting kinda grating that the system had to rub it in with the 'again' part.

"Yes," I whispered.

[-15 Swag Points, 220]

Louder, I said, "Uh, actually, Maude, I can code a lot of things like... I can take us to the beach..." My fingers were at it again, working faster than my mouth or brain.

[System Query: Please Input Code]

[<Action Input: Export Scenery. Create Landscape Greenscreen With Effects Of Real Life Beach: Blue Sky, Sand, Rolling Surf, Relaxing, Gulls Crying Overhead>]

[<Enter>]

And, suddenly, we were no longer standing in the office courtyard, overgrown with ivy. Our toes were buried in deep, white sand as ocean waves brought frothy surf rolling towards us with crashing, gentle thunder. A beautiful, blue sky spanned overhead. Just like I'd imagined. *Who'd gotten an A+ in coding? Yep, this guy...!*

"*Oh my God!*" The girl exclaimed—clearly excitement and wonder this time.

[System Alert: Try Again Received, +10 Swag Points, 230]
[System Alert: Way to Go! You Impressed Her, +5 XP,
1419/1500]

Elation rushed through me as Maude rushed towards the water, crouching to run her hands through it, "It's even warm!"

But my eyes darted to my watch.

0007
0006

My breath hitched. Six minutes to get the girl? Could I do it? Only one way to find out. I began typing rapidly.

[<Action Input: Create Budding Flowers, Weaving
Upward And Into An Arch…Make It Fancy…>]

That was a technical term…kidding.

[<Enter>]

And flowers started to grow upward from the sand, just like I'd input—delicate, white and pink buds opening, forming an archway shape. Then, blocks appeared and stacked to make an arched column—

0005

Wait—

I froze. What was I doing? I was just asking the girl out. This wasn't a wedding or a proposal. This wasn't—

I'd gone too far. I'd taken this too far again. I was gonna creep her out—I needed to backtrack!

0004

"*Sorry!*" I burst out.

I dropped the code.

I hit enter without thinking.

And we were back in the office courtyard, the girl crouching by a pile of rocks that was no longer the ocean. She turned, confused, "What…"

0003

[System Query: Would You Like To Ask Out MAUDE, APPRENTICE? Use 100 Swag Points To Ask Her Out?] [Yes, Ask Her Out] [No, Thank You]

Oh my Grand Dragon, this was it. This was do or die time. Did I even have enough swag to pull it off?

[System Unable To Understand Query…Recognizable Word = 'Swag'. Linked To Swag Points. Loading Swag Points Now…] [Current Swag Points / DORMOUSE, CODER 14 = 230]

Just enough to pull it off—hopefully. I had one try. Ask her out, I commanded the system internally even though I was shaking like a leaf. My stomach plummeted.

[-100 Swag Points, 130]

"Maude, I've been wanting to—" I stumbled, my hands twisting together in front of me, "I mean, I wanted to for a long time, but I just never had the courage—"

0002

She was staring at me weird. Why was she staring at me weird? I had to get this out. I still had one rose pre-programed in the code. I hit enter again, extending the single flower in one hand towards her with the words I'd been wanting to ask *forever* trembling on my lips—

"Maude, I—"

0001

"Dorrat, you're freaking me out," she blurted, backing away from the extended rose.

And, as I looked down, I realized I had a sixth finger.

And there was an eyeball on the finger.

Blinking at her.

Whhhaaaa??? The code—

I'd hit the wrong button? Of all the times to mess up the minutiae—

[System Penalty: Ask Out Rejected -200 Swag Points, -70]
[System Penalty: Congratulations, You Scared Off The Hot Girl -10 XP, 1409/1500]
0000
[System Penalty: Failure To Complete Side Mission Objective. Side Mission Failed.]
[System Penalty: No Points Awarded]
[Side Mission Aborting...]

NO! Shit! My points were almost low enough to make me go down a level & my Swag Points were negative—

And, just like that, the world went black. And I was standing back at the Hindu temple with a confused Rosabella squinting into my lowered face.

Welcome Back ROSABELLA, GAME MAKER 6 & DORMOUSE, CODER 14 To The Game

Rosabella blinked at the pop-up that appeared between us and my probably devastated face.

"*Dormouse?*" she prodded, "...you okay?"

No. I wasn't fucking okay.

Maude couldn't even remember my name!

"I fucked it up," I whispered, barely audible, "I had one chance, and *I fucked it up.*"

Rosabella

Dormouse and I were back in The Game, but what started as such a carefree jaunt had layered the kid's face in defeated ash.

"Hey," I shook his limp shoulder, "it was just a side mission. It *wasn't real*."

But his smile wasn't as elastic as it usually was. He shrugged half-heartedly, tendrils of his dark hair falling into his eyes as he ducked his bashful head again, "I fucking hate simulations anyway—"

"Guys, it's all clear!" Callen rounded the corner of the overgrown temple with Rainer and Joy, waving an arm towards the two of us, "Looks like the place has been uninhabited for a while now and, luckily, no squatters."

Rainer adjusted the axe on his back while Joy ran a gloved hand through her long hair. "*What's with Dorkus?*" the pink-haired girl's pursed lips interrupted with a scowl and a sideways glance at the sullen boy, "He looks like he got run over by an eighteen-wheeler—"

"You know it'd be mega helpful in this moment if *someone* would get my name right," Dormouse sulked.

I walked past Joy, nudging her slightly in the arm as I did. "*Be nice to him,*" I whispered. "Long story." Her eyes narrowed at me, but she didn't push the kid any further.

"So…this temple…" I circled my arms around me at the looming, golden building over us, trying to take the spotlight off Dormouse for a second.

"You should see the view from the inside," Rainer chimed in, his deep voice echoing in the hallway he'd just ducked into. He waved me over.

I trotted his way, trying to ignore the unease churning in my stomach as I dodged the falling ivy covering the opening. My boots met with polished, though grimy, floors. I didn't know what significance this building held for the group or the Gamers, but I did know that they wanted me to do the magic here—the magic that was supposed to fix their world. …*And saying I was nervous about it was putting it lightly…*

I swallowed all the dryness in my throat and tried to still my swirling head as my eyes adjusted to the dim hallway. This place was *gorgeous*—or once was, at any rate. Even in its fallen state of decay and disrepair, the intricate carvings in the walls stood out like this was once royalty among buildings. Numerous columns and archways stretched overhead, holding an equally etched and beautiful tray ceiling, and the weavings of turquoise and white tile underfoot were like a story crafted in artwork beneath the dusty toes of my boots. I almost felt bad standing on it. Gold shone through in little, winking bits overhead like stars of what was probably its former, streaming glory.

"The real show is over here," Rainer called from somewhere up ahead. I wove around the plethora of carved columns, trying to find him.

"Here," the burly warrior's arms spread wide as his deep voice rang in the labyrinth. And my jaw…*dropped.*

Open.

Like the wall.

Seriously. The back wall of an expansive room, which appeared to once have included three enormous, rounded fountains—their basins now dry and stained with dirt and leaves—opened with a giant arch to an extensive, outside balcony. ...Where the world dropped off like a cliff except for the landing of three bridges which crossed the chasm, connecting the balcony to the ridge on the horizon. *Enormous* bridges, coming to a point together at the temple.

"There used to be railings but..." Rainer trailed off as I inched my feet closer to the edge, peering over and only finding ragged rocks and darkness there, beyond the ruins of a fallen barrier.

"Hey, look, there's something on that ledge," I pointed to a bobbing triangle icon on a rocky jut out. The picture of a turquoise diamond was emblazoned on the front. "Is it Creator Magic?"

Rainer leaned past me to see, "No, that's a spell. You gotta remember what all these icons look like. You'd better pick it up. It's no good to the lot of us."

I squatted, reaching off the ledge—

Beep.

[System Reward: Spell Acquired +10 XP, 581/600]
[VACU-ROCKET]

Vacu-Rocket? Now, that sounded a little more promising than the others I had...

"Well, what does it do?" Rainer prodded, raising a bushy eyebrow and nodding at the Examination Opportunity which now bobbed over the name of the spell.

"Examine," I commanded.

[System Object Examined... +1 XP, 582/600]
[A Spell Stat Sheet Pulls Up As You Get Closer. This'll Tell You What It Does!]

Spell: **Vacu-Rocket**

Required Class, Level & Ability For Use: CM 2	Game Maker Or Dragon L6,
Description:	Tired Of Dingy, Dirty Carpets? Get Rid Of The Shit With This Vacuum-Packed Spell! Point At The Mess & Watch It Be Sucked Into Oblivion. There's No Mess Too Messy! No More Cereal Crumbs Under The Table Or In Your Couch.
How To Cast:	Speak 'Goodbye Messafuss'
Augment Capacities:	None
Learning Curve Required:	1 Use
HP Needed To Cast:	-1
Baddie Points:	+0

Another useless L1 spell? This was getting old fast. I'd have to find more CM Diamonds so I could start to collect something actually useful. I rolled my eyes and swiped out of the spell stats.

"This temple is called Meherna," Callen stepped out of the shadows, clearly giving me some kind of class lecture I hadn't realized I was behind on, "It means 'The Meeting of the Hearts'. It's the one neutral place in The Game—without alliance. We're standing at the very center of our land where North, South, East and West meet. Each bridge and the temple represent each one of those directions. This was always a place of discussion and treaty. It's sacred ground. They say any magic done here is magnified."

"So, you think my Creator Magic will magnify here too?" I asked tentatively. My voice shook. *Was I ready for this with a handful of terrible, useless beginner spells and hardly any knowledge of magic?* Could anyone ever be ready for this—to test their unconfirmed skills in the deep end? To dive out of their comfort zone in the hopes greatness would flow out—bring them and those they cared about bobbing to the top like a sea? …Maybe not.

Callen seemed to sense my trepidation. He placed a solid hand on my shoulder, his eyes warm and level like the steadiness I couldn't seem to find in this moment—like freaking dry land in the storm of my mind. "You can do this, Rosabella."

And I wanted to believe him; I really did.

I turned and found the group shuffling their feet forward to form a circle around me—not creepily, just…expectantly. And I was in the center of that circle.

I was what they were all here for. …Why they'd been searching all these years.

This was the moment that had brought them hope—hope that their world could be fixed. And, now, it was time to test that theory. *God fucking help me.*

I took a huge breath, trying a casual smile and shrug of my shoulders, but failing. "It's time, isn't it?" I asked—more of a squeak.

Callen nodded.

And, suddenly, an empty feeling overwhelmed me—an alone feeling.

Because they were all looking at me.

This was only something *I* could do as the last Game Maker. And Sparo wasn't here this time to guide me through it. I was…*truly by myself here…*

I closed my eyes. I tried to calm my rocketing heartbeat as I dropped into my mind, attempting to find a quiet thread. *I could do this. I was supposed to amplify my magic here. I guess that meant I should start with a spell…*

System, what are the spells I can choose from? I asked inwardly, squeezing my eyes together.

[System Understands Query…Loading Response…]

[System Answer: Available Spells Include:]
[NO MORE NOISY NEIGHBORS ABSORPTION HEX]
[FIND THINGS HOPELESSLY LOST HOCUS POCUS]
[VACU-ROCKET]

Well, I was hopelessly lost. Could the second spell help with that? I'd already cast it once, so it shouldn't mess up this time...

"Cast FIND THINGS HOPELESSLY LOST HOCUS POCUS," I whispered.

[System Alert: FIND THINGS HOPELESSLY LOST HOCUS POCUS Used]
[-1 HP, 51/53]

You're not alone, child.

A voice? Had the spell worked?

I scrunched my closed eyes up further, attempting to focus on the swirling, meshing colors that had finally materialized. And it, strangely, felt familiar reaching through the levels of magic—moving through the ocean of swaying colors around me and honing in on a pulsing orb of light at the center...

...Like a song that I'd sung a hundred times.

...Or a story... Why did it feel like a story I'd told?

Did MRP work with my Creator Magic? I knew this place.

I'd certainly hope so. Welcome home, dear one.

The voice again, neither female or male, but, strangely, both. In my mind...*it could—hear me? My thoughts? Like the dragons...*

Who are you? I asked it, demanding.

[Draconic Telepathy Used... +1 XP, 583/600]

The voice chuckled a bit—a slow, drawl, like it was smiling.

The better question is: who are YOU, dearest? The answer lies in that orb.

It meant the orb glowing right in front of my face? The object's blinding light bobbed up and down in front of my eyes, beckoning—like the CM Diamonds but…

Different.

It felt like…

Strength.

Courage.

Resiliency.

Like holding my chin high.

Like…L1 Determination, Bounce Back skill…and fighting dragons…thinking out of the box and never giving up…

<u>*Yes, that's it. Your understanding is keen.*</u>

The voice purred.

<u>*That is your soul, beloved. And I am the Grand Dragon.*</u>

Shock rolled over me. <u>*The Grand Dragon? The dragon from the tale Sparo told me about the very creation of The Game world?*</u>

<u>*The same.*</u>

The dragon answered breezily. I swallowed nervously.

<u>*And you…*</u>

The dragon continued.

<u>*Are Game Maker Rosabella.*</u>

There was such strength in the way the beast said my name.

<u>*And it is time you take your rightful place as the last Game Maker.*</u>

Frustration and desperation tumbled over me at the same time in a wave I'd rather hide my head under than face. *I'm trying!* I protested, clenching my teeth and fists. The orb wouldn't absorb into my fingers when I touched it.The glowing sphere spun like a globe, showing burned holes in it—dark. Whenever I tried to reach a hand out towards the magic there, it burned me.

The magic isn't working! I complained.

Those who surround you influence your magic. Negativity in the mind is not amenable for augmenting magic. The Temple will augment when only light resides. Dig out the darkness, and there will be light enough for all in this world.

I don't know how! I'm brand new to all this! I bit back tears now. *Surrounded by this swirling, opulent magic, and I was reduced to tears?* It felt silly...childish...

There is little time, child.

The Grand Dragon's voice sounded patient, but warning.

So, show me what to do! I pouted, throwing my hands down at my side. *Just—show me! I want to fix this! No one ever taught me—*

Goran taught you. Remember…?

[System Searching MRPs To Select & Display Correct Memory...]

"Have you ever been in a dragon's mouth, Rosie?"

Goran's voice—

I flinched at the sound. *He murdered my Mom and Dad!* I all but screamed in my head.

Yes, and you have killed many creatures since you've been in The Game.

I swallowed, feeling a lump growing there in my throat. *I'm just trying to survive. You get XP for it—*

I know. It is my brother's inadequacies shining through in the system.
I understand you are trying to survive.

The voice was kind.

Sparo's not here to do the magic with me, I told it. Before, he had me put my hand in his mouth, and it would augment it—*combine our strength and magic, somehow. I was alone in this now...*

You're not alone.

The Grand Dragon repeated, and I realized that that was something it'd said earlier.

I don't understand. I felt like I was floundering, losing myself in the nauseating, pulsing waves of magic surrounding me. *Wasn't I supposed to be finding something—not losing something? Hadn't that been the spell? It hadn't worked.* The colors were so bright that they hurt my eyes— like a million pieces of striped candy, swirling around my head like I was in a bad commercial.

Close your eyes, child. Focus within you. I am a dragon—the Grand Dragon. First Creator. I am always with you when you create too. The magic connects us both. Breathe in.

I did. I couldn't help it; it felt natural. *Finally, something felt easy and natural.*

You are in the dragon's mouth whenever you create—whenever you try to do something bigger than yourself, whenever you step into the flames with a brave face. You are in the dragon's mouth as you step into me—as you step into yourself for we are one; you are a Creator, a Game Maker. You make your game. And your magic is augmented here, in this space. You become bigger when you face your fears. When you put your hands on jagged teeth for the sake of something greater. I am proud of you, child, but there is very little time. Move quickly, dear. Move through the fear, and you will taste victory.

And I blinked my eyes open as an electric charge rolled through my limbs, strengthening me.

The Grand Dragon's words.

The Grand Dragon's intention—*magic? My* magic? They were too entwined to tell apart. I felt it coursing through my veins—swifter and more powerful than the life of blood.

[System Reward: Damn Girl, You Connected With The Grand Dragon! +30 XP, 613/600]

Over 600 XP? That meant… The world froze. Emerald plus marks spiraled all around me. *It meant Level Up.*

[System Alert: ***Congratulations, You've Advanced To Level 7!***]

Name	Rosabella	
Class & Level	Game Maker 7	
XP	613/700	
MRP	3795/6209	
HP	50/62	
Baddie Points	90	
Armor Class	15/20	
ABILITIES /20		
Strength	+0	11
Agility	+0	10
Endurance	+0	10
Intelligence	+1	13
Awareness	+1	12
Presence	+3	16
CM		3

[+9 HP & HP Extended By 9, 60/62. Reminder: System Has Cached Additional +2 Ability Points In Your Inventory From Prior Level Up. Furthermore, You've Been Awarded The Ability To Select One Of The Following Extras:]
[Mystery Spell] [Mystery Object]

Oh man, I'd forgotten I had 2 Ability Points still to award.

"System, add one point to Endurance and one to Strength," I told it.

[System Alert: +1 Strength, 12/20, +1 Endurance 11/20]

There, solved, but...what were these options? The typical Examination Opportunities hovered over each one—*easy XP at this point.* I clicked on the first shield and magnifying glass option.

[System Option Examined... +1 XP, 624/700]
[A Closer Look At The Fine Print Explains The Option Further:
MYSTERY SPELL: A Spell Chosen At Random By The Game Which Will Be Explained Further Upon Receipt. This Spell May Only Be Used Once But Does Not Require A Learning Curve To Cast.]

...Well, that was the most nicely-put vagueness I'd ever read—completely useless in the way of telling me anything about what I'd actually be choosing. Would the other be any different?

"Examine," I said. Another paragraph of text bounced into view:

[System Option Examined... +1 XP, 625/700]
[A Closer Look At The Fine Print Explains The Option Further:
MYSTERY OBJECT: An Object Chosen At Random By The Game Which Will Be Explained Further Upon Receipt. This Object May Only Be Used Once.]

...Apparently, it was the same there except an object and not a spell. I raised a finger, wobbling over the two buttons. Which should I choose? I needed magic to save The Game world, but the spells I'd gotten so far had proved entirely pointless...then, again, I had no idea that the object would be useful—

Beep.

[System Alert: Mystery Object Selected. Object Will Be Placed In Your Inventory.]

Wait, what?! My finger had slipped! My freaking finger had—

"System, pull up my inventory," I growled, annoyed—Level 7 and I accidently chose my reward?

[System Understands Query...Loading Response...]
[System Alert: Per Request, Inventory Opened.]
- **1 Rosabella's Mother's Silver & Gold Broadsword**
- **4 CM Diamonds**
- **1 The Game Map**
- **1 Mystery Object**

A shield and magnifying glass symbol hovered next to the Mystery Object. *Show me what the hell this is,* I thought, but I said, "Examine".

[System Option Examined... +1 XP, 612/700]
[A Closer Look At The Fine Print Explains The Object Further:
MYSTERY OBJECT = ERASER OF NONENESS: A Magical Object Which Allows A Gamer To Erase A Singular Object In The Game. This May Be 1 Gamer, 1 Object, Or 1 Creature. This Eraser Can Only Be Used Once.]

Whoa. I could erase something? Maybe I wasn't so mad at the choice after all.

The world unfroze and a system pop-up reminded me that I was coming out of my CM magic and the conversation with the Grand Dragon, back to the reality of the Temple Meherna...

[System Reward: A Gift From The Grand Dragon. 1 CM Diamond Acquired +10 XP, 635/600, Object Will Be Placed In Your Inventory Unless You'd Like To Equip. Would You Like to Equip?]
[Yes] [No]

"Yes," the word rolled off my tongue like I'd known it was mean to be there.

[System Alert: 1 CM Diamond Equipped]

And my eyes locked suddenly on Rainer, across from me. And the swirling magic of the CM Diamond showed me a huge, blurry, black patch over his heart—like a mournful raincloud.

The dragon had said that those around me influence my magic. They'd said to cut out any negativity, and light would come—my Creator Magic! I looked around and quickly realized there weren't any other black spots on the other individuals in the group. *Rainer was the black spot. I had to figure out how to fix whatever darkness lived in Rainer, so the Temple would augment my CM…*

…And I suddenly knew what I had to do. *I'd already been given the tools! I'd done it with Joy before—lessened the darkness on her through the side mission! The dragon was right! I DID know how to do this!*

I whipped around, breathless, my eyes flying open, "*Dormouse!*"

The kid's glum, pale face barely looked up.

"I know you're dealing with everything but"—I was so excited I could barely get the words out—"Can you patch Rainer and I into a side mission? Quick, can you do it quick?"

Blubbering excuses drooled out of the kid's mouth, "I—yeah, I mean, I can—"

"Good," I snapped, already spinning towards Rainer and clamping both hands down on the Nomad's arm. He looked at me with questions written underneath his furry eyebrows, but I had more than he did. *Why was the darkness affecting him so much? At any rate, I was about to find out.*

"Is this really necessary—" Rainer protested.

"Now, Dormouse, *the code!*" I prodded.

"Okay, okay! *Pushy much?*" he brushed a wave of dark hair out of his face as his fingers flew mid-air.

[System Query: Please Input Code]
[*SideMissionStart101*]
[<Action Input: Start Side Mission Without General
Restrictions>]
[<Begin Reboot>]
[<Initialize>]

"The dragon said we don't have much time," I explained as I felt his code integrating and my surroundings shifting. An electronic beep ensued.

[System Alert: Work Around Utilized]

"What dragon?" he called.

It was the last thing I heard before I was standing in Rainer's world.

Goran

Time.

Time was tricky—*sticky*.

You could weave it, or you could get stuck in it, much like a spider's web.

This time, *time was mine*—just like Rosabella. Just like the spider, I'd set the perfect trap and Rosabella's discontinued Game Wardens all would fall into it—with this world.

With the greed that made and had already destroyed this world...

And only Rosabella and I would escape together. I'd made sure it was part of the dragon's vow—just another part of my ingenious plan. I fingered the handle of the emerald-encrusted dagger near my pocket as a strange sort of relish flooded over me, making me smile. Yes, yes I had it all locked down very nicely this time; there would be no mistakes.

This time was *my* time—not Ford's.

Mine.

Now, I didn't have to pretend to be his goodie-two-shoes, rule-following, princely self to make them follow me. This time, they could see who I was from my outside: the black warpaint streaking the defined lines of my cheeks and nose...the fires of their villages reflecting in my eyes as we paraded into the night, victorious as the cheers of the Commandress's army bellowed behind us and the flap and thaw of dragon wings sounded overhead…their smoky breath—their shapes trailing like a hundred black crows in the brooding clouds above. I was done hiding the blackness that'd taken over my life long ago; it'd been running, coal-colored, through my veins for too long. Some people ran from fear. I'd made it my flag. I'd held it high over my head and dared anyone to come near me. Because I'd killed my own brother. *What wouldn't I do for Rosie? What wouldn't I do to get her back?*

The Commandress thought she had the better end of this trade—that I was protecting her from the Game Maker. But it was merely a selfish task. I wanted Rosie back, and this dragon's army was how I got her. We'd overwhelm anything in the path.

To Rosie.

The dark dragon had let me borrow armor. In fact, she'd had her war generals suit me with the finest, black body armor and camouflage cape they had. It was heavy on my shoulders—like the weight of pulling all this off—and dragged behind me with every crunching step through the knee-high grass.

A woman's wails filled the distance. *Did we kill her baby? Her husband? Her dog? Maybe. If she were to see them there, alive again, would there be more nails-on-a-chalkboard moaning? …Wasn't it ironic that we screamed for both pain and pleasure?* I gritted my teeth. I didn't care what others had lost, only what I had. Because I'd lost *too much*, and I was going to get it back if I had to step on everyone here's back to do it—crush them like the skeletons of a past that hated me under the soles of my animal-skin boots. I was through with this world.

Only the power in it interested me.

And Rosie.

Of course, Rosie.

Small rocks pinched through the thin soles of my boots.

We were getting out of here.

We're getting close.

The Commandress's voice filled my ears, nearly like I could hear her enormous, beating wings. But it was my imagination. She was so far above the clouds I could barely make out her engulfing shadow if I tilted my head back into the dying daylight.

You were right about the dragons and the towns, man who killed his brother. They have all fallen as we met them. You have proved very useful. Power suits you. Perhaps, if you continue to prove loyal, I should promote you to a general under my watch.

General.

General Goran.

I liked the ring of it but kept my thoughts neutral and paced ahead; I didn't need the dragon honing in and reading them now while I was scheming.

The Discontinued Game Wardens will take the Game Maker to the Temple Meherna, I told the beast swiftly in my mind. They're going to fight to fix The Game and gain control that should be yours. We'll need to throw everything we have at them.

[Draconic Telepathy Used... +1 XP, 1168/1200]

She laughed in my head, a malicious, clanging rattle of cymbals.

Good thing we have everything to throw.

I grinned. That we did.

I went over the plan again, feeling the dragon slip from my mind. The discontinued Game Wardens were strong and well-trained, but they didn't stand much of a chance against the makeshift army we'd formed roving over the countryside to get here. The Creator Magic was the only unknown in the equation. If Rosie had figured out how to wield it, she could be a problem. But I was prepared for the challenge. It was like how I'd taught Rosie to braid her own hair when she was little. I'd taught her the motions. I'd walked her through it over and over, but her movements were slow and messy at first. If she'd braided her own hair, it was all too easy for me to unbraid it. Quickly. Efficiently.

[System Searching MRPs To Select & Display Correct Memory...]

I smiled, thinking of the moment...

My huge hands lingered on her small ones. I grabbed her little hand with chubby fingers, going over the motions again and helping her hold the different strands of her hair.

"Like this, Rosie—over, under," I instructed her gently.

I watched her fingers struggle to stretch the elastic out, twisting it around the ends of her hair.

"There, now it's right," I told her, patting her soft locks as she grinned up at me.

I shook the memory away. This was no different.

If Rosie came against me, I'd have no choice but to make things right.

Even.

Clean.

And she *would* come with me. It was the only way to ensure she was protected. We both knew this. I just wondered if Rosie had accepted it yet, or if her group had poisoned her mind.

Because if they'd turned Rosie against me—if she believed their lies and had lost herself in The Game—I just might crack the whole world open with my anguish.

"System, how much CM and MRP does Rosabella have?" I murmured under my breath. "Show me the Game Damage Points too."

[System Understands Query...Loading Response...]
[Current CM / ROSABELLA, GAME MAKER 6: 4/20]
[Current MRP / ROSABELLA, GAME MAKER 3:
3795/6209]
[GDP – 90/100]

My eyes scanned over the neon text. So her MRP and CM were alarmingly high, but I could deal with it. ...At least The Game was going to royal shit—

Clear a landing area!

The Commandress bellowed from overhead.

The dragons must descend, or the discontinued Game Wardens will see us. I can see them on the sacred ground—

No, I told her in my mind. *I refuse to hide. They asked for this; they will get it.*

I am the Commander. I decide.

The dark dragon's words reverberated in my head.

We stay hidden for now and attack at nightfall.

'Stay hidden'. I shook my head. It was something I wasn't good at. ...*Like following orders.*

I took a step towards where the earth fell away from my feet, peering through the thick bushes there. *Surely, this hiding was folly—couldn't the discontinued Game Wardens already see the smoke from the burning towns behind us? But, maybe, they were too far away.* I gazed across the chasm, peering at the figures, standing in a circle on the temple balcony across the craggy valley. From here, they look like tiny figurines:

The discontinued Game Wardens and—

My breath caught in my throat—lodged there.

Because I'd been right: Rosie was there with her hair streaming back from her scalp in the wind—rigid. Unmoving as she clasped one of the Nomad's arms with both hands. *She must be in the Creator Magic. Did that mean I could guess where her allegiance lie?*

But I didn't want to. Not yet. For now, I just wanted her to continue to be the sweet, small Rosabella in my mind.

The one who still loved me.

Untainted by this Game that hated us both.

Untainted.

Till I had to acknowledge otherwise.

Callen – 1 Hour Later

Nothing was moving—that was what bothered me most. There was usually birdsong even as the sun fell, hawks or Kenchee circling in the misty clouds fading from midnight blue to pink along the wavering horizon…

But tonight, there was no song.

Just the whisper of the wind over my broad shoulders, wrapping around my neck with trailing fingers—like nature itself was holding a hushed secret. And it made every muscle in me tense as I watched the ridgeline across the bridges. Because the smell of smoke had been wafting into my nostrils, and smoke, here, didn't mean campfires and marshmallows…

It meant dragons.

"*Keep your eyes sharp,*" I told Joy, shifting again on my feet as I scanned the tree line once again.

Silent.

Still.

Eerie.

…How long had Rosabella and Rainer been in there—in the side mission?

My eyes flickered to the pair's stiff, statue-like forms—locked together, almost, in an embrace. Their eyes were chalky-white and their breathing, shallow.

It was times like this that I hated my sixth sense—hated for it to be right. Because something felt…*off.* And, if things went south, I'd only have the pink-haired girl as a capable warrior in this fight. Dormouse could code, but he was only as good as his fear. I wouldn't count on him to stick around if there was a chance to run. I'd caught him in the shadows too often whenever danger reared its head. *Was that what I smelled in the air now? Danger? Rearing?*

I squinted up at the clouds. *Were those dark wings slithering behind a cloud, or did I have a morose imagination?*

"System, show me the GDP chart," I growled, my eyes never leaving the ridge across the valley.

[System Understands Query…Loading Response…]
[GDP – 90/100]

Current Gamer Population:	332 Million
Current Darken Population:	178 Million
Darken To Gamer Ratio:	~53.61%
Darkness Cover:	86/100
Dilapidation Cover:	94/100

Significantly worse stats than two days ago. Something was up. Something was—

Whizz—thud!

Joy shrieked.

I turned to see the shaft of an arrow protruding from the pink-haired girl's shoulder blade. Her face was shock-white as her hand flew to cover the wound. Dark red stained her fingertips when they returned—

[JOY, WARRIOR, 12:-20 HP 90/172]

Shit.

"Take cover!" I screamed, "Dormouse, help me drag Rosabella and Rainer beneath the roofline!" I lunged for their stiff bodies.

Arrows pelted down like the hailstorm this quiet night had been brewing for hours now.

Across the valley, an army roared to life with cries of blood and rage—their shadows moving like the darkened trees along the edge had come to life.

Fuck it! I'd been right. And, if the Game Maker died, so did our very chance of survival.

Rosabella

I stared at the pop-up with confusion. *'Honor and respect?'* *What did that mean?*

Ca-Thunk!

Ca-Thunk!

—*What?* I blinked, squinting into the streaming sunlight which was so bright it bit through my pupils, shining over the horizon and off of a glinting—

Was than an axe? Was someone swinging an axe high over their head—?

"*Rainer!*" I shouted at the man right beside me as I recognized him. *It was Rainer! He was…chopping wood?*

The burly warrior heard my cry, but he wouldn't look at me. His face turned away, tucking near his chin as he lowered the axe from its next wood victim on the cut tree trunk, makeshift, slicing bench. …He looked different. His beard was gone—his chin, clean-shaven. He looked strange without it and…*younger?*

He was clad in layered deerskin with the arms of the shirt cut off to reveal biceps shining with sweat. A pile of jumbled, different-sized wood pieces surrounded his legs, evidence that he'd been at his wood chopping for a long while, and droplets of rain spit down on my cheeks from a navy-blue sky overhead where the surrounding evergreens didn't quite reach the Heavens. I glimpsed the outline of a small, sleepy town through the break in the trees. It actually looked rather peaceful and quiet here—a sentiment which conflicted greatly with the wincing pain on the Nomad's face. *Was that a—tear?! Rolling down his cheek?* He quickly swiped it away with an urgent hand before I could determine.

"Rainer?" I tried again, more softly this time as I approached him. I cast a wary glance at the enormous blade of the axe, but he let it slip from his fingers and thud into the dense grass.

[RAINER, NOMAD 9: System Alert: Object Discarded.]

"*It's no use,*" he huffed, his deep voice gruff and deeply troubled, "I thought the side mission would let me stop it, but I know this scene. This was afterwards—"

"After *what?*" It felt a little strange to be reaching out to put a comforting hand on the man's huge shoulder, but something inside me knew he needed it this moment. His face was tortured—twisted in emotions I couldn't pin down. I noticed, all at once, that his hands were shaking. From where my hand touched his shoulder, I felt him take a shuttering breath.

"It was *me,*" he admitted sullenly, shaking his head, "I didn't mean to, but I did it—"

He was speaking rapidly and rapidly losing me. *Did what? What did he do?*

My fingers clamped down on the skin of his arm if only to get the man to breathe for a minute. His face was sliding into hyperventilation.

"Rainer, I don't understand—*hey*—hey, *breathe for a second,*" I told him, leaning in, hoping that he could see me—hold onto the image of my face—even as his eyes glossed over like all he could see was whatever was tormenting him.

"It was *my fault*, Rosabella," he panted, running a huge, frazzled hand through his hair as his face shut down even further, "Oh Grand Dragon, *it was my fault! I didn't mean—*"

"*Rainer!*" I grasped the huge man by both biceps, trying to shake him back to reality and not the churning thoughts it seemed he was facing, "*Tell me what's going on.*"

This was a side mission—Rainer's world. The Grand Dragon had said I didn't have much time. I had to figure out why the darkness was so concentrated on Rainer's heart and fix any negativity that might be clogging up the Temple's ability to augment my Creator Magic, so I could fix The Game world...

But the man was despondent.

His chest convulsed.

This huge warrior, reduced to mush before me—*a freaking out puddle? What was I going to do?*

Aggravated, I lifted my face to the sky to shake strands of hair out of my eyes but—but my gaze locked on shadows drifting overhead. I squinted into the sun. *Were those...?*

A shield with a magnifying glass symbol over it followed the curves of one of the birds in the air: an Examination Opportunity. *Maybe it could tell me something?*

"Examine," I whispered.

[System Object Examined... +1 XP, 636/700]
[You Crane Your Face Up To The Sky And Discover Those Aren't Just Birds, They're Kenchee.]

...Weird. Why would the system want me to know that?

"Rainer," I tried again, speaking into his face with a leveler tone, "There's Kenchee circling above—those zombie vulture things?

They're drawn to magic, aren't they? Is this your hometown? Is there magic nearby?"

The man's face hardened then and cracked open.

Simultaneously.

He shook his head back and forth, his cleft chin twitching with the movement, "Rosabella, I never meant—"

"I know that, I know," I cooed—while suppressing every sudden need to shake him again and demand what the fuck was going on. "Tell me, Rainer," I said instead. "Please tell me."

Tell me why we were in these woods, near this town?

Tell me what I was doing out here chopping wood, and how a great warrior with infinite weapons could be reduced to a sobbing child?

Tell me why the Kenchee were circling overhead.

Please let him tell me.

He swallowed; I watched. His jaw clenched—his fists did too. Finally, he spoke, "It's—this is a memory of the past. I have a CM Diamond in my inventory."

My forehead scrunched up, confused.

"I don't understand—" I tripped over my own tongue. "I thought only dragons and Game Makers could use CM." I hated the way the words sounded, coming off my tongue—far too lofty or self-important.

Rainer sighed, shaking his head. "It was on the dare of a girl. I wanted to impress the young lass. When the Reordering happened, the Creator Magic was taken from all humans and given only to one; they banned creation. They mandated no one could create. But I was a blacksmith; it was my trade—my life."

Tears swam in the big man's eyes; I saw the emotion there.

"I was young, I didn't know there'd be consequences! A girl I was sweet on dared me to sneak into the cave of a Green Rinkeclaw and grab a CM Diamond so I could create, not knowing that I couldn't, you know? I was foolish, a wee lad. I snuck out in the dark of night. I wanted to make myself a sword," his chest puffed out a bit at that. "I was a right good Nomad even being a youngin, so I stole from that dragon but," his gruff voice broke, "I put the CM Diamond in my inventory, and the Kenchee followed me back home through the wood. I didn't know that the dammed birds attract Darken. The zombies began trickling in after me. There was too many to stop. I hid. I hid with that stupid CM Diamond I could do nothing with in the cupboards of the old blacksmith shop—pressed my hands over my ears as the town screamed…as they died. Everyone died that night or ran away. Everyone except me. And I did that. I killed—children."

He hated himself. I could see it in his eyes. A tear escaped them, running down the folds of his face. Oh my God. He'd been living with this shame—the guilt of being the death of his town—for years now. …Something that was an accident? We could fix this. We could fix this together. Maybe the side mission was supposed to give him a second chance.

"Where's the CM Diamond now?" I asked, "I mean, in this side mission, is it still in your inventory?"

"I don't know," the man admitted, his face listless. He gestured around at all the wood, spanning around his ankles. "This was where I was after I ran from town when everyone was dead—even the bloody girl I liked. Seeing her limp body—the Darken gorging—I got so angry," he started, his brows creasing, "I chopped wood for days after the last death, trying to understand what had happened—"

"It was a mistake," I interrupted, but the man wouldn't let me finish.

"Yes, but the next part wasn't." His face was solemn. "I took all this wood and I—I couldn't look at everything…this place…all the diseased, rotting flesh with the Darken still milling around. I had to get rid of it—of the evidence that I'd killed…that I—" he swallowed.

"I burned it. I burned my whole town and all of the bodies in it in one giant bonfire. I tried to cover the place up like a town had never existed here. And the bodies—I mean, if they had relatives, they'd never know where their loved ones were buried. And I did that on purpose."

His face was hard.

And, suddenly, understanding dawned on me.

"Rainer, bring up the side mission objective again," I told him. He swiped it into view half-heartedly.

[Side Mission Objective: Honor and Respect.]

"I think I get it," I told him. "You weren't brought back to this memory to save your town. What happened, happened. It truly was a mistake. But you were brought back before you burned it. Maybe you're not supposed to—maybe that's the regret that's hurting you most. Maybe you should make a different choice this time."

The Nomad's head shot up, "Bury them?"

I nodded, "With honor and respect."

And something changed in Rainer's eyes then—something shifted. And, although weariness was evident in every crease in his face, something else was too. ...*Relief?*

"It will take all day..." he griped, wringing his hands, like trying not to convince himself, "And, if it's anything like that day, the Darken will still be swarming about."

"I have an idea about that," I told him, smiling grimly out of the corner of my mouth. "We'll do this...together." Because I suddenly knew that this was the right way forward. *We had to do this.* "Check your inventory and see if the CM Diamond is still there," I prodded.

The man pulled up his account.

[Rainer - System Alert: Per Request, Inventory Opened.]
- **1 Custom Steel Broadsword**
- **1 Set of Matches**
- **1 Blacksmithing Tool Kit**

- 1 Rope
- 1 Canteen
- 1 CM Diamond

My eyes latched onto the last item. *It was there!*

"Give me the Diamond," I told him. I'll distract the Kenchee by running away from town with it. The Darken should follow, right? Then, I'll help you bury your town, properly." My last words sobered what I thought was actually a pretty genius idea.

The mad nodded, "Here." In his hand, he extended a glowing, turquoise CM Diamond. Somehow, even just seeing it made everything within me buzz.

[System Alert: RAINER, NOMAD 9 Has Gifted You 1 CM DIAMOND. Will You Accept?]
[Yes] [No]

"Yes," I breathed as wind from the object warmed my cheeks and blew my hair back.

[System Alert: 1 CM DIAMOND Acquired, +10 XP 646/700. Object Will Be Placed In Your Inventory Unless You'd Like To Equip. Would You Like To Equip?]
[Yes] [No]

"Yes, Equip," I told the system again.

[System Alert: Object Equipped.]

The CM Diamond flew, spinning to my hand, floating above it. When I moved my palm, the hovering Diamond moved with it. *Cool. Now time for the show.* I thrust the Diamond up towards the sky.

"See this? You see this, you awful terrible birds?!" I screamed as loudly as I could, my voice scraping up my throat.

The Kenchee's rotting necks snapped towards me—*well, towards the magic.* But I didn't wait for them. Holding my breath, I swiveled on my heel and dove into the underbrush—

"Careful!" Rainer called after me.

But the air rushing by my face and my heartbeat ricocheting in my ears blurred out any other sounds. *If I could just lead them far enough away—*

Caw!

Something dove at me: black wings, diseased flesh, foul smell. Oily feathers brushed against my neck and face as a sharp beak missed, stabbing over my shoulder—

"Ew! *Off!*" My hands threw the bird as hard as I could downward.

[KENCHEE, UNDEAD 4: -1 HP 57/58]

Where was my sword? My fingers fumbled at my belt.

[System Reward: You Successfully Dodged A Kenchee Attack +2 XP 648/700]

+2 XP for almost getting pecked to death? Where the fuck was my sword?!

"System, equip my mother's broadsword!" I yelled. The system beeped.

[System Understands Query...Loading Response...]
[System Alert: Weapon Equipped.]

The heavy blade appeared in my other hand. I swung it around me like the tip was a barricade against the squawking ball of feathers rolling around in the ferns, attempting to get its spindly feet under it. *The bird was bigger than a cat. I didn't know why the Grand Dragon had been so bent out of shape about killing creatures like this; these things were parasites—*

I sprinted around it. I expected my long strides to give me some headway but—

My right leg hit air instead of earth. I pitched forward—*fuck of fucks!*

Brown.

Green.

Fern leaves and dirt blurred in my vision as I rolled down a steep incline.

Pain.

[-1HP 59/62]

Exploding—body complaining...

[-1HP 58/62]
[-1HP 57/62]

Shit, if I broke something from a dumb misstep—

"Ouch!" I griped as my back hit the solid form of a tree, and I rolled to a stop next to some gnarly-looking rocks. My hand flew to massage my back, but I still had the stupid CM Diamond attached to it. A system pop-up fizzled into my vision:

[System Query: It Appears You Would Like To Discard 1 CM DIAMOND. Would You Like To Discard?]
[Yes, Discard] [No, Place In Inventory]

Discard? Leave the CM Diamond here? My eyes traced the slope all the way back up. This, honestly, was the perfect spot. The Kenchee would swarm. The Darken would stumble into the ravine if they even got close, which would give Rainer and I time to bury the bodies.

"Yes, discard," I told it.

An electronic beep sounded as the CM Diamond fell out of my palm and to the ground.

[System Alert: Object Discarded.]

I swallowed, looking at the magic there, bobbing in rays of light only a foot away from my face. It felt…almost bad to leave it—leave its warmth. But I pried myself away like I pried my aching body from the forest floor. As I dragged myself back up the slope, I watched the Kenchee descend on the magic like the plague they were, and I knew the Darken would follow.

Neon words bobbed in front of my eyes.

**[System Reward: Excellent Job Employing A Decoy +10
XP 658/700]**

Mission accomplished. Sort of. We only had a whole town to bury.

***

Rainer and I worked in silence in the still morning as the peaked silhouettes of the town's roofs hung over us like the shadows of the past. Rainer grabbed the head and shoulders of the bodies. I grabbed the feet. And we towed them outside, one by one, onto a grassy field on the outer perimeter of the town, laying them each down with dignity in the tall grass…as our backs ached and our feet complained. We searched every nook and cranny in each house, double-checking wallpapered rooms and unmade beds, making sure we'd found them all. And, when we were sure, Rainer handed me a shovel.

And we dug.

The only metal here was not sharp swords, digging into flesh, but the blades of our shovels, meeting dirt. Over and over. In a rhythm. And, although my shoulders pinched and my back complained, there was something soothing about doing the right thing…even when it was finally doing it. …And helping a friend.

Rainer didn't talk, and I didn't push him.

Not as we eased the bodies into the holes.

Not as we covered them with mounds of earth, carefully piling it on and over flesh.

When we did finish, he opened his mouth.

"I don't have any flowers or anything to adorn the graves with," he told me sadly. "The Darken trampled our gardens."

But I had something better than flowers. I took a deep breath and closed my eyes, attempting to dig into the recesses of my mind and remember the words to cast the spell.

"Ift Wilbafound," I whispered.

[System Alert: FIND THINGS HOPELESSLY LOST HOCUS POCUS Used]
[-1 HP, 56/53]

That was it. My eyes shot open to see flowers, floating up from places they'd been discarded through the town and drifting towards me. *The Darken hadn't trampled ALL the flowers…*

The petals coasted downward, one coming to rest on the crest of every burial place.

"*It's beautiful,*" the burly Nomad murmured. I looked up to realize that his face was different. Its creased folds were smoothed out in a calm sort of acceptance. "It's what they would have wanted," he amended, "I know this is just a side mission and not reality but…*thank you.*" There was such gratitude in his eyes as he turned to me. …And there was, also, an electronic beep. I watched a system message appear over Rainer's head.

[RAINER, NOMAD 9: System Alert: Honor and Respect Attained. Side Mission Objective Completed. Victory Established. +30 XP, 1020/1000]
[RAINER, NOMAD 10: System Alert: ***Congratulations, You've Won The Side Mission!*]**

Rainer's stats populated, as did a Level Up, and I watched him accept the system reward. …But I knew what came next. I steeled myself. I stood there patiently as Rainer's world disintegrated in front of my eyes. Replaced by—

Welcome Back ROSABELLA, GAME MAKER 7 & RAINER, NOMAD 10 To The Game

WHAT????

Callen was in my face, shaking me, squatting down to peer into my blinking eyes, "Rosabella? Are you there?!"

And, as I watched, something hit him in the back—an arrow?

[CALLEN, TRADER 10: -75 HP 7/100]

I saw the shaft quivering from over his shoulder as he slumped towards me, shock and confusion on his face.

"Callen, no!" *Was that Joy's scream from somewhere to the side?*

I tried to swivel my head to see, but Callen's face was so close, his fingers clutching both my arms…

As crimson blood dripped from his mouth.

"Rosabella," he mouthed, gurgling, his eyes glossing over as more blood came up and down his chin. He gasped for breath, "Save us all."

Rosabella

What could I do?

What could I DO?!

Callen slumped forward, the entire weight of his suddenly ridged body pressing into my chest, his head lolling on my shoulder. I felt his blood seeping into the fabric of my body armor and saw the feathered arrow shaft anchored in his back, bobbing up and down. Oh, God, I was gonna be sick.

"Callen?" I tried, shoving him backwards as panic and desperation laced my voice tighter than an ice skate. "Listen, Callen," I grasped his waning face between both of my hands, trying to get his wandering, glossing-over eyes to focus on me. My hands left red fingerprints on his white flesh from blood I didn't know was there. Neon letters popped over his head, indicating just how much red there was:

[CALLEN, TRADER 10: -3 HP 4/100]

"Callen," I prodded him, "you have to be okay—I *need you*."

"We need *YOU*," the man whispered; his voice was so grating and faint that I had to nearly press my ear to his forehead to hear it.

Tears welled up in my eyes.

No.

NO! The man was the one person in the group who understood how hard it was to be me—to have to shoulder everything my parents unknowingly left behind:

The truth of Goran's treachery—

My own magic—

…He got the internal struggle. He'd sat outside my bathroom door in NYC and patiently waited for me to figure everything out.

[System Searching MRPs To Select & Display Correct Memory...]

My eyes brimmed with tears as the memory took me under.

My hand swiveled the cold doorknob, and the door creaked open, displaying Callen's brow wrinkled in concern as he hunched over his knees on the side of the bed, pausing in rubbing his hands together. He looked…as troubled as I felt.

"Hey there, kid," he started with a half-hearted smile, "You okay?"

. . .

"Callen, tell me this," I began tersely, "you let me go? Why? I'm the only one who can fix your world, right? The Last Game Maker."

…He looked down at his feet for the briefest minute as his voice cracked, but I caught it, "Well, the system offered you a way out, and I thought—damn, if I was her, I'd take it. I'd take it and run. I wanted you to have a chance at normal life again—if you wanted one."

My throat was thick. My desperate eyes racked over his face. He'd been there to offer me a way out when no one else had even presented that as an option, and I was…I was grateful to him.

"Callen, please," I begged, sobbing even as I tried to hold back the crashing emotions.

I heard Joy running across the balcony to get to us, each thud of her boots a muffled boom.

I heard Dormouse take a sharp breath in over me.

—Saw the ends of Joy's pink hair and Rainer's pricklish beard as they both leaned over us.

But none of it was important in this moment.

Only Callen's beseeching eyes.

Only the number decreasing over the man's head:

[CALLEN, TRADER 10: -2 HP 2/100]

"Use the Creator Magic," he wheezed, "Save everyone…just not me." And the edge of his lips curled up in a little, sad humor at the comment.

No. No, I wouldn't accept it—

"System—system, use the Eraser Magic Object thing!" I commanded. "Equip it—whatever. Erase the arrow in his back," I begged.

[System Understands Query…Loading Response…]

I held my breath.

[System Query: System Understands That You'd Like To Use The ERASER OF NONENESS To Delete The Arrow In CALLEN, TRADER 10's Back? Is This Correct?]
[Yes] [No]

"Rosabella, don't!" Joy yelled, "He's bleeding out. If you delete the arrow, the blood only flow faster."

No, no, no. I had to try to do something. I had to—

Joy reached out and selected 'no' from the system prompt. The system beeped. My chest shuttered as more blood flowed. *I couldn't stop it. I couldn't stop this…*

[CALLEN, TRADER 10: -2 HP 0/100]

[GREATBERD, NOMAD 17: System Reward: CALLEN, TRADER 10 Eliminated +15 XP, 1756/1800]

The light leaked out of the man's eyes. His gray head became heavy in my hands. And tears blurred what was left of my vision. *Target eliminated? The same message that'd came up when I'd killed a Snargel and a Kenchee and—* But death looked so different now. *No. This couldn't be happening—*

"Callen—" I tried to shake him—to wake him—"*Callen?!*"

Rainer put a warning hand on my arm, "Rosabella, he's…"

But not even the burly Nomad could say it.

I'll admit, I dropped the gray-haired man. I let go and scurried backwards, hugging my knees to my chest in the shadow of the temple roof overhang—away from his lifeless body. Like, if I moved quickly enough, death couldn't get me too. And Callen pitched forward—

But Joy stopped him from faceplanting. With a swift movement, she broke off the arrow from his back. "Fucking barbarians," she swore with a heated glance over the ravine as she turned Callen's body to lay on its back. Her fingers grazed over his eyelids, shutting them with a gentleness I didn't know the girl fully possessed. But her face was hard and streaked with pain. I noticed, for the first time, the arrow jutting out of her own shoulder.

"Oh my God, Joy!" I reached up to gesture at the arrow, but she shrugged.

"Like I told you, never remove an arrow from the wound; you might bleed to death," she lectured Dormouse and I swiftly. I glanced over and noticed the nerd's face was even whiter than the balcony floor. My body felt numb from grief. Like I could barely lift my limbs or process what was happening—like everything was in slow motion. *…Except, we didn't have time for grief or slow motion.*

"Rosabella," the pink-haired girl turned swiftly to me, "You need to do something. Use the Creator Magic. Heal the damage in our world. Make it work. There's an army out there on the ridge. I'm a damn good Warrior, but I'm not *fucking Houdini*, and we're gonna need a lot more than a white rabbit to get through this."

I gritted my teeth, hoping I could do what she was asking, "Understood."

"I'll cover your back," Rainer promised both Joy and I, his head swiveling between the both of us.

...And, then, we all looked at Dormouse who seemed frozen in both fear and uncertainty.

"Nerd," Joy called shortly, "Do what you do best."

The dark-haired boy nodded shortly, ducking as a volley of arrows whooshed overhead again, plinking on the metal roof like the jab of a thousand needles.

"The bridges are the only pedestrian way over from the other side," the geeky boy began rapidly, "I'll take them out with my code, but I'm going to need constant concentration—"

Rainer nodded, "You got it. Joy, positions." He drew his bow, tight, lowering to one knee and aiming at the opposing ridge with one eye shut. "We take out anyone who tries to cross the bridges and give Rosabella enough time to figure out the Creator Magic to fix this," he growled.

Gulp. Why did this fucking sound familiar? All the weight was on me...again? But—then again—I'd rather not end up like Callen today. The tears had barely dried on my cheeks even though a night wind was kicking up from the valley. Across it, in the dark, it looked like the forest on the other side of the chasm was alive—figures darting, the dark silhouettes of trees and bushes, moving. ...And the glinting of metal and skin and death...advancing on us all while the twinkling stars overhead left little in the way of light to mark our targets. *Why were they coming after us when all we were trying to do was fix The Game?*

"Rosabella!"

I spun around. It was Joy's harsh voice, and her expression was harsher as I met it. "No deer-in-the-headlights, more Creator Magic. You'll be the reason we live or die today. Make sure we live," Joy snarled. The inflection in her voice traveled up my arms in goosebumps. *She was right. What was I doing standing here bemoaning things? I had to move. I had to fight!*

The Creator Magic.

I wedged myself against the back wall, under the cover of the roof ledge, pressing my back to the firm stone there as another volley of arrows clattered on the metal overhead.

"There's too many of them!" Joy shouted to Rainer over the hailing noise, "We need to focus on the ones in front—"

The panic in her words wanted so desperately to seep into me—into my shaking breaths and hands…into the sweat on my forehead and the dryness of my mouth. But I couldn't let it.

I needed to figure out how to harness this Creator Magic. NOW.

I had to save The Game world and, hopefully, us.

My heartbeat crashed against the inside of my chest repetitively as I carefully closed my eyes.

Breathe. I could do this—could I do this? I pushed down the utter terror. And, when I did, a door in my mind stood tall before me:

Brown.

Arched.

And I grabbed the wrought iron hand and opened it.

Quiet.

The world was silent.

No more panicked shouts or war cries. No more zinging arrows just…

…

Still.

Stagnant. …*What was this place?*

469

I was in my bare feet. Grass tickled the exposed soles, poking and prodding like wanting me to move forward. But my eyes flashed up from my toes. I blinked, turning my head to look around and finding an extensive...garden?

Everything was lush, green and full. Ivy climbed up the hedge walls enclosing the space and plush grass stretched ahead like carpet. Mature trees and blossoming flowers crowded the way forward, layering over the paths that seem to be cut through the garden. The sweet scent of buttercups and honeysuckle tickled my nose. This place would be the perfect sanctuary if my mind would allow me to have any. ...Because the nagging realization was there again: I had to figure out how to use my Creator Magic to fix The Game world. I had to save us all.

Shit.

My feet picked up speed as I brushed past lilies sagging with rainwater and ornamental grass. *What was this place, and what was I supposed to find here? The Grand Dragon, before, had told me that the starlike orb was my soul. Maybe I was looking for something similar here...?*

Ouch!

Blinding light suddenly caught my pupils, then, faded, just as quickly. I swiveled in the direction it came from to find a purple flower...glowing on a nearby bush... No, the flower was holding a star at the very center! Its delicate petals fluttered in the wind under the glow.

I moved towards it, and I felt the breeze too—it was coming from the star. It blew my hair back from my neck, and I, suddenly, wanted nothing more than to touch the brilliance. Because, somehow, I knew that it would envelop me in warmth. And I needed that warmth; I'd been looking for it—longing for it my whole life. I needed to know if I could have it—if I could feel it here...finally.

I stretched my hand out. My fingertips wobbled just above the glowing orb—

[System Query: Would You Like To Try To Touch The Star Orb?]

Did the system read minds? Yes, yes, I wanted to.

Heat zapped through my fingers—up my arms—as the star absorbed into my hand.

[System Reward: Secret Unlocked 1/5 +20 XP 678/700]
[Portal Activated.]
[System Processing Location Transfer...]

What the heck did that mean? The star was a portal? I blinked.

And the sound of gurgling, rushing water met my ears as water droplets splashed up onto my hands. I was standing next to a fountain? The scenery had changed. My eyes took a minute to adjust. I stood in the center of a clearing within the garden—tall hedges, blooming with ivy created an alcove which their colorful cousins filled: beautiful flowers of every type. I leaned against the stone sides of a round, ornate fountain. The water inside was crystal, turquoise blue, and copper pennies shone at the bottom, glinting in the sun up above.

But that wasn't the most startling thing—not the shift in landscape.

Not the fountain.

My heart stopped and my breath hitched because, from the other side of the fountain, a girl stared at me.

And that girl...

Well...

She looked exactly like me...

Rosabella

What the fuck??? Something must have been wrong with my eyes. There *had* to be something wrong with my eyes unless this place was a mirror or something. But I knew, suddenly and clearly, that that wasn't the case just by looking at the girl…at the other me.

We were wearing different things. I was still dressed in my body armor and the other girl donned a white, flowing jumpsuit—almost bright-looking against the foggy-green garden landscape around us. We shared the same eyes, but hers were clearer than mine. And the same chin but hers was lifted higher in confidence. Her hair was the same deep brown but longer and smoother. Her skin was smooth too, creamy white—or, maybe, it was just her expression: calm… no, *serene* without the edge of fear or question.

This was trippy—like a dream…but it was real if I was experiencing it in The Game while trying to use my CM, wasn't it? Who was this girl? I was getting icy deja vu from when I'd found out my dad was a twin…

The garden around us glowed in an ethereal light. Soft waves of sun warmed my cheeks and the scene around me. The splendor of the blooming bushes and trees and the gurgling of the ornate fountain created a Garden of Eden picture. This place was…*perfect*, like the girl standing just a few paces away. In that moment, I wasn't so sure that an arrow just hadn't hit *me*, and I was in some sort of Heaven.

"…Are you my twin?" I whispered at the girl, allowing my fingers to trace the rounded edge of the stone fountain as I took a few steps forward and around it.

She shook her head.

No.

Of course, we couldn't be twins; she looked, somehow, older.

"You know who I am," she breathed, standing still even as I approached with slow steps.

But she was wrong. I was lost. I really had no idea—

Grand Dragon, I started, silently praying in my mind, *If you're there, can you help me find the Creator Magic—*

[Draconic Telepathy Used… +1 XP, 679/700]

"The Grand Dragon sent me to help you," second me said smoothly.

Second me….that was it! Could the girl be me just…a future version of me? My future? My eyes widened as I stared at her with renewed respect and understanding and, as though she could read my thoughts like a book, she nodded.

And I'd never been more sure in my life.

She was me.

She was the *real* me—*who I was becoming.*

[System Reward: Secret Unlocked 2/5 +20 XP 699/700]

A sly smile slid onto second me's lips, curling them upward. "We made it to CM 20," she admitted.

CM 20? Like 20/20? I marveled at her words for a minute as a smile broke open my lips, "Of course we did," I told her—*myself?*—"*Of course, we fucking did.*"

She chuckled.

But my core sobered quickly. Because I suddenly *really needed to know*. More than anything, I needed to understand if what I thought I saw in her glassy eyes could be true—

"There's no more pain?" I blurted before I'd registered that I was going to, "*You don't feel any more pain?*"

And I held my breath.

Till she shook her head.

No? No more pain? I could barely breathe at the concept. *How was that even possible?* My heart had hurt for longer than I could recall—first from the moving around and the lack of money, then, the Goran debacle…finding out my father was murdered by his twin brother and my mom's death was an accident that—*that he lied about forever?! Lied to my face.*

It was a dull ache in my chest. …Sometimes, so tight I could barely breathe.

What would it feel like if that wasn't there? Would it be a hole which would just consume me or…or could I breathe again, freely? *Live* again? Without weight? Weightless? Guiltless? *What would it be like to feel like Goran had never even existed in my life?*

I blinked at the girl—at second me. I could see she was being patient, but her eyes were bright and intelligent, quickly scanning my face. "Do you want to find out?" she asked, reaching a hand out towards me.

I jolted back from my thoughts at her voice, feeling my cheeks flush as I realized I didn't know what she was asking about, "Err, find out what?"

"What it feels like"—her voice was so calm and soothing—"*Not to hurt.* To stand in your power."

My heartbeat lit my chest. My body froze as the system prompt appeared—

[System Query: She's Waiting For Your Answer. Would You Like To Feel What It Feels Like Without The Pain?]
[Yes] [No]

"*Yes*"—I could barely choke the word out, stumbling all over myself and, suddenly, feeling like a preschooler—"Yes, *I want to know.*"

[System Reward: You Just Jumped Into The Deep End Without Training Wheels. Way To Be Brave! +5 XP 704/700]

My throat went dry at the words there—*shit, what did that mean?! Was this the wrong choice?* But the world froze. I panicked before I realized it was only a Level Up.

[System Alert: ***Congratulations, You've Advanced To Level 8!***]

Name	Rosabella
Class & Level	Game Maker 8
XP	704/800
MRP	3795/6209
HP	65/71
Baddie Points	90
Armor Class 15/20	

ABILITIES /20		
Strength	+1	12
Agility	+0	10
Endurance	+0	11
Intelligence	+1	13
Awareness	+1	12
Presence	+3	16
CM		4

[+9 HP & HP Extended By 9, 65/71. You've Been Awarded The Ability To Select One Of The Following Extras:]
[+500 Baddie Points] [Increase AC To 15/20]

Yes! I'd reached the level I needed to save The Game world! I looked at the options. Not so great this time. My AC was already at 15. It was kind of rewarding to see my 4 CM Diamonds recorded though.

[Please Select Which Extra You'd Like.]

"System, select +500 Baddie Points" I said. *Maybe they'd help me later somewhere anyway…*

[System Alert: +500 Baddie Points Selected, 590]

The world unfroze, and I noticed the second me reaching out towards me, "Take my hand then." *Oh, I'd forgotten. She was going to show me what it felt like with no pain…*

Her skin looked soft and smooth—*if I survived here, I should ask her what bodywash we'd been using. …That was a stupid thought. Take her hand!* I told myself. *There was only so much time!*

With trembling fingers, I extended my arm too. And our skin met.

And there was a zap of energy—

And I looked down to see—

Whoa. I was her.

I was in the white jumpsuit—no body armor.

Her luscious locks now trailed down my shoulders and my heart felt—

God, my heart felt…

…Healed.

There was a lightness in my chest—a levity which nearly glowed. And, she was right, there was no pain—*anywhere*. My body—*her body?*—felt energized and calm. And I, suddenly, realized I could do *anything* from this state. I could literally command armies in the darkest battle and *still be okay—*

[System Reward: Secret Unlocked 3/5 +20 XP 724/800]

Wait… That might be what I had to do next: command armies… Normally, my stomach would have dropped and twisted, but, now, I just felt my arms jittering at the thought—a strange, moving energy, but nothing sickening like before.

I glanced up. It appeared we'd done a bit of a Freaky Friday dance because old me stood only a few feet away, blinking at me from the side of the still-gurgling fountain.

"You are ready," she said simply, "but don't be fooled; this isn't the hard part. Your fight is just beginning, but you hold the power, now, to fight it. It's in here." Old me stepped forward, placing a hand on my heart. I could feel the warmth of her skin through the thin fabric of the jumpsuit. She nodded at me, and, with her nod, vines began to sprout from the grass near my feet. They snaked up my legs, to my arms—

What was it—?

Around my wrists securely.

Tightening around my ankles—*noooooooooooo!*

I tried to yank free, but the green cords were thick and strong. They squeezed harder at my skin as my heart leapt into panic-mode—

"*Hey!*" I shouted at the girl who had turned and was walking slowly away from me, her—*my?*—brown hair swishing down her back, "*Hey! What the heck?!* Get me out of this—"

"You are ready," she called over her shoulder, "Good luck."

What—?

What the FUCK was wrong with her? Good luck?! I wouldn't need luck if she didn't trap me in these vines! New me was really uncool. Fuck, I didn't even want to be her anymore—GET ME OUT OF THIS! I tugged against the plant, but it was strangely strong—

Think, child. Calm yourself.

I stopped thrashing against the tightening vines for the briefest second. *That voice! It was—the Grand Dragon?!*

Yes.

It confirmed, booming in my mind.

She is right, you are ready. This is meant for you; don't fight it. Look inside. You have everything you need.

The beast's voice was so soothing, but it would be more so if I'd actually thought it was telling the truth. *I had everything I needed?* I looked down at my open palms, firmly secured at the wrist by wrapping, snarled vines. *I had everything I needed?!...But, then, again, who was I to contradict the grand beast?*

With an annoyed huff of a breath, I closed my eyes. The lush garden around me faded to black and, instead, I saw myself standing in that darkness, in my mind.

And the vines were there.

But...

I felt my forehead crinkle up as I stared at their source. The vines were no longer coming from the ground...They were coming *from me*, sprouting out from my ankles. They were...*I was trapping myself?*

The realization hit me like a dump truck of bricks, and my body instantly relaxed. *If I was trapping myself, I just had to stop...*

The vines...

They slithered off.

...If I was controlling them, could I...???

I used the force of my mind to make the right strand rear up—pushing energy towards it. The vine obeyed, snaking upward. I threw that same energy forward.

Snap!

The vine attacked the air like a viper...*just like I'd wanted!*

478

[-25 CMP 375/400]
[CMP Fully Activated. Congratulations, ROSABELLA,
GAME MAKER 8.]

CMP? I didn't think I'd seen that stat before.

"System, what is CMP?" I asked, hoping it'd still hear me in this dream of a dream.

[System Understands Query...Loading Response...]
[System Answer: CMP, Creator Magic Points, Is A Magic
Meter Which Indicates How Much Creator Magic You
Can Use In A Given Timeframe When Not Using Spells. It
Is Based On CM Ability Points. For Example, Possessing 3
CM Diamonds Equates To 3/20 CM Ability Points And
300 Available CMP, Meaning That You Have 300 Points
Available For Use Until You Need A Long Rest To
Recharge Your CMP To Full Again.]

Whoa. That was a lot but... The joy of using the magic coursed through me in excited, shivering tingles. *This was insane! What else could I make???!*

A unicorn! A unicorn popped into my head, so that was what I focused on. Immediately, I heard a whinny and a beautiful, pearl-white stallion trotted into view, its hooves making splashing sounds in the dark backdrop. It shook its silken mane, and I realized that there was a horn there! *There was a horn in the middle of its head!!!*

[-50 CMP 325/400]

...Oh, damn, the unicorn had cost me 50 CMP? I'd better save the magic for saving The Game world. I guessed it only repopulated after a long rest whatever that meant?

The unicorn's hooves clicked as it stepped towards me, nuzzling my shoulder. And the contours of its huge face slid through my hands as I absent-mindedly stroked its velvet-soft skin and ran my fingers through its silky mane. I began braiding the hair there, chewing on the inside of my lip.

I'd done something here. I'd unlocked some sort of CM capability with the CMP. I had to get back and save my friends—save The Game world. Shit! I was here braiding pony hair when they could be dying— when those monsters across the ridge were decimating everything that my parents loved??? I had to get back!

"How do I get back to where my friends are, on the Temple balcony in The Game?" I bellowed into the surrounding darkness, hoping the Grand Dragon could hear me. "…Also, is it possible for me to get a 'long rest' before going back?" I squeaked, hoping the request wasn't too much.

I felt it, more than saw it—the Grand Dragon's smile.

I thought you'd never ask.

Joy

Luck had never been enough for me in battle—only skill. Sheer determination, will-to-live and skill had gotten me through more rough patches than I cared to count—more fenced-in corners and backed-between-a-rock-and-a-hard-place moments…

And, yet, here I was facing one again.

Another rush.

Another all-out.

As much as I hated it, *I was born for this shit.*

I gritted my teeth as the wind picked up, as rain began to torrent down, pelting my cheeks. And I stared at the Nomads now rushing the bridge towards the Temple—towards us—swords raised high.

"*I'm going in!*" I screamed.

From behind, Rainer grabbed me by the back of my body armor, swinging my kicking feet off the ground, "Like hell you are—*ooff*—"

That was the sound of me kicking him squarely in the nuts*; he wouldn't try that again.*

[RAINER, NOMAD 10: -1 HP, 150/151]

"*I said,*" I leaned near his face, grabbing his ear and growling into it, "*I'm going in.* It's our only chance, and you know it. Dorkus is taking way too long to destroy the second bridge, and Rosabella's still under…" My gaze flashed to the brunette girl hidden by shadows in the corner. Her eyes were still milky white. *All this was taking too long. Shouldn't she be equipped to perform the Creator Magic by now? Shouldn't the nerd be able to take out the bridges faster?* We'd watched him puncture a hole in the first; it was now crumbled into a pile of rubble in the dark valley below, but the second and third bridges still stood. A few gutsy warriors had made it almost three quarters of the way over the bridge with their sprinting war cries and outstretched weapons before Rainer or I could take them out by bow.

What if they figured out we were way underpowered and a few of them tried at once? What if they all rushed us? There was only Rainer, Dormouse and I… What if they just rushed a bridge and killed us all? …If three or more made a run for it, one might get through, and I couldn't have that.

Callen was gone. I needed to step up and protect us all. …Our whole world.

Because I really couldn't go back to the other one—I'd rather *die* here.

But the big, ole, teddy-bear-hearted Rainer was proving harder to dissuade than I'd imagined. Even from his bent over, wincing position, he reached for my arm. "Joy, you're hurt," he started, his eyes brimming brown with worry as he stared at the protruding arrow in my shoulder.

I shook my head, tugging my arm free with gentle appreciation, "It's nothing, really."

Just stung like hell. My shoulder was on fire with that hand basically disabled. Whenever I tried to move it, the arrow ripped through more flesh. *I'd had worse before. I could still best these assholes with one hand.* I shook out my good hand in front of me, feeling the rain pelt further at my face.

"What if Dormouse finally takes out the bridge and you're on it?" Rainer shouted around the storm in a last-ditch effort.

I chewed on my bottom lip. *I'd already considered that and was okay with the outcome. As long as Rosabella was safe, we still had a chance…*

"We'll cross that bridge when we get to it…*literally*," I joked sarcastically, reaching to wrench the heavy, wet strands of my pink-hair up into a high ponytail as the rain continued to douse my face, blurring my vision of the bulky man, but only strengthening my resolve.

I was a Warrior.

I got this.

I slung my bow over my bad arm, my eyes ducking towards the quiver also there.

"System, how many arrows do I have left?" I spat, rapid-fire.

[System Understands Query…Loading Response…]

Rainer eyed me warily. "Joy—"

But the system answer popping up cut him off.

[Current Inventory Level Of Long Bow Arrows / JOY, WARRIOR 12: 15/30]

It'd be enough.

"System, equip Dragonblade Broadsword," I commanded. The sword hurled out of my belt and into my hands with a swishing noise.

[Weapon Equipped]

I narrowed my eyes as I looked into the deluge and saw nothing but hopelessness and blood up ahead. *That was my bus. Time to go.* I took off at a brisk trot into the darkness, letting my hair whip out behind me—

"*Joy!*"

Rainer's voice again? I whipped around; *what did the guy want?!* I glared at him through the sheeting rain. Even this close, his form was blurred by the storm.

"Thank you!" he yelled back, his deep voice as sincere as they came. It—

It *surprised me.*

Caused a lump in my throat which I, instantly, shoved downward.

[System Reward: Damn, You've Just Wowed The Hell Out Of Your Friend With Your Selfless Move +10 1297/1300]

"Don't thank me yet," I whispered under my breath and only loud enough for me to hear. I turned again and faced the end of the first bridge and the dark horizon. *Here went nothing.*

Swallowing, I broke out into a gallop, my sword raised high in front of me. The firm, wood plank floor of the bridge clunked under every thud of my boots, matching my thundering heart. Each running step jostled my wounded shoulder so that I had to bite down on my lip to stop myself from crying out. The copper taste of blood filled my mouth but, worse, the stench of smoke filled my nostrils. My HP popped into view like a reminder to slow down, but I wasn't heeding that shit.

[-1 HP 89/172]

My feet trotted to the center of the bridge as my chin tilted up, and I suddenly felt smaller than an ant.

Tiny.

On that bridge.

Looking up.

Because, over me, in the sky, I heard a roar—saw the swish of an enormous tail slice through a cloud bigger than a cruise ship. And heard the whoosh and flap of leathery wings.

Dragons? They had dragons?

…We were so fucked.

A beast's sharp cry overhead cemented my fears, and heat washed over my frame even in this wet rain.

Fire.

[-2 HP 87/172]

I was prepared. I'd trained for shit like this. Breathless, I rolled forward, out of the blaze. I heard the flames crackling and snapping behind me, consuming the bridge where I'd stood only seconds ago—*and there went my escape route… Perfect…ly terrible.*

The only way to go was forward—

"*Argh!*" A male cry. I felt air brush along the back of my neck—*movement behind me?* My instincts cracked into immediate gear. I swirled around, bringing my sword up with all my strength.

[-2 HP 85/172]

Clang.

Metal hit metal as my sword clashed with his even larger one.

I was right. The asshole had been aiming for a clean run through. Not on my watch.

I heaved all my weight against the weapon, trying to slide my blade up towards his throat, but he was a big guy—your typical West Side brute: A-Z muscle mass covered in drenched furs, the remainder of the heavy camouflage they wore….and black eyes reflecting an ego as big as Texas. He grinned at me, his eyes perusing my form.

"A little lady," he purred, his teeth showing gaps I'd like to make larger for him, "Sure you can handle such a big sword?"

I clenched my jaw. Couldn't they all come up with something else to ask me? The recurring question was more than insulting at this point…

"Sure you can?" I countered. Searching for every inch of determination in me, I reached up with my injured arm, grabbing the tip of his blade with the flat of my palm. One shove of that arm—pain ripping through my shoulder—and my blade was free. I thrust the metal deep into his skull, watching both of our HP take a hit.

[-4 HP 81/172]
[RUTHMOORE, NOMAD 9: -90 HP 0/90]

The big man fell.
In shock.
To his knees.
They always did.

[System Reward: RUTHMOORE, NOMAD 9 Eliminated
+15 XP, 1312/1400]

The world slowed to stationary. Green plus marks spiraled upward from the ground. The Level Up gave me time to look ahead, sizing up three more Nomads who were frozen, racing towards me. *Rainer's Class was royally pissing me off.*

[System Alert: ***Congratulations, You've Advanced To
Level 13!***]

Name	Joy	
Class & Level	Warrior 13	
XP	1312/1400	
MRP	2009/7306	
HP	91/182	
Baddie Points	2840	
Armor Class 13/20		
ABILITIES /20		
Strength	+3	16
Agility	+3	16
Endurance	+2	15
Intelligence	+1	12
Awareness	+0	9
Presence	+5	20

[+10 HP & HP Extended By 10, 91/182. You've Been Awarded +2 Ability Points. Please Select Which Ability You'd Like To Increase.]

Kind of busy, System. My eyes glossed over the numbers before locking my sword buried in the body—*I needed to yank that out...* I brushed the prompts away.

[System Alert: System Will Cache Additional +2 Ability Points In Your Inventory For Future Application. Inventory Updated.]

The world came back to life as another prompt slid into view. My hands tugged at the hilt of my sword—

[System Reward: You Looked Fantastic Swinging That Sword. Way to Be a Beast +40 Baddie Points, 2880]

System, seriously, leave me alone! I swiped to clear my vision again—
The world went sideways.
Beside me, something exploded—*shit!*
—Rock flying, rubble scratching at the skin of my cheeks.

[-10 HP 81/182]

—Men shouting.
—Dragons bellowing overhead.
The second bridge! The brainiac WAS good for something! Now there was just one more...the one I was standing on...

[RAINER, NOMAD 10: System Reward: NORMAN, NOMAD 7 Eliminated +15 XP, 1035/1100]

An arrow whizzed past my face, thudding into one of the three barbarians flying towards me—*good shot, Rainer!*—but the other two were clearly mine.

I lunged forward, meeting blades.

Metal crashed and zinged in my ears…

My arm *burned* from the effort.

[-3 HP 78/182]

Each thump of my heart matched the hit and cover of each strike. Dust swirled around my face, mixing with rain and smoke—*damn these warriors!*

"*Ughhhh!*" I thrusted.

I cut.

[BREWTON, NOMAD 12: - 50 HP 0/108]
[System Reward: BREWTON, NOMAD 12 Eliminated +15 XP, 1327/1400]

Blood pooled, running red across the wood planks, but, when I looked up, there were more coming. Not just three this time—it was exactly what I'd been worried about.

The entire mob—*the entire army!*

Racing towards me.

One against more than I could count.

Dragons hissed and bellowed overhead. Panic rushed through me as I swung a desperate look back at Rainer.

The burly Nomad waved me back, "*Fall back, Joy! Fall back! There's too many of them!*"

And I had to agree.

My fingers scrabbled for my weapon, closing around the handle. As if I was in slow motion, I scuttled towards the raging fire that was the path back. But there was no way through it. *There was no—*

A sonic boom vibrated the ground.

My ears rung—

The wind kicked up my soaked hair—*an earthquake?*

An—

"Dormouse, *NO!*" I heard Rainer scream, "*Joy's still there!*"

But the rumble always came before the explosion.

The blast threw me.

My body catapulted forward—

Heat—

Fire—

[-30 HP 48/182]

Rocks scraped against me—

Falling—

NO. I would live!

I grabbed for the rocks as I fell—

Any sort of ledge.

But my fingers came up empty…

Rosabella

I gasped, coming back with a start, but the noise—no matter how loud—was barely audible in the deafening, breaking thunder shattering my eardrums. I clapped both hands to my ears, sinking further against the hard temple back wall, feeling it press into my spine. *Oh my God, what was happening? It sounded like the whole world was erupting!*

My eyes adjusted quickly to the smoky blackness. Rain splattered up on an angle from where it pelted the balcony stone dark brown and soggy. Fire climbed into the sky in the valley, making the jagged rocks there glow red in the dark, navy-blue chasm and—

And the three bridges lay in piles of rubble. *Dormouse did it?!*

But elation sizzled out of me like a grill in a deluge as I saw Rainer's frantic, scrabbling form…reaching for something off the edge of the cliff—

My eyes quickly scanned the balcony for Joy, but the pink-haired girl wasn't anywhere to be found. *What happened while I was gone?*

I ran towards the edge of the cliff, not caring as rain battered my face with the force of hail. I squinted down at the craggy ledges of rock there, the ends of my drenched hair falling forward as I leaned—

What—! My breath snagged sharply in my throat.

Because a pale, white hand clutched at the edge of a rock there. And a steep drop lay below the pink-haired girl's swinging legs. I watched as her HP flashed over her head—*damn, if it wasn't MRP, it was something else*—

[JOY, WARRIOR 13: -2 HP 46/182]

Her fingers slipped. Rock beside her crumbled and fell into the chasm below. *She was hurt and barely holding on.* Her face clenched in immeasurable pain as she struggled to hang onto the rock ledge.

Rainer was already on hands and knees, ready to scrabble down the cliff face to reach her. "I'll get her," he assured me gruffly, but it was hard to imagine the burly Nomad being able to do anything without causing some sort of landslide—

"*Wait*," I told him, cutting him off with an urgent hand, "…Let me try something."

And, before I'd assured myself this was the stupidest idea in the world, I took a deep breath, closed my eyes, fell into the blackness there and imagined vines, breaking out of the side of the cliff wall, reaching towards Joy's slipping fingers—

[-25 CMP 300/400]

Crack!

My eyes flew open.

And it wasn't a bad crack; it was a good one. Because, as my eyelashes fluttered open, I realized that the vines I'd created in my mind had come to life! Green sprouts burst forth from the dirt and rock side of the cliff, entwining and getting thicker—stronger. …Reaching like fingers towards Joy's hand as the CMP system update appeared at the corner of my vision to tell me how much magic it took:

[-10 CMP 290/400]

Rainer staggered back. "*Well, I'll be damned...*" he muttered incredulously under his breath.

And a little bit of pride filled me, even in the panic. Because *I'd found it.* I found my Creator Magic even with what felt like two, whole worlds against me; I'd found my *power*, and I was finally standing in it—finally standing firm with something to offer. *...Now, I just had to figure out how to wield it...*

I bit down on my lip, forcing my energy into moving the plant's tendrils towards Joy. I remembered how strong the vines were when they'd been around my arms and legs. *Maybe that would work for me in this case...*

The sturdiest of the vines moved quickly, snaking forward where I wanted it and wrapping around the girl's thin wrist.

[-10 CMP 280/400]

Please, please work, I prayed in my head. *If this failed, I'd drop her.* I imagined her body falling...her screams—*no.* I attempted to cut off the thought in my mind. *I couldn't let that happen—not after Callen. I could do this.* I took a shaking breath and yanked the energy upward with all my might.

[-25 CMP 255/400]

The vine pulled.

Lifting Joy up, over our heads.

And placing her carefully down on the balcony floor, which she quickly crumpled to. Her face was flushed with both relief and adrenaline. I supposed it was how you looked when you were that close to death.

"Thank you," she huffed, coughing and holding her injured arm to her chest, breathing heavily.

…And my eyes widened because…*well, it was the first time I'd heard the girl thank…anyone.* I allowed myself the satisfaction of a smile. *I'd done it! I'd saved her—*

"*Duck!*" Rainer bellowed.

All of us hurried to drop to the ground, flattening out, torsos level with Joy's still heaving face as a dragon's huge shadow passed overhead. I glanced up just long enough to see it opening its mouth, ready to spew fire—

No!

I clamped my eyes closed and imagined a glass ceiling over us—a shield just like Dormouse had programmed during his duel with Maude.

[-25 CMP 230/400]

And I felt heat on my face—

But, when I cracked one eye open, I saw flames leveling out, spreading over an invisible surface…unable to reach us. *This Creator Magic stuff was awesome!*

[-5 CMP 225/400]

My CMP lessened the longer I held the force field?

[-5 CMP 220/400]

Sweat popped onto my forehead from the effort.

[-5 CMP 215/400]

I gritted my teeth—
There.

The dragon passed. I dropped the shield, letting my cheek sink to the cold, rain-soaked ground. *Thank God for rest—for relief.* The icy temperature and the rain still hitting my cheeks felt glorious.

"You okay, Rosabella?" Rainer asked, attempting to tug me upward, but my limbs felt so heavy. *This CM stuff was no joke...*

The Nomad was speaking into my face, his eyes urgent as he ran a troubled hand through his brown hair—*what was he saying?* He helped both me and Joy to our feet, letting us lean against him for support as we moved towards the shelter of the shadow of the Temple. "There's too many of them," he grunted, "If they have dragons, they'll find a way across. We have to get back under cover—"

"Wait."

The word tumbled out of my mouth.

I had to stop Rainer's speech...because I had to stop in general.

And it was because I'd caught sight of him—the only man who could make me stop.

Flat out.

Freeze.

Goran.

He rode an enormous, bronze dragon—sitting, upright, in the saddle confidently, like a king. His chin was held high, and his eyes shone black over streaks of warpaint on his cheeks of the same hue. The massive dragon landed on the edge of the Temple balcony, creating a tiny rockslide as its huge talons clawed into the rocky ledge. The beast waited for the man to dismount, which he did swiftly. The huge creature shook its head, snapping a little in Dormouse's direction and sniggering as the pale-faced boy darted away. The monster perched, flapping its massive wings in the air, whipping my hair back from my scalp as though to further terrify me of the man standing before it. ...But even under all the fur and armor...

It was him.

Goran.

Traitor.

Fake Dad.

My jaw hardened although the rest of me desperately wanted to slink into the shadows someplace and hide.

"Rosabella, you want my help, you have it; you want me to leave, I'll leave it," Rainer mumbled under his breath for my benefit. I nodded, acknowledging him, but waved downward, trying to gesture discretely for him to cool his jets.

"Just give me a minute," I told the Nomad, whispering as I stepped forward and away from the group, towards Goran.

"Make that *30 seconds*," Joy snarled lowly, "What I wouldn't do to run his traitorous ass through—"

"*She said a minute*," Rainer quieted the girl with a hand and a glare.

And they fell a few steps back.

And I was face to face with…

Him.

I could barely look at him. Because part of me still desperately wanted to race to him—to wrap my arms around his middle and bury my face in his shirt like a kid…anything to have those arms of safety and warmth fall over me.

But they were *NOT* arms of safety or warmth.

Those same hands that clenched and unclenched—those same fists—killed my dad…murdered my parents in cold-blood.

For what?

My protection?

I didn't feel protected. I felt lied to. I felt like I hated him. The emotion swirled in my belly, tightening my face and hardening my eyes just like his voice when the man said the one, inevitable thing… When he tried to gloss this all over by just saying my name…

"*Rosie!*" His arms opened wide like he'd hug me if he had the choice.

495

But it just made me want to retreat from him further; he'd murdered the chance of a reunion when I'd found out he'd murdered my parents.

"*What's your problem?*" I spat the words, sounding more immature than I would have liked. "...*What?*" I griped. "You didn't get enough the first go around when you killed my parents, so you have to come here to kill me?"

Goran's face got serious then. His eyes darkened further—if that was possible; they were like jagged shards of coal now. "Rosie, I would never hurt you. Everything I've ever done has been to protect you. Even right now, this—" he spread his arms wide, gesturing at the army on the other side of the chasm, "this is for your protection—"

"*Bullshit!*" I barked, my hands flying out of control in the air around me, "Your side was firing arrows *directly at us!* One of them could have hit me! One of them *killed my friend!*"

Callen.

I swallowed the bitter bile in the back of my throat as I remembered his dead body—still warm in my hands. The life draining out of him.

Why? Why?!

But Goran was chuckling—sneering. His lip curved up in open disdain. "*Friend?*" He scoffed. "Oh, Rosie, what little you know of this world. These people aren't your friends! They used to be Game Wardens! Do you know what Game Wardens did?" His tone was belittling. It made something under my skin squirm. *Was I...wrong? Why did it feel like he was convinced I'd give the incorrect answer here?*

No.

No, I knew what Game Wardens did! Dormouse told me himself, and he'd always been the most honest one from the start. Goran was just trying to twist my thoughts. I was right. I knew I was right.

"Of course, I know what Game Wardens did," I told him, trying to hide the quiver in my voice, "They protected The Game—"

Goran clicked his tongue, cutting me off and shaking his head, "You are so naive, Rosie; it's not your fault, you're so good-hearted...so caring about everyone. You can't see when you're being lied to."

I narrowed my eyes, feeling my insides boil. I clenched both fists at my sides and suddenly wished I'd let Joy deal with the man, "*I know when I'm being lied to.*"

"Then, you know it isn't true," Goran remarked.

What? I suddenly felt lost.

Winded.

Turned around and backwards. *Where was he going with this?*

"*What* isn't true?" I demanded.

"That your merry band of discontinued Game Wardens are here to save The Game," Goran started, "They're not trying to save The Game. They're trying to save their own asses—their power. Their Class, job titles and their status. Without a Game Maker in power who will reinstate them as Wardens, they go back to being Sue and Harry. ...But me. *I'm* the real one trying to save you, Rosie. Because you're worth more to me than any world. I convinced this *entire army* to stand down, so I could talk with you. Stop letting these Game Wardens involve you in their politics. You don't want to be a ruler, a Game Maker. I know you. You want a quiet life, a *safe* life. *I can give you that, Rosie.* I negotiated a deal with the dragon for safe passage—me and you, back to New York. Back to normal life, what do you say?"

Goran stared at me expectantly, but I didn't have an answer for him because...

...Did he say my group of friends wanted me to be...*a ruler?*

Rosabella

A ruler?

…Did Goran just say that the discontinued Game Wardens needed me so they could reinstate their Class, keep their job titles and their power which required…my power? Me? A ruler? I wanted to laugh at the absurdity. I wanted to laugh it off confidently so sure that Goran'd lost his mind and stepped off the deep end here but—

But something hitched in me—doubt?

Definitely my breath.

…Because, for a minute, I wondered, could it be true??? I stood there in the pelting rain, looking at the man who turned my rosy world upside down and…wondering if he was telling me the truth? The guy who'd lied to me my whole life and, yet…I needed to know. Because the discontinued Game Wardens had a knack for only telling me bits of the puzzle at a time…and this seemed like a pretty important piece to have left out up to this point…

"They want me to be a ruler?" I hissed under my breath, taking care to make sure my group was a step out of earshot. A sideways glance at the anxiously milling Joy, Rainer and Dormouse told me they hadn't heard.

But Goran had. His eyes locked on me like a Kenchee's—sniffing out my doubt? As much as I didn't like the man right now, I had to know if he was telling the truth—

"They don't want you to be a ruler. They need you to be," Goran leaned forward, "They're power-hungry sons of bitches. Game Makers are rulers of The Game. Their ability to create makes them law. My brother was always trapped by responsibilities. It's why I had to do something—save you—give you a better life. His responsibilities to The Game were strangling the relationship he had with you. It was disgusting." The man's face grew harder, annoyed, under the dark war paint, "You'd think he'd have made more time for his absolutely perfect wife and daughter—the family I'd always wanted, and he just pushed it to the side—"

"Don't you dare talk about my dad," I growled.

Goran didn't get to sit here and act noble; I didn't want to hear his justified reasons for murder. What he did was irreconcilable; the discontinued Game Wardens were right to want to lock him up in prison but… But was what he was saying…true?

Because, in my MRP, it had looked like my real dad was busy. He'd had to pass me off to Goran. …Was he a ruler?

I couldn't be a ruler—I wasn't that person. I was perfectly content just living a simple life—living, in general, if I could get out alive from this terrible battle. I just wanted to restore order to The Game world—fix it of the darkness and, then, be on my way. I'd just wanted to do right by my parent's legacy but…

If they were expecting me to lead…

The very thought made me want to run and hide in a closet somewhere.

No. I wasn't cut out for it. They were wrong if they thought they can trick me into it. I wouldn't. I'd fix their world, but I wouldn't—

"You understand now," Goran shook his head, his eyes leveling out like there was a conclusion hanging between us that we were both reaching together, "I've taught you since you were little: you can't trust strangers, only me. I always protect you, Rosie—"

"Will you cut it out?!" I snapped. I stared at him.

Because something had snapped inside me, allowing me not to care that I was yelling at the adult that had practically raised me, backed by a skyscraper-tall, bronze dragon.

Because he was a liar. He could tell himself all day that he protected me, but he didn't!

Not when he'd killed my dad.

Not when he'd tried to imprison me in that underground bunker.

He could fool himself, but he could no longer fool me. I was putting my foot down. I refused to lie to myself anymore about this man.

"You don't protect me," I spat. "This army behind you is not protecting me—"

"I can protect you," he countered, insistent and side-stepping my accusations, like typical, "I told you, I can get you and me safe back to New York, away from this shit, for a quiet life together—"

"Would you just stop talking?! …For once!" The words burst out of me—out of my lips.

Just for a minute, I needed to think. I needed him to stop jabbering, so I could figure out what I wanted to do here—who was telling the truth. …What lie I wanted to teeter on…Who could I trust more?

Myself.

The answer came in sharply.

Like a thought.

And a prod: I could fully trust myself.

And it was a strange sort of realization, rushing in all at once. Because, for so long, I'd been unsure of myself—my own direction. I'd had to place my trust in others just to find my way out of the maze of everything and, yet…yet, I couldn't trust them.

I couldn't let them lie to me.

I couldn't take their word as truth till I knew…till I knew for sure. Till I felt it in my gut and I…

I knew the way forward—me!

I could trust myself.

[System Reward: Secret Unlocked 4/5 +20 XP 744/800]

All of a sudden, I was a different person standing there. I stood taller. I held my chin higher—maybe closer to the stance of the second Rosabella from my mind. And my boots were firmly planted in the ground here. Finally, I was standing firmly on both feet. Finally, grounded in what I knew to be true: myself. How I felt about things.

And I wasn't going to tiptoe anymore; I was gonna lay it out bare. The wind kicked up around me, throwing more rain in my face, but I didn't care.

Not anymore.

"You're the one that's full of shit," I said to Goran, quietly at first, "And I don't need your help. I don't *need* protecting. I've done more on my own here than I ever did back in New York and…and I did that all myself. By *myself.*" Saying the words—actually saying them out loud—meant more than I'd thought it would…it held more weight.

Because Goran heard me.

He had to finally hear me in this moment.

And he did.

[System Reward: Way To Stick Up For Yourself +50 XP 794/800]

[System Reward: The Sexiest Girls Are The Ones That Know Their Worth +30 Badie Points, 620]

Thanks, System.

I watched my words soak into his face as his eyebrows raised and his mouth tightened and…well, I didn't know how I'd expected him to react, but it didn't look like he was going to agree with me…

"You're making the wrong choice here, Rosie," he warned, his voice hardening and wavering for the smallest moment—unless I imagined the waver?—"you don't want to do this."

"Yes, I do," I whispered.

Because he was right about one thing; I'd made a choice, and I wouldn't back down now.

I'd trapped a dragon.

I'd negotiated with another. I'd beat an entire swarm of Darken. I'd killed a Snargel, bested the Kenchee, even helped three of my friends navigate side missions… I'd got and activated my CM. And I wasn't going to let the man who'd killed my parents tell me what to do with it. I was going to fix The Game world. And, if it turned out my friends wanted me to be their ruler, they could forget about it. It was like the Grand Dragon had said: I was the Game Maker. I made The Game. I made the rules. I made my life. And I wasn't about to let someone else make those decisions for me.

I had 215/400 CM. I should be able to fight him with that. What spells could I use against him? I'd use every last bit of everything if it took it.

[System Understands Query…Loading Response…]

Thank God the system read minds…

[System Answer: Available Spells Include:]
[NO MORE NOISY NEIGHBORS ABSORPTION HEX]
[FIND THINGS HOPELESSLY LOST HOCUS POCUS]

[VACU-ROCKET]

Beginner spells, but I'd do what I had to—

"Don't make me do this, Rosie. That army just over that ridge will wipe you all out." Goran's tone sounded pleading, but his face was still granite hard.

"Let them try," I barked, taking a step back towards the Game Wardens while attempting not to notice the insane amount of warriors on the other bank. "You don't have to do anything; this is your choice. You can let us go. You stopped them from attacking. …What does the army even want?"

"—Everything to stay the same as it's been since the death of the last Game Maker," Goran hissed, shuffling his feet on the floor of the balcony, "That's why we have to get out of here to keep you safe—"

And I gritted my teeth.

Because there was no more 'we'.

And no more 'safe'.

"I wasn't safe the minute you killed my parents," I sputtered, "You made that decision for me. They're all wrong. The Game can't stay the same way it's been since the death of the last Game Maker because that never happened. I'm the last Game Maker, and I'm alive. I'm the only one who can fix this world. If you take issue with it, you're on the wrong side of this chasm—"

"Argh!"

Goran's frustrated shout.

I flew backwards.

Because something hit me, shattering my core.

[-5 HP 60/71]

My ass slammed into the ground. My spine, followed it, as I blinked upwards at the man, stunned. *What hit me? A dark forcefield?*

A wall of smoke-like blackness swirled between me and where Goran stood like an enormous coiling python. ...And... And it was trailing out of the man's fingertips...well, out of the hand that wasn't squarely in the bronze dragon's mouth. *Magic? He was using the dragon's CM?*

I heard the swish of metal swords draw behind me as I scrambled to my feet. I knew it was Joy and Rainer, running to my aide.

"Oh, you're going down!" Joy bellowed, her eyes sparking like her glinting sword as her pink hair swirled out around her. But I held up an arm to stop the girl's advance—to stop both of them.

"No," I said shortly, drawing up the Creator Magic within me and feeling its satisfying hum reach down through my fingertips, "He's mine."

Rosabella

Goran and I circled each other like eagles in the air, planting our feet on the hard floor of the balcony, readying our hands. *If he could use the dragon's Creator Magic to destroy everything good and fight us, I could use it to do the opposite. I could save us all, just as Callen had said. I had to believe it.*

[System Alert: Dragon Spar Initiated.]
[System Alert: Please Manually Enter Your Battle Song Or
The System Will Sync With Your Mood To Select
Automatically. Allow Automatic System Sync For Battle
Song Selection?]
[Yes, Auto Sync] [No, Manual Selection]

Dragon Spar? Battle song? Hold on—

"What is this?" I whirled around, my eyes locking on Dormouse's white face.

"It's a Dragon Spar—two CM wielder's battling like you saw with Sparo and that purple dragon in the forest. Music is an assertion of dominance. Goran's challenged you, and, somehow, internally you must have accepted. It's the only way one will start. I'd auto sync the battle song by the way," he shouted, running a hand through his wind-tousled hair, "It's just easier—"

"Auto sync," I commanded. What the fuck was I doing? This was so out of my league. I only had baby spells!

[System Auto Sync Initialized...Response Loading]
[System Alert: Survivor by 2WEI Selected As Battle Song...
Waiting for Challenger To Select]

I swallowed nervously, finding my throat almost completely parched—from nerves? Maybe this was a stupid idea...challenging Goran. I'd seen his stats. I knew he knew magic...but, then, again I had to try. I couldn't back down, not when I'd been standing for this long. Finally, here was my chance—my chance to prove I wasn't weak.

[GORAN, PRISONER 11: System Alert: Not Afraid by
Eminem Selected As Battle Song]
[Begin Spar]

Both of the songs clashed in the air—each biting thread of their melody like a cry against the other. Except my song had a softer intro as Goran's loomed, threateningly in the air. His dark eyes stared at me as the rap music seemed to tear through the oxygen in my lungs.

But I wouldn't blink. I wouldn't be intimidated.

"System, *turn up the volume for my song,*" I spat.

[System Understands Query...Loading Response...]
[System Alert: +5 Volume Of Battle Song]

I closed my eyes, allowing the thrumming music to swell within me and attempting to focus there. And I readied my own magic—

Hiss.

My eyes flew open as an enormous snake slithered out of Goran's fingers—made of his dragon's magic. Its charcoal-black form shimmered in the air, swimming massive coils towards me, blinking slitted, ruby-red eyes. Its jaw unhinged with a hissing snarl, displaying rows of thin, razor-edged fangs... *Oh God. Could magic...bite me?* The unicorn I'd created before had felt real... *I didn't want to wait around and find out!*

I dove inwards, summoning my CM, balling it into my hands and fists—

"Rosie, I told you I don't want to hurt you," Goran insisted, interrupting my concentration behind closed eyelids so that I was forced to open them again. When I did, I saw his hands shaping the black magic like a puppeteer, slithering the reptile forward, towards me, "The venom in this snake's teeth is a sedative. It'll knock you out, not kill you, and I'll take you back to NYC with me like you should have agreed to in the first place—"

The giant snake reared its head, lunging for me. I felt it's hot breath on my forehead even as I brought my hands up to protect my face, clamping my eyes shut for the inevitable—*no! ...That was when I got the strangest idea—*

"*Shirtaloon Mufalato!*" I bellowed desperately into the snake's face—

[System Alert: NO MORE NOISY NEIGHBORS
ABSORPTION HEX Used]
[-1 HP, 59/71]

I felt magic spiral out of my fingers. The black behind my squeezed-closed eyelids glowed yellow. Something scratched against my palms—

Snap. The beast's fangs came together with a scream but—

My face...

My face was...*okay...???*

I opened my eyes, wincing like there would be pain even though I didn't feel anything. Instead, something jumped, jubilant, inside of me. —*What? Did I do it?!*

The snake was held captive by the massive, corrugated sponge my spell had created—its teeth stuck in the holes. The yellow sponge stuck firmly to the roof of its mouth. The animal tried to shake it off, but couldn't do anything with a sponge stuffed in its fangs. Squirming and writhing in annoyance, the thing danced around in the air completely harmless.

[System Reward: Successful Spell! You Showed That Snake! +5 XP 799/800]

Breathless, I stifled a chuckle, but the smile still got through. I DID do it. This was hilarious: L1 Spell met real life circumstance that had nothing to do with muffling noise—

"You think this is funny?!" Goran spat, frustration lining his face, "Creator magic is not something to play around with—"

He whipped a dagger out of his belt, chucking it at the head of the snake, seeming to want to put it out of its misery...or use it as a dartboard for his. The throw wasn't aimed at me, but I was having too much fun showing off.

"Shirtaloon Mufalato!" I cast again.

[System Alert: NO MORE NOISY NEIGHBORS ABSORPTION HEX Used]
[-1 HP, 58/71]

I wiggled my fingers in the air, engorging the sponge so that it all but engulfed the knife as well as the snake.

"—Says the man who broke the world playing around with Creator Magic," I threw back, proud of my snarky retort. I raised a determined eyebrow, trying to steady my breath and bracing myself for another attack. "I wouldn't *have* to use CM this way at all if you'd leave me and my friends alone while I fix The Game—"

"That's *not going to happen*." Goran clenched his jaw and threw his arms out at me. "*Fontanous Windomagno!*" he yelled.

Oh shit. All of the bravo drained out of me quick.

[GORAN, PRISONER 11: System Alert: WIND FUNNEL OF
DEATH Used]
[GORAN, PRISONER 11: -4 HP, 20/117]

All of a sudden, sand stung my eyes and a windstorm kicked up my hair, thrashing it around my head. I tried to gasp in air, but found it clogged with rough particles that scratched at my throat and nose. I coughed, hacking—

[-1 HP, 57/71]

It was his magic!

[-1 HP, 56/71]

I couldn't open my eyes to see it, but I knew it. *Think, Rosabella, I* told myself, *What would get rid of a sandstorm? What spells could I use?* I clamped my eyes shut and tried to ignore the howl of the wind and the pain in my eyes as I struggled to tap into the Creator Magic again, so I could remember the words to initiate the magic…

"Goodbye Messafuss!" I recited. *It was the first time I'd used the spell. It'd probably backfire but—*

[System Alert: VACU-ROCKET Used]
[-1 HP, 55/71]
[System Alert: VACU-ROCKET Ineffective. Try Again In 5
Seconds. Initiating Countdown For Reference.]
[5]

Five seconds?! The spiraling sand caked into my eyes, grated past my cheeks, coating my hair—

[-2 HP, 53/71]
[4]
[3]

Fuck! 5 seconds felt like forever!!

[-2 HP, 51/71]
[2]
[1]

I parted my dried lips, readying myself to scream the incantation again—

[0]

"*Goodbye Messafuss!*" I shouted. Pain exploded in my chest from the spell kickback—

[System Alert: VACU-ROCKET Used]
[-1 HP, 50/71]

There!

Overhead, a loud, mechanical noise sounded. The sand spiraled faster for a minute and, then, began to dissipate as a seeming vacuum overhead sucked the sandstorm upward—damn, the spell really DID clean up a mess. I peeled my smarting eyes open, just barely able to make out my surroundings. My throat was bone dry and my eyes, watery, even though I currently wanted them to be opposite.

Goran said he wasn't going to leave us alone? …Well, then, there was only one thing left to do.

"If you won't let us be," I rasped. "Then I'm going to keep stopping you. Every punch you throw. Everything you do. I'll stop it. Just like this." My voice was so frail, but my chin was held high in determination as I pushed a strand of sandy hair out of my eyes, "You're going to have to face it, Goran; I'm stronger than you think." I glared at the man.

[System Reward: Damn, Girl, What A Show Of
Determination, +20 XP 819/800]

The world stopped—froze. Sand, magic and green plus marks swirled in my vision. Goran's face paused, twisted in a strange, unafraid sneer that I wanted more than anything to wipe right off.

[System Alert: ***Congratulations, You've Advanced To Level 9!***]

Name	Rosabella	
Class & Level	Game Maker 9	
XP	819/900	
MRP	3795/6209	
HP	59/80	
Baddie Points	620	
Armor Class 15/20		
ABILITIES /20		
Strength	+1	12
Agility	+0	10
Endurance	+0	11
Intelligence	+1	13
Awareness	+1	12
Presence	+3	16
CM		4

[+9 HP & HP Extended By 9, 59/80. You've Been Awarded The Ability To Enable The Following Option: EASY MODE.]

Easy Mode? I squinted at the text. *Well, that had to be good, didn't it?* The shield and magnifying glass icon for an Examination Opportunity bobbed over the option,

Okay, I'd humor the system. Anything would help in this fight. "Examine," I said.

[System Option Examined... +1 XP, 820/900]
[A Closer Look At The Fine Print Explains The Option Further:

EASY MODE: When Enabled, This Tool Alerts Gamers To
Potentially Helpful Objects And/Or Situations By
Supplying Hints. Once Turned On, Easy Mode Will Last
For 5 Minutes. This Option Can Only Be Used Once.
Would You Like to Enable?]
[Yes] [No]

Hell yes. If there was a way out of this that didn't end with all of us dead and a demolished Game world, I needed to find it. "Enable!" I shouted.

[System Alert: Easy Mode Enabled. 5 Minute Countdown
For Use Initiated.]
...5 Minutes Remaining...

The world unfroze, and I was met with Goran's smug face. He didn't look disturbed that I'd bested him with two beginner spells. Instead, he looked rather like he'd won a stuffed animal at a carnival game, and I hadn't seen him do it. It set me off-balance as I wondered why his eyes were gleaming black like that. *What was his next move? Would Easy Mode be able to tell me before time ran out?*

"System, volume up!" he raged.

[GORAN, PRISONER 11: System Alert: +5 Volume of Battle
Song]

Goran's lifted his face grandiosely to the sky as his music blared louder. "I don't need to *face* anything," he snickered, "but you and your so-called friends are going to have to. Have it your way."

Dragons! Emerge!

[GORAN, PRISONER 11: Draconic Telepathy Used... +1 XP,
1169/1200]

His words echoed through my mind as my stomach dropped. *Draconic telepathy? This couldn't be good.*

The colossal, bronze wings of the dragon on the ledge beat in the night air—so large they obscured the moon above. And the dark clouds above parted—the whole sky was full of them.

Hundreds of dragon silhouettes.

And they were carrying Nomads on their backs, waving weapons and shouting—their army. *Who needed bridges when you had dragons? —Goddamn! They were easily—literally—flying over the damage that Dormouse inflicted!*

Shock and hopelessness coursed through my limbs in a sickly toxin called desperation.

"*What do we do?*" I whispered as I noticed Goran slip sideways and out of view.

And I didn't know if Rainer had moved up or I'd moved back, but the burly Nomad was close enough to hear my plea. He turned to me, his brown eyes intense and pleading over his red beard, "If there ever was a moment to fix The Game, it's right now, Rosabella. Callen said you could do it. *I stand with Callen.*"

And there was such resolve in his voice—such *belief.*

…In *me.* He believed in *me.*

And I was the last shot—the last hope of a miracle.

And it was now or never.

I closed my eyes again—ignoring the doubt rising in my heart.

Ignoring the flutter of the organ there.

Only listening.

To me. To the strength inside. To the Creator Magic.

And I felt it roar to life, ready again even after taking the battering from Goran. *Could I do this?*

...3 Minutes Remaining...

And something started then—a green glow at my belt. *Was my inventory...glowing? Was this the Easy Mode hint?*

"System, show me my inventory." A pop-up fizzled into view:

[System Understands Query...Loading Response...]
[System Alert: Per Request, Inventory Opened.]
- **1 Rosabella's Mother's Silver & Gold Broadsword**
- **4 CM Diamonds**
- **1 The Game Map**
- **Eraser of Noneness**

My eyes scanned the objects to realize that the Eraser of Noneness and the Game Map were glowing the same neon-green as my inventory just had...

"System, is the green highlight the Easy Mode hint?" I asked rapidly.

[System Understands Query...Loading Response...]
[System Answer: Yes.]

...Wow, that was the briefest answer I'd ever gotten. Okay, so I guessed I could use the Eraser of Noneness and the Game Map for something? I'd forgotten about the eraser, but there were rules...what had they been?

"System, tell me about the Eraser of Noneness again," I hurried.

[System Understands Query...Loading Response...]
[System Answer:
ERASER OF NONENESS: A Magical Object Which Allows A Gamer To Erase A Singular Object In The Game. This May Be 1 Gamer, 1 Object or 1 Creature. This Eraser Can Only Be Used Once.]

Okay, one thing. I could erase one thing—

...2 Minutes Remaining...

My thoughts spun. *What could I do? How could I use what I had to fix this world?* "Open The Game Map, system—" My voice wobbled.

[System Understands Query...Loading Response...]

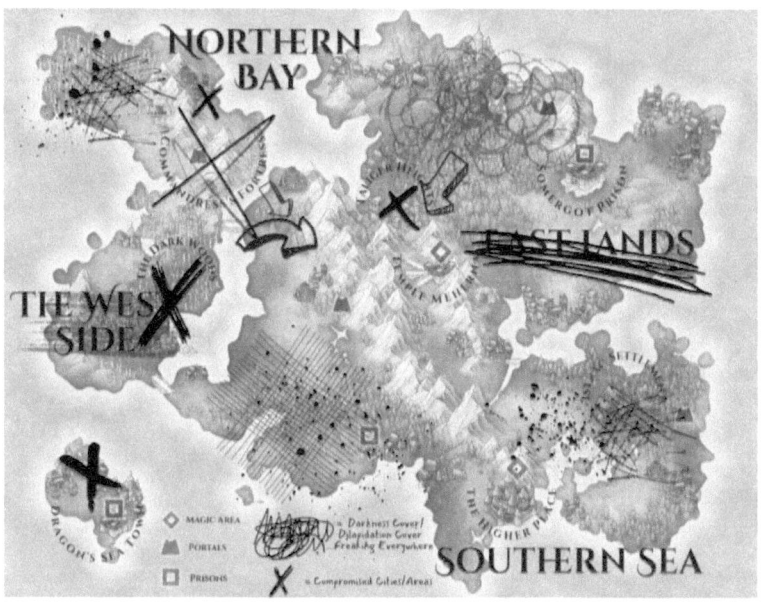

I stared at the map: the bodies of water and the land—some green, some desert-brown—showed where the darkness and Darken had infiltrated with black pencil marks. The city names were written in script, but some of them were crossed out with red x's which almost looked written in marker or crayon. A hand drawn legend on the bottom marked them as 'compromised'. Those were probably the ones that were affected by the earthquakes and were all but deserted piles of rubble now... There were, also, black, scribbled lines scrawled across whole sections of the topography. I squinted at them. It looked like the Darken had taken over those areas...

...1 Minute Remaining...

Grand Dragon? I asked inwardly to the echoing abyss around me, *Are you there?*

[Draconic Telepathy Used... +1 XP, 821/900]

Yes, child; I'm here.

A wave of security washed over me just hearing the beast's voice in my mind.

Where am I on the map now? I asked, waiting in the stillness for a reply.

Here.

A red dot appeared, glowing briefly on the map in about the middle. *If I could only scroll in—*

Oh! There!

I used two fingers in the air, moving them outward like I would on my cell phone in reality to enlarge something, and it zoomed the image in.

I could easily read the words around a turreted building symbol: 'Temple Meherna'.

Yes! Three bridges were marked to the side…and all the black hatching and the 'x' over what looked like a nearby city.

Rid the land of darkness and you will win this fight.

The Grand Dragon told me clearly.

Rid the land of darkness… I stared at the black, scribbling marks across the page. *But how did I fix it? And how did I know that, even if I DID fix it, the army wouldn't have already decimated Joy, Rainer, Dormouse and I?* I had less than a few minutes while they held them off—

Do you trust me?

Trust?

The Grand Dragon?

I wasn't sure. All I knew was that I had to trust someone right now—I had to trust myself. Yet something felt so familiar about the dragon's voice…so warm…like when… A memory tugged at me…

[System Searching MRPs To Select & Display Correct Memory…]

She is right, you are ready. This is meant for you; don't fight it. Look inside. You have everything you need.

The Grand Dragon's voice echoed.

What it'd said before in the garden? What did that have to do with now? I squeezed eyes even further shut, trying to think.

You have every tool you need.

Repeated the dragon.

Tool.

My eyes flashed open.

Tools were kept in my inventory. And my inventory held…the eraser. The Game Map showed dark marks written in pencil. *Could I get rid of the darkness by erasing the dark lines on the map? Would it work like that? Did the darkness count as one thing?* Nerves jumped in my arms and fingers. I had to try.

[System Alert: Easy Mode Timed Out And Disabled.]

"System, equip the Eraser of Noneness," I commanded.

[System Understands Query…Loading Response…]
[Object Equipped]

The pink eraser flew into my hand. Yes! Good! Now was the tricky part…

"System, I'd like to use my one use of the Eraser of Noneness to delete the dark pencil marks on this map which represent darkness." My voice shook. *This was crazy, I was literally using the one useful tool in my arsenal to erase pencil lines? What about erasing a dragon or Goran?* The pencil lines could have nothing to do with the actual, real darkness. The Grand Dragon could be tricking me, or I could be tricking myself into thinking I had this when I really didn't—

Shut up, I told my mind.

[System Understands Query…Loading Response…]
[System Alert: ERASER OF NONENESS Used.]

An electronic beep sounded. *Shit—shit, this was the moment of truth!* I looked at the map as the eraser worked its way across its form. It left white blotches in its wake—where it had erased the dark…like there was a void there. And something inside me suddenly knew I needed to fill it.

I closed my eyes. And I imagined greenery, flooding the land there instead of white.

[-50 CMP 165/400]

Vibrant trees.

Lush grass. Life.

I imagined bringing life.

Blossoming flowers.

Running, clean water…

[-50 CMP 115/400]

My eyes darted back and forth in my imagination —rebuilding— underneath my closed eyelids with my CM. And I was vaguely aware of an audible murmur running through the valley like a thousand voices seeing the same thing at the same time.

But the clanging of metal on metal and the smell of smoke was still there too.

An image of the decimated city I'd first entered in The Game in flashed to life. And it stuck out like a sore thumb that I needed to fix. Gathering all my energy into my mind, I began dismantling the broken buildings and stacking them upward again—like working with little toy blocks.

I righted the crumbled skyscrapers.

[-50 CMP 65/400]

Damn! I was running out of CM! I repaired the cracking sidewalks.

[-10 CMP 55/400]

I replaced building signs, fixed broken parks and vending stands and planted lush plants…designed landscaping and streets…

[-15 CMP 40/400]

There was a busy ease to the work, like playing a world-building video game. Sweat rolled down my forehead as I concentrated, using the Creator Magic that was almost gone…

I hastily added one last thing—one last thing the city street needed: a Chinese restaurant on the corner.

[-10 CMP 30/400]

And everything was finally as it should be.
Standing.
Upright.
Good.
…Now, for the final touch.
I flipped a switch in my mind, and the power went on.

[-10 CMP 20/400]

And I flipped my eyes open at that exact moment, watching as a million, tiny windows flickered into brilliance on the horizon.

And the army froze. I watched as all the dark shadows fighting Joy, Rainer and Dormouse turned to stare, unabashed, at the glowing city in the distance—a city that had been dark for years, now, lit up like a towering Christmas tree on the night horizon.

And I heard metal hitting the ground as they dropped their weapons. I balked at it. The entire army was frozen in shock, staring between others and their repaired world.

I'd done it, but it felt like some darkness still might be lingering…in the Gamers?

I gathered the last of my CM magic around me, relishing the feeling as I collected it, swinging it easily in my hands. And I pulled any last remaining darkness towards me. Joy stood close enough to watch the last of the Darken rash peel off her neck. The blackness dribbled towards me in the air like loose paint, and I whisked it away.

[-20 CMP 0/400]

And that was the last of my magic—the most I could do before a long rest…

[System Alert: Gamer MRP Restored Within A 15 Mile Radius]

"System, show me the GDP," I commanded, breathing heavily.

[System Understands Query...Loading Response...]
[GDP – 50/100]

Current Gamer Population:	332 Million
Current Darken Population:	10 Million
Darken To Gamer Ratio:	~39.12%
Darkness Cover:	48/100
Dilapidation Cover:	52/100

Whew! I'd dropped it! I'd taken it way down from 90/100! Their world was...saved. I'd done it. Relief coursed through me. I watched others in the army staring down in awe at healed hands and arms, bumping each other and grunting as they showed the proof of their clear skin to each other. I saw them bring up their MRP to check, their jaws dropping when they saw it restored. *I'd done that?* And everyone turned to gawk at me as my hands begin to glow—

As my *body* began to glow and tingle with radiating light—

Keep attacking! You fools!

The enormous bronze dragon roared overhead, but the crowd barely responded except for muffled exclamations of 'Look, she's a Game Maker! She's wearing white like the Game Makers of old!'.

One Warrior shook his thick fist at the sky and the looming dragon, "Why should we fight for you?! You burned our home—killed our loved ones unless we agreed to join you!"

"*Yeah!*" A host of voices shouted in agreement.

It looked like the dragons were in agreement too. A group of smaller ones circled the large, bronze beast, all spitting and hissing, forcing it backwards and down to the ground.

And I turned in shock towards Joy, Rainer and Dormouse.

My friends.

To find their jaws almost on the ground.

"She's—" Rainer stumbled, gesturing at me. "Rosabella, *you're glowing*—"

Joy leaned a jesting elbow on the burly warrior's shoulder, "*How come no one ever says that about me?*"

Dormouse stifled a giggle. And, for a second, it was almost like everything was okay.

Like we were still all in one piece.

Like I'd just saved the world.

I stifled a blooming smile. "Guys, I—*I think I did it!*" I squeaked. And my cheeks hurt from the wide grin, but the rest of me was okay. The rest of *us were okay!* A familiar chart popped into view:

[System Alert: Dragon Spar Completed.]
[System Reward: You're The Winner! Winner, Winner, Chicken Dinner! You Showed His Ass! +50 XP, 871/900]
[System Alert: ***Congratulations, You Won The Dragon Spar!***]

Name	Rosabella	
Class & Level	Game Maker 9	
XP	871/900	
MRP	3795/6209	
HP	59/80	
Baddie Points	620	
Armor Class 15/20		
ABILITIES /20		
Strength	+1	12
Agility	+0	10
Endurance	+0	11
Intelligence	+1	13
Awareness	+1	12
Presence	+3	16
CM		4

And I looked at the stats there, and I…I felt…*proud.*

I'd done this. I'd won the Dragon Spar, but, more importantly, I'd, finally, taken control and made something beautiful. It was an amazing feeling. I let it wash over me—*warm* me. *I'd saved my friends. I'd saved the masses still milling about confused in front of me. …My parents would have been proud.*

…I could have stood there, feeling like that for days…*weeks?* I could have relished the feeling forever, just sinking into it, but I caught Dormouse out of the corner of my eye.

…And his face looked…frazzled. He threw an anxious hand through his wavy, black hair, "Hey—uh, guys. *You might want to see this.*"

It only took three, large steps to get to the wall the kid was gesturing towards, and I reached it first, glancing at the nerd while I did—*why is his face so white?*

That's when I saw it—a message, cut into the plaster wall of the Temple in jagged, red letters:

IF I CAN'T HAVE HER, NO ONE CAN. I WILL DESTROY YOU ALL. GOODBYE, GAME.
GOODBYE, ROSIE.

My heart hammered in my chest. My stomach twisted. *Goddammit, Goran!*

About The Author

Keegan Eichelman is a lover of all things books and the author of over 50 of them, including her bestselling, young adult paranormal *Wisteria Rebel Series*. As a kid, she read the library dry of dragon books. Her passion for fantasy and enjoyment of classic survival horror video games catapulted her into the LitRPG genre, and she hasn't looked back since—besides to keep the zombies at bay. She fills her free time with writing, outdoor adventures with her fiancé, Greg, including hiking, biking, off-roading and boating, snuggling her calico feline and encouraging budding authors. In her opinion, life's too short to do anything but have some proper fun doing what you love; therefore, you can expect she'll be doing what she loves, churning out some more fun novels for you to read!

Find her online: linktr.ee/keeganashleylive